On the Farm

Enid Blyton

Enid Blyton

On the Farm

EGMONT

Enid Blyton

EGMONT

We bring stories to life

The Children of Cherry Tree Farm first published in Great Britain 1940
The Children of Willow Farm first published in Great Britain 1942
More Adventures On Willow Farm first published in Great Britain 1943
This edition published 2014 by Egmont UK Limited
The Yellow Building, 1 Nicholas Road, London W11 4AN

ENID BLYTON ® Copyright © 2014 Hodder & Stoughton Ltd.
Text copyright for The Children of Cherry Tree Farm © 1940 Hodder & Stoughton Ltd.
Text copyright for The Children of Willow Tree Farm © 1942 Hodder & Stoughton Ltd.
Text copyright for More Adventures on Willow Tree Farm © 1943 Hodder & Stoughton Ltd.

ISBN 978 1 4052 6906 3

www.egmont.co.uk

A CIP catalogue record for this title is available from the British Library

Printed and bound in Great Britain by the CPI Group

55944 /1

MIX
Paper
FSC FSC® C018306

EGMONT LUCKY COIN

Our story began over a century ago, when seventeen-year-old
Egmont Harald Petersen found a coin in the street.

He was on his way to buy a flyswatter, a small hand-operated
printing machine that he then set up in his tiny apartment.

The coin brought him such good luck that today Egmont has
offices in over 30 countries around the world. And that lucky
coin is still kept at the company's head offices in Denmark.

The Children of
Cherry Tree Farm

Contents

1

A Great Surprise

One early spring day three children looked out of a window in a tall London house. Below them was a busy street, and not far off was a patch of trees and grass with a tall railing round them.

'The trees aren't even budding yet,' said the biggest boy, Rory. He was the oldest of the family, black-haired and brown-eyed. 'How I do hate to be in London in the springtime!'

'Well, we always have been, and I suppose we always shall be,' said Sheila. She was twelve, a year younger than Rory. Her hair was fair, but her eyes were as brown as Rory's.

The other boy rested his chin on his hand and looked thoughtfully down at the London square below.

'What are you thinking about, Benjy?' asked Sheila. 'Wondering if there are any birds nesting in those trees, I suppose? Or if you might suddenly see a rabbit in the street, or a fox slinking by? You'll have to wait till our summer holidays to see those things.'

'I wish we were rich enough to have a cottage in the country, as some people have,' said Benjy. 'Wouldn't I just love to see all the spring flowers coming out and to watch for frog spawn in the ponds!'

Benjy was ten – a thin, quiet boy who spent all his

spare time reading about animals and birds. He was not the youngest; there was Penelope, who was only seven. She was downstairs with her mother, who was bandaging a cut finger for her.

And it was whilst she was there that Penelope heard the Great News. She listened with all her ears whilst the grown-ups were talking; and as soon as her finger was bandaged she flew up the stairs, bursting to tell the news!

She flung open the door, and stood there panting. The others turned round in surprise and saw Penelope's blue eyes shining.

'You'll get into a row if you make such a noise,' said Sheila. 'You came upstairs like a dozen elephants.'

'Rory! Sheila! Benjy! Listen! I've heard something marvellous!' cried Penelope.

'What?' asked the others.

'Well, we're all going down to Cherry Tree Farm to stay with Auntie Bess for at least six months!' shouted Penelope, and she danced round the table in joy.

'Penny! Are you sure?' cried Rory.

'Oh, Penny! It can't be true!' shrieked Sheila.

'But what about school?' asked Benjy in surprise.

'Mummy said that the doctor advised a good long holiday for all of us,' said Penny, still skipping about happily. 'She said . . .'

'Penny, do stop still and tell us everything properly,' begged Rory. So Penny sat down on a stool and told her brothers and sister what she had heard.

'Well, we've all had measles, and then we had the flu, and then Benjy and I got that awful cough, and Mummy said we were all so thin and pale, and we didn't eat enough, and the doctor said the only thing to do was to let us run wild down in the country, and Mummy said, 'What about Cherry Tree Farm?' and the doctor said, 'Splendid,' and Daddy said, 'Just the thing,' and I listened and didn't say a word, and . . .'

'Oh, Penny, it's too good to be true!' said Benjy. 'No school! Just going wild in the country. I'd like to go wild. I wish I could go down the rabbit-holes and live wild there. I wish I could get into a hollow tree and live wild there. I wish . . .'

'Benjy, don't be silly! It will be much nicer to live at Cherry Tree Farm with Auntie Bess and Uncle Tim!' said Rory. 'Golly! Cream every day! And those apple-pies with cheese that Auntie Bess makes! And strawberries straight out of the garden! What do people live in a town for?'

'Oh, to ride on buses and go to cinemas, I expect,' said Sheila. 'When are we going, Penny?'

Penny didn't know any more, but Mother soon came up and told them all about it.

'You go on Thursday,' she said. 'You have all had such a lot of illness, so there must be no more school for you for some time. Just the country air and good food and lots of walks. I can't come with you, because Daddy wants me to go to America with him – but Auntie Bess will look after you well.'

What an excitement there was for the next two days! The children were given one small trunk between them in which to pack any toys or books they wanted to take with them. Mother packed their clothes, but she said they might pack their toy trunk themselves.

Sheila wanted to take her biggest doll, but Rory would

not let her. 'It will take up half the trunk,' he said. 'Take a little one.'

Then Penny wanted to take her whole family of teddy bears. She had seven.

'Well, if you take those bears, you can't take anything else at all,' said Rory firmly. 'Not a thing. No, not even that dreadful rabbit without any ears.'

In the end they all took what they wanted most. Rory took pencil-boxes, paint-boxes, and painting-books, for painting was his hobby. Sheila took her work-basket, some puzzles and a small doll. Benjy took nothing but books. Penny took three teddy bears, and as many other soft toys as she could squeeze in.

And then they were all ready. They were to go down by train, so Mummy and Daddy drove them to the big London station where their train waited for them. Cherry Tree Farm was far away in the heart of the country, not very far from the sea. It would take them all day to get there.

'Goodbye, my dears!' said Mother. 'Be good!'

'Goodbye!' said Daddy. 'Remember that you will be in someone else's house, so do exactly as you are told, and help whenever you can!'

'Yes, we will!' shouted the children in excitement. 'Good-bye, Mummy! Goodbye, Daddy! Have a good time in America! Don't forget to write to us!'

The engine whistled. Doors slammed. The guard waved a green flag and the train began to move slowly along the platform, chuffing as it went.

The chuffing grew faster. The platform came to an end. Mother and Daddy were only black specks in the distance, and the train came out of the big dark station into brilliant golden sunshine.

'We're off to Cherry Tree Farm!' cried Rory, and he banged on the seat so that dust flew up in a cloud.

'We're going to go wild, we're going to go wild, we're going to go wild!' chanted Penny, in time to the noise that the train made. That made all the children laugh, and they sang Penny's funny little song for a long time. It was a good thing they were all alone in their carriage!

2

Off to Cherry Tree Farm

It was a very long journey, but most exciting. For one thing, Daddy had arranged that they should all have lunch in the dining-car, and it was quite exciting to walk down the rushing, rattling train and find their places at the little dining-tables. Rory had to hold on tightly to Penny, because she nearly fell over when the train swayed about.

The knives and forks rattled on the table, and Penny's bread jumped off its plate. Rory's water spilt on the table-cloth, but it wasn't his fault. It was funny to eat inside a train that was going at seventy miles an hour.

'If the train keeps up this speed it will soon be at Cherry Tree Farm, I should think,' said Penny, looking at the hedges and telegraph poles rushing by in a long line.

'We don't get there till after tea,' said Sheila. 'We've got to wait for tea till we're there, Mummy said. She said Auntie Bess would be sure to have it ready for us, and it would be a pity to spoil it by having tea on the train. So I guess we'd better eat as much dinner as we can, in case we get hungry.'

They ate such an enormous meal that they all felt very sleepy afterwards. They staggered back along the rushing train, and found their carriage. Rory had promised his mother that he would make seven-year-old Penelope lie down after the midday meal, so he made a kind of bed for her on one seat.

'Come on, Penny,' he said. 'Here's a bed for you! Look, I've put my coat for a pillow, and I'll cover you up with this rug.'

'But I want to be big like you, and talk,' said Penny, who hated to be treated like a baby. But Rory was firm, and she had to lie down. In two minutes she was fast asleep.

And so was Rory! He leaned his head against the window, and although the train whistled and roared, he heard nothing of it – he was as fast asleep as little Penny.

It wasn't long before Sheila curled herself up like a kitten in her corner, and shut her eyes too. It was delicious to sleep in the swaying carriage. The noise it made crept into her dreams and made a song there – 'We're going to go wild, we're going to go wild!'

Benjy stayed awake for a little while, thinking joyfully of the lovely holiday they were all going to have. Of the four children he was the one who most loved the country, and who longed most for the feel of animals and the song of the birds. The children had never been allowed to keep pets in London, so all that Benjy had been able to do was to make friends with the dogs in the park, and to feed the ducks there.

'Perhaps I shall have a puppy of my own,' thought Benjy dreamily. 'Perhaps there will be calves at the farm that will suck my hand – and maybe I shall find a badger's hole – or a fox's den.'

And then he was fast asleep, and found himself sitting outside a fox's hole with his arm round a most peculiar yellow fox, who was smoking a pipe and saying that he wanted to go to America! Yes, Benjy was certainly asleep!

So, what with talking and having lunch and sleeping, it didn't really seem very long before the train drew up at a smally breezy station, and the porter there cried 'Cherry Woods, Cherry Woods! Anyone for Cherry Woods!'

'That's our station!' yelled Rory, in delight. 'Come on, get your hats! Here's your bag, Sheila. Come on, Penny! Hie, porter, there is some luggage of ours in the van!'

'It's coming out now, sir!' said the porter. And sure enough it was. Then Rory caught sight of Auntie Bess hurrying on to the platform, the wind blowing her dark hair into tight curls.

'Auntie Bess! Here we are!' yelled the four children, and they rushed to meet her.

'We had dinner on the train!' shouted Penny.

'Where's Uncle Tim?' asked Sheila, who loved her big, burly country uncle.

'Waiting outside with the trap,' said Auntie Bess, kissing them. 'My goodness, what pale cheeks! And what sticks of legs Benjy has got! I wonder you can walk on them, Benjy!'

Benjy went red. He hated his thin legs. He made up his mind to eat so much that his legs would be as fat as Uncle Tim's! And there *was* Uncle Tim, outside in the trap, waving his whip to the children.

What a noise there was as the four children clambered up into the pony-trap! Their luggage was coming along later in a farm-cart. The fat little brown pony turned round and looked at the children. She neighed joyfully.

'Why, even Polly, the pony, is pleased to see you!' laughed Uncle Tim. 'Hallo, Penny! You've grown since I saw you!'

'Yes, I have,' said Penny proudly. 'I don't have a nanny now. I'm as grown-up as the others.'

It was a very happy party that drove along the pretty country lanes to Cherry Tree Farm. Here and there a tiny splash of green showed, where early honeysuckle leaves were out. Golden coltsfoot flowers gleamed on banks in the evening sunshine, and Penny and Benjy saw a sandy rabbit rushing away over a field, his white bobtail flickering in the sunlight.

'I'm so hungry,' said Rory, with a sigh. 'I ate an enormous dinner, but I'm hungry again.'

'Well, there's high tea waiting for you,' said Auntie Bess. 'Cold ham, and apple-pie and cheese, and buttery scones, and my own strawberry jam and those ginger buns you loved last time you came, and . . .'

'Oh, don't tell us any more, it makes me feel I can't wait,' begged Penny.

But she had to wait until Polly, the pony, had trotted three miles to Cherry Tree Farm. And there it was at last, shining in the last rays of the February sun, a rambling old farmhouse with a snug roof of brown thatch coming down so low in places that it touched Uncle Tim's hat.

The children washed and sat down to their meal. They ate and ate and ate. Benjy looked down at his legs to see if they had got any fatter – he felt as if they really must have grown already! Then up to bed they all went, much to their disappointment.

'Your mother said so,' said Auntie Bess firmly. 'You can go later tomorrow, but tonight you are tired with a very long journey. This is your bedroom, Sheila and Penny, and this one, opening off nearby, is the boys' room.'

The two bedrooms were snuggled under the thatch, and

had big brown beams running across the ceiling and through the walls. The floors were uneven, and the windows were criss-crossed with little panes.

'I do like a ceiling I can bump my head on in the corners,' said Penny.

'Well, don't bump your head too often or you won't be quite so fond of my ceiling,' said Auntie Bess. 'Now hurry up and get into bed, all of you. Breakfast is at a quarter to eight. The bathroom is across the passage – you remember where it is, don't you? You can have either hot or cold baths in the morning – but please leave the bath clean and the bathroom tidy, or I shall come roaring at you like an angry bull!'

The children laughed. 'We're going to go wild, you know, Auntie Bess!' called Penny.

'Not in the house, Penny, my dear, not in the house!' called back Auntie Bess, and she went downstairs, laughing.

'I'm so happy!' sang Benjy, as he slipped off his boots. 'No more London! No more noise of buses and trams! No more poor sooty old trees! But clean sweet bushes and woods, bright flowers, singing birds and little shy animals slipping by. Oh, what fun!'

3

The First Day at the Farm

Early next morning the sun slipped into the children's bedrooms and lay slanting across the walls. It was glorious to wake up in strange bedrooms, and to hear the hens clucking outside, and ducks quacking on the pond in the distance.

It didn't take the children long to bath and dress. Then down they went as the breakfast bell rang, and took their places at the white-clothed table.

Uncle Tim had been up for two hours, and came to breakfast as hungry as a hunter. 'Hallo, sleepyheads!' he said. 'I've been up and about for ages! A fine morning it is, too, though it was pitch-black when I slipped out of the farm door.'

'Uncle, have you any calves?' asked Penny.

'Yes, two,' said Uncle Tim. 'You can see them after breakfast. And there are little lambs in the long meadow, and a foal in the field.'

The children hurried through their breakfast and then went out to see everything. Sheila loved the little long-legged foal that shied away from her timidly when she held out her hand to it.

Benjy loved the two calves. He put his hand into the mouth of the little white one and it sucked it gently and lovingly. The brown calf butted its head against him and looked at him with soft brown eyes.

Then Shadow, the collie dog, came running up to him and rubbed against his legs. All dogs loved Benjy, and all cats, too! As soon as Shadow had gone to answer Uncle Tim's whistle, three cats slipped out of the dark corners of the barn and mewed to Benjy.

'What a collection of cats!' said Benjy in his soft voice, and he scratched their heads.

Sheila and Penny had gone to see the lambs. There were thirty-three of them in the long meadow with their mother sheep. How they frisked and jumped! How they wriggled their long tails and maa-ed in their tiny high voices.

'Penny! Sheila!' suddenly called their aunt's voice. The two girls turned and saw Auntie Bess waving to them. 'Will you do something for me?'

'Yes, of course!' shouted the girls, and they ran to see what it was that their aunt needed.

'You will find three little lambs by themselves in that pen over there,' said Auntie Bess. 'They have no mother, so I feed them from a milk-bottle. Would you like to feed them for me?'

'Oh *yes*!' cried the children, and they took the feeding-bottles that Auntie Bess held out to them.

'They are just like babies' bottles,' said Sheila. 'Do they really suck from these?'

'Yes,' said Auntie Bess. 'Come back to me for more milk when they have finished. They will need more than I have given you.'

Penny and Sheila climbed through the fence and three

16

tiny lambs came frisking up. When they saw the milk-bottles they were most excited. The biggest lamb of all put his front feet up on to Penny and tried to get at the bottle at once.

'Well, I'll feed you first,' said Penny. 'Oh, Sheila, do feed that tiny one. He looks so hungry.'

But the tiny one didn't get a chance at first, for his brother pushed him away, took the teat of the bottle firmly into his mouth and sucked away so hard that in a minute or two the bottle was quite empty! Then Sheila ran back for more milk and fed the tiny lamb. He was gentle and sweet, and Sheila had to keep pushing his big brother away. The girls gave the lambs two bottles each and then went to wash them out ready for the next meal.

'I'd like to feed the lambs always, Auntie Bess,' said Penny. 'And the chicks too – and the ducklings. Oh, do look at those tiny ducks! Can I pick one up?'

'So long as you don't drop it and hurt it,' said Auntie Bess, going indoors. Penny picked up a bright yellow duckling. It crept under her coat and huddled there. Penny wished she could keep it there all day and night. It felt so soft and warm.

That first day was a very happy one. It seemed so long, and so full of sunshine. The children made friends with all the animals except Bellow, the bull, who was kept in a strong fenced paddock.

'He doesn't like strangers,' said Uncle Tim. 'Wait till he is used to you before you go and sit on his fence and talk to him. If you like you can go with Taffy when he walks him every day.'

Taffy was one of the farm-men. He took the big bull for a short walk every day up the lane and down. Bellow had a ring through his nose, and Taffy had a hooked stick through his ring. He led the bull by this, and Bellow stepped proudly up the lane and down, his red eyes gleaming round at the watching children.

'I'd like to lead the bull for you one day, Taffy!' called Rory, dancing up.

'I reckon it would be the bull that led *you*, Master Rory!' said Taffy, with a grin. 'Now don't you go dancing round Bellow like that. He doesn't like it.'

So Rory and the others went off to see the cows milked, and Bill and Ned, the two cowmen, let the children try their hands at milking.

Benjy was the best, for his hands were both strong and gentle. It was lovely to hear the creamy milk swishing into the pail. Penny was afraid of the cows at first, so she wouldn't try.

'You don't need to be afraid of Blossom and Daisy and Clover,' said Ned, patting the cows' big sides.

Daisy looked round at Penny, and swished her tail gently. It hit the little girl and made her jump.

'She smacked me with her tail,' said Penny indignantly. Everybody laughed.

'Well, you smack old Daisy with your hand and she'll be pleased enough!' grinned Ned, who was milking the big gentle cow.

When bedtime came at last the four children were more tired than they had been the day before. Penny could hardly undress herself and Sheila had to help her.

'My legs won't hold me up any more!' said Penny, and she fell on to her little white bed.

The others stayed up a little while, talking to their aunt and uncle round the lamp that gave a soft yellow light over the table. It was peaceful in the parlour. Shadow, the collie, lay at Uncle Tim's feet. A big white cat washed herself by the fire. Auntie Bess darned a stocking, and Uncle Tim listened to the children's chatter.

'Uncle, can we go for walks beyond the farm?' asked Benjy. 'When I know all the animals on the farm I'd like to go and find some wild ones in the hills and woods.'

'Yes. You can go where you like,' said Uncle Tim. 'But if Penny goes, you must take care of her, because she might fall into the river or ponds, or get lost by herself.'

'Oh yes, we'll take care of Penny,' promised Rory. 'She can't always come with us, though, Uncle – because her legs are not as strong as ours are, and she couldn't walk as far as we do.'

It was a good thing that Penny was in bed for she would not have been at all pleased to hear that! Although her legs were not so long as those of her brothers and sister she felt sure that they were just as good at walking and running. Poor Penny – she was always wishing that she wasn't so much smaller than the others! She didn't at all like being the baby of the family.

'Uncle, are there any badgers or otters about here?' asked Benjy, looking up from the book he was reading.

'There used to be badgers when I was a boy,' said his uncle, lighting his old brown pipe and blowing out a cloud of blue smoke. 'Those woods beyond the hill are called Brock Woods, you know, Benjy, and Brock is the old country name for badger.'

'Perhaps there are still some there now,' said Benjy, his eyes shining. 'Is there anyone who could tell me, Uncle Tim?'

'I should think old Tammylan, the wild man, would know,' said Uncle, and the children looked up in surprise.

'A *wild* man,' said Sheila. 'Are there wild men in this country then?'

'No, not really,' said Uncle Tim. 'We call him the wild man because he doesn't live in a house; he lives wild in the fields, and he looks odd – long hair and long beard, and funny clothes, you know. But people say that what he doesn't know about the animals and birds around here isn't worth knowing.'

'I *wish* I knew him,' said Benjy longingly. 'What did you say his name was, Uncle?'

'Tammylan, he's called,' said Uncle Tim, blowing out another cloud of smoke. 'But don't you go hunting him out now, or you'll get into trouble. Last year he caught two boys and threw them into the river, and the year before that he caught young Dick Thomas and shook him so hard that his head nearly fell off.'

'Why did he do that?' said Rory in surprise.

'We never really knew,' said Auntie Bess, joining in the talk. 'But we did know that the three boys were real rascals and deserved all they got! Still, it would be better if you didn't go hunting out old Tammylan, my dears. I wouldn't like you to be thrown into the river – especially if you can't swim!'

Well, of course, all three of the listening children at once made up their minds that they *would* go and hunt out the wild man of the hills as soon as they possibly could. They wouldn't go too near him – oh no! They would just watch out for him, see where he lived, and what he did. That would be fun. But they wouldn't let themselves be caught.

'We'll go hunting for old Tammylan next week,' said Rory to Benjy, as they went upstairs to bed that night. 'We'll find out from Taffy or Bill or Ned where he lives – and we'll go and see what he's like. Fancy – a real wild man!'

4

The Hunt for the Wild Man

The next few days were full of farmyard adventures, and for a time the children forgot about the wild man. Rory was chased by Bellow, the bull, and nearly got into serious trouble. Benjy just pulled him over the fence in time!

Rory had sat on the fence to watch the bull, and somehow he had fallen over. Bellow had seen him and had come rushing up in a trice, making a noise like his name! Rory had scrambled up, and Benjy had helped him over the fence just as the bull tore up to it.

'That was a near squeak!' said Rory, pretending that he wasn't at all frightened. 'I say, won't the girls tremble to hear about that!'

They did tremble – but unluckily Penny told Uncle Tim, and Uncle Tim was not at all pleased. He sent for Rory and gave him a good talking-to.

'Don't play the fool,' he said. 'That sort of thing isn't funny. I'm in charge of you, and if you go and hurt yourself, I'm to blame. You're thirteen years old and I thought you could be trusted.'

'I can, Uncle,' said Rory, very red. 'I won't go near the bull field again.'

Then Penny was chased by a goose and tried to squeeze

through some barbed wire. She tore her coat and scratched her arms very badly. She rushed in to Auntie Bess, screaming and crying.

'Well, I don't know who is the bigger goose,' said Auntie Bess, putting some ointment on to the scratches. 'The goose is a silly goose for chasing a harmless little girl, and *you* are a silly goose for being frightened and running away. If you had said "BO" to the goose, it would have gone off at once. Surely you are not one of those people who can't say "bo" to a goose?'

'I *could* say "bo",' said Penny at once, 'but I just didn't think of it. I'll go right away now and practise saying "bo" to that big grey goose over there.'

All the same, she went to find Rory to take her, and how he laughed to hear Penny saying 'Bo' as loudly as she could to a most alarmed goose, clinging on to his hand tightly all the time. The goose waddled away, cackling in fright, and Penny was simply delighted.

Sheila found a hen's nest out in the hedge, full of brown eggs. She was most surprised, and ran to tell her aunt.

Auntie Bess was pleased. 'That's my naughty little hen, Brownie,' she said. 'I knew she was laying away, but I didn't know where. Bring in the eggs for me, Sheila. If Brownie wants to sit she shall, and we will have some more chicks then.'

Benjy didn't get into any trouble. He was a quiet, dreamy boy, and he followed the farm-men about and watched them, fed the animals and birds, went walking across the farm with his uncle, and wished he was old enough to smoke an old brown pipe. Uncle Tim looked so contented and comfortable as he leaned on a gate, looking at his wide fields, with his pipe in his mouth. Benjy leaned too, and pretended that he was puffing away at a pipe, though his pipe was only a bit of twig.

After the excitement of the first few days had worn off the three older children began to think about Tammylan again.

'I saw a little spire of blue smoke this evening, away on the hill over there,' said Rory, waving his hand to the distant woods. 'I think it must have been Tammylan cooking his supper.'

'Who's Tammylan?' asked Penny at once.

'A wild man,' said Sheila.

'Fibber!' said Penny.

'No, really, it's true, Penny,' said Benjy, and he told her what Uncle Tim had said about Tammylan. 'And we are going to find him one day and see what he's like!' said Benjy.

'Oh!' said Penny, in excitement. 'Can I come too?'

'I don't think so,' said Rory. 'You see, it might be a long way. And Tammylan might be very wild and frighten you.'

'I don't care how far away it is, and I know I wouldn't be frightened!' said Penny obstinately. 'I'm coming. You're not to leave me out.'

'Well, we'll see, Penny,' said Rory. Penny sulked. She knew what 'We'll see,' meant. It meant 'You won't come.' But she was quite determined to go, and she made up her mind that she would not let the others out of her sight at all. Wherever they went, she would go.

'I may be only seven, but I'll just show them I'm not a baby!' thought Penny fiercely. 'I'm as strong as Rory, and he's thirteen. I *won't* be left out!'

So for the next day or two the little girl followed the others about everywhere till they got quite tired of her.

'Can't you go and find something to do on your own?' said Sheila at last. 'You just come tagging after us all the time, and you'll get so tired.'

But Penny wouldn't go off on her own. So when the others did decide to go and look for Tammylan they had to talk about it when Penny was in bed.

Sheila went to sit on the boys' big white bed, whilst Penny was lying asleep in the other room. They talked in whispers.

'We'll get Auntie Bess to give us sandwiches to take for our lunch,' whispered Sheila. 'We'll go off for a picnic. We'll make for Brock Woods. Taffy told me today that Tammylan is most often seen there.'

'Good!' said Rory, hugging his knees. 'But what about Penny?'

'We can't take her,' said Benjy. 'She's too little. I know, Sheila – you can tell her she may feed all the lambs tomorrow morning by herself. She will be so pleased – and whilst she is doing it we'll slip off.'

'Well, I hope she won't mind too much,' said Sheila. 'She does so hate being left out of things because she's younger – but we can't make her older, however much we want to!'

Well, the next day Rory begged Auntie Bess to give them a picnic lunch, and she nodded her head at once.

'It's a fine sunny March day,' she said, 'and if you promise not to sit on the damp grass, I'll let you have a picnic. But what about Penny?'

'She'd better stay behind with you, Aunt Bess,' said Sheila. 'She really isn't big enough to walk for miles.'

'Well, I'll make it up to her somehow,' said Auntie Bess.

'Come for your sandwiches in half an hour and they will be ready.'

So in half an hour the three children went to fetch their picnic lunch. Auntie Bess had put it into two bags. One had the eatables, and the other carried two big bottles of creamy milk.

Penny was feeding the three lambs, happy because she was doing it all by herself. Rory, Sheila, and Benjy slipped off with their lunch and made their way down the sunken lane towards the far-off woods. The March sun shone down and warmed them. The celandines in the lane lifted up their polished faces and smiled. It was a lovely day for an adventure.

'I wonder if we'll find Tammylan!' said Sheila, skipping along. 'I wonder what he'll be like. I'd love to see a wild man.'

'Sheila, if you're going to skip like that you'd better give *me* the milk,' said Benjy. 'You'll turn it all into butter before we get to the woods!'

So Benjy carried the milk and Sheila skipped like a month-old lamb, whilst Rory plodded along with a crook-stick that Uncle Tim had given him.

'It's fun to be in the country like this!' said Sheila. 'Fancy – all we'd see in town now would be a few trees and a bit of grass, unless we went to the parks. And out here we're going to look for a wild man!'

They came to the end of the lane and climbed over a stile. They went across the field and over another stile. Then the path led into Brock Woods. It was dark under the evergreen trees, but when they came to where oak and hazel grew the woods were lighter.

A farm-boy came along whistling, Rory stopped him. 'I

say!' said Rory. 'Do you know where Tammylan lives?'

'No, I don't, and I don't want to, either,' said the farm-lad. 'You let him be. He's wild, he is.'

'Oh, but do tell us whereabouts he lives,' begged Benjy. 'We just want to see him, that's all.'

'He's much more likely to see you than you are to see *him*,' said the boy. 'Well, I don't rightly know all his hiding-places, but folk do say he has a cave or two in the hill yonder.'

'Oh, thank you!' said the children and went on their way through the wood. They came to the steep hill at last, covered with heather, birch trees, gorse, and bracken.

'Now we must be quiet and look for the caves,' whispered Rory. 'Come on!'

The children went in single file round the hill, looking for caves. But to their surprise, no matter how carefully they looked, they could find no cave at all. Not one.

'Well,' said Rory, after about half an hour, 'I don't believe there's a cave larger than a rabbit's burrow anywhere in this hill! That farm-lad was telling stories.'

'Let's sit down and have our lunch,' said Sheila. 'I'm so hungry I could eat the paper round the sandwiches!'

'All right,' said Benjy. 'You eat that, and we'll have the sandwiches, Sheila!'

Auntie Bess had made them a lovely picnic lunch. There were ham sandwiches, hard-boiled eggs in their shells, each with a screw of salt beside them, slices of sticky gingerbread, last autumn's yellow apples, and half a bottle of milk each.

'I wonder why food tastes so much nicer out of doors than indoors,' said Rory, munching hard. The children had spread out Rory's mackintosh and were sitting on it, leaning back against a big old oak tree, with the March sun shining warmly down through the bare branches.

'What shall we do after our lunch?' asked Sheila. 'Shall we look for Tammylan again?'

'Yes,' said Benjy. 'And we'll pick some primroses and violets for Aunt Bess. And if I can find some frog spawn I'd like to take it home and put it into a jar. I've never seen tadpoles turn into frogs.'

'How are you going to take the frog spawn home?' asked Rory.

'In my hands,' said Benjy.

'You *are* silly!' cried Sheila. 'It's like a lump of jelly. You'll never be able to carry slippery jelly all the way home.'

'Well, I'll have a jolly good try,' said Benjy. 'Come on, you others. Haven't you finished yet?'

'Yes, but I wish I hadn't,' said Sheila, with a sigh. 'That was a gorgeous meal.'

They all got up and brushed the crumbs from themselves. The empty milk-bottles went back into the bag. The paper off the sandwiches and cake blew away through the trees. Not one of the children thought of picking it up and taking it home again, so that the woods might be clean and tidy.

They set off to look for a pond, keeping a sharp look out for the wild man all the time. But they didn't see a sign of him – though, if they had looked very carefully indeed, they would have seen a pair of sharp brown eyes peering at *them* every now and again through the bushes.

After a long time they came to a pond. There was a little moorhen on it, swimming fast, her head bobbing to and fro like clockwork. The children laughed to see her.

'Any frog spawn here?' said Benjy. He stooped down to look. He could see the blunt noses of the frogs poking up here and there – and then, in a far corner, he saw a floating mass of jelly – the frog spawn.

Benjy ran round to the other side of the pond. He balanced carefully on an old log and crept out to where he saw the frog spawn. He bent down to pick it up in his hands.

He lifted a big patch of it. It slipped from his hands and went flop into the water! He tried again – but no sooner did he get hold of it than it seemed to wriggle out of his hands like a live thing. Rory and Sheila shouted with laughter at him.

'Try again, Benjy!' they laughed. 'Try again!'

Benjy tried and tried, but it wasn't a bit of good. At last he grabbed a piece in both hands and held it tightly against his coat to keep it from slipping – and just at that very moment a startling thing happened.

There came a scream, loud and frightened, not very far off – and the scream was Penny's! All the children knew it at once, and they looked at one another, alarmed and surprised.

Benjy tried to jump back from his log – his foot slipped, and into the pond he went, flat on his face! He floundered there for a moment and then came up, gasping and spluttering. Rory rushed round to help him out.

'You idiot, Benjy!' he said. 'Just look at your coat! You *will* get into a row!'

'Quick! Help me up! Was that Penny we heard?' gasped Benjy, spitting out bits of frog spawn from his mouth. 'Don't bother about *me*. What's the matter with Penny?'

All three children rushed in the direction of the scream. And then, far away, they saw somebody carrying Penny, and on the breeze they could hear the sound of crying.

'It's Penny all right! She came to look for us, I expect – and oh, do you think Tammylan has got her?'

'Quick! Quick! We must rescue her!' shouted Rory. And off they ran at top speed to find poor Penny.

5

Penny has an Adventure by Herself

When Penny had been left alone at the farm feeding the three lambs, she had felt very happy. It was the first time she had fed them all by herself and she was pleased.

But when she had finished, and had washed the milk-bottles well, she began to look for the others. Then she was *not* so pleased.

'Rory!' she shouted. 'Where are you? Sheila! Benjy! Oh, do come and play with me!'

Auntie Bess came out of the farmhouse and called to Penny.

'They're gone for a very long walk, darling. It was too far for you to go. I want you to come and help me make some tarts this morning. Would you like that?'

'No, thank you,' said Penny, almost in tears. 'I do think it's mean of the others to go off without me. My legs are quite as strong as theirs.'

Nothing that her aunt could say would make Penny any happier, so in the end Aunt Bess gave it up. 'Well, just play round the farmyard and have some fun,' she said, and went indoors to her baking.

Angry and hurt, Penny wandered round the farmyard for a while. But she didn't feel like playing with anything. Shadow, the collie, came up and licked her hand but she pushed him away. Snowy, the big white cat, came and rubbed against her legs, but that didn't please cross little Penny either.

And then she made up her mind to go and find the others! Yes – she would go all by herself and just show them that she could walk as far as they could!

'I guess I know where they've gone!' said Penny. 'They've gone to find Tammylan, the wild man! They think he lives over in Brock Woods there, away by the hill. That's where they've gone. Well, I'll go too! I'll just show them how I can walk.'

The little girl said nothing to her aunt. She slipped away through the gate, out into the lane and ran down it as fast as she could. She began to puff and pant after a while, and she slowed down. She sat for a moment on the stile, then jumped down and began to run again.

'I hope I don't meet the wild man,' she thought to herself. 'I don't think I'd like that. Now, is this the path to the woods?'

It was. Penny ran down it, and after a long while she came to the hill which the children had searched for caves some time back. They had had their lunch and had gone to find frog spawn. But Penny knew they had been there.

'There's the paper wrapping from their sandwiches!' said the little girl to herself. 'Oh dear – it does make me feel hungry to think of sandwiches. I wish I'd got something to eat. I wonder if they've got any left.'

Penny didn't know what to do next. She had no idea where the others had gone. She was hungry and tired – and lost! She didn't know the path home. She only knew she was very tired and miserable. She wished she hadn't gone to look for the others now.

'I know what I'll do,' said Penny, trying to be brave. 'I'll climb up a tree! Then maybe I shall see where the others are – or perhaps I shall see Cherry Tree Farm, and then I can make my way home.'

Penny was not used to climbing trees. There were very few to climb in London. But she ran to a tree that looked easy to climb and did her best to get as high as she could.

But Penny did not know the right way to climb trees. She didn't know how to test each branch before she set her weight on it, to make sure that it would bear her. And suddenly, when she was half-way up the tree, the branch she was standing on broke beneath her!

Penny clutched the branch above her in fright. She was standing on nothing! She screamed long and loudly – and that was the scream that the others heard.

'Oh help, help!' wept poor Penny. 'I shall fall. My arms won't keep me up any longer!'

And then a voice below her spoke clearly. 'Let yourself fall, little girl. I will catch you. You will be quite safe.'

Penny tried to look down, but she couldn't. She didn't dare to let herself fall – but she had to, because her arms gave way, and down she went.

Yes, down she went – but not to fall on the hard ground and perhaps break her leg. No – she fell straight into two strong arms that were ready for her! Somebody caught her, somebody held her, and somebody comforted her.

Penny looked up through her tears. She saw a dark-brown face out of which looked two brown eyes with unusual yellow flecks in them. A curly brown and grey beard grew from the chin, and the man's hair was rather long, and curly too.

'You're quite safe!' said her rescuer. 'I caught you beautifully, didn't I! Don't cry any more.'

'My arm hurts,' said Penny, sobbing. She had scraped her arm on a sharp twig as she fell, and it had made a deep cut. Her arm was bleeding under her torn coat.

The man who had caught her set her on the ground and looked at her arm. 'A nasty cut,' he said. 'We'll soon put that right, though. Come along with me.'

But Penny was so tired and hungry and had had such a shock that her legs wouldn't walk. So her friend had to carry her in his arms, down the hill through the bracken and heather. Penny sobbed as they went, and felt very sorry for herself indeed.

'Why did you come out all alone, so far from home?' asked the man. 'You shouldn't do that.'

'The others went off by themselves to look for Tammylan, the wild man,' said Penny, rubbing the tears from her cheeks.

'Why did they want to look for him?' asked her friend.

'Oh, they thought it would be fun to see a real wild man,' said Penny. 'But I would be afraid if I met him.'

'No, you wouldn't,' said her friend.

'Yes, I would,' said Penny. 'I would run and run and run!'

'And instead of running and running, do you know what you did? You jumped right into my arms!' said the man, with a laugh.

Penny looked up at his face in surprise. 'What do you mean?' she said. '*You're* not Tammylan, are you?'

'Yes, I am,' said Tammylan. 'I don't know why people call me the wild man. All I do is to live by myself in the woods and hills, and learn the ways of my little furred and feathered friends. Well, little girl – are you afraid of the wild man?'

'No!' said Penny, beginning to feel really excited. 'Oh, Tammylan – I've found you, and the others haven't! Aren't I lucky?'

'I don't know about that,' said Tammylan. 'Now – can you stand down for a minute. Here we are, at one of my little hidey-holes!'

Penny stood and looked. Tammylan was moving a curtain of bracken away from a hole in the hillside. Behind it a cave showed its dark mouth – a cave with heather dropping down from the top edge, and close-growing plants trimming the sides. It looked exciting.

'I want to see inside,' said Penny. 'And oh, Tammylan, have you got anything I could eat? It does seem such a long time since my breakfast!'

'I have some soup made from all kinds of plant roots,' said Tammylan in his clear, low voice. 'I will make it warm for you.'

Penny bent down and went inside the cave. It opened out widely inside, and the ceiling became high. A rocky ledge ran along one side and on it was a rough bed of dried bracken and heather. On a rocky shelf were a few tin plates and other things.

At first Penny could see nothing inside, but as soon as her eyes grew used to the half-darkness she could see everything clearly. She liked it. It was really exciting. She was in the cave of the wild man!

'Wouldn't my brothers and my sister be jealous if they could see me here!' said Penny. 'Oh dear – my arm does hurt me, Tammylan!'

'I'm just getting some water to bathe it with and some of my special ointment to put on the cut,' said Tammylan from the back of the cave. 'I believe I saw your brothers and sister this morning.'

'Oh, I wonder where they are now,' said Penny. 'I'd really like them to share this adventure with me, although they did leave me out of their walk!'

Rory, Sheila, and Benjy were not very far away! They had tracked the wild man and Penny almost up to the cave. Now they were whispering together behind a bush to decide how to rescue their little sister.

'We'll all make a rush, and we'll shout and yell like Native Americans!' said Rory. 'Then, in the excitement, we'll grab Penny and run off with her. Now, are you ready?'

'Yes,' said Sheila and Benjy. They ran to the mouth of the cave, shouting and yelling, and forced their way inside, looking for Penny.

But it was so dark that at first they could see nothing. They stood there, blinking – and then they heard Penny's voice.

'Oh Rory! Oh Sheila – and Benjy! You did make me jump. How did you find me? Oh Rory – what do you think? I've found Tammylan, the wild man!'

'Where is he?' asked Rory, his eyes getting used to the dark cave. 'We thought he had caught you, Penny. We heard you scream, and we came to rescue you.'

'I screamed because I was climbing a tree and the branch broke,' said Penny. 'Tammylan held out his arms and I fell into them. Then he carried me here to see to my cut arm. I caught it on a twig.'

The three children began to feel rather silly. A deep voice

came from the other end of the cave. 'Please sit down for a moment. I am glad you wanted to rescue your sister – but she really isn't in any danger at present!'

The three children sat down on the heather bed. So Penny had found the wild man, and they hadn't! They were simply longing to ask dozens of questions, but there was something in Tammylan's voice that stopped them. They suddenly felt that they must be on their best behaviour. It was puzzling.

So there they all sat, waiting for the wild man they had wanted so much to find.

6

Tammylan and His Cave

Tammylan came out of the darkness holding a small bowl of water. Penny was surprised.

'Have you got a tap at the back of the cave, Tammylan?' she asked. Tammylan laughed.

'No,' he said. 'But a little spring comes from a hole in the rock there, and then runs down through the floor of the cave. It is very cold and clear, and I use it for my drinking-water. Now, where's that arm?'

Penny slipped off her coat, which was badly torn. Tammylan bathed her arm gently and then put some odd-smelling yellow ointment on it. Penny sniffed at it.

'What is it?' she asked. 'I like the smell.'

'Oh, it's made of all kinds of herbs and roots,' said Tammylan. 'You wouldn't know any of them. It will heal your cut more quickly than anything out of a chemist's shop.'

'It feels nice,' said Penny. Tammylan took her handkerchief and bound up her arm neatly. Penny looked up at Rory.

'I suppose you haven't any sandwiches left?' she asked. 'I haven't had any dinner and I'm so hungry.'

'Not one,' said Rory. 'I'd have saved you some if I'd known, Penny.'

'You shall soon have some food,' said Tammylan, and he

lit a little fire at the doorway of his cave, on a flat stone that had been often used before. He cooked some broth in a pot, stirring it with a twig. It smelt simply delicious.

The others gazed enviously at Penny when the soup was ready and she was eating it. It made them feel hungry even to smell it. Penny said it was the nicest soup she had ever had in her life.

Tammylan suddenly saw that Benjy was wet and was shivering. He felt the boy's coat.

'So you fell into the pond where you were looking for frog spawn!' he said. 'Go to the back of the cave and take off your wet things. You will find an old rug there. Wrap yourself in it and come back to the fire. I will dry your things for you. You can't go home like that.'

Very soon Benjy was sitting by a roaring fire, wearing an old red rug. He said he only wanted a few feathers in his hair to feel like a real Native American.

'You live a sort of Native American life, don't you, Tammylan?' he asked. 'Do you know, we heard all sorts of dreadful stories about you.'

'Did you?' said Tammylan, as if he was not at all interested.

'Yes,' said Rory. 'We heard that you had shaken a boy called Dick Thomas till his head nearly flew off!'

'That was quite true,' said Tammylan. The children stared at him in surprise. Tammylan seemed so gentle and kind.

Tammylan spoke sternly. 'Dick Thomas found a bird with a broken wing,' he said. 'And the poor thing couldn't get away from him – so he tormented it. I won't tell you how, but he was very cruel. That is why I shook him as I did.'

'Oh,' said Rory. He thought for a moment and then asked

Tammylan another question. 'Why did you throw two boys into the river?'

'Dear me, so you heard that too, did you?' said Tammylan. 'Well, they had a dog they didn't want – so they tied a brick to him and threw him into the river to drown. I came by, took out the dog – and threw the boys in. That's all.'

'Could they swim?' asked Benjy.

'Of course,' said Tammylan. 'I didn't tie bricks to them! Don't you think they deserved a ducking?'

'Oh *yes*,' said Rory. 'I do.'

There was a pause – and suddenly Tammylan lifted up his hand to stop everyone from speaking. He had heard a small sound that had escaped everyone else's ears.

The children sat still and looked towards the cave entrance. They saw a pair of big ears – then a pair of large, anxious eyes – and then a brown rabbit slipped round the fire and came into the cave. When it saw the children it stopped in fear. It sat up on its hind legs, its nose sniffing and woffling, and its whiskers trembling.

'Well, Bobtail,' Tammylan said in his deep, clear voice. 'Have you come to pay me your usual visit? Don't be afraid of the children.'

The rabbit came a little nearer, sniffed at Tammylan's outstretched hand, and then, frightened at a sudden movement made by Sheila, he turned and fled, his white bobtail showing as he went.

'Oh!' said Benjy, too delighted for words. 'Tammylan! Is he a tame rabbit?'

'No,' said Tammylan. 'He is a wild one. One night he got into a trap, and his leg was broken. He squealed pitifully, and

I went to free him. I set his leg and it healed. Now he is one of my friends and comes to see me every day.'

'*One* of your friends?' asked Benjy at once. 'How do you mean? Are other animals your friends too?'

'Oh yes,' said Tammylan. 'Birds as well. They all come to me. They show me their homes and their little ones. I share their lives. I am as wild as they are, you see!'

'Tammylan, please, Tammylan, will you show me your friends?' begged Benjy, taking Tammylan's brown freckled hand, that seemed more like a paw, it was so thin and brown. 'I've read books about birds and animals for years, but I've always lived in London till now. I'll never get a chance like this again – so will you please, please let me know your friends!'

'And me too?' asked Penny.

'Do you want to make friends with badgers and foxes, with toads and frogs, otters and wild birds?' asked Tammylan. 'No! You children don't care for any of those things nowadays! You want toys of all kinds – cinemas – bicycles to ride – roller skates. Oh, *I* know! All you want of animals is to tease them and frighten them – to take their eggs, to throw stones at them. No – my friends are my own, and I share them with nobody.'

'Oh, Tammylan, you are wrong!' cried Sheila. 'Children aren't all like that. Just because you've seen a few that were cruel and stupid doesn't mean that we are all like that. Can't you give us a chance and see? Anyway, give Benjy a chance. Benjy has been mad on animals and birds all his life but he's never even had a dog to call his own.'

Tammylan didn't say anything for a minute, and his eyes looked far away.

'Even Benjy cared so little for my woods this morning that he let the wind blow away your papers,' he said at last. 'They will go pulpy with the rain. They will wrap themselves around my primroses and violets, and will make my woods look ugly and untidy.'

The children went red. They remembered that Auntie Bess had told them not to litter the countryside with paper or bottles.

'We shouldn't have done that,' said Benjy. 'I'm sorry, Tammylan. We'll look for the papers on our way home and pick them up. We'll never spoil the country again like that.'

'I have picked up your papers already,' said Tammylan. 'You didn't see me, but I was there.'

The children all felt ashamed – except Penny, who had had no papers to throw away. But she was ashamed for the others.

'Benjy may come and see me again,' said Tammylan at last. 'He has the low voice and the quiet hands of those who love the wild creatures, Benjy may come – and maybe, if my friends like him, I will let you others come sometimes too.'

'Oh, thank you!' cried Benjy, his face shining. 'I'll come! I won't make a single noise or movement if you'll let me see the friends that come to visit you. I'll tell the others all about it, and then maybe you'll let them come too, another time.'

'I won't make any promises,' said Tammylan. 'Now, Benjy, your clothes are dry and I am sure it must be long past your teatime. Get into them and go home. Come again after tea the day after tomorrow – by yourself.'

Benjy was overjoyed. He got quickly into his almost-dry clothes. Then they all said goodbye to Tammylan, and left his exciting cave, talking nineteen to the dozen.

'Well, that *was* an adventure!' said Benjy. 'Fancy the wild man turning out to be such a grand person. Before you know it, I'm going to be friends with all the otters and badgers and hares and rabbits in the countryside!'

'Don't be so sure,' said Rory, half-jealous. 'Tammylan won't stand any nonsense. You might get thrown into the river.'

'I shan't,' said Benjy, and he knew quite well he wouldn't. 'I say – is that Uncle Tim coming to meet us?'

It was – he had come to find Penny, for when she had not gone in to her midday meal Auntie Bess had been very worried indeed. Now it was almost teatime.

Auntie Bess didn't want to hear about Tammylan – she wanted to know where Penny had been, and what she had been doing! Penny found herself being well scolded!

'Why didn't you come and tell me you were going?' scolded Auntie Bess.

'Because I knew you wouldn't let me,' said Penny, beginning to cry. 'Don't be cross with me. I climbed a tree and I fell down, and I cut my arm, and I didn't have any dinner . . .'

'Well, that was your own fault,' said Auntie Bess. 'Now don't you do such a thing again. Come along in and have tea. You must be as hungry as hunters.'

They were! There wasn't much left of the veal and ham pie, the jam tarts and the cherry cake when the four children had finished!

'What an adventure we all had!' said Benjy that night when they went to bed. 'I did enjoy it – and to think it's only just beginning! Aren't we lucky!'

43

'*You* are!' said Rory. 'You're the one that's going to have the luck, it seems to me.'

'Well, I'll do my best to share it with you,' said Benjy sleepily. 'I'll tell you everything.'

Then off he went to sleep, to dream of a tame rabbit that came to clean his shoes and cook soup for him and dry his clothes!

7

Benjy Pays a Visit

After tea two days later Benjy said goodbye to the others and slipped off to Tammylan's cave. He felt excited. What was he going to see?

As he came near to the cave he saw Tammylan sitting outside. Tammylan nodded to Benjy. 'So you are none the worse for your soaking!' he said. 'Come along in. I am expecting visitors this evening!'

Benjy was soon sitting on the bed of dry heather and bracken. 'Don't talk,' said Tammylan. 'And don't move, no matter what you see!'

Benjy sat quite still. He even tried not to breathe, but he just *had* to do that. And suddenly someone appeared at the cave opening! Someone with large upright ears, big eyes and a furry coat.

'The rabbit!' whispered Benjy in delight.

'No. A hare,' answered Tammylan, and he made a low animal-like noise. The hare scudded in and sat at Tammylan's feet, his whiskers quivering. Tammylan's lean brown fingers caressed the long ears, and the hare sat perfectly still, enjoying the quiet fondling. Benjy longed to put out his hand and touch the hare too, but he did not dare to. It might frighten it and make it leap away.

Tammylan began to speak to the listening animal. At first he said a lot of nonsense that Benjy couldn't understand – and then he slipped some sense into his talking, and Benjy listened because Tammylan was telling him all about the hare.

'You should know a hare from a rabbit, Benjy,' said Tammylan, still caressing the hare's long ears. 'See these long, long ears with their black tips – and see how long the hare's hind legs are. Soon you will see a rabbit and you will notice the difference.'

The hare stirred under Tammylan's fingers and the wild man ran his fingers down the animal's spine. 'Now don't stir, little brown hare. I am only telling your story to this young friend of mine. Speak in a low voice to the hare, Benjy – maybe he will not be afraid of you, now that he is used to your smell.'

Benjy spoke in his softest voice. 'Little brown hare, don't be afraid of me. Where do you live?'

The hare started when Benjy spoke, but Tammylan's fingers went on stroking his ears and he sat back again, looking up at Benjy out of his enormous eyes.

'So you will be friends with Benjy, brown hare?' said Tammylan. 'Shall we tell him where you live?'

'In a burrow, like the rabbits?' asked Benjy, longing to feel the hare's long ears.

'No, no,' said Tammylan. 'The hare is no lover of under-ground ways. He likes the fresh open air. He lives in the fields, in a hiding-place called a "form" because it takes the shape or form of his body. Sometimes he makes his form among the thickets of briar and gorse – but this hare has his home in one of your uncle's fields. Ah, he is a clever fellow, this little brown hare. Many a time he has been chased by the sly red fox, and has thrown him off the scent.'

'How does he do that, Tammylan?' asked Benjy.

'I have watched him,' answered Tammylan. 'If the red fox is after him, he will suddenly leap twelve or fifteen feet to the side, and break his track in that way. The fox finds that it comes to a sudden end – and by the time he has found the new track, my little brown hare is far, far away. When he leaves his form at dusk to go and feed, he plays the same trick – he leaps suddenly to one side, and so breaks the trail to his hiding-place.'

'Clever little hare,' said Benjy. 'Oh, look, Tammylan – here are some more visitors!'

Some small creatures appeared at the mouth of the cave. Against the setting sun they seemed dark – but their long ears told the two watchers what they were.

'Rabbits this time,' said Tammylan. 'They always come at dusk. They do not mind the hare – but if the red fox is here, or the striped badger, they will not even come near the entrance.'

'Oh, does the fox . . .' began Benjy, in surprise – and then he stopped. He had raised his voice, and the rabbits had fled. The hare too started in alarm and would have gone if Tammylan's hand had not restrained it.

'Sorry, Tammylan,' said Benjy. 'I forgot.'

'Say no more for a while,' said Tammylan. 'I will sing my song and maybe they will come back.'

Tammylan's song was strange. It wasn't really a song at all. It was the sound of the wind in the trees, the noise of a babbling brook, the rustle of leaves in the hedge – all the sounds that animals know and trust.

And soon the rabbits came back again, their long ears outlined against the fading light. 'Come!' said Tammylan. 'Come little friends! I am here!'

The rabbits scampered in. There were three of them. They came to Tammylan's feet, but they would not even touch Benjy. He was there with Tammylan, so he must be all right, but he was not yet their friend.

Tammylan lifted the smallest rabbit on to his knee. In the evening light that streamed into the cave Benjy could see its twitching, never-still nose, its long ears and wide eyes.

'You will see that this little rabbit's ears are not so long as the hare's,' said Tammylan, and he stroked them. 'Nor have they the black tips. Ah, little rabbit, you were not really made for an underground life, with these large ears, were you?'

'What does it do with its ears when it goes underground?' asked Benjy in wonder.

'It lays them flat over its back, like this,' said Tammylan, and he placed the rabbit's ears down on its back. 'Now, little rabbit, shall we go to see your home? Will you show us how you build it, with your strong forepaws?'

The animals seemed to understand what he said to them. They ran to the entrance of the cave, sat upright there for a moment or two, and then scampered away, their white bobtails showing clearly as they ran.

'Where have they gone?' asked Benjy, disappointed.

'To their playground, outside their home,' said Tammylan. 'Come, we will follow them.'

In a few minutes Tammylan and Benjy were sitting behind a big gorse bush. On the other side, clearly to be seen, were rabbits of all sizes – playing, feeding, running. Benjy felt as if he could watch them all night long!

The hare appeared beside them again, and watched the rabbits too. One rabbit sat up and began to wash itself, putting down first one ear and then the other to clean them thoroughly.

'See, Benjy,' said Tammylan in a low voice, 'there is a rabbit scraping a new hole in the hillside! See how he does it!'

Benjy watched. The rabbit scratched at the earth with its strong forepaws, and sent it flying behind it with its hindpaws.

'Is the hill full of rabbit-burrows?' whispered Benjy.

'Yes,' said Tammylan. 'If you were small enough to explore them you would have a fine time, Benjy! You could go from the top of the hill to the bottom by their underground passages. You would see that here and there they have been sensible enough to make the passages a bit wider – for passing-places.'

'Oh, how I wish I could go inside and see,' said Benjy. 'Oh, listen, Tammylan – what is that rabbit doing?'

One of the big rabbits was drumming on the hillside with his back legs. At the sound, all the rabbits looked up in alarm. Then one by one they fled to the nearest burrow, their white scuts bobbing up and down behind them. The hare silently disappeared.

'Why have they gone?' asked Benjy. 'Did I make a noise?'

'No. They have smelt the red fox!' said Tammylan, getting up. 'He is about now. Come, it is time for you to go home to *your* burrow too, Benjy! I will take you part of the way – and you shall see the hare's form as we go.'

The boy and the man went down the hill and into the

dark wood. Tammylan moved as surely as a cat in the dark of the trees, but Benjy could hardly see. Tammylan had to take his arm and guide him.

They came to the open fields. Tammylan walked swiftly towards the middle of one. He made a curious noise, and the hare appeared silently beside them again.

'We have come to see your form, brown hare,' said Tammylan. 'Where is it? Are we near?'

The hare gave an enormous leap sideways and disappeared for a moment. Then Benjy saw his long ears a good way away.

'He has broken his trail, as I told you he does,' said Tammylan. They went towards the hare, who led them a little way farther, and then they came upon his form – a cosy dent in the ground, well hidden from prying eyes.

The hare lay down in it to show Tammylan that it was his. Benjy thought he was a marvellous hare. 'Has he got a wife?' he asked Tammylan. 'Does she have a form, too?'

'Yes,' said Tammylan. 'And soon after they are born her little ones make their own tiny forms, and lie there hidden safely – as safe as the baby rabbits that are born underground. Now come, hare, let us see you run!'

The hare came with them over the field – and then, at a sign from Tammylan he ran in the dim light across the big field. Benjy could see his white bobtail.

'I know why we say "as swift as a hare" now,' said the boy. 'I never saw anything run so fast before! Why do we say "As mad as a March hare" sometimes, Tammylan? Are hares mad in March?'

'Quite mad!' said Tammylan. 'They kick and buck, they box with one another, they leap and bound about in the most ridiculous way. Perhaps you will see them this month, Benjy. Now I will leave you here. Come and see me another day and meet some more of my friends. Bring little Penny. Good night.'

'Good night,' said Benjy. He stopped and watched Tammylan slip away in the dusk. He heard the wild man give a curious call, and the hare answered it. 'Ohnt, ohnt!' said Tammylan, and the hare said the same. Then, with the hare at his heels, Tammylan disappeared over the evening fields, and Benjy, tired and happy, ran back to Cherry Tree Farm, full of his unusual adventure.

8

Tammylan and the Snakes

Penny, Rory and Sheila were never tired of hearing Benjy tell about his evening with Tammylan. They decided to tell their aunt and uncle all about it too.

Auntie Bess and Uncle Tim were astonished. 'I'll go along and see this strange fellow,' said Uncle Tim. 'I'd better see if he's all right for you to go about with.'

So he went along. The children were rather cross about it. 'Suppose Uncle says we mustn't go with him!' said Benjy. 'I really can't obey him! I do like Tammylan so much, and I mean to learn all he can teach me about his furred and feathered friends!'

'You can't disobey Uncle Tim,' said Penny. 'We are staying in his house. We *must* do what he says.'

Luckily for the children Uncle Tim liked Tammylan. 'He's a strange chap,' he said to Auntie Bess. 'Says he doesn't like the way men behave to one another, so he prefers to live with the animals. He says he can trust *them*. Well, well – his ideas about rabbits and foxes are not mine. He wouldn't want to make friends of those tiresome rabbits if they spoilt his crops as they spoil mine – and he wouldn't think the fox such a fine creature either, if it killed his chickens! Well, we don't all think alike, and it won't do the children any harm to learn a bit about the ways of our animals and birds. There's Penny here wanted to know if goats laid eggs the other day!'

Rory, Sheila, and Benjy screamed with laughter. Penny went red. 'You shouldn't tell tales of me, Uncle,' she said.

'No, I shouldn't,' said Uncle Tim, patting her head. 'Never mind! I could make you laugh at some of the things the others have said to me too. Now, let me see, who was it wanted to know where the turkeys' pond was?'

It was Sheila's turn to go red. Auntie Bess laughed. 'Well, you can't expect town children to know much,' she said. 'If Tammylan can teach them something they will love it. You and I are too busy to take them about much.'

'I've got to take Penny with me next time I go,' said Benjy. 'It's her turn. Can I take her, Aunt Bess?'

'Benjy will get more turns than anyone,' grumbled Rory.

'Well, you'd better practise moving and speaking quietly,' said Benjy. 'You and Sheila are such noisy creatures. A rabbit would run a mile as soon as he heard you coming!'

'Benjy, when can we go to see Tammylan?' asked Penny eagerly. 'Can we go today?'

'Not today!' said Auntie Bess. 'It looks too much like rain. Wait for a really sunny day.'

Two days later the sun shone down and felt as hot as in July. March had come in like a lion, and was going out like a lamb.

'It's the last day of March today,' said Benjy. 'We'll go and find Tammylan if you like, Penny. Let's go this morning.'

So off they went together to the cave in the hillside. But no Tammylan was there. The cave was empty.

'Bother!' said Penny. 'Where do you suppose he is?'

53

'Look! Isn't that Tammylan down there!' said Benjy, his sharp eyes spying someone far off. 'Yes, it is. He's near the pond where I fell in that day, Penny. Come on.'

They ran down the hillside and made their way to where Tammylan was sitting. As they came near he held up his hand to stop them – but it was too late. They saw the quick movement of some animal – and it was gone.

'Oh, sorry, Tammylan,' said Benjy. 'I didn't know.'

'He'll come back again,' said Tammylan. 'Hallo, Penny. Is your arm quite better now?'

'Yes, thank you,' said Penny. 'What was the creature that will come back again, Tammylan?'

'A snake,' said Tammylan. Penny gave a cry of horror.

'Oh! A snake! Really and truly? Oh, don't let it come back. It will sting me.'

'Don't be so silly, Penny,' said Tammylan, in such a cross voice that Penny felt really hurt. 'Snakes don't sting – they bite. And this one doesn't even bite. But you don't need to wait for it unless you want to. Go away and play, and Benjy and I will wait for it to come back.'

Penny stared at Tammylan. 'I thought snakes were horrid creatures,' she said. 'People always shiver when they talk about snakes. I've always been afraid of them.'

'Well, go on being afraid of them then,' said Tammylan. 'If you prefer to shiver when you hear snakes spoken of, shiver! What about you, Benjy?'

'Oh, I want to stay, please,' said Benjy eagerly. 'I want to know how snakes get along without feet. I want to know how they get out of their skins. I . . .'

'So do I,' said Penny, blinking away tears. 'You needn't be

so cross with me, Tammylan. I was only saying what other people said.'

'And that's the silliest thing in the world to do!' said Tammylan, stretching out his hand and pulling the little girl down beside him. 'Don't listen to what other people *say*. Find out things for yourself. They say snakes sting, do they? Well, find out from someone who really *knows*. You'll be telling me you're frightened of spiders next.'

Now Penny *was* afraid of spiders – but she was even more afraid of telling Tammylan so at that moment. So she said nothing, but sat on the sunny ground beside him.

Presently there was a tiny rustling noise nearby and a long snake came softly up to Tammylan, wriggling his body from side to side. Penny was so excited that she quite forgot to do what she had felt sure she *would* do – and that was shiver. She sat just as still as the others.

Tammylan began to whistle to the snake. It looked at him out of wide-open eyes. Benjy saw that the eyes had no eyelids, so the snake couldn't possibly shut its eyes even if it wanted to!

The snake put out its black tongue and ran it quickly over Tammylan's brown hand. It was an unusual tongue, forked into two branches at the tip. Penny gave a scream.

'It's putting out its sting!' she cried. The snake hissed, and began to glide away. Tammylan whistled gently and softly and it slowly came back, putting its forked tongue in and out.

'You are a silly little girl, Penny,' said Tammylan. 'That is only the snake's tongue. It uses it to feel things – it likes to run its tongue over its food before it eats it, to feel its shape. It is split into two at the end to help it to feel things easily – its forked tongue is like two sensitive fingers. Don't let me hear you call it a sting again.'

'No, Tammylan,' said Penny, glad that the wild man was not really angry with her. Benjy put his hand slowly towards Tammylan's. The snake flickered its quick tongue over his fingers. Benjy's face was a sight to behold. It was shining with joy! To think that a snake would be friendly enough to do that to him!

'This is a grass snake, a great friend of mine,' said Tammylan. 'For three years it has come to me. Look at it well. Its family are ill-used by man, for people kill it whenever they see it.'

'Oh why?' asked Benjy, remembering to keep his voice low.

'Like Penny here, they think all snakes are terrible!' said Tammylan. 'This pretty grass snake is perfectly harmless. It has no poison. It never attacks anyone, not even the smallest child. It is a harmless, friendly creature. Look at its large eyes, Penny, with its round pupils circled with gold. Look at its pretty patches of orange just behind the head, rather like a bright collar.'

Penny and Benjy looked. The snake looked back at them. Penny began to feel that it was rather a nice creature after all.

'It's a good long snake,' said Benjy, looking at it.

'Just over three feet I should think,' said Tammylan. 'The female snakes are even longer. Grass snakes are graceful things – their bodies taper gradually from the waist to the tip of the tail. See its long narrow head, and look at the lovely patterning of spots and bars along its olive-brown back. Touch its body, Benjy, and feel the curious scales that cover its body, overlapping each other.'

Benjy touched the snake and felt the scales. Penny hardly dared to and Tammylan did not make her. The snake drew back at Benjy's touch but did not go away.

'Where has it been all the winter?' asked Benjy. 'Snakes sleep in the winter, don't they?'

'Yes,' said Tammylan. 'This one slept curled up with two or three others among some underground roots. The hot sun of the last day or two has awakened them. Ah – our snake spies a meal!'

The snake suddenly slid down the bank and entered the water. To the children's enormous astonishment it swam easily in the pond.

'Gracious! I didn't know snakes swam!' said Penny. 'Whatever next?'

The snake had seen the movements of frogs and toads in the water. It caught one and brought it back to the bank, its scales glistening with water.

'The frog can't escape once it is in the snake's mouth,' said Tammylan. 'It has teeth that point backwards!'

'Look!' said Benjy, in excitement, 'Is that another snake, Tammylan – just over there?'

'Yes!' said Tammylan. 'Your eyes are getting sharp, Benjy. It's a smooth snake this time. If you felt its scales you would not feel the roughness that you felt when you touched the grass snake.'

'Tammylan, whatever is it doing?' asked Penny. 'It is pushing its head against that stone. Is it hurt?'

'Oh no!' said Tammylan. 'It is just going to take off its skin, that's all.'

Penny stared at Tammylan to see if he were joking. 'But

why should it take off its skin?' she asked in astonishment. 'I never take mine off.'

'No, because yours grows as *you* grow,' said Tammylan. 'But there are creatures whose bodies grow and whose skins don't – and then they have to take off their tight skins and wear others they have grown underneath. Watch this smooth snake and you will see it take off its whole skin, just as you might take off a stocking, inside-out.'

The smooth snake rubbed its head against the rough stone until the skin was loose. Then, when the head-skin was off, the snaked glided out of the rest of its body-skin, turning it neatly inside-out as he went! The children stared in amazement.

Penny gave a shout. 'Can I have the skin?'

The snake gave a frightened glance round and glided away into the undergrowth.

'You are a silly, Penny,' grumbled Benjy. 'Now you've frightened the smooth snake away and I wanted to feel its smooth body.'

Tammylan picked up the snake-skin. He showed it to the children. 'It's called a slough,' he said. 'See how perfect it is – even to the eye-covering! You were very lucky to see such a thing today. It is few people who see a snake casting its skin.'

Benjy looked at the skin carefully. 'However does a snake get along?' he asked. 'It hasn't any feet at all, has it?'

'Not one,' said Tammylan. 'But it manages very well indeed without them – it walks on the free ends of its many ribs! It puts a few of them forward, pressing on the skin – then others behind follow – and then the rest – then the front ribs move forward again, and so on. So it performs that curious gliding movement which is really fascinating to watch.'

'Are there any more snakes in our country besides the smooth snake and the grass snake?' asked Penny.

'Yes – one more – and a poisonous one this time!' said Tammylan. 'Come with me and I'll show you one.'

Penny wasn't at all sure that she wanted to go. 'I don't want to be stung – I mean bitten,' she said in a low voice.

'You won't be stung *or* bitten,' said Tammylan. 'But don't come if you don't want to. You come, Benjy.'

Well, of course, as soon as Penny was told that she needn't come, she wanted to! So off they went, leaving the pond behind, and climbing the warm southern side of the heather-covered hill. Tammylan sat down. His sharp eyes had caught sight of a movement. He began to whistle what Benjy secretly called his 'snake-tune'. Benjy was already trying to practise it in his mind, hoping that he too would be able to call snakes from all over the place, just as Tammylan seemed to do.

There was a rustle near them. Penny and Benjy saw a short, thick-looking snake gliding up to the wild man. It was only about two feet long, and its coppery-red eye looked unwinkingly at Tammylan.

It was a brownish snake, with a line zigzagging down the middle of its back. On its head was a mark that looked like a V. Its tongue flickered out as it came.

'I don't like this snake so much as the others,' said Penny.

'It isn't so pretty, certainly,' said Tammylan, letting the snake feel his fingers with its tongue. 'Its body is not so long and graceful – and do you see the mark on its head, rather like a V. V for viper – or A for adder if you look at it the other way! This snake is a viper or adder – our only poisonous snake.'

'How does it bite, Tammylan?' asked Benjy, staring at the snake.

'Watch, Benjy, what the snake does when I show him this stick,' said Tammylan. 'Watch carefully.'

The children watched. Tammylan picked up a short stick and brought it suddenly in front of the snake's head. In a trice it reared up its head, opened its mouth and showed two large teeth or fangs. It struck – and its fangs bit the stick. Tammylan laughed, and threw away the wood. He whistled his snake-tune again and the snake wavered its head to and fro in the air, quite peaceful and happy once more.

'Did you see those two fangs?' asked Tammylan after a moment. 'Well, those were the poison-fangs. They lie back in the mouth usually, but when the snake wants to strike they get into position for biting, and bite like lightning.'

'Where is the poison – is it on the fangs?' asked Benjy, staring at the snake.

'No – it is kept in a kind of bag or gland at the base of the tooth. When the fang strikes an enemy, and so presses on the bag of poison, it squeezes some out – and this runs down a passage in the fang, and into the wound made by the bite. So you see,' said Tammylan, 'a snake bites – but does not sting!'

'I shall be afraid of coming out on the hillside in case a viper bites me,' said Penny fearfully.

'They rarely bite,' said Tammylan, 'and anyway, you are sensible enough to wear shoes, aren't you? Barefoot people, who might accidentally tread on a sleeping viper might possibly get bitten – but you may be sure that in the usual way a viper hears you coming long before you get to him, and slides away to safety. He is far more afraid of you than you are of him!'

A dog barked in the distance – and the viper at once glided off without a sound.

'There!' said Tammylan. 'You see how the least noise sends it to hiding? You need not be afraid, Penny. And now I think it is time you went home, or your Uncle Tim will be coming after the wild man with a gun!'

The children laughed.

'Who can I bring next time?' asked Benjy.

'You can bring both the others,' said Tammylan. 'And you may ask your aunt if she will let you come at night, next week, when the moon is up.'

'Ooh – what fun!' said Benjy.

'Can't I come too?' asked Penny, thinking that a moonlight adventure sounded very thrilling.

'Not this time,' said Tammylan, 'but you may keep the snake's cast-off skin for yourself, because you were quite a sensible little girl after all, and didn't run away when the snakes came!'

Penny was very pleased. How the others would envy her the snake's skin! She thanked Tammylan very much for it, and Benjy took her hand to take her home.

All the way home Benjy whistled a curious little tune. Penny looked at him in surprise.

'What tune is that?' she asked.

'It's the snake-tune that Tammylan whistled,' said Benjy. 'I'm going to practise it and call the snakes to me for all the others to see.'

Well, when the others heard of the snakes and saw the snake's cast-off skin, and heard Benjy's odd whistle they were thrilled. 'Auntie Bess! Benjy can whistle snakes to him!' cried Sheila. 'Come and listen!'

So everybody sat still near Benjy whilst the boy whistled the strange monotonous tune – but alas, no snakes came at all, much to Auntie Bess's relief. Only Shadow, the collie, came rushing up and licked Benjy wetly on the nose.

'Don't, Shadow! Do you think you're a snake, you silly dog?' cried Benjy crossly. 'Now you've spoilt my whistle!'

'And a good thing too!' said Auntie Bess. 'I don't really feel that I want my farmyard full of snakes just at present, with all my young chicks about! Come along and have your meal, all of you. The cats will be eating it, if we don't go in and have it soon!'

9

A Moonlight Adventure

Rory and Sheila were wildly excited when they heard that they were to go and see Tammylan in the moonlight.

'What friends will come to see him in the moonlight?' said Sheila. 'Foxes, do you think – or otters?'

'Maybe badgers,' said Rory. 'Look – here's a picture of a badger, Sheila, in this book of Benjy's. Isn't he an odd-looking creature?'

All the children looked at the picture. 'He's got such a funny face,' said Rory. 'Striped white and black – very easy to see! If he comes out at night I could see him a mile off in the moonlight!'

Auntie Bess wouldn't let the children go until a really warm night came. The moon rose bright, and the countryside was flooded with light. The three children were so excited. Penny was sad.

'Well, Penny, don't forget you've got a real snake's cast-off skin,' said Benjy. 'That ought to make up to you for anything!'

Penny cheered up. The others were not likely to see a snake throwing off its skin that night – and anyway they would tell her all that happened. Uncle Tim had promised to let her help him wash the new-laid eggs for a treat, and Penny was looking forward to that after breakfast the next day.

Benjy, Rory, and Sheila set off to Tammylan's cave. Tammylan was sitting outside with some of his friends. The children saw that they were rabbits, who fled as they came near.

'I wish animals wouldn't run away from us,' said Sheila. 'Hallo, Tammylan – we're so excited. What are we going to see tonight?'

'I hope you will see the gentleman who gave his name to our woods,' said Tammylan, showing his white teeth in a smile.

'What gentleman?' asked Sheila puzzled.

'Master Brock, the Badger,' said Tammylan. 'Years ago the badger was far more plentiful here than he is now, and his country name of brock was given to our woods. He has been sleeping fast this cold winter, but now he should be about. Come along.'

'Do you know where he lives, then?' asked Benjy, trotting along beside Tammylan.

'I know where all the badgers live in Brock Woods,' said Tammylan, with a laugh. 'Look – there goes the red fox, out on his evening hunt. I hope he is not after your uncle's chickens!'

In the moonlight, outlined against the bright sky, the three children could see the graceful figure of a fox on the side of the hill. He stood there, listening and sniffing.

'He can smell *me* – but he can smell you too,' said Tammylan. 'If I were alone he would come trotting at my heels, like a dog.'

Benjy sighed enviously. 'He's rather like a beautiful, bushy-tailed dog to look at, isn't he?' he said. 'Oh – he's gone.'

They made their way deep into Brock Woods. Soon they

came to a big bank, and Tammylan stopped. An owl hooted loudly and made Sheila jump.

'Speak quietly now,' said Tammylan. 'Stand over here, so that the wind blows from the bank to us, then the badger will not smell us.'

The children stared at the bank. In it, showing clearly in the moonlight, was a very dark hole, quite big.

'That is the doorway to the badger's "sett", or "den",' said Tammylan. 'He may come out in a few minutes. We will watch for him.'

Outside the badger's den was a big mound. 'What's that?' whispered Sheila.

'That is the earth that the badger turned out when he dug his hiding-place,' said Tammylan, in a voice like the wind in the trees. It was marvellous the way he could make words sound like the wind blowing.

'And what's that huge pile of old leaves over there?' whispered Rory.

'That is old bedding of the badger's,' said Tammylan. 'In the autumn he collects a great many dead leaves and takes them into his den for bedding. They keep him warm and cosy. But if he wakes up to have a little stroll in a warm spell he often turns out his bedding and brings in fresh.'

'Oh look – look!' whispered Sheila, clutching hold of Tammylan's arm. 'Something's coming out of the hole!'

Sure enough something was! A striped face looked out and sniffed the night air. It was Brock the Badger.

Not one of the four made a sound or a movement. The badger put his head out a little farther, and sniffed loudly. He was sniffing for the smell of enemies. He never came out if he smelt anything strange or frightening.

The wind was blowing from him to the children, so he could not smell them. Neither could they smell him, for their noses were not trained to smell the scent of animals' bodies. But Tammylan could smell him. Tammylan knew the smell of badgers and he liked it, for they were cleanly beasts. Tammylan sniffed Brock – but the badger could not sniff Tammylan's smell because of the wind.

The badger shuffled right out of his 'sett' and the children could see him clearly in the moonlight – but as he went into the shadows he seemed to disappear!

'How funny!' whispered Sheila. 'I can't see that striped face of his now. It seems to have gone – and yet I know he's there among those shadows, because I can hear him.'

'His face is striped like that so that he may not easily be seen in the moonlit wood,' said Tammylan, in his low voice. 'For the same reason the zebra is striped, Sheila. White and black stripes look like white moonlight and black shadows. Now, here he comes, look – see his stout body and his rough, reddish-grey coat. Look at his pointed muzzle. Brock! Brock!'

The badger stopped dead and looked towards Tammylan. He sniffed hard and smelt the smell of the children as well as of his friend. He turned to go lumbering back to his sett. Then Tammylan spoke badger language – grunts and curious noises that Benjy knew he would never be able to make if he tried all his life long! The badger paused and looked doubtfully at Tammylan.

Tammylan left the children and went alone to Brock. The badger rolled over on his back like a dog and gave a grunt of pleasure as Tammylan knelt beside him to poke him and prod him just where he liked it most. The children hardly dared to breathe at such an extraordinary sight.

Tammylan spoke to the badger, and grunted to him, and in between he spoke to the children in the same kind of voice. 'See his big claws, children? See how black he is underneath! See what a stout, broad body he has, this little badger of mine?'

Benjy could bear it no longer. He felt as if he must join in or burst. Surely, surely the badger would let him tickle it and tease it as Tammylan was doing?

He ran forward to join in the game – but before he reached the badger it had gone, and Tammylan was kneeling there alone! Benjy could hear the badger making its way through the wood. 'Oh!' he said, disappointed. 'It's gone.'

'Of course!' said Tammylan. 'Did you expect to do in one minute what has taken me years? And surely you know that no animal, wild or tame, will stand a rush like that! Even Shadow, the collie, would have jumped to his feet!'

'Yes – I know,' said Benjy. 'But oh, Tammylan, I wanted to touch that badger so much. How did you manage to make it so tame?'

'I once had three badger cubs,' said the wild man. 'When they grew, they left me to live their own lives. That was one of the grown cubs. They still know me and are friends with me. Come nearer to Brock's den, children. Look inside. You cannot see much – but it is a big place if only you could get in and see!'

'How big is it?' asked Rory, kneeling down and almost putting his head inside.

'Rory's going in to look!' said Sheila, with a laugh. 'Mind

67

you don't meet two or three more badgers, Rory!'

'This sett goes in about nine or ten feet,' said Tammylan. 'There are passages and galleries too, and Master Brock has provided himself with a convenient back entrance right away at the back there, behind those bushes. I believe the red fox used to live in one of the passages, but the badger turned him out. He hates the fox's smell.'

'Good gracious! It's a real underground house!' said Rory. 'I do wish I was small enough to go in it. Where has the badger gone, Tammylan?'

'To find some food,' said Tammylan. 'He has slept nearly all the winter, and he is hungry. He blocks up this entrance and the back entrance too, when he goes to sleep.'

'I should have thought he was too clumsy to hunt his food properly,' said Benjy.

'He usually picks up wounded or ill animals,' said Tammylan. 'I know where Master Brock has gone tonight, I am sure. He has gone down to the rookery not far from your uncle's farm to see if any young rook has fallen from its nest!'

'Is he ever caught in a trap?' said Rory.

'Not very often,' said Tammylan, leading the children away from the badger's home. 'The badger that you saw to-night will never, I am sure, be caught in any trap. He has a curious way of dealing with traps.'

'What's that?' asked Benjy.

'He rolls heavily on them!' said Tammylan. 'He waits till he hears the spring go, then he knows the trap is safe. After that he calmly takes the bait and walks off with it!'

'He is cleverer than he looks!' said Sheila, admiringly. 'Are you going to show us anything else tonight, Tammylan?'

'Only the way home,' said Tammylan, with a chuckle. 'There it is – look! Come and see me again another day some of you.'

Then, off they went back to the farm in the moonlight, keeping a good look out for badgers and foxes and any other creatures that might come along. As for Benjy he tried to make the badger noises that Tammylan had made – until the others said he would have to buy them cotton-wool to put in their ears if he didn't stop!

10

Tammylan's Tree-house

One morning, when the children went down to breakfast, they heard Auntie Bess grumbling. 'My nice lawn is quite spoilt,' she said. 'Just look at it!'

The children looked out at the grass. It was a nice lawn, and their aunt was proud of it. But this morning it certainly looked very odd.

'It's all up and down!' said Penny, in surprise. 'It looks as if someone has made tunnels underneath and thrown up little hills and banks all over it. What's happened, Auntie Bess?'

'You'd better ask your friend Tammylan!' said Uncle Tim, looking up from his newspaper. 'I've no doubt he would call up a whole lot of the little wretches who have spoilt the lawn, and let them tell you a wonderful tale – but all *I* can say is – I'm going to get the mole-catcher here and tell him to trap the little pests who are mining under my lawns and my fields too!'

'Oh – so moles did it?' said Rory. 'Well, I've never seen the work of moles before. I don't even know what they are like to look at.'

'I do,' said Benjy. 'They are made for tunnelling, aren't they, Uncle Tim? Their front paws are really spades.'

'Spades!' said Penny, in surprise. 'Do you mean real

spades like we have when we go to the sea?'

The others laughed. 'Don't be such a baby, Penny,' said Rory. 'Benjy means the paws *act* like spades. We'll go and see Tammylan this morning and ask him a few questions.'

'And tell him that if he can find any good words for moles as far as farmers are concerned I'll be surprised!' said Uncle Tim. 'Pesky little creatures!'

The children were pleased to have an excuse to go and see Tammylan. They had been busy at the farm for two or three weeks, and when they *had* gone to see their friend he was nowhere to be found. Perhaps they would be luckier today. So after they had done their various jobs of feeding the farmyard creatures, washing the eggs, and giving fresh water to hens and others, the children set off to find the wild man.

But again the cave was empty, and again there was no sign of Tammylan. The children were disappointed. 'Perhaps he isn't wild any more. Perhaps he has gone tame,' said Penny.

Sheila giggled. 'You do say silly things, Penny,' she said.

The sun shone down warmly. Chaffinches carolled madly, and larks sang their sibilant song high in the sky. The music came dropping round the children as they stood wondering about Tammylan.

'I like the larks,' said Sheila, looking up at them. 'If I were a bird I'd fly as high as I could to sing. Listen to that lark – you can almost catch his song as it comes tumbling down from the sky!'

Penny put out her hands to catch the notes of the song, and the others laughed at her. 'Come on,' said Rory. 'We can't stay here all morning. Let's wander round a bit and yell. Perhaps Tammylan will hear us calling and shout back.'

71

So every now and again they shouted for Tammylan – and at last, away in the distance, they heard an answering cry.

'That's old Tammylan!' cried Benjy in delight, and the four children raced off over heather and bracken to where the call had sounded. Tammylan sent his call at intervals to guide them – and soon they came to his hiding-place.

It was by a backwater of the river – a quiet peaceful place, where moorhens bobbed about, and fishes jumped for flies. 'A Tammylanny sort of place,' Benjy thought to himself.

Their friend was there, and on his shoulder was a red squirrel, with a bushy tail and bright black eyes. When they saw the squirrel the children stopped their rush and walked quietly. They had learnt enough of animals now to know that even the tamest ones hated too sudden an arrival.

The red squirrel did not leave Tammylan's shoulder. Tammylan smiled at the children. 'Hallo,' he said. 'I wondered where you had all got to. I haven't seen you for some time.'

'We've been helping our uncle and aunt,' said Rory, 'and when we *did* come to find you, we couldn't. But now we have, and I'm glad.'

Tammylan was very busy at something. Penny looked hard at what he was doing. 'Tammylan!' she cried. 'Are you making a house?'

'Yes – a tree-house!' said Tammylan. 'I always live in a tree-shelter in the warm months of the year. This is the house I made two years ago – I am just trimming it up to make it right for me again now.'

'But the house is growing!' said Sheila, looking at it. 'Oh, Tammylan, do you really live in a growing house?'

'Why not?' said Tammylan. 'If my walls grow buds and my roof grows leaves, so much the better!'

It was a most extraordinary house. Tammylan had planted quick-growing willows close to one another, and used their trunks for the walls. He had trained the top of their branches across for a roof! Between the trunks of the willows he had woven long, pliable willow twigs, and had stuffed up all the cracks with heather and moss. It was the cosiest house imaginable.

But it was alive and growing! That was what amazed the children. The roof was green with leaves. Buds and leaves grew from the walls too. Tammylan was busy trimming the twigs and branches to make his house neat.

'Oh, if only I could have helped you to build your house!' said Benjy. 'I wish I had a growing house like that. Where's the door, Tammylan?'

'There is no door,' said Tammylan. 'The south side is open to the wind and the sun. There is a flat screen of woven twigs over there, which I use to shut up the house occasionally – but I do not need a door.'

The backwater of the river flowed by Tammylan's house, murmuring as it went. Primroses grew almost to the doorway. Bluebells pushed up all around it. The four children looked and looked – it was like a house in a fairytale.

Penny went quietly into the house. There was nothing inside but a few pots and an old rug. 'Are you going to have a bed, Tammylan?' she called.

'You can make me one if you like, Penny,' said Tammylan. 'All I want is plenty of dry heather. It smells so sweet at night!'

'Penny can make you your bed soon,' said Sheila, undoing a packet she carried. 'We'll have something to eat first. Look, Tammylan – chocolate cake baked by my Auntie Bess yesterday. It's for our lunch. Will you share it?'

'I should love to,' said Tammylan, seeing that there was a whole cake there. He took out his knife and cut it into enormous slices. 'Let's sit down by the river and have a talk.'

The little red squirrel had been sitting on Tammylan's shoulder all the time. When it saw the cake it made a little chittering noise.

'You don't like cake, Bushy!' said Tammylan. The squirrel took a bit of cake, bounded off Tammylan's shoulder, and disappeared with its prize behind a tree.

'He'll come back,' said Tammylan, seeing Benjy's disappointed face. 'And probably bring a friend too, if I know anything about Master Bushy.'

The children hoped he would. They munched their delicious chocolate cake and talked to Tammylan.

'Tammylan, Uncle is very cross because moles have tunnelled across his lawn,' said Benjy. 'He said he'd be surprised if even *you* could find a good word to say for moles where farmers were concerned.'

'Really?' said Tammylan. 'Well, we'll see. Finish your cake and we'll go and pay a call on a few moles I know.'

Penny almost choked in her excitement. Really, you couldn't mention *any*thing to Tammylan without hearing that some creature or other was his friend.

'I believe that if you lived in a jungle all the tigers would follow you round like dogs!' she said, with her mouth full.

'I should feel a bit uncomfortable with tigers behind me

all day long,' said Tammylan, laughing. 'Have you finished? Well, come along then.'

Just as they were leaving, the red squirrel came bounding back – and with him were two other red squirrels, their bushy tails streaking out behind them.

'Too late, Bushy, too late!' said Tammylan, shaking his head. 'The cake's all gone.'

'No, it isn't, Tammylan, no it isn't!' cried Benjy. 'I saved a bit in *case* Bushy did bring a friend. Here's a bit of cake, squirrels!'

To Benjy's joy all three squirrels scampered up to his outstretched hand. One stood on his hind legs and sniffed at the cake. One jumped on to Tammylan's shoulder – and oh, my goodness me, the third one actually ran all the way up Benjy's back and sat on the nape of his neck! Benjy was so thrilled that he couldn't move. He just stood there, half-bent, his eyes shining.

'Well, Benjy seems to have turned into a statue!' said Tammylan, with a laugh. 'Come on, Benjy – the squirrel will stick on all right if you walk! He likes you.'

'Oh, I wish he'd like me too!' cried Penny. And Rory and Sheila wished the same. Benjy began to walk – a bit stiffly at first, in case the squirrel took fright and bounded away. Then, as he got used to feeling the warm furry bundle at his neck, he walked properly, and the squirrel balanced itself easily.

'The third one's gone,' said Penny. 'I wish it had stayed with us and let me carry it.'

They left the strange growing house behind them, and followed Tammylan. He led them away from the river to a grassy field – and there, all around them, were the hills and tunnels of many moles.

'And now we'll catch a little velvet miner, and see what he's got to say for himself!' said Tammylan.

11

The Velvet-coated Miner

The sun shone down hotly on the field. There was a bank nearby where primroses grew in big patches of yellow, and where white violets scented the air. Tammylan sat down on the bank and the children sat by him. The two squirrels sat still, their bright eyes watching everything.

'Now,' said Tammylan. 'There are moles at work here. I saw their work when I came by this morning. If we sit quite still for a while, we shall see the earth being thrown up, and maybe I can get a mole for you to see. Keep quiet now.'

So they all sat as quiet as mice. Tammylan's squirrel sniffed and sniffed at Penny's hair, and the little girl was delighted. The sniffing tickled her, but she didn't move. Benjy's squirrel kept brushing the boy's ear with his whiskers, and it felt lovely.

Suddenly Tammylan pointed. The field was ridged here and there with the tunnels of the moles and with small hills of earth – but as the children watched, a new ridge appeared bit by bit. The grass seemed to be forced upwards as if something was tunnelling underneath and pushing it up.

'There's a mole at work there,' said Tammylan. 'He's not far under the surface either. The soil is rich and soft just here so the moles do not go very deep. Keep still and I'll get him for you.'

What happened next the children found it difficult to see because it all came so quickly. Tammylan knelt down by the newly made run, just at the end of it. There was a scraping and scrabbling – and then Tammylan turned round, his hands covered with earth – and in them a struggling little body dressed in grey-black velvet! It made no sound at all and the children crowded round to see it.

'Quiet, little Mowdie Mole,' said Tammylan, stroking the struggling body with his strong brown hand. In a moment or two the mole stopped wriggling and lay quite quiet. The two red squirrels, after a disgusted sniff at the mole, tore back to the woods, much to Benjy's dismay.

'Here is our little miner!' said Tammylan. 'Stroke him. Feel his soft velvet coat. See how the hairs grow, thickly and straight up. They do not lie all one way as a dog's hairs do, or a cat's. He can go either forwards or backwards as he pleases, you see, without his coat being ruffled up the "wrong way". That is important to him in his tunnelling underground.'

'Where are his eyes?' asked Penny, stroking the fat little miner.

'Buried deep in his fur,' said Tammylan. 'He has no use for them underground, and he rarely comes above the surface. But look at the most important part of him – his front paws.'

Penny looked at them, still half-expecting to see a sort of seaside spade! She saw a pair of wide-open hands, the palms facing outwards for digging. They were very large hands, for such a small creature, and they were set with big strong nails for digging. Penny could just imagine how well the mole could use them in the earth.

Rory touched the strong little spade-hands gently. At

once they moved as if they were digging, and the long snout quivered and shook.

'What a long loose nose he's got,' said Sheila. 'What does he use that for? Smelling out his food?'

'Yes – and to turn up the earth when he has loosened it with his paws,' said Tammylan. 'When you saw him tunnelling just now, he was loosening the earth and then forcing it upwards with his snout – and so you saw the ridge of earth appearing on the surface of the field. He has a good sense of smell too, and finds his nose very useful indeed.'

The mole began to wriggle again and Tammylan stroked it gently. 'We'll put him down here, where the earth is soft,' he said. 'Then little Mowdie Mole will show you how he can use his spades!'

Tammylan put the mole down – and at once it set to work digging in the soft earth. How it dug with those spade-like hands! The earth seemed to sink away under the mole – and in a very short while the velvet-coated creature had gone completely underground!

'I wish I could do that!' said Rory. 'Just dive into the earth and disappear! It looks so easy!'

'What does the mole look for when it tunnels?' asked Penny. 'And why does it tunnel, Tammylan? Does it like living in the dark, under the ground?'

'It doesn't think about whether it likes it or not,' said Tammylan. 'Its food is there – and to get it, it must tunnel through the earth! It eats earthworms, and grubs of all kinds – the leather-jackets, the cockchafer grubs, the harmful wireworms – and if it smells snails or slugs above ground it will come up and get those too!'

'Does the mole have a nest or a den?' asked Rory, watching another ridge appearing in the field, and wondering if it was made by their little mole.

'Yes – he makes a nice little nest for himself,' said Tammylan. 'I'll show you where there is one on the way back. It is quite a big hill, as you will see.'

'Isn't it funny to think that moles are making a sort of underground world below our feet?' said Sheila. 'I suppose the people who made the Underground Railway copied the moles and the rabbits.'

'I shouldn't be surprised,' said Tammylan. 'You know, the moles have their own system of main roads and highways in the fields – ways which they know as well as you know your own roads. From these highways they branch off in their hunting, making new tunnels to find food. But they come back to the main roads whenever they want to. I have sometimes dug into a mole's highway, and they are just about the size of the mole's body, and are worn quite smooth and hard by the continual passage of hurrying moles!'

'A real little world of their own!' said Benjy, wishing he were small enough to go hurrying along a mole's road, down the side-roads, up the tunnels, and see whom he would meet. 'Where's that mole's nest, Tammylan?'

'Come along and look,' said their friend, and the children followed him down the field. Tammylan stopped and pointed to a bush. Half-hidden under the brambles was a hill of earth, about a foot high and about three feet across. 'That is where our velvet-coated friend nests,' said Tammylan. 'Inside you would find his sleeping-chamber, and above it little tunnels leading upwards, through which he pushed the earth he dug out when he made his nest. This hill is made of the earth. He is a clever little fellow, isn't he?'

'Yes,' said Rory, wishing he could see inside the hillock. 'Well, I think I shall know what these hills of earth are now, when I see them again! I saw one the other day and couldn't think what it was.'

'You must go now,' said Tammylan. 'It's getting late.'

The children ran off – but they hadn't gone far before Benjy stopped. 'Bother!' he said. 'Tammylan didn't tell us what to tell Uncle Tim – surely there must be good things to say to a farmer about a mole?'

'Well, we can't go back and ask Tammylan now,' said Rory impatiently. 'We shall be late. Surely we can think of something for ourselves. We know all about moles!'

So all of them thought hard as they went home. Uncle Tim was in the farmyard, on his way in to his lunch.

'Well!' he said. 'Have you been mole-hunting?'

'Yes!' said Rory. 'We've seen a mole, and how it digs.'

'It wears a velvet coat, Uncle!' cried Penny.

'And has Tammylan any good to say about the tiresome little creature?' said Uncle Tim with a laugh. 'I've been to the mole-catcher this morning, and he'll be along soon with his traps.'

'We forgot to ask Tammylan what to tell you,' said Benjy, 'but Uncle, the mole catches earthworms – isn't that a good thing for you?'

'No,' said Uncle Tim at once. 'Earthworms are good for our fields.'

'Oh,' said Benjy. 'Well, what about leather-jackets and wireworms and grubs?'

'Ah, now you're talking!' said Uncle Tim. 'Yes – I'm thankful to any creature that eats those pests for me. They ruin many a good crop!'

'And Uncle, they make tunnels everywhere under the fields!' cried Rory. 'Surely that must help to drain them!'

'Quite true,' said Uncle Tim.

'And I should think it's very good for your land to have the under-soil thrown up to the air,' said Benjy solemnly. 'It must air it nicely.'

Uncle Tim shouted with laughter. 'You'll make a farmer yet, Benjy!' he said. 'Come along in. You've said some sensible things to me – but all the same I'm going to rid my land of the moles if I have to have the mole-catcher here every week!'

But what do you think Tammylan said when Benjy told him that? He said, 'No mole-catcher ever yet got rid of all the moles in a field, Benjy – and never will!'

'Why doesn't he?' asked Benjy. 'Can't he?'

'He may catch all the grown moles!' Tammylan said. 'But *he leaves the youngsters in the mother mole's nest.* Would a mole-catcher rob himself of his living, Benjy? No, no – there are always some left to grow up and have families – and then the mole-catcher is sent for once again!'

And when the mole-catcher came to set his traps, Benjy comforted himself and thought of the many nests of baby moles scattered here and there under the ground. The youngsters would soon grow up, and then once more the highways under the fields would be alive with the smooth velvety bodies hurrying to and fro on their endless hunt for worms and grubs.

12

An Exciting Morning

The children settled down so well to their life at the farm that it began to seem years to them since they had left London. Their mother and father had sailed to America, and jolly picture post cards kept arriving. At first these seemed very thrilling to the children and they wished they had gone to America, too – but soon the happenings at the farm began to seem far more important than things in faraway America.

By the end of May all the children had fat legs and rosy cheeks. Penny had grown such a lot that her aunt thought she really must get some more clothes for her.

'We'll send Penny back to London, and ask her friends there to take her to buy some new clothes,' said Uncle Tim slyly. Penny gave a screech.

'I won't go back to London! I won't! I'll wear nothing but a bathing-suit. I don't want new clothes!'

All the same, something had to be done, so Penny and Sheila were put in the pony-trap and driven off to the nearest town to buy bigger clothes and shoes.

The boys were all right – their jerseys and shorts did not matter. So they were left at home, and as soon as they had done their jobs, they looked at one another.

'I vote we go and see old Tammylan,' said Benjy. 'I'm

simply longing to feel a squirrel on my shoulder again! Shall we go?'

'Yes,' said Rory, cleaning out a pail, and putting it back in its place. 'We'll just tell Uncle. Perhaps we could take our dinner.'

Jane, the cook, put them up a picnic lunch in a few minutes, and the boys set off. It was a lovely day and Brock Woods were still blue with bluebells. The gorse was blazing on the hillside, its yellow blossoms sending out a delicious smell.

'Vanilla!' said Rory.

'Hot coconut!' said Benjy. 'Oh, look – there's a snake! Sh! Do keep quiet, Rory. I want to see if I can make it come to me!'

Rory stood perfectly still. Benjy began his 'snake-whistle'. It was a funny kind of whistle, and at first the snake seemed to listen. But then it uncoiled itself, gave Benjy a funny look out of its wide-open eyes, and glided softly away.

'You'll never be a snake-charmer!' said Rory, laughing at Benjy's cross face.

'It nearly came,' said Benjy. 'I saw it just thinking about it. It was a grass snake, like the first one that Penny and I saw.'

Tammylan was not in his cave, so the boys made their way to the tree-house. It was as strange and as lovely as ever. The boys peered inside. Tammylan had a bed of heather now, and a few of his things were arranged neatly on a kind of shelf.

'Let's sit here and wait for Tammylan,' said Benjy. 'I'm tired.'

So down they sat, leaning against the doorway of the little green house. The sun shone between the trees, and golden freckles of sunshine lay on the ground, moving as the wind shook the leaves above. It was all very peaceful and quiet.

Presently a moorhen swam to the bank and clambered up on its strong legs. 'How funny!' whispered Benjy. 'It is a swimming bird but it hasn't got webbed feet!'

'Sh!' said Rory. 'It's coming here!'

So it was. It came half-running, half-walking to the tree-house, as if to make a call on Tammylan. Then it suddenly saw the two boys and stopped. With a squawk it rushed back to the bank again, dived into the river – and disappeared!

'It's completely gone!' said Benjy, in astonishment. 'Where is it? It must be under the water.'

A series of small ripples began to show on the surface of the water, and soon made a little trail on the river. 'It must be the moorhen that is making that trail,' said Benjy. 'Oh look – it's stopped – and it's sticking just its beak out. Can you see it, Rory?'

'Yes,' said Rory. 'Keep quiet now, Benjy. Let's see if anything else comes. This is fun.'

The boys sat quietly. Somewhere a warbler sang his quaint little song. Somewhere a blackbird fluted like a musician composing a new melody all for himself. The wind moved in the trees and the sun-freckles danced on the ground.

Rory nudged Benjy. Two bright black eyes were looking up at the boys from a tuft of long grass nearby. The eyes stared unwinkingly. The boys kept perfectly still. The eyes still stared – and then a brown nose came up and sniffed the air gently to get the smell of the boys. As soon as it smelt their scent, nose and eyes disappeared in a flurry and a tail appeared for half a moment, and then disappeared too.

'Another of Tammylan's friends, I suppose,' whispered Benjy. 'I wonder what it was. A mouse of some sort, I think.'

'Sh! Look over there,' whispered Rory, slightly nodding his head to the right. Benjy looked. A wild duck in all the beauty of its early summer plumage had come from the water, and was preening itself in a patch of sunlight. The sun fell on its brilliant feathers, and the colours shone as brightly as a rainbow. The duck heard the boys and looked towards them. It thought that the noise was only Tammylan and the big bird settled down on the bank in the sun, tucked its head under its wing and slept.

A large fish leapt out of the water at a fly. The boys jumped at the splash. 'Look at those funny flies, Benjy,' whispered Rory. 'They've got three tails, like stiff hairs, hanging down behind them. What are they?'

'May-flies,' whispered back Benjy, proud that he knew. 'Fish love them. Those must be early ones. Look – there goes another fish jumping at the flies. Do you see how the flies rise up in the air altogether when a fish jumps and then go down again altogether? It seems as if they are dancing, doesn't it?'

A robin flew down and looked sideways at the boys. He had bold black eyes, and he hopped nearer on his long thin legs. He opened his mouth, swelled out his throat and warbled such a rich little song that the two boys were enchanted. Then it flung a dead leaf over its shoulder, gave a kind of bow and bob, flicked its wings and flew to a nearby branch to keep watch.

'I say, Rory, wouldn't it be marvellous to live in a growing house like Tammylan does, and know all these creatures?' said Benjy longingly. 'What shall we see next?'

They saw a baby rabbit! It had disobeyed orders and had come out in the daytime instead of waiting for the dusk.

Maybe it wanted to speak to friend Tammylan – anyway, there it was, quite suddenly, almost at the boys' feet! It looked at them out of big surprised eyes.

'*Oh!*' cried Benjy. 'You're like a toy rabbit we've got at home! Come here – do come here!'

But Benjy's surprise was too much for the young rabbit. It disappeared as quickly as it had come, and the boys saw its white bobtail flash – and then it was gone.

A swan sailed by down the stream, its white wings curving about its back. Its head was held proudly and it looked with dignity from one side to the other.

'It reminds me of those old sailing-ships somehow,' said Benjy. 'Isn't it marvellous? Look at its big feet paddling it along at the back, Rory. They act like oars.'

The swan heard Benjy's voice and looked enquiringly at the bank. Thinking that Tammylan was there, with a titbit for him, he sailed majestically to the grassy bank. He shook his wings then clambered clumsily up the bank. He waddled up to the two boys.

To tell the truth, Rory was rather frightened. The swan was a very big bird, and he didn't much like it quite so near him. But Benjy, as usual, was only too delighted to have anything alive close to him. He made no movement except to slip a sandwich out of his lunch packet. He held it out to the swan with a slow movement.

The swan took it quickly in his beak. He dropped the sandwich on the ground, pecked at it, and then gulped it down. He looked up for more.

'Give him one of yours, Rory,' said Benjy. But Rory was really rather afraid of the swan's beak! So Benjy gave him another of his own sandwiches.

The swan liked them. It wanted more. 'Oh no, my dear, greedy, beautiful swan,' said Benjy, reaching out his hand to run it softly down the swan's graceful neck. 'I want my dinner, you know – and you've already had a good bit of it!'

The swan pecked at Benjy's packet of sandwiches, and broke the whole lot up! Benjy tried to save them but it was no use.

'Oh, Benjy! Make him go away!' said Rory, afraid that his own lunch would go too. 'He's too greedy. Send him away.'

'Well, how do you send a swan away without making it angry or frightened?' demanded poor Benjy, looking with dismay at his spoilt lunch. 'Goodness! Now he's pecked my chocolate. Swan, go away. Go and swim on the river. You look beautiful there!'

The swan came even closer. Benjy wondered if he dared to push it away. He tried – but the swan had far more pushing power than Benjy. The boy rolled over.

Then Rory had a good idea. He took one of Benjy's sandwiches and threw it a little distance away. The swan waddled after it. Then Rory threw another sandwich a bit farther off. The swan went after that. And then there was no more of Benjy's lunch left, so Rory had to begin on his own! He took a sandwich and threw it into the water.

The swan looked at it, and turned and hissed at Rory as if to say, 'Bad shot! Now I shall have to go in and get it!'

He slid down the grassy bank and entered the water with a splash. And at once he changed from a clumsy waddler into a graceful swimmer, and the boys watched him admiringly. Rory had to throw the swan half his lunch before the lovely white bird was satisfied and swam off down the river in a stately manner.

'Well!' said Rory. 'I agree that it's fun to meet all Tammylan's friends – but I think, Benjy, I prefer the shy ones!'

'Tirry-lee!' said the robin from its branch, and it flew down almost on to Rory's foot, to peck up a crumb.

The boys watched it – and then they heard somebody laughing. The laughing went on – and then Benjy looked up and saw Tammylan lying on a branch up in a tree not far off!

'Tammylan!' he cried. 'You've been there all the time!'

'Yes,' laughed Tammylan. 'I wanted to see how my friends liked you – but I couldn't help laughing at you and the swan. He liked you a bit too much, didn't he?'

'He liked our *lunch* too much,' said Benjy, pulling a face. 'We thought we had brought enough for you too, Tammylan – but now there isn't even enough for one of us.'

'You shall have lunch with me today,' said Tammylan, and he leapt lightly down from the tree. 'I went out hunting this morning and I have found all kinds of strange and delicious roots, leaves and buds! Wait till I prepare them and cook them for you!'

The boys watched Tammylan peel roots of all colours and shapes. They saw him shred leaves into his pot. They knew none of them except young nettle leaves.

'Are we going to eat nettle leaves?' asked Benjy in dismay. 'Won't they sting our tongues?'

'Wait and see!' said Tammylan, with a chuckle. 'Look – suck this whilst you are waiting!'

He tossed the boys what looked like tender green shoots

of rose briars. He had peeled them and taken off the thorns. The boys put them into their mouths, not really liking the idea of chewing them – but to their surprise they had a most delicious taste.

'I should never dare to chew stalks and leaves and roots in case I was poisoned,' said Benjy.

'Quite right,' said Tammylan, putting the pot over a fire he had made outside his green house. 'A great many things are poisonous – and also a great many things are good and delicious to eat – but unless you know them, as I do, you must never make silly experiments.'

They had a strange but delightful meal. There was enough chocolate left for them all to have, and it seemed that Tammylan was as fond of that as the two boys were.

'The girls have gone to buy new dresses,' said Benjy. 'They are like the animals and birds – want new clothes in the springtime!'

'And very nice too,' said Tammylan. 'I love to see the birds put on their brilliant spring coats, and to see the animals freshen themselves up and become lively.'

A chittering noise made the boys look up. A red squirrel sat on a branch above them. Tammylan smiled. 'He is cross with me because I picked some of the juicy buds he loves for himself,' said the wild man.

The squirrel gave a tiny bark and stamped on the bough with his feet. Then he bounded off.

'He is building a nest for his wife,' said Tammylan. 'Would you like to see it?'

'Oh *yes*!' said the boys, knowing that this meant climbing a tree. 'Come on, Tammylan – where is it?'

13

Tammylan's Squirrels

Tammylan led the way through the wood. The hazels and oaks gave way to pine-trees, standing rather dark and sombre in the summer sunshine. The boys saw three or four red squirrels racing about. Some were on the ground, others shot up into the trees.

'Watch how they leap from twig to twig!' said Tammylan. 'See how clever and light-footed they are – they seem almost to fly without wings!'

Rory and Benjy stood and watched. The red squirrels chattered at them. Then two began to chase one another and they scampered through the trees, leaping from the end of one twig to the beginning of another without a pause.

'Don't they ever fall?' asked Benjy, in wonder. 'What happens when they miss their footing – or the twig breaks, Tammylan?'

'Watch and see,' said Tammylan. 'There – did you see that squirrel? He wanted to leap from one tree to another but the twig he sprang to broke beneath his foot! But did he fall?'

'No!' said Benjy. 'He simply dropped to the next twig below – but that broke too – and he dropped to another – and that held – so off he went up the tree as quick as lightning!'

'They use their tails to help them to balance themselves,

don't they?' asked Rory. 'Aren't they quick and light? Oh, how I'd love to play about in the trees like that!'

'Look, Tammylan – what's the squirrel doing over there?' asked Benjy, nudging Tammylan. 'Is he eating the grass?'

All three of them looked towards a patch of long green grass. The red squirrel that Benjy was speaking of was busy pulling up the grass with his front paws. He rolled it into a ball with his clever paws, and then stuffed it into his mouth.

'It *is* eating it!' said Benjy. 'Gracious, it's pulling some more and stuffing it in!'

'It isn't eating it, Benjy. It is the squirrel's way of carrying it,' said Tammylan. 'He is going to take it to his nest, and make a cosy lining with it! He is pleased to find such nice long grass – it will make a good lining. And look – here comes another squirrel with his mouth full – what is sticking out of his lips?'

'It's hay in *his* mouth!' said Rory. 'Has he been fetching hay for his nest?'

'Yes,' said Tammylan. 'He has evidently found a haystack near enough to rob, and he knows it makes a cosy lining! Now – what about looking at the nest itself, boys?'

'Oh yes!' cried Benjy. 'Where is it?'

Tammylan led them to a fir tree. The boys looked up. Half-way to the top they saw a big erection of twigs.

'Can you climb this tree?' asked Tammylan. 'The first part is rather straight. But you can use those old bits of broken boughs for your feet, if you feel them carefully before you put your weight on them.'

'Of course we can climb the tree!' said Rory scornfully. 'We may be Londoners, but we can climb all right!'

All the same Tammylan had to watch them at first, and

give them a bit of a help. But when they were well up in the tree it was easy to climb. They came to the big nest – and a red squirrel appeared at the opening to the nest and gave tiny barks at them to make them go away!

'Now, now, Bushy!' said Tammylan in his low voice – and the squirrel quietened down and leapt to his shoulder. Nearby was another squirrel – Bushy's little wife. She chattered at them as they looked at her nest.

'See how well it is made,' said Tammylan. 'Sometimes squirrels use old nests made by birds – a magpie's perhaps – but this time Bushy has made one entirely himself. He has worked very hard!'

Benjy looked closely at it. 'Are these bits of bark?' he asked, pulling out a thin strip.

'Yes – the squirrel strips off tree-bark with his sharp teeth and weaves it into his nest,' said Tammylan. 'And look – here is moss – and leaves. It is a fine nest. We call it a drey – did you know? A squirrel's drey.'

'It's a pretty name,' said Benjy, fingering the moss. 'What's the drey like inside, Tammylan?'

'Feel and see,' said Tammylan. So Benjy and then Rory put in their hands and felt the softness inside. It was well lined with grass – the grass that the boys had seen the squirrel pulling down below.

'This drey is dome-shaped, and has a roof,' said Tammylan. 'Sometimes they are cup-shaped, and then they are just resting-places. This will make a fine nursery for squirrel babies. It is a good sight to see four or five little bright-eyed squirrels peeping out of the nest-opening at me when I pass by!'

'I'm going down now,' said Benjy. 'Bushy, you can go

into your drey! We've finished looking at it!'

Bushy was pleased. He waited till all three were down on the ground again, and then he and his wife popped into the big drey to make sure that no damage had been done!

'Last year Bushy made his nest in a big hole in the trunk of an old tree,' said Tammylan. 'But it was cut down in the autumn, so he had to find a new tree this year. He rested all the winter in an old drey in that tree nearby – but it wasn't suitable for a proper drey for himself and his wife. That is why he has been so busy this spring!'

'Do squirrels sleep all the winter through, as the snakes do?' asked Rory.

'Oh no!' said Tammylan, sitting down to watch the squirrels playing in the wood. 'They only sleep when the weather is very bitter. They love to come out in a warm spell, even though snow may be on the ground! In fact, last winter they played in the snow just as you do – I half-expected them to roll up snowballs and throw them at me!'

The boys laughed. 'What do they eat, then, if they wake up in the winter?' asked Rory. 'They hide nuts, don't they?'

'Yes – nuts, beech-mast, acorns,' said Tammylan. 'But they often forget where they have hidden them. And sometimes the mice find them and take them away for themselves. It is funny to see an anxious squirrel scrabbling about in corners and under leaves for his hidden store – feeling quite sure he *did* put it there! And perhaps a bright-eyed mouse not far off watches him from a hole in a tree-trunk, knowing quite well that the nuts will never be found, because he has eaten them himself!'

'Do squirrels eat birds' eggs?' asked Benjy.

'Sometimes,' said Tammylan. 'And sometimes they are bold enough to carry young nestlings from the nest to eat, too. The wise mother-bird will never remain away from her nest too long in a wood where squirrels live – she knows her young ones will be in danger if she does.'

'They like toadstools, too, don't they?' said Rory.

'Some kinds,' said Tammylan. 'You know, I love the edible toadstools myself, and . . .'

'Tammylan! But toadstools are deadly poison!' cried Benjy in horror.

'Some are poisonous, and some are good to eat,' said Tammylan, smiling. 'Don't you go trying any, though – you are sure to choose the poisonous kind! But I know which are safe, and I make many a delicious meal from them. You shall share some with me later on. But what I was saying was that sometimes when I go hunting for the particular toadstools that I love, the squirrels see that I am picking them, and they come and scold me – because, you see, they are what they want for themselves!'

'I'd like to see them scolding you!' said Benjy.

'They not only chatter at me, and stamp their tiny feet in anger on the tree branches above, but they even run down and scamper across to me – and help themselves out of my basket!' said Tammylan.

'Will you tell us when there are baby squirrels to be seen?' asked Rory. 'And, by the way, Tammylan – aren't there any *grey* squirrels in these woods? I've only seen the red ones. There were lots of grey ones in London, and they were very tame, too. But not nearly so pretty as these red ones.'

'Those are descendants of American squirrels that were

let loose in London years ago,' said the wild man. 'They have spread outwards, and now in many places they have driven away the little red squirrel. But we have not yet had any of the grey ones – and I hope we shan't, for I like my happy little red friends, and would hate to see them forced away by grey strangers!'

It was pleasant to sit in the woods, listening to the calls of the birds and watching the friendly squirrels at play. Bushy was on and off Tammylan's shoulder all the time, and his little wife visited Benjy, too. Rory was not so lucky. He could not remember not to make quick movements, so the little creatures avoided him. At last, seeing his disappointed face, Tammylan put Bushy on to Rory's shoulder.

Bushy sat there for two seconds, and Rory was delighted – but then the small creature was off and up a tree in a twinkling.

'Tammylan, I shall be eleven next week,' said Benjy. 'Aren't I getting old?'

'You are, rather,' said Tammylan, looking at the boy, with a smile. 'So you are going to have a birthday? Well, I wonder what birthday treat you would like from me?'

'Oh! I don't want a present or a treat!' said Benjy at once.

'Well, I'd like to give you a treat of some sort,' said Tammylan. 'Think now – you can choose.'

Benjy thought. Then his face went red and he looked up at Tammylan shyly. 'Well,' he said, and stopped. 'Well, Tammylan . . .'

'Go on,' said Tammylan. 'Is it something so difficult?'

'Oh no,' said Benjy. 'You see . . .'

'*I* know what he wants to say!' said Rory, taking pity on

Benjy. 'He's often said it to us. He would like nothing better than to come and spend a night with you in your tree-house, Tammylan – and hear the night-owls hooting, and the splash of the river going by, and see the stars through the doorway of your house.'

'Is that right, Benjy?' asked Tammylan, looking very pleased. Benjy nodded.

'I hope you don't think it's awful cheek,' he said.

'Why should I?' asked Tammylan. 'Very well – that shall be your birthday treat from me. Come any night next week, the warmer the better. It will be moonlight, and we will have a few visitors, I hope!'

Benjy was thrilled. He couldn't have wished for anything better. Rory looked at him enviously.

'You are jolly lucky!' he said.

'I *am*!' said Benjy, and he rubbed his hands in glee. What a treat to look forward to!

14

Benjy has a Birthday

When the others heard what Benjy's birthday treat from Tammylan was to be, they wished and wished that their birthdays were near too. Sheila and Penny had come back thrilled with their new dresses – but they forgot all about them when they heard the tale of the squirrels and their drey. Penny wanted to go off to the woods at once, and climb the tree.

'What! In your new frock!' cried Auntie Bess. 'Certainly not, Penny. No climbing trees for *you*, please. Or for Sheila either. What's all this about spending the night with Tammylan, Benjy? You'll have to ask your uncle.'

But he didn't need to, because Tammylan spoke to Uncle Tim one morning as he went round his fields. Uncle Tim was quite willing to listen. He agreed to let the boy spend the night with Tammylan. 'But he must take a mackintosh sheet with him, to spread on the ground,' said Uncle Tim. 'It may be all right for you to live as you do – but the boy might take a chill. He's not used to it.'

Benjy was overjoyed when Uncle Tim told him he had seen Tammylan and agreed to the birthday treat. He danced round the farmyard like a mad thing and the hens fled squawking to hide.

'Have pity on my hens, Benjy, for goodness' sake!' called Auntie Bess. 'You'll frighten them out of their feathers!'

Benjy's birthday dawned fair and warm. The sun shone down hotly, and not even a wisp of cloud sailed over the sky. It was perfect birthday weather. Benjy was very happy.

He had lovely presents. Uncle Tim and Auntie Bess gave him boots and leggings just like Uncle Tim wore. How grand he felt when he put them on!

Sheila gave him a new book about animals. Rory gave him six tomato plants that he had bought at the market especially for Benjy. Benjy loved tomatoes – and now he could grow and pick his own!

'Thanks, Rory,' said Benjy. 'I shall take them out of their pots and plant them in that sunny spot by the wall where Aunt Bess said we could have a garden. And you and Sheila and Penny shall have the first three tomatoes! Golly, shan't I love picking my own tomatoes!'

Penny gave him a big tin of toffees that she had bought out of her own money. Taffy gave him a stick of his own that he had cut from the hedge for Benjy. That was a great surprise, and the boy was proud of his fine hazel stick.

His mother and father sent him some money to spend. He put it away safely in his purse. He didn't want anything at the moment, but it would be very useful when he did.

Uncle Tim took all the children in the pony-trap to market that morning. This was a treat they simply loved. It was good to see the fat cows, and to smell the rich market smell. It was fun to see the cackling geese, and to look at the grunting pigs in their pens. The market-women had golden butter to sell, and fresh brown eggs, bright green gooseberries, pots of homemade jam, greens from the garden, and many other things.

'Things feel *real*, somehow, out in the country,' said Rory, staring round at everything, his eyes wandering off to the blue hills in the distance. 'There's plenty of room, for one thing, and your eyes can look for miles. And there's the good animal, earthy smell – and everybody's doing something that matters – you know – milking cows, or selling eggs, or driving geese. I shall hate to go back to town!'

'Don't let's think about it!' said Benjy. 'Come on – I shall spend some of my birthday money on ice-creams!'

At teatime there was an enormous cake covered with pink and white icing. On it was written in Auntie Bess's handwriting, 'Many Happy Returns to Benjy'. Eleven coloured candles stood proudly upright in sugar roses.

'This is the loveliest birthday I've ever had!' said Benjy, with a sigh of happiness. 'Thank you, Aunt Bess, for making such a lovely cake. I usually have shop birthday cakes, and they aren't nearly so nice as this.'

The cake was gorgeous, and each of the children managed two pieces. 'I don't know what your mother would say if she saw you eating now,' said Aunt Bess, looking at the fat, rosy faces round the table. 'She told me you picked at your food, never asked for second helpings, and fussed over everything – so I thought I was going to have really difficult children!'

The children thought back to their London days. 'Well, I never felt hungry,' said Penny, remembering.

'And nothing ever tasted really nice to me,' said Benjy. 'I say, Aunt Bess – could I take a piece of my birthday cake to Tammylan? He'd be so pleased.'

'Of course,' said Auntie Bess. 'Take him a nice big piece.

He'll enjoy it – always eating those roots and toadstools and wild fruits! I wonder he keeps well!'

'He's awfully strong,' said Benjy, munching at his cake. 'He can climb a tree in a trice, and jump over the widest streams, and carry a fallen tree over his shoulder.'

'Marvellous man!' said Uncle Tim. 'Well – I suppose you'll soon be going off to spend the night with him? Got your mackintosh sheet out?'

'Yes,' said Benjy. 'But I wish I didn't have to take it. I'd like to feel the heather tickling me all night long!'

'I suppose we'll see you back tomorrow sometime,' said Auntie Bess. 'Well, you're a lucky boy – you've had a marvellous birthday, and, although most children's birthdays end when they go to bed, yours will still go on tonight!'

Benjy felt happy every time he thought of spending the night with Tammylan. He hugged himself in a funny way he had, and the others laughed at him.

'Mind you tell us *everything* when you come back,' said Sheila. 'Every single thing!'

'Of course,' said Benjy, and he went to get his mackintosh sheet. It was in a tight little roll and he slung it over his shoulder on some string. He took a pocketful of the toffees that Penny had given him, and a big piece of his birthday cake wrapped up in paper. He had on his new boots and leggings, and in his hand was the stout hazel stick that Taffy had given him.

He felt very important and grand. Leggings made him feel manly. He wasn't very big for his age, but now he felt twice as old as he shouted goodbye to the others, and strode away down the lane, his stick swinging in his hand.

Benjy whistled as he went, and hoped he would meet the farm-men. He tucked his stick under his arm as he had seen his uncle do. Then he fished a toffee out of his pocket, and after that he couldn't whistle any more because the toffee took a lot of managing.

The sun was sending slanting rays between the trees as he came near to Tammylan's little growing house. The river shone gold, for it reflected the western sky. Blackbirds were fluting clearly, and a yellowhammer somewhere sang its monotonous little song. 'Little bit of bread and no *cheese*! Little bit of bread and no *cheese*!'

Tammylan was waiting for him, sitting at the open doorway of his little green house. 'Many happy returns!' he said to Benjy.

'Thanks,' said Benjy. 'I've had a fine birthday. See my new leggings?'

'Grand!' said Tammylan. 'And that's a new stick, I see. Well – here's my present for you!'

He dropped a tiny bundle of warm fur into Benjy's hands. The boy gave a soft cry, and looked down.

'A baby squirrel!' he said. 'Oh, how lovely! Where did you get it?'

'It's one I've been keeping for you,' said Tammylan. 'The mother was accidentally killed – caught in a trap, poor thing – and of her three babies, two died. But this one was still alive in the nest when I found it. So I brought it here and fed it – and kept it for your birthday. It will be like a little dog, always with you, always at your call.'

'Oh, Tammylan, I couldn't want a better present!' said Benjy, really overjoyed. He had never in his life had a pet –

and now here was the quaintest, softest ball of fur, ready to become his faithful little friend. It should live on his shoulder! It should come at his call. What should he call it?

'Shall I call it Scamper?' he asked Tammylan. 'Squirrels scamper over the ground and up the trees so quickly. And I could call it Scamp for short, if it's a rascal of a squirrel.'

'Good idea,' said Tammylan. 'Now, Scamper, cuddle down for a while in your new master's arms. We want to watch the sun go down. There will be a marvellous sunset tonight.'

Scamper had already cuddled into the crook of Benjy's right arm. Its bright black eyes closed. Its little furry tail coiled round its nose. It was asleep.

Benjy sat hugging his new pet, feeling its tiny heart beating quickly against his arm. He leaned against one side of the doorway and Tammylan sat against the other side. The tree-house had grown leaves to such an extent that they made a completely green roof, and hung down the sides.

Benjy peeped inside the house. To his great delight he saw that Tammylan had made up another bed, opposite to his. Dried moss and heather were banked up, and an old rug was thrown at the end.

'I can see my bed!' said the boy. 'Isn't it a pity – I've got to have this silly mackintosh sheet to lie on. It will spoil the feel of the heather.'

'No, it won't,' said Tammylan. 'We'll put it on the ground, *beneath* the heather – and pile the bedding on top! Then you won't get the damp striking up from the ground – and you'll still lie on the heather and moss!'

'Oh, good!' said Benjy, pleased. His squirrel stirred in his arms and he stroked its back gently. The little thing stretched itself and fell asleep again.

'And now let us be quiet, for I am expecting a visitor tonight,' said Tammylan. 'When you hear his whistle keep quite still.'

'*Whistle!*' said Benjy, amazed. 'Is it a man, then?'

'Oh no,' said Tammylan.

'But no animal whistles,' said Benjy. 'Oh, you mean a bird?'

'Not even a bird!' said Tammylan. 'Now, be quiet, and wait.'

15

A Night in the Tree-house

Benjy sat perfectly still, the baby squirrel asleep on his knee. The sun sank lower, and the sky became pink and gold. The quiet backwater of the river reflected the sky, and Benjy was almost dazzled as he looked at it. A buttercup field across the river shone and glowed in the last rays of the sun – and then the big round disc sank half-way over the sky-line.

The light went out of the buttercups. The clouds faded from pink to grey. Two bars of gold remained in the sky – and then, just as Benjy was watching them fade to a pale blue, he heard the whistle.

It was clear as a flute, and it came echoing over the water. There was something bird-like in it, and yet it wasn't a bird Benjy felt sure. It came again, fluting over the water, clear and lovely.

Tammylan answered the whistle. He sent out a call so exactly like the whistle that Benjy had to look at him to make sure it came from him. Tammylan nodded towards the water. 'Here he comes,' he said.

Benjy looked eagerly at the darkening water. He saw, coming gradually towards them, a dark blunt head just on the surface. The body belonging to the head was swimming below. Benjy couldn't make out what it was at all.

With hardly a ripple to show that anyone was swimming there, the creature moved towards the bank. It clambered out – and Benjy saw that it was a big dark-brown animal, with a long tail and strong webbed feet.

'An otter!' he said. 'Oh, Tammylan!'

Tammylan whistled to the otter again and it shook itself and came towards him, moving easily over the ground. Its small, bright eyes looked at him, and then at Benjy.

'All right, friend, you are safe with Benjy,' said Tammylan, in his special voice – the one he always used for animals and birds. The otter moved closer to him and lay down, its head on Tammylan's leg. Tammylan ran his fingers over the otter's small, rounded ears.

'Have you had good hunting, friend?' he said. 'Have you eaten fish today? Did you catch them by swimming below them, and darting upwards more quickly than they could swim? Did you turn over the river stones and hunt for the crayfish you love? Did you find the frogs and skin them for a meal?'

The otter made a snickering noise, and moved its head a little higher up Tammylan's leg. Benjy watched enviously, wishing that the otter would come to him too.

'Feel him, Benjy,' said Tammylan. 'Feel his thick fur. He has two coats of hair – one a thick, short undercoat to protect his body from the water, and the other a coat of much longer hairs. You can feel them growing out of his short coat.'

Benjy felt them. 'Doesn't he ever get cold and wet swimming like that?' he asked.

'No,' said Tammylan. 'His body never gets wet. He is a marvellous swimmer, Benjy, as graceful as any fish.'

'What does he do when he swims under the water?' asked Benjy. 'Doesn't the water get into his ears?'

'No. He closes both his ears then,' said Tammylan. 'See his thick, strong tail, Benjy. He uses it as a rudder in the water. He is a beautiful beast in the river, and when he gambols there for fun he is a joy to watch.'

'I saw that he had webbed feet,' said Benjy. 'They help him to swim fast, of course. What a lovely whistle he has!'

'Yes,' said Tammylan. 'I hear it often at night now, coming down the river. The night-sounds are lovely to hear – the bark of a distant fox – the whistle of the otter – the hoot of the owl. This friend of mine visits me often at night, and sometimes, if he is near, he comes in answer to my whistle.'

'How did you first know him?' asked Benjy. 'He is so tame!'

'Three years ago his father and mother made a nesting-place in a hole among the alder roots, a little way down this backwater,' said Tammylan. 'It was a good hole, with an entrance below the water and one above it on the bank at the back. In this hole the otters brought up three cubs – fur-covered youngsters eager to learn to swim and hunt fish.'

'Eager to *learn*?' asked Benjy. 'Did they have to be taught, then? Didn't they know it without being taught, as birds know how to build nests, and ducks know how to swim?'

'No – the young otters had to be taught, Benjy,' said Tammylan. 'I used to hide in the bushes and watch the parents take the three cubs into the water and teach them the business of hunting. They could not stay under the water for very long at first without breathing – but they soon learnt that trick. Then they learnt to chase the fish and swim below them. They were taught to bring their catch to the bank and eat it there – but to leave the tail! It is not good manners in the otter family to eat the tail of a fish.'

Benjy laughed, and the little squirrel stirred, settled itself again and slept. The otter looked at Benjy with glittering eyes. Tammylan ran his fingers down its neck, and it snickered and rolled against him.

'Well,' said Tammylan, 'the otter hounds came to hunt the otter one day. The parents fled away, swimming for dear life. The dogs caught two of the cubs – they killed them. And then this one, who was the third cub, tried to make its way to a hiding-place across the river, unseen. But the hounds saw the slight ripple he made – and two of them caught him. They bit his back legs cruelly. He fought hard, and they let him go.'

'Poor little cub,' said Benjy. 'I wish things needn't be so cruel to one another.'

'The cub managed to crawl back to his old nesting-hole,' said Tammylan. 'And there I found him after the hunt was over. He crawled to me out of the back entrance, and I brought him here and looked after him till his legs were better and he could swim again. That is how he and I became friends.'

'It's a fine story,' said Benjy. 'Penny would cry over that, I know. She can't bear anything to be hurt.'

'This otter has travelled far in the winter days,' said Tammylan. 'He wandered over the land at night, for he is a good traveller. But now he lives in the river, and knows every inch of it from the source to the mouth!'

Benjy sat quiet, thinking over the story of the otter, wondering where the parents had gone. What a good thing Tammylan had been about at the time of the hunt! How many creatures had he healed and saved? Benjy was proud to have him for a friend.

The moon rose up, and the river changed from black to silver. Pools of cold moonlight lay on the ground. Rabbits came out everywhere. Owls hooted weirdly, and once there came such a screech that Benjy jumped violently and awoke the squirrel.

'Whatever's that?' asked the boy.

'A barn-owl across the water,' said Tammylan. 'They always screech like that. Now Benjy – what about some supper – and then bed?'

'I could stay here for hours,' said Benjy, with a sigh. 'Doesn't the world seem strange and unreal by moonlight, Tammylan? Oh – I nearly forgot – I've got some of my birthday cake for you!'

The boy gave the slice to Tammylan. He was very pleased, and ate it as he sat, giving a few crumbs to the otter at his feet. Then he lit a small fire and cooked the boy a strange but delicious meal. They ate it in the moonlight, and then drank something that Tammylan called Nettle-gingerbeer. It was made of nettle leaves and tasted funny but cool and sweet.

'And now for bed!' said Tammylan. 'I bathe in the morning, Benjy. Will that suit you? We will take a plunge in the river then. Take off your coat and shorts and I'll roll you up in the rug.'

The mackintosh sheet was laid flat on the ground under Benjy's bed of heather and moss. When he was ready Tammylan rolled him up in the rug, and then the boy cuddled down on his heather bed. It felt soft and springy, though a few sprigs stuck into him here and there. Benjy arranged them comfortably, and then let himself sink down into the unusual bed. It smelt nice. The squirrel curled up on his tummy, still sleeping.

'Where's the otter going to?' asked Benjy sleepily. 'Is it going back to the river?'

'I think he wants to sleep here for the night,' said Tammylan. 'Do you mind? He sometimes likes company, you see.'

'Do I *mind*!' said Benjy. 'Why, I'd love it! I never, never thought I'd go to sleep with a squirrel on top of me, a wild man near me, and an otter at our feet!'

Benjy didn't want to go to sleep at all. He wanted to stay awake and feel the strange delight of the little growing house, the breathing of the otter, the warmth of the squirrel – he wanted to lie and look at the moon which was now shining straight into the open doorway of the house. He wished he could hear the owls all night long – and the plash-plash-plash of the water nearby, and the whispering in the trees above.

But his eyes wouldn't stay open. They closed and he slept as peacefully as Tammylan, the otter, and the tiny furry squirrel.

16

Two More Friends

Benjy awoke first in the morning, because the squirrel was trying to sit on his nose. Benjy couldn't think what was happening. His eyes shot open, he gasped for breath – and sat up. The squirrel fell off and leapt to the ground. Benjy picked it up at once – he didn't want it to scamper out of the doorway and be lost!

The otter was gone. Tammylan lay on his side, sleeping peacefully. Faint daylight shone into the open doorway. The splash of the water against the bank sounded like a little tune – plishy-plash-plash, plishy-plash-plash.

'I wonder if the sun is rising yet,' thought Benjy, lying on his back and looking up into the greenness of the roof. 'Oh, isn't it lovely to wake up like this, in a wood by the water! I shan't wake Tammylan. I shall just enjoy it all quite by myself – with my squirrel!'

The squirrel had curled up on a warm part of Benjy's neck, and was now asleep again.

A few birds began to sing. The light grew stronger. A breeze got up and made the trees say 'Sh! Sh! Sh!' to one another – at least, that is what Benjy thought it sounded like.

Then a small animal appeared in the doorway, and stood up on its hind legs, sniffing gently. It was quite surprised to see Benjy looking at it. Benjy moved his squirrel and sat up, leaning on an elbow to watch the newcomer.

'I think it's a rat,' thought Benjy. 'I don't like rats. I really don't. They are about the only animal I don't want to be friends with.'

He watched the furry creature as it ran quickly to Tammylan's couch. It put one paw on the wild man's bed and stood there, waiting to see if Tammylan would move or speak.

But Tammylan slept on. The little creature scratched itself behind the ears, and seemed to think a little. Then it made up its mind that its friend was asleep – and it ran to the doorway. Benjy made up *his* mind to see where it went.

So he cautiously got up and went to the open doorway. The furry animal had run to the river bank. Benjy followed. The little creature did not seem to mind him in the least. It slipped down to a small ledge, near the water, and began to nibble at some juicy horsetail stems. Every now and again it looked up at Benjy as if to say, 'Try a bit! It's good!'

There was a noise behind Benjy, and he looked round. It was Tammylan. He had awakened, missed Benjy, and had come to look for him. He saw him at once, by the river.

'Hallo, Tammylan,' said Benjy eagerly. 'I did love waking up in your tree-house! Look – do you see that rat down there? It came to visit you – but you were fast asleep. I don't think I want a rat for a friend. *Is* he your friend?'

'That little creature down there is a great friend of mine,' said Tammylan, squatting down on the bank beside Benjy. 'But he is no rat!'

'I thought he was!' said Benjy. 'I know lots of people

who would have killed him if they could – everyone seems to hate rats.'

'Yes – rats have a bad name, and they certainly deserve it,' said Tammylan. 'But this poor little animal should not be made to suffer because he happens to be just a little like a rat to look at!'

'What is he, then?' asked Benjy in surprise.

'He is a water-vole,' said Tammylan. 'A quiet and harmless little animal, who loves the water and only wants to live at peace. But as soon as anyone sees him they cry, 'A rat! A rat!' and throw stones at him to kill him. Watch him as he nibbles that stem – he is a dear little thing, harming nothing and no one!'

The water-vole looked up at Tammylan. It sprang up the bank and ran on to Tammylan's knee. The wild man stroked the long glossy fur. It was a rich reddish-brown with grey hairs here and there. Tammylan rolled the vole over to tickle him and showed Benjy the yellow-grey fur below.

'He is not *really* like a rat,' said Tammylan. 'Look at his head – it is thicker and shorter than a rat's – and see his rounded muzzle. You know that the rat has a pointed one, don't you? And look at the vole's hairy tail – not nearly so long as the rat's bare, scaly one.'

'Yes – now you say all these things, I can see that the vole isn't like a rat,' said Benjy, stroking the tiny head with its round ears. 'What a shame that it is killed in mistake for a rat! You say it's a *water*-vole, Tammylan. Can it swim, then?'

'Watch and see,' said Tammylan. He set the vole down gently on the bank and gave it a little push. The vole at once leapt down to the water and entered it with a little plop.

'When you walk along the river bank and hear that 'plop' you will know that a water-vole has seen you and gone home!' said Tammylan.

'Where does he live?' asked Benjy, trying to see whereabouts in the water the vole was. But he could see nothing.

'He has a cosy hidey-hole in the bank over there,' said Tammylan, pointing to where reeds grew thickly. 'The entrance is under the water – but, like the otter, our vole has a back entrance above ground. Come and watch him peep out of it.'

They got up and went to the reeds. Tammylan parted them and showed Benjy a small hole. He pursed up his lips and made a curious sucking noise. At once the rounded furry head of the water-vole appeared, and two black eyes looked up inquiringly at Tammylan.

'All right, old fellow,' said Tammylan. 'We just wanted to see you at your back door! He swam to his underwater entrance, Benjy, ran up his burrow – and, when he heard my call, popped up to see us.'

The water-vole popped back and disappeared. 'Does he sleep all the winter?' asked Benjy as they went back to the tree-house.

'Oh no,' said Tammylan. 'He comes to see me during the darkest days of winter. He sometimes lays up a little store of food for himself – and in the New Year I have seen him chewing the tender willow shoots. He has two little cousins you must look out for, Benjy – the small field-vole, which we often call the short-tailed field-mouse, and the little bank-vole. Now – what about a bathe?'

The sun was shining warmly now. The river looked cool

and inviting. It wasn't long before Benjy and Tammylan were having a fine time in the water, splashing one another and shouting. Tammylan could swim like an otter. Benjy wished he could do the same – but he couldn't!

They dressed, and Tammylan cooked a strange but delicious breakfast. The tiny squirrel sat on Benjy's shoulder all the time. Tammylan picked some tender shoots for it, and it held one in its hands and nibbled it.

'I do love Scamper,' said Benjy, rubbing his head against the furry mite. 'Do you think he will be happy with me?'

'He will soon run off into the woods if he isn't!' said Tammylan. 'I will show you what shoots to feed him on. Later on he will love acorns and nuts. I will tell you the toadstools he likes, too.'

'I *have* had a lovely time,' sighed Benjy, looking round at the tree-house, the river, and the sunny freckles on the ground. 'I wish I could stay here always.'

'I would like you to,' said Tammylan. 'It is not many boys who have the feeling for the wild creatures that you have – but you belong to your family – and it is time you went back to them, Benjy. They will be wondering what you are doing.'

'Yes – I must go back, I have my jobs to do,' said Benjy, standing up. 'I'll come and see you soon again, Tammylan – and thanks for a lovely time – and a lovely pet! I'll bring Scamper to see you whenever I come.'

'I'll come with you a little way,' said Tammylan. 'It's such a lovely morning.'

The man and the boy walked together through the green woods. They came to where bushes of yellow broom were waving in the summer breeze. As they passed near them a tiny creature ran across their path. They stopped, and Benjy pointed to where it ran.

'What's that?' he cried. 'A mouse? Isn't it small!'

'That was a tiny harvest-mouse,' said Tammylan. 'Almost the smallest of all our animals! Let us look in this broom bush . . . it ran there. Perhaps it has its nest there. We could see it.'

Tammylan looked into the bush. He made a funny chirping noise, rather like a bird. Benjy listened in astonishment when he heard someone chirping back! Surely a mouse didn't chirp!

But the harvest-mouse apparently did – for Tammylan beckoned to Benjy, and showed him the nest. It was really marvellous. It was built among the stems of the broom, about seven or eight inches from the ground. The mouse had cleverly used some of the stiff stems to hold up her nest, which she had made in the shape of a little ball. It was made of split blades of grass, very neatly plaited together to make a cosy, strong nest.

'It's the best nest I ever saw in my life,' said Benjy, full of wonder. 'I couldn't make such a beauty myself! Where's the entrance?'

'Oh, just anywhere!' said Tammylan, and he showed Benjy how he could force an opening in any place, between the woven grass. 'There is a family of six or seven inside, I should think – and the mother too!'

'But how can they all get into that three-inch nest!' said Benjy. Tammylan gently forced a space in the outside of the nest and Benjy caught a glimpse of a closely packed family, small and frightened.

'We won't disturb them any more,' said Tammylan. 'It is only because the mother heard me chirping to her that she knows I am friendly. Listen – she will chirp back again!'

Tammylan chirped loudly – and from the nest the little harvest-mouse answered with a softer chirp. Benjy tried the chirp, too – but it was not so easy as it sounded!

'Another noise to practise!' thought Benjy. 'The snake noise – the otter whistle – goodness, I shall be a walking menagerie of noises soon!'

'Watch for the little harvest-mouse as you go about the fields this summer,' said Tammylan. 'Especially in the cornfields, Benjy. The mouse is so small that it can climb up a stalk of corn, hold on by its tail, and nibble the grain! It is really a pretty sight to see, with its thick, yellow-red fur, blunt little nose, and bright black eyes.'

They came to the stile and Tammylan swung off up the hill, and called goodbye. Benjy went back to the farm with Scamper on his shoulder.

The others came running to meet him.

'What did you do? Did you sleep in the tree-house?' cried Penny.

'What's that on your shoulder!' called Rory.

'It's a baby squirrel!' squealed Sheila. 'Oh, where did you get it from, Benjy?'

'It was my birthday present from Tammylan,' said Benjy proudly. 'Aren't I lucky?'

The squirrel looked at the three children with bright black eyes. It did not seem in the least frightened. It lay against Benjy's neck as the boy told all about his adventures of the night before.

'Oh! Fancy sleeping with a squirrel and an otter!' said Penny, her eyes as wide as the squirrel's. 'Oh, you are the luckiest boy in all the world.'

'Yes, I am!' said Benjy, patting Scamper. And he really meant it!

17

The Tail that Broke Off

The little squirrel was very happy with the children. They made a fuss of it, fed it with all kinds of dainties, as well as the food that Tammylan had told Benjy to give it, and it became as much a pet as Shadow, the collie.

It usually lived on Benjy's shoulder, and it always slept on his bed. It leapt here and there, bounded up the curtains and down, and gave Auntie Bess a hundred shocks a day. But she liked the pretty little thing, and was only afraid that the cat might catch it.

'I think Tammylan would like to see how Scamper has grown,' said Benjy one fine sunny day. 'Let's go and see him, and take the squirrel with us.'

'Take your tea with you and have a picnic,' said Auntie Bess.

'Oh yes – let's take our tea!' cried Penny, who was always ready for a picnic. So Aunt Bess packed up tomato sandwiches, egg sandwiches, ginger buns, and milk, and they set off for their picnic.

They went first to Tammylan's cave and then to the tree-house but Tammylan was not to be found. So they decided he must have gone on one of his explorations, or to visit one of his friends, and they chose a nice sunny place in the heather for their tea. Scamper nibbled at the tomato sandwiches in delight, but he couldn't bear the taste of the ginger buns. He scolded Sheila for giving him a bit, and stamped his little feet hard on Benjy's shoulder.

'Oh, what a naughty temper you've got!' laughed Sheila. Then she suddenly gave a squeal, and pointed to something that lay basking in the sun nearby.

'Look!' she said. 'A snake!'

They all looked. They saw a creature about eighteen inches long. Its head was small and short, and the tail tapered gradually to a point. It was covered with scales. The bright eyes gleamed in its head.

'Well – but what *sort* of a snake!' said Benjy in wonder. 'It isn't a viper, that's quite certain. And it isn't a grass snake, because its body is so different – and I'm sure it isn't a smooth snake. Tammylan said there were only three snakes in this country – and he must be wrong!'

'I wonder if it bites,' said Sheila, not at all sure that she liked the look of it.

'No, I shouldn't think so,' said Benjy. 'Tammylan did say very clearly that we only have one poisonous snake here – and this one is most certainly not the viper!'

'Catch it, Benjy,' said Rory. 'Then we can show it to Tammylan. We can tell him he's wrong – there's a fourth kind of snake in our country!'

'Well – I can't think Tammylan is wrong,' said Benjy, puzzled. 'But I really must find out about this. Hold Scamper, Rory. I'll see if I can catch the snake. Keep quiet, all of you!'

Benjy crept quietly over the heather. The creature did not seem to hear him coming. It was enjoying the sunshine, and lay there, its long body stretched out to the warm rays.

Benjy got very close – closer – and then he made a grab at the snake. In a trice it wriggled through his fingers – but Benjy had hold of it by the tail!

'Got you!' he cried.

But had he? What was this? The frightened creature wriggled away in the heather, and left behind in Benjy's hand – a tail! It jumped about in a most peculiar manner.

'I say! Just look at that!' said Benjy, in the greatest astonishment.

'Oh, Benjy! How cruel of you! You've broken its tail off!' said Penny, almost in tears.

'I *didn't*!' said Benjy indignantly. 'I just held it, to catch it – and its tail broke off in my hand. You saw it! Do you suppose it did it on purpose, to get away?'

'Lizards do that, but not snakes,' said Rory, staring at the jerking tail-end in Benjy's hand. 'I wish Tammylan was here. He would be sure to know about this.'

Scamper sniffed at the tail-end and then jumped on to Benjy's shoulder in disgust. He didn't like the look of the tail at all. Neither did anyone, really. Benjy put it away in his pocket and tried to forget about it.

But although they went on with their picnic, nobody felt really hungry now. Somehow it seemed spoilt. They couldn't help wondering if the creature had been hurt – and Benjy felt really very guilty. Suppose Tammylan called him cruel and was angry with him?

Just as they were finishing they saw Tammylan in the distance. Rory got up and waved to him. He came over to the children, smiling.

'Tammylan, does it hurt a snake to have its tail broken off?' asked Penny as soon as he came near.

'Whatever do you mean?' asked Tammylan in surprise. 'A snake never breaks its tail off.'

'But it *does*!' said poor Benjy; and, very red in the face, he pulled the tail-end out of his pocket.

Tammylan looked at the tail, and then he looked at Benjy's guilty face. Then, to the children's surprise and relief, he began to laugh.

'Oh dear!' he said at last. 'So you really thought you'd been strong enough to pull a snake's tail off. No – that's not a snake's tail.'

'But it *is*, Tammylan,' cried all the children. 'It is, it is!'

'Listen!' said Tammylan. 'I told you we only had three kinds of snakes in our country, didn't I? Well, this isn't one of them. It belongs to the lizard family, not to the snakes. It is a slow-worm, or, to give it another of its silly names, a blind-worm.'

'Oh!' said the children. Benjy blushed. 'I ought to have known,' he said. 'I've read about it in my books.'

'Now, what about looking more closely at a slow-worm?' said Tammylan. 'Not the one who made you a present of his tail, Benjy – he won't appear again today! But I dare say we shall see another, if we search about a bit.'

The children watched Tammylan as he quietly hunted on the sandy banks for another slow-worm. At last he spied one. The children watched him in excitement.

'I guess this one will break off its tail too!' whispered Rory. But it didn't. No – Tammylan knew how to catch slow-worms! He caught it just behind the head, not by the

122

tail, and brought it over to the children.

The slow-worm did not seem in the least frightened. That was the strange part about the wild man. No animal or bird ever showed fright when he spoke to it or touched it. The slow-worm lay in his hands, and even when Tammylan no longer held it by the back of the neck it did not glide away.

'Here is our slow-worm,' said Tammylan. 'I am afraid that far too many people make the same mistake as you did, children, and think it is a snake! So the poor old harmless slow-worm is killed by any passer-by. It can't sting. It can't bite. It eats worms, slugs, and insects, and does no harm to anyone! If only people would learn a little more about our wild creatures, no slow-worm would ever be killed.'

'Why is it called a *slow*-worm?' asked Rory. 'You know, the one that wriggled away from Benjy wasn't slow – it was a quick-worm!'

Tammylan laughed. 'I will tell you the three names that foolish people have given to this legless lizard,' he said. 'One is slow-worm – but, as you said, it *isn't* slow. Another name is blind-worm – but, as you see, it has remarkably bright eyes – and please notice the eyelids, which a snake never has! The third name, even sillier, is deaf-adder. It isn't deaf, and it certainly isn't an adder!'

The slow-worm put out its tongue and Benjy gave an exclamation. 'Look! Its tongue isn't forked like a snake's.'

'No,' said Tammylan. 'It is only notched. I am glad you noticed that, Benjy. Good boy!'

'But, Tammylan, why did the slow-worm break off its tail?' asked Benjy. 'Will it grow again?'

'It broke its tail off because it knew it could escape that

way,' said Tammylan. 'A snake cannot do that, of course! Yes – it will grow again, though it may not be quite so nicely fitting a tail as before! Look, children – do you see that slow-worm over there? It has just come out on the bank. Look at its tail – at some time or other it has been broken off. Do you see where the new one began to grow again, at the break?'

'Oh yes!' said Sheila. 'I can see it quite easily! Well I *am* glad we didn't hurt the slow-worm, Tammylan. I do hope it will soon grow a very nice new tail.'

'It will take it a little time,' said the wild man. 'But it will grow it all right! And what is more, it would grow a third one if it had to!'

Tammylan let the slow-worm he was holding slip to the ground. It wriggled away like a flash and disappeared. 'A *quick*-worm, as you said, Rory!' said Tammylan. 'Yet it isn't a worm either. It *does* suffer from a lot of stupid names, doesn't it! I wish you could see its young ones, later on in the summer. They are amusing little things. Last year I kept a whole family of them.'

'What were they like?' asked Benjy.

'Oh – like wriggling silver needles!' said Tammylan. 'They were perfectly lovely, and I didn't need to feed them myself at all. They could catch their own food even when they were not much bigger than a darning-needle!'

'Do you know where any lizards are?' asked Benjy.

'Good gracious, yes!' said Tammylan. 'I can call any amount of lizards for you! Would you like me to?'

'Oh *yes*!' cried everyone in delight. 'Call them – and we'll watch them come!'

Tammylan got up. He led the way to a sheltered part of

the hillside. Heather grew all around, and the scent of gorse came warmly on the breeze. Tammylan pointed to a small patch of warm sand.

'Watch that patch,' he said. 'I'm going to whistle.'

He whistled – a curious low whistle, on one or two notes. On and on and on went the strange whistle, till it seemed part of the breeze and the rustling of a nearby birch tree. The children watched and waited, thrilled.

And then, from out of their hiding-places came the little lizards! First one came running, a little thing about five inches long. With its tiny fingers and toes it ran over the heather and went to the sandy patch. It stood there, slightly raised on its two front arms, its head on one side as if it were listening – as indeed it was.

'Isn't it sweet!' whispered Penny. 'Look how it winks at Tammylan!'

It really did seem as if it were winking, for it flashed its eyelids up and down over its bright eyes. Then another lizard ran out with a gliding motion, and it too stopped suddenly and listened.

'They run as if they are clockwork,' said Benjy. 'Oh, here's another – and another!'

Soon the patch of hot sand was full of listening lizards – at least, they all *looked* as if they were listening! Tammylan stopped his whistling, and the lizards began to play about, rushing from one place to another, just as if their clockwork started and stopped very suddenly! They were fun to watch.

'That lizard's got a very peculiar tail,' said Benjy. 'The one at the edge of the sand.'

'He has broken it off, just as the slow-worm did,' said

Tammylan. 'But it hasn't mended very well – it is rather rough and ready! The new one doesn't seem to fit.'

The lizards ran at any insect that appeared. The children were near enough to see their notched tongues, and to marvel at the tiny, delicate fingers and toes they had.

'I do wish I could hold one,' said Benjy. 'I'd like to feel those little fingers and toes on my hand.'

'I'll catch one for you,' said Tammylan. He slid his hand quietly along, and then made a firm grab at the nearest lizard. He caught it behind the shoulders and put it on his other hand.

'It's no use making your little body go all stiff like that!' said Tammylan to the lizard. 'I am not going to allow you to break off your tail!'

The lizard soon recovered from its fright and lay quietly on Tammylan's hand. He whistled softly to it and it listened, its eyes blinking every now and again. Then Tammylan put it gently on to Benjy's hand and the boy felt the touch of the tiny fingers and toes. It was lovely. Scamper, the squirrel, who had been on Benjy's shoulder all the time, did not at all like to see the lizard in Benjy's hand. He suddenly ran down Benjy's arm and made a grab at the lizard.

But in a trice the little thing was off and away, hidden in the heather.

'Oh, jealous little Scamper!' said Tammylan. 'Look, Benjy, more lizards have come out again. Do you see that one climbing up the heather-stalk? See its pretty underside of bright orange?'

'Oh yes!' said Benjy. 'I do like the lizards, Tammylan. I wish I had one for a pet.'

'I had one two years ago,' said Tammylan. 'It made itself very useful to me, for it lived in my cave and ate all the flies that bothered me! But when the winter came it went away to sleep.'

'I suppose there was no insect food for it in the winter-time,' said Penny, wisely. 'So it *had* to go to sleep.'

'Quite right, Penny,' said Tammylan. 'Well now, I must go. I have to get something to eat, for I've had nothing today so far. I must hunt for the things I like best!'

Tammylan stood up. Rory looked at his watch. 'We must go too,' he said. 'Well, good hunting, Tammylan – and a fine meal when you've finished!'

18

The Strange Frog-rain

One morning the children were sent to another farm with a message from Uncle Tim. It was fine when they set out, but on the way back a great purple cloud blew up and covered the whole of the sky.

'Gracious! What's going to happen!' cried Sheila, half afraid. 'Is it a storm coming, do you think?'

As she spoke, there came the roll of thunder some distance away. A few large drops of rain pattered down. Then more and more, like big silver coins. They struck the children quite hard.

'It feels as if someone up in the sky is *throwing* rain-drops at us,' said Penny. 'Goodness, I *am* getting wet!'

Then the rain came down properly, in long silver lines, slanting over the fields and woods. The thunder rolled again, but was not very near. Penny didn't like it. She was afraid of storms.

She began to cry. 'What shall we do? We mustn't shelter under trees in a thunderstorm because it's dangerous – but, oh Rory, I shall get so wet! I've only got this little thin frock on.'

Rory stood still and looked round. 'I believe we can't be very far from Tammylan's cave,' he said. 'I don't know this way very well, but I believe if we go down that lane, cut across that field, and go over that patch of heather, we'll come to the cave from the opposite side. Come on – run down the lane!'

The children began to run – but before they had gone very far they slowed down in surprise. The lane was absolutely full of small frogs! They covered the road, they hopped from the ditches, they made the wayside quite dark with their hopping bodies!

'Look, look!' shouted Rory. 'Did you ever see so many frogs?'

A lady came by on a bicycle. She too was astonished, and tried her best to ride without squashing the crowd of little frogs.

'It's frog-rain!' she called to the children. 'It's raining frogs! That's where they're coming from!'

The children stared at her in astonishment, forgetting the rainstorm. They looked up into the sky to see if they could spy frogs coming down – but the rain was too hard for them to keep their heads up – and all the time more and more frogs filled the road till it really seemed as if they must be falling with the rain.

'It's most extraordinary!' said Benjy, gulping down some raindrops. 'The frogs can't *really* come from the sky! How would they get up there? And yet there are thousands!'

'Of course they're coming down with the rain!' said Penny. 'Why, look – plop, plop, hop, hop, you can almost seem them coming down with the raindrops!'

The lane was moving with frogs. They hopped around the children's feet, and it was very difficult to go through them without hurting them. At last they got to the end of the lane and set off across the field. The thunder was nearer now, and Penny began to cry again.

There were frogs in the field too, hundreds of them, though they could not be seen quite so clearly as on the road. Rory took Penny's hand and helped her along, for she could not run so quickly as the others. Benjy had got Scamper, the squirrel, tucked safely away in his pocket. Scamper hated the rain.

At last they came to the cave – and Tammylan was there! 'My goodness, what drowned little rats!' he cried. 'Come in – there's going to be a marvellous storm. I'm glad you were sensible enough not to shelter under a tree. Ah – there's the lightning. Did you see it tear that dark cloud in half?'

'Do you like storms, then, Tammylan?' asked Penny in surprise.

'I love them,' said Tammylan. 'Grand things! The roll and crash of thunder, the sharpness of the lightning, the sting of the rain! Don't tell me you are afraid of a storm, Penny?'

'Well, you see,' said Penny, 'I once had a nurse who went and hid herself in a cupboard when there was a storm, so I thought it must be something very dreadful, and I always feel afraid too.'

'And now here is someone who loves a storm and thinks it's one of the loveliest sights in the world, so you will be able to think differently!' said Tammylan, taking the little girl on his knee. 'Goodness, how wet you are! Let's take off this thin little frock and wrap you in one of my rugs.'

So, wrapped in a rug, Penny sat at the cave entrance to watch the storm. And because Tammylan loved it and was not in the least frightened, Penny saw the beauty of it too.

'Long, long ago men thought that the thunder was the noise made by great wooden balls rolled over the floor of heaven,' said Tammylan. 'Listen to the next rumble, Penny, and tell me if you think it sounds like that!'

The thunder obligingly rolled round the hills and the children laughed. 'Yes – it's exactly like big wooden balls rolling over a great floor!' said Benjy. 'Isn't it, Penny?'

Penny suddenly remembered the frogs. 'Oh, Tammylan,' she said, 'whatever do you think happened as we came running here? It rained frogs all around us!'

'It couldn't do that,' said Tammylan. 'Rain is only rain.'

'But, Tammylan, it really *was* raining frogs!' said Penny. 'I saw them plopping down all round me – thousands and thousands of them! And a lady on a bicycle told us it was raining frogs, too.'

'Well, Penny, her eyes must have deceived her just as much as yours deceived *you*!' said Tammylan with a laugh. 'Your own common sense will tell you that frogs do not live in the sky, and so they can't drop from there! You know where frogs come from, don't you?'

'From tadpoles,' said Penny.

'Yes, and where do tadpoles live?' asked Tammylan. 'In the clouds?'

'No, of course not – in the ponds,' said Penny, beginning to feel rather silly.

'What do the others think about it?' said Tammylan, turning to them. 'Did any of *you* think you saw frogs flying gracefully through the air, each riding on a silver raindrop?'

The children laughed – but they were puzzled all the same.

'No, Tammylan, none of us actually *saw* the frogs in the

air,' said Benjy honestly. 'It only seemed very odd to see them in such thousands on the ground when the rain began. They weren't there before, I know.'

'Quite right, Benjy,' said Tammylan. 'Well, there is a very simple explanation of the curious sight you saw. I'll tell you. You know that the frog spawn turned into tadpoles, and the tadpoles grew into small frogs, don't you?'

'Yes,' said everyone.

'Well,' said Tammylan, 'there comes a time when all those thousands and thousands of small new frogs need to leave the pond and find somewhere else – a nice moist place in a ditch, perhaps, or in long meadow grass, where they may catch flies and grubs for their food. Now, no frog will leave the wet cool pond on a dry sunny day, for all frogs need moisture when they travel. So what happens? They wait until a terrific downpour of rain comes along – and then the same idea pops into the head of each restless frog!'

'And they all climb out of the pond and go travelling!' cried Benjy. 'Of course! And that's how we saw so many all at once. It was their travelling time!'

'Yes,' said the wild man. 'They had left their home pond, where they had been born, and were hopping away to find a new home for themselves on land. And there they will stay, in ditches and moist places, all the summer through, feasting on flies and grubs, growing large and fat until the autumn – when they will once more return to their pond to sleep.'

'And we thought it was raining frogs!' said Rory. 'What stupids we are!'

'You are, rather,' said Tammylan. 'Never believe stupid things without first making quite sure they are right! This idea of frog-rain comes up every year – but if everyone really thought hard about it they would know there couldn't possibly be such a thing.'

'There are plenty of frogs outside your cave, Tammylan,' said Penny, watching them. 'They are nearly all small ones, though. Where are the big ones?'

'Oh, the big ones have left the water some time ago,' said Tammylan. 'Those that you see are this year's crop of frogs! It takes a frog five years to grow up, you know. But some, if not most, of the creatures you saw in the lane must have been toads, not frogs, I should think. Look – there are some tiny toads over there, in a little batch together.'

'They look exactly like frogs to me,' said Rory. 'I don't know the difference!'

'Oh, Rory!' said Tammylan, pretending to be quite shocked. 'Aren't you ashamed of knowing so little!'

Rory grinned. 'Not a bit,' he said, 'when I've got someone like you to explain things to me!'

'Well, it's easy to show you the difference between a frog and a toad!' said Tammylan. He went out into the rain, which was now not nearly so bad, and fetched a frog. Then he did such a funny thing. He put his finger into his mouth, slightly blew out his cheeks, made a kind of humming noise, and jiggled his finger quickly from side to side of his mouth.

'Why, Tammylan, what are you . . .' began Penny in surprise. And then she stopped. For *someone* had heard the strange call! And that someone was a large old toad. He was under a big mossy stone just outside the cave. He came crawling out, and made his way to Tammylan.

'A very old friend of mine,' said Tammylan, smiling round

at the astonished children. 'I won't tell you how old he is, for you wouldn't believe me. Would they, Bufo?'

Bufo, the toad, looked up at Tammylan out of coppery eyes. Penny knelt down to look at him closely.

'Tammylan! He has got the loveliest eyes!' she cried. 'They are like jewels – and they look so wise and kind.'

'Yes – he's a wise old fellow is Bufo,' said Tammylan. 'Come along, old chap – up on my knee.'

The toad levered himself up and stood on his hind-legs, resting his forepaws on Tammylan's leg. Then he crawled slowly up to the knee. Tammylan took a piece of heather stem and gently tickled the toad on his back. Bufo at once put an arm behind himself and scratched where Tammylan had tickled. The children laughed.

'Now see the difference between this frog and my toad,' said the wild man. 'See the frog's smooth, shiny, rather moist body, and its greeny-brown colouring – and now see the toad's earthy colour, and his dry, pimply skin. He is quite different. Look at his back legs, too – they are much shorter than the frog's. The frog's long hind-legs give him the power of jumping very high in the air, to frighten his enemies and to escape easily – but the toad can only hop with difficulty and usually crawls.'

'Well, how does he get away from his enemies, then?' asked Benjy. Tammylan was just about to answer when the toad replied for him – for Scamper, the squirrel, suddenly dropped down on the toad in play – and then, in a trice, the squirrel gave a distressed cry, rubbed its little mouth, and leapt to a ledge above the children, its mouth open, and foam and bubbles dripping out at the sides.

'Oh! Whatever's the matter with Scamper?' cried Benjy in dismay. Tammylan laughed.

'Don't worry about him!' he said. 'Old Bufo, the toad, has just taught him that toads cannot be played with in that manner! As soon as Scamper dropped down on him the toad sent out an evil-tasting fluid from some of those pimples on his back – so horrible that no enemy will take a second lick, and certainly not a bite!' Scamper will soon be all right.'

The toad lay crouched on Tammylan's knee, keeping quite still, as if it were dead. 'It's an old trick of the toad's, to pretend that it is just a clod of earth,' said Tammylan. 'Now – do you see that bluebottle fly? Watch what happens when it perches near the frog or the toad.'

The bluebottle fly buzzed around. The frog heard it and became alert. The toad heard it, too, but made no sign. The fly flew down on Tammylan's knee.

And then, it just wasn't there!

'What's happened to it?' cried Sheila. 'I didn't see it fly away!'

'*I* saw what happened,' said Benjy. 'The frog flipped out its tongue, struck the fly with it – and flipped it into its mouth. It blinked its eyes and swallowed. Isn't that right, Tammylan?'

'Yes,' said Tammylan. 'You have quick eyes, Benjy! The frog's tongue is fastened to the *front* of his mouth, not to the back as ours is – so, when a fly comes, the frog opens his mouth, flips out his tongue to its full length, and strikes the fly with the sticky tip. That's the end of the fly. It all happens so quickly that it really seems as if the fly has disappeared by magic!'

'There's another fly!' said Benjy. 'It's going near the toad – oh – it's gone!'

135

That time it was Bufo, the toad, who had flicked out a tongue and caught the fly. It was all done in the twinkling of an eye, so fast that it was difficult to follow.

Benjy tickled Bufo's back. The toad liked it. Penny tickled the frog – but, with a bound, it was off Tammylan's knee, and leapt towards a patch of wet grass as fast as it could go.

Tammylan put the toad down on the ground. 'You can go home, Bufo,' he said. The toad crawled to its hiding-place under the stone and disappeared.

'He lived there all last summer, slept there all the winter, and now lives there this summer,' said Tammylan. 'I am fond of him – a quiet, wise old thing, who never hurries, never worries, and just gives a croak now and again to remind me that he is near me!'

A croak came from under the stone. The children laughed. 'He heard what you said,' said Penny.

'When you next go by the pond, look for the other member of the frog family – the newt,' said Tammylan. 'He has a long tail, but please don't mix him up with the lizards you saw the other day! Maybe you will be lucky enough to see the great crested newt, which looks like a miniature dragon, with its toothed crest running all down its back, and its brilliant under-colouring.'

'We'll look,' promised Benjy. 'I think we ought to get back now, Tammylan. It's stopped raining, and the storm has quite gone. There is blue sky over there.'

The wind had almost dried Penny's frock, but Tammylan said she had better keep his old rug wrapped round her. The others had had coats, which they had taken off to dry, but Penny had come out without one. So, clad in Tammylan's old red rug Penny went home with the others, feeling rather like a Native American as she capered along.

The lane was almost clear of frogs and toads when the children once more ran down it.

'They've each found a little place for themselves,' said Benjy. 'Somewhere they are hiding, and watching for flies. How I wish I had a tongue I could flip out like a frog's.'

They practised tongue-flipping all the way home, much to the surprise of everyone they met. Auntie Bess soon stopped them!

'It may not be rude in frogs!' she said, 'but it's certainly not good manners in children. Stop it, all of you!'

19

Flittermouse the Bat

The summer days slid by, golden and warm. It seemed to the children as if they had always lived at Cherry Tree Farm. London seemed to them a misty place, not quite real.

Their mother and father were having a grand time in America, and were supposed to come back at the end of the summer. Then the children would have to return to London.

When September came in, with its ripening fruit, its peaceful blue skies and heavy morning dews, the children were very happy. They were allowed to pick what ripe fruit they liked, so they had a glorious time.

But gradually Benjy became quiet and sad looking. The others couldn't understand it. Was Benjy ill?

'He just won't laugh or make jokes any more,' said Rory. 'I think he *must* be ill.'

But Benjy wasn't ill – he was just thinking that soon, very soon, the four of them would have to say goodbye to the farm and go back to town. He was counting the precious days. He wondered if Scamper would be allowed in London. He looked at the solemn cows he knew so well, the quacking ducks, the old brown horses with their shaggy heels, and inside him was a horrible ache.

Aunt Bess was really worried about Benjy – and she

thought that he must be homesick for his home in London and his father and mother! So she kept talking in a very bright voice about London, and that it wouldn't be long before he was back there, and things like that; all of which made Benjy feel a hundred times worse, of course!

And then one day Auntie Bess got a letter from America at breakfast-time, and read it with a very surprised look.

'Is it from Mother and Daddy?' asked Rory.

'Yes,' said Aunt Bess. 'I am afraid you will all be very disappointed with the news – they aren't coming back until Christmas!'

'Oh!' said Penny, looking ready to cry. 'Oh, I did think they would come back soon.'

Rory frowned. 'I think they might come back this month, as they said they would,' he said.

'We've been without them such a long time,' said Sheila.

Benjy said nothing at all. Auntie Bess wondered what he was thinking.

'Poor Benjy,' she said. 'I'm afraid it will all be a great disappointment to you. You can't go back to London now, and I know you wanted to.'

Benjy stared at his aunt as if he couldn't believe his ears. 'Can't go back to *London*!' he said. 'Are we going to stay on at Cherry Tree Farm, then?'

'I'm afraid so,' said Aunt Bess. 'I shall love to have you, but I know that you . . .'

What she was going to say nobody ever knew, for Benjy suddenly went quite completely mad. He jumped up from the table, knocking over the salt and the pepper, and capered round the room like a Native American doing

139

a war-dance. He shouted and sang, and everyone stared at him in amazement.

'So you *didn't* want to go back!' said Aunt Bess, in surprise. 'And all this time I've been thinking you've been so quiet and glum because you wanted to go home!'

'Oh, Aunt Bess, no, no, no!' shouted Benjy. 'You're quite wrong. 'I never, never want to leave Cherry Tree Farm for London. Oh, oh, to think we'll be here till Christmas now! How gorgeous! How marvellous! How . . .'

Everyone began to laugh, for Benjy looked so funny leaping round the breakfast table. Scamper, the squirrel, was quite scared and rushed to the top of the curtain, where he sat barking and stamping.

'Well, now we've settled that, come back and finish your breakfast, Benjy,' said Uncle Tim, who was just as amused, and as pleased, as Aunt Bess. 'What about their schooling, Bess? They can't miss another term.'

'I'm to make arrangements for them to go to the vicar's for lessons,' said Aunt Bess, looking at the letter. 'You know, he already has five other pupils, and our four can join them. They will like the walk across the fields each day – won't you, children?'

'Oh *yes*!' cried everyone, hardly able to believe so much good news all at once. Lessons at the lovely old vicarage – Cherry Tree Farm all the autumn – it was too good to be true. The only pity was that they wouldn't see their parents for so long. Still, they could look forward to Christmas!

'We must go and tell old Tammylan the good news as soon as we can,' said Benjy after breakfast. 'We'll go tonight. He said he would be away over the hill all today.'

So that evening, when the sun sent slanting yellow rays over the fields, and the trees had long shadows behind them, the four children and Scamper set out to Tammylan's tree-house. They took their supper with them – big bottles of creamy milk, and hunks of new bread with homemade cream cheese to eat with it. They took some for Tammylan too, for he loved milk and cheese.

Tammylan was sitting outside his house, watching the fish jumping in the river. He smiled at the children, and saw at once that they had news.

'Tammylan – we're staying till Christmas! What do you think of that?' said Benjy, grinning. 'We're to have lessons with the vicar – not to be sent away to school! Are you glad?'

'Very,' said Tammylan. 'There will be time for you to have a few more lessons with *me* too!'

'Lessons with you?' said Penny in surprise. 'What sort of lessons?'

'The same as I've given you before,' said Tammylan. 'Teaching you to make friends with the little folk of the countryside! There are still a few more people you don't know yet, Penny.'

'But there *can't* be!' said Penny. 'Why, we know the squirrels, and the snakes, the badgers and the otter, the water-vole and the slow-worm, the . . .'

'Well, here's one you don't know yet!' said Tammylan, as a little bat swooped down near Sheila. It almost touched her and she screamed.

'Oh! Oh! A bat! Make it go away, quick!'

The bat came back again and fluttered round Sheila's head on its curious wings. Sheila screamed again, and hit out at it

141

with her hand. 'Tammylan! Don't sit there like that! Make it go away! It will get into my hair!'

Tammylan looked cross. He didn't move at all. 'The only time I ever feel I want to give you a good telling-off is when you screech like that about nothing,' he said. 'Be quiet!'

Sheila got such a shock. She stopped squealing and looked ashamed. She went very red and tried not to look at Tammylan. 'Sorry,' she said.

'I should think so!' said Tammylan. 'Now, will you please tell me exactly why you behaved like that, squealing and screaming at a tiny creature that can neither sting nor bite?'

'Well, Tammylan,' began Sheila. 'I'm afraid of bats.'

'Why?' asked Tammylan.

'Because . . .' said Sheila and then she stopped and thought. She really didn't know why she was afraid of them! 'Well, you see . . .' she went on, 'I've seen people cower away from bats, and I've heard people say they get into your hair.'

'Well, they don't get into your hair, and they are perfectly harmless,' said Tammylan. 'Please don't act like that again, Sheila. It's no wonder animals and birds won't make friends with you. All animals sense when anyone fears them – and see what your squealing has done to Scamper. He's really scared!'

The squirrel was sitting on the top of the house, trembling. Benjy got up and lifted him off. The little creature cuddled under his arm-pit, digging his paws into Benjy's shirt.

'We'll show Sheila what an extraordinary little thing a bat really is,' said Tammylan, getting up. 'If she sees one closely maybe she won't be quite so frightened. They are marvellously made!'

142

'Can you make them come to you, Tammylan?' asked Benjy, surprised.

'I can make them fly near me, but I cannot make them come to my hand whilst you are here,' said the wild man. 'I am going to get my net – I can easily catch one with that.'

He went into the tree-house and came out with a kind of butterfly net. He stood by the doorway, and made some extremely high-sounding squeaks in his throat. Benjy pricked up his ears. 'I've heard the bats squeaking like that,' he said.

'Then you have sharp ears, Benjy,' said Tammylan. None of the others could hear the bats answering Tammylan. Only Benjy's sharp ears heard them. They came fluttering down around Tammylan's head. With a quick dart of his net he caught one. He sat down, and took the little quivering creature from the net.

Whenever any animal felt Tammylan's gentle, strong hands about it all fear left it and it was peaceful and safe. The bat lay in Tammylan's brown hand, and the children crowded round to look at it.

'It's not a kind of bird, after all,' said Penny. 'I thought it was!'

'Oh no,' said Tammylan. 'There is nothing of the bird about it, except its aerial life. It has no feathers.'

'It's like a tiny mouse with big black wings,' said Benjy.

'Country folk call it the flittermouse,' said Tammylan, 'and it's really not a bad name for it. Look at its tiny furry body.'

'And look at its big wings!' cried Sheila. 'What are they made of, if they are not feathery wings, Tammylan?'

Tammylan gently spread out the bat's strange wing. 'Look,' he said, 'do you see how long the bat's fingers have grown?

143

It is those that support the wing, which is simply a broad web of skin, stretched over the finger-bones and joined to the bat's little body. The bat flies with its fingers, over which the skin has grown!'

'How strange!' said Rory, who, like the others, had never seen a bat closely before. 'What's this little hook thing at the tip of the wings, Tammylan?'

'That is the bat's thumb, one on each wing,' said Tammylan. 'That little hook, with which the bat can hang on to any surface, is all that is left of its thumb – but it finds it very useful.'

'Well, I never knew what a peculiar thing could be done with fingers and thumb before!' said Sheila, who was not a bit afraid of the bat now that she could see it closely for what it was. 'Look – there's a little pouch between the legs and tail, Tammylan. What's that for?'

'That's where the bat puts his beetles and flies, when he catches them!' said Tammylan. 'It's his pocket! Watch the bats that are flying overhead, Sheila – when they suddenly swoop and dip down, you will know they are catching an insect and pouching it!'

The four children watched. 'I think they fly almost better than birds do,' said Benjy. 'That bat up there stopped in mid-air just now – just completely stopped! I've never seen a bird do that.'

'They certainly fly marvellously well,' said Tammylan. 'They are a joy to watch. Do you see how closely they fly to the trees and yet never touch them? They have a wonderful sense of the nearness of things.'

Tammylan set free the tiny bat he had caught. It flew

off to join the others. 'That was a little common bat,' said Tammylan. 'There are plenty of other kinds, but unless we catch them and examine them it is difficult to point them out in this twilight.'

'I never see bats in the winter,' said Benjy. 'They sleep then, don't they?'

'Yes,' said Tammylan. 'They get nice and fat in the autumn, and then hide themselves away in some cave or hollow tree or old barn. Do you know that old tumble-down barn at the end of the long field, at Cherry Tree Farm? Well, hundreds of bats sleep there, not only during the winter, but during the daytime now, as well.'

'I shall look in and see!' said Benjy, pleased.

'Well, you won't stay long!' said Tammylan. But he wouldn't tell Benjy why.

They had their supper outside the tree-house in the September twilight. Tammylan enjoyed the bread and cheese and the creamy milk. He gave the children a basketful of sweet wild strawberries to eat. They were delicious.

'I picked them today for you,' said Tammylan. 'I hoped you would come tonight.'

When the first stars came out Tammylan said they must go, so they said goodbye and walked slowly home in the deepening twilight.

'I shall just look in that old barn as we go by,' said Benjy. So when they came to it they all went inside – but, just as Tammylan had said, they didn't stay long!

'Pooh! The *smell*!' said Benjy, holding his nose. 'Well, if that's what bats' sleeping-places smell like I shan't ever want to spend a winter with *them*.'

The bats squeaked round his head as if they were laughing at Benjy – and this time even Sheila did not mind them. She had learnt her lesson, and would never be so silly as to squeal and screech again!

20

Penny's Prickly Pet

There was one thing that Penny longed and longed for – and that was a pet of her own. She loved Scamper, the squirrel, who was growing fast now and was a real pet of the family, though it was always Benjy he cuddled up to. She loved Shadow, the collie, and the big white cat by the fire. She liked the stable-cats too, but they were half-wild and wouldn't stay to be stroked.

'But none of them really belong to *me*,' thought Penny. 'I want something of my own – and I'd like a wild animal, like Benjy has.'

She wondered if she could find a young badger, or a fox-cub. But Uncle Tim put his foot down at once.

'A fox-cub!' he said in disgust. 'What next? It's all very well whilst they're cubs – nice little playful things they are then – but they grow up, Penny, they grow up! And what are you going to do with a full-grown tame fox, I'd like to know? Keep it on collar and chain, like a dog?'

'Oh *no*!' said Penny, shocked. 'I'd tame it properly and let it run loose, Uncle Tim.'

'And do you know what it would do?' said her uncle. 'It would catch all your aunt's hens and ducks! It would go to the farms around and eat the hens and ducks there too. It would be the greatest nuisance in the world, and it would have to be shot.'

'Oh, I won't have a tame fox then,' said Penny. 'I didn't think about it eating hens and things. I promise you I won't have a fox-cub, Uncle.'

And then Penny found a pet, quite unexpectedly. What do you suppose it was! A hedgehog!

Penny got up early one morning and went round by the tennis-court to pick a ripe plum. As she ran round the tennis-netting she noticed what looked like a big brown lump of earth rolled up in the edge. She went to it – and to her great surprise she found that a hedgehog had got caught in the netting and was so tangled up that it couldn't get out! It had curled itself up tightly and lay as if it were dead; perfectly still.

'Oh, the poor thing! Oh, quick, come and help it!' shouted Penny. 'Benjy, Benjy, where are you?'

But nobody came. So Penny fetched a pair of garden scissors from the tool-house and hacked away at the net until she had freed the hedgehog.

Still it didn't move.

Penny tried to lift it up. It was very prickly indeed. It was just like a round ball of spines, and the little girl had to put the funny animal into her overall before she could carry it.

Then she noticed that fleas were jumping from it and she dropped it in horror.

Benjy came running up just then and was surprised to see the hedgehog. 'You needn't worry about the fleas,' he said. 'They aren't the kind to bite *us*. But, wait a minute – I'll just dust the hedgehog with the insect powder that Aunt Bess uses for Shadow. That will soon clean up the hedgehog!'

He got the tin and dusted the powder over the hedgehog. The fleas all leapt off in horror and died. The hedgehog couldn't bear the smell of the powder and he uncurled himself very suddenly.

'Oh!' cried Penny, 'look at him! He's undone himself! Hasn't he got a dear little face – and such bright eyes. I like him. Look, he's running along – doesn't he go fast? Benjy, he shall be my pet!'

'Goodness! What a funny pet!' said Benjy with a grin. 'You'll need to wear armour whenever you want to cuddle him, Penny. I'll go and get him some boiled egg and water. I've heard the hedgehogs love that. See that he doesn't get too far.'

But before Benjy came back Penny had had to put the hedgehog into a hen-coop, for he got along so fast she was afraid she might lose him! There he was, sitting in the hen-coop, looking at Penny with bright eyes.

He loved the egg and water, and almost tipped it over to get at it. The children watched him in delight.

'I shall take him to Tammylan this morning,' said Penny. 'He will like to see my new pet. Let's go and tell Auntie Bess.'

Aunt Bess laughed when she heard about the hedgehog. 'They are useful creatures in a garden,' she said. 'They eat all kinds of insects, and slugs and snails. I once had a plague of cockroach beetles down in the cellar – and your uncle got me a hedgehog and put him down there. Well, in a week there wasn't a cockroach to be seen!'

'I think he'll make a nice pet, don't you?' said Penny. 'I'll give him eggs and water every day.'

But a great disappointment was in store for poor Penny –

for when she went to take her hedgehog from the hen-coop to show him to Tammylan, he was gone!

The hen-coop was quite empty. The little girl stared through the bars of the coop in dismay. 'Has anyone let out my hedgehog?' she cried. But nobody had. It was most mysterious. And then Uncle Tim explained it all.

'He could easily get out between the bars, Penny,' said her uncle. 'All he would have to do would be to put down his spines and squeeze through! You've lost him, I'm afraid. Never mind!'

But Penny did mind. She didn't say anything, but she went into the dark cowshed and cried by herself. Then she decided to go and see Tammylan and tell him about it. So she slipped off by herself to the tree-house – but she met Tammylan long before she got there. He was sitting by the stream, watching some water-hens.

'Hallo, Penny,' he said. 'You've been crying! What's the matter?'

'It's my hedgehog,' said Penny, sitting down beside the wild man. 'I meant to keep him for a pet – and now he's gone.'

Tammylan listened to the whole story. He didn't seem at all surprised to hear that the little girl's hedgehog had gone.

'You know, Penny, it's rather difficult to make a pet of a grown hedgehog,' he said. 'You should begin with a baby – then you can teach him to know you and not to escape.'

'But how can I find a baby one?' asked Penny.

'Oh, I can easily get you one,' said the wild man. 'Come along – we'll see if we can find you a tiny one to take home!'

Penny skipped along beside Tammylan in the greatest delight. You never knew what he was going to say or do – he was the most exciting man in the world!

Tammylan led Penny over a field, and came at last to a steep bank, which was overhung by bushes and briars. Tammylan pressed back some brambles and Penny saw the opening of a small hole, partly hidden by some green moss.

Tammylan put aside the moss and made a small grunting noise. At once a blunt nose looked out, and Penny saw the bright eyes of a hedgehog looking up at her and Tammylan.

'This is a mother hedgehog,' explained Tammylan. 'She has five youngsters in this hole with her. They are about a month old, perhaps a little more. She made a cosy home for them in this old wasps' nest-hole. She took moss and leaves into the hole with her mouth, and her small family live there happily. She will soon take them out at night to teach them how to hunt for beetles and slugs – and perhaps to nibble a few of the toadstools that are coming up everywhere now.'

Tammylan put his hand into the hole, and felt about. He brought it out again and in it Penny saw a very small hedgehog indeed!

'Oh, its prickles are quite soft and pale!' cried Penny.

'Yes,' said Tammylan. 'They will gradually darken and become stiff, but the hedgehog will have to wait many months before it can erect its spines properly and protect itself with them. Now, Penny – would you like this tiny hedgehog for a pet? It will soon know you and will stay in the garden or somewhere nearby when it grows up.'

'Oh, I'd love it,' said Penny. 'The others will laugh at me, I know, for having such a prickly baby, but it will be *mine*! What shall I feed it on?'

'Chopped boiled egg, minced meat and water,' said

Tammylan, putting the tiny creature into Penny's hands. 'When it has grown a little it will hunt around the garden for beetles and slugs.'

'Does it sleep in the winter?' asked Penny, carrying the hedgehog very carefully.

'Oh yes,' said Tammylan. 'It likes a hole rather like the one we took it from – but if you make it a sleeping place in a box, lined with dead leaves and moss, it will sleep there till the spring. What will you call it?'

'Prickles,' said Penny at once. 'I'll take it home now, Tammylan, and give it some food. Thank you so much for giving it to me. I shall take great care of it and make it just as happy as Scamper, the squirrel, is.'

She went off with the hedgehog – and the others were half-jealous when they looked at it and heard Penny's story. Then Benjy went off to make it a kind of cage to run about in, and Rory and Sheila hunted for little stones and moss.

Its home was soon ready – and the children were pleased to see the tiny animal curl up on the moss and go to sleep quite happily.

'It doesn't seem to miss its mother,' said Sheila. 'Well, Penny – you've got what you wanted – a pet of your own, though I do think it's a funny one. I hope you'll never ask me to cuddle it for you!'

21

The Battle of the Stags

In late September the children began to have lessons again.

They walked across the field to the vicarage, and loved the peaceful autumn countryside. They liked their lessons in the quiet study of the old vicar, who, with four or five other pupils, enjoyed teaching the four children from the farm.

They could not go and see Tammylan quite so often now, for they had homework to do. They saw him one afternoon, on their way to the farm for tea, and called to him.

'Tammylan! Wait for us! We want to ask you something!'

Tammylan waited. They ran up to him.

'Tammylan! We found such a lot of funny little dead creatures in the fields this week!' cried Benjy. 'They had long noses. What are they?'

'Do you mean little creatures like that one on the bank?' asked Tammylan. The children looked – and there, on the bank, lay a little dead animal, looking rather like a mouse with a long nose.

'Yes,' said Benjy. 'What is it?'

'It's one of the smallest of our animals,' said Tammylan, picking it up. 'It's a little shrew. You can always tell a shrew by its long, movable nose. Now, just keep quiet for a minute. I think I saw one moving here.'

They kept quiet – and sure enough a tiny shrew came out from its hiding-place, moving its long flexible nose. It was a dear little thing, and did not seem to see the children and Tammylan at all.

'They are short-sighted,' said Tammylan in a low voice. 'See this one looking for a caterpillar or beetle. He is always hungry!'

'Why are there so many dead this autumn?' asked Benjy. 'I don't like to see them.'

'They only live for fourteen or fifteen months,' said Tammylan. 'They have a busy, happy little life, and then, before the bitter winter comes to visit them for the second time, they lay themselves down and die.'

'Tammylan, I saw a dormouse yesterday evening,' said Penny. 'It was in one of Uncle's frames!'

'Oh, that reminds me – you must meet a new friend of mine!' said Tammylan. He wriggled himself a little, and a bright-eyed mouse came down from one of his sleeves. It was a fat little dormouse!

The children were thrilled. Really, you never knew what Tammylan was going to produce next! Benjy tickled the pretty dormouse down its back.

'Isn't it fat?' he said.

'Yes – like most of the winter sleepers the dormouse likes to get itself fat and healthy before its nap,' said Tammylan. 'I expect the one you saw in your uncle's frame was looking about for a warm place for the winter, Penny.'

Tammylan took a hazelnut from his pocket and cracked it. It was not yet quite ripe, but the little dormouse took the white kernel and ate it in delight. Then it ran back up

Tammylan's sleeve and disappeared.

'Where is it?' asked Penny, and she prodded the wild man's arm till she found where the dormouse had curled itself up. 'I do wish I had a dormouse living up my sleeve too,' she said. 'Tammylan, my little hedgehog is growing. He is getting more prickly, and he drinks such a lot of milk now!'

'Good,' said Tammylan. 'Well, perhaps I shall see you all soon again. Don't come on Saturday because I am going over the hills to see the red deer.'

'The red deer!' exclaimed Benjy. 'I'd like to see them too. I knew there were some about because Uncle told me once he had a whole field of turnips spoilt by them. They came in the night and ate them.'

'Very likely,' said Tammylan. 'Well, if you want to come with me be at the stile at nine o'clock sharp. It's a good long walk, so you'll have to bring your lunch.'

All the children wanted to go. They had never seen deer except in the Zoo. They made up their minds to ask Aunt Bess for a picnic lunch and to meet Tammylan at the stile without fail on Saturday.

It was a marvellous October day when the children stood at the stile waiting for Tammylan. It had rained every day since they had seen him, but now it had cleared up and the sun shone almost as hotly as summer. A few trees had turned colour and they shone brilliantly in the autumn sunshine.

'The sunshine always looks much yellower in the autumn than in the summer,' said Sheila. 'I say, look at those enormous blackberries! Let's pick some whilst we're waiting.'

They were so busy eating the juicy berries that they didn't notice Tammylan till he was just behind them. 'So you've come!' said Tammylan. 'Good! We ought to see a bit of fun today! The red stags have their wonderful antlers now, and maybe we shall see them using them as weapons! It is the time of year when the red deer fight for leadership.'

'I say! How thrilling!' said Rory. 'Come on, let's hurry!'

Tammylan led the way over the hill and across a wide stretch of common. Then there came another set of heather-covered hills. Penny was quite out of breath at the top, for her legs were not so long as the others were. They sat down at the top for a rest. The countryside spread out below them, green and gold, changing to a purple blue in the distance.

'Do you see that dip in the moors over there?' said Tammylan, pointing to a wild-looking stretch of moorland. 'Well, I think we shall find our deer there today.'

No sooner had he finished speaking than a strange noise came on the wind. It was like a loud bellow, a ringing sound that echoed all around.

'What's that?' asked Penny, looking startled.

'That's a stag sending out his challenge to all others,' said Tammylan. 'Come along. I know there are two or three stags about here, as well as a good many hinds – those are the mother deer, you know. We shall be in time to see the stags battling with one another if we hurry.'

Another bellowing cry came over the moors as the children followed Tammylan, and then another and another.

'Look!' said Benjy, 'there's a stag!'

They all looked – and there, on the brow of a small hill, stood a magnificent red deer, his great antlers standing up proudly on his head.

'Oh!' said Rory, 'what a splendid animal he is!'

'Will he hurt us?' asked Penny, rather anxiously.

'Well, we certainly won't go too near him!' said Tammylan. 'Ah, look – here comes another stag to challenge him!'

A second deer came slowly up the hill. He threw back his antlers and sent out his cry. The first stag pawed the ground in excitement – then he ran straight at his enemy! The two put down their heads and there was a loud clash as their enormous antlers crashed together.

'Their antlers have caught in one another!' said Rory, excited.

So they had. The two stags pushed and pulled, stamped and strained at each other – and the antlers at last freed themselves. But not for long – once again the stags rushed at one another, and the antlers rattled.

'I wonder they don't break!' said Sheila. 'Why are they fighting, Tammylan?'

'They are fighting to see who is the strongest and who will be leader of the herd,' said Tammylan. 'Only the strongest guards the hinds. Both these stags are young and strong, and each wants to be the leader.'

'Look! Are those the hinds over there?' cried Benjy, pointing to a hill not far off, where a group of deer stood watching the fierce battle. They had no antlers, and were rather smaller than the stags.

'Yes,' said Tammylan. 'Ah, look – one stag is winning. He is pressing the other down the hill. He is the stronger of the two!'

For a while the two stags struggled and panted, but gradually the weaker one gave way, and when he saw a chance, he fled. The victorious stag sent a ringing cry after him, then stamped over to the herd. He was king for that season!

'I wish I could see the stag's lovely antlers a bit closer,' said Benjy. 'They look like a tree on his head. Does it take years and years to grow them as long as that, Tammylan?'

'No,' said Tammylan, 'it usually takes a stag ten weeks.'

'Ten weeks!' cried Benjy, in surprise. 'No, Tammylan, you're joking – those enormous antlers would take ten years to grow!'

'A stag's antlers are a marvellous growth,' said Tammylan. 'He throws them off each year, and grows them again – and each year they are a little bigger, to show that he is older!'

'Did that stag who won the battle grow new antlers this spring then?' asked Rory.

'Yes,' said Tammylan. 'On his head, if you could have seen him this spring, you would have been able to feel two very hot knobs. From these knobs the antlers began to grow – as fast as the bracken grows in the wood! Then the growing antlers branch out – more branches come – and by the time that the ten weeks are gone he has on his head the great antlers you see now! At first these growing antlers are covered by a mossy kind of skin, called the *velvet* – but when the antlers are full grown the stag rubs off the velvet against the trunk of trees. I have often seen it hanging there in the summer.'

'Well, cows don't throw away their horns every spring!' said Rory. 'I wish they did. I'd make a nice collection of them!'

'I should think the stags must find their antlers a great nuisance when they run through the woods,' said Sheila. 'They must catch in the tree-branches.'

'Well, they don't,' said Tammylan. 'The stags throw their heads back so that their antlers lie on their back – they don't catch in the trees at all – in fact, the antlers save them from many a bruise!'

'Where do stags put their horns when they throw them off?' asked Sheila.

'Would you like to see if we can find some?' asked Tammylan. 'Well, come along. The stags always feel ill and weak when they are shedding their antlers, and often they go to some cave and lie there. I know an old cave near here where I found a pair of antlers one year. We'll go and see if there are any this time.'

So off they went to a nearby hill where there was a narrow cave. It opened out into a wide chamber at the end, and smelt of bats. Rory had a torch and flashed it round. He gave a shout.

'Here's one! Look! A fine antler!'

He took it out into the sunshine to see. It was a magnificent antler, quite perfect. 'It is the antler of a full-grown stag,' said Tammylan, looking at it. 'Count the points – I should think there are about forty.'

'Can I keep it for myself?' asked Rory, in excitement. 'My word – what will the boys in London say to this!'

'I wish I could have one too!' said Sheila, and she took Rory's torch. She ran back into the cave, trying not to smell the sour bat-smell there. She flashed the torch round – and to her great delight saw a fallen antler in one corner. She picked it up and raced outside with it.

'Here's the pair to your antler!' she cried. 'Look!'

'Oh, give it to me – now I shall have two!' cried Rory, and he snatched the other antler from Sheila. She gave an angry cry.

'No, Rory! It's mine. I found it and I want it!'

'But it's a pair. I must have a pair!' cried Rory. 'Mustn't I, Tammylan?'

'It would certainly be nice to have a matching pair of antlers,' said Tammylan, in a dry sort of voice. 'But that isn't a pair. It is two odd ones.'

'How do you know?' said Rory – but almost at once he saw what Tammylan meant. The antler that Sheila had found was not so big nor so branched. It certainly could not have been worn by the same deer that wore Rory's antler.

'This antler was worn by a four-year-old stag,' said Tammylan. 'It doesn't show the fifth-year branch. Well, you can keep it, Sheila. It's an odd one, like Rory's.'

Sheila was thrilled. She tucked the antler under her arm and danced round.

'Benjy's got a squirrel, Penny's got a hedgehog, and Rory and I have antlers! Now we've all got something.'

Scamper, the squirrel, chattered a little and tried to get inside a bag of food that Benjy was carrying. Benjy laughed.

'Scamper says it's time for a meal!' he said. 'Where shall we have it?'

'I know a sunny place, where there are many birds and voles to watch,' said Tammylan. 'Let's go there. It will be fun to eat and watch things at the same time.'

'Come on, then,' said Rory. 'I'm hungry enough to eat all we've got!'

22

An Odd Performance

It wasn't long before they were all sitting down on a grassy bank, sheltered by great clumps of gorse and bramble. Penny's mouth watered when she saw the clusters of ripe blackberries on the brambles and she made up her mind to do a little picking afterwards!

It was a gorgeous lunch. Aunt Bess had made ham sandwiches with a dab of mustard on each, and there were late tomatoes to bite into, nice and juicy. There were slices of plum cake, spicy and rich, and some eating plums as sweet as sugar. Scamper sucked a tomato, and made such a noise.

'I shall really have to teach you manners, Scamper!' said Benjy.

There were plenty of birds about, just as Tammylan had said. A robin flew down at their feet. Some chaffinches flew over the hedge, crying 'pink-pink!' A blackbird cocked a bright eye at them, and some thrushes sang a little from nearby trees.

There were voles too, running here and there, and even a daring rabbit, who came out of his burrow to watch the children. A tiny mouse ran under the hedge and another peeped at them from a tuft of grass. It was fun to eat and look round at so many little creatures.

'I wonder what's in that pile of brushwood over there,' Rory said, as he ate his plum cake. 'I am sure there's something. I thought I saw some eyes looking at me just now.'

'I'll go and see,' said Sheila, who had finished her lunch. She got up and went slowly to the heap of old wood. As she got there, a snake-like head looked out at her, and she heard a loud hissing noise. She ran back to the others at once.

'I think it's a snake,' she said. 'It hissed at me.'

'I don't think it is,' said Tammylan. 'We'll wait for a minute and see.'

So they all sat quiet and waited. Presently a tiny vole ran across the grass near to the brushwood. A long slender body immediately threw itself from its hiding-place, and pounced on the vole. But, with a squeak, the vole turned sideways and darted into a small hole.

'It's a weasel!' said Tammylan. 'The farmer's friend. He will rid a farm of rats and mice if he is given a chance, though he will not say no to a chicken if the hen-house has a place for him to squeeze inside!'

The weasel looked at the group of children and hissed again. He really was rather snake-like, for he had a small head, long neck, short legs and slender body, and he moved with an easy gliding motion.

'I've no doubt Master Weasel is hungry today, for some reason or other,' said Tammylan. 'He doesn't look in very good condition – perhaps he is getting old and finds it more difficult to hunt. Weasels, as a rule, are marvellous hunters, quite fearless and very fierce.'

The children looked at the hissing animal. It wasn't very

big, only about ten inches long, with a short tail. It wore a red-brown coat, and was white underneath.

'I say, look! There's another weasel!' said Rory, nodding towards a hedge. Sure enough, a second animal was there, looking as fierce as the weasel. Tammylan took a look at it.

'No – that's a stoat,' he said. 'They *are* a little alike – but the stoat is distinctly larger. Look at his tail too – it's longer and has a black tip.'

'Well, I can see the difference now, when *both* the creatures are there to look at,' said Rory. 'But I'm sure if I met one alone I wouldn't know which it was!'

'I'll tell you an old rhyme about the stoat and the weasel,' said Tammylan. 'I don't know who made it up, but it's very good. Listen.

> *'The stoat can be easily*
> *Told from the weasel*
> *By the simple fact*
> *That his tail is blacked*
> *And his figure*
> *Is slightly the bigger!'*

The children laughed. 'That's very good!' said Sheila, and she repeated the rhyme correctly, for she had a very good memory. 'Now I shall never forget which is the stoat and which is the weasel – whenever I see one I shall just say the rhyme to myself and I'll know!'

The stoat had seen the weasel and was angry. It snarled and ran into the open, taking no notice of the group of children. It, too, looked rather snake-like as it went, for it did not exactly run, but went along with low bounds.

'Will they fight?' asked Rory, thinking that it would be a real day for fights, if so.

'No,' said Tammylan. 'The stoat won't waste its time on a weasel. It knows that the weasel would simply fight till both creatures were dead! It is angry to see it here because it probably thinks that this is its own private hunting-ground. It doesn't want to share it with a fierce little weasel!'

'I suppose it hunts all the year round,' said Benjy. 'I can't imagine either the weasel or the stoat going to sleep for long!'

'You're right!' said Tammylan. 'They are fiercer in the winter than in the summer. In the cold north country the stoat does a curious thing in the winter – he changes to white, and becomes the ermine!'

'How funny!' said Penny, staring. 'Why does he do that?'

'Well, I really think you might find out the reason for yourself!' said Tammylan.

Penny thought. 'Yes – I know why,' she said. 'It's because snow lies on the ground in the north for a long time, and the stoat would be easily seen in his *brown* coat – so he puts on a white one to hide himself!'

'Good girl!' said Tammylan, pleased. 'Yes – his coat changes like magic. But down here, where it is warmer and we do not often have a winter where the snow lies for long, the stoat does not bother to change his coat. I have sometimes seen him when he has changed to an ermine up in the north, and is all in white – all I could see against the snow was a pair of eyes and the black tip of his tail!'

The stoat suddenly sniffed the air. He evidently smelt

something good, for in a trice he was bounding off, and disappeared through a hole in the hedge.

'He smelt his dinner somewhere!' said Benjy with a laugh. 'The weasel is glad to see him go.'

'I think the weasel is just about to perform for us,' said Tammylan. 'Keep quite quiet now and you will see something strange.'

The weasel was certainly behaving very oddly. He had come out farther into the open, and was doing most extraordinary things. He ran round and round as if he were chasing his own short tail. He jumped up in the air and down. He wriggled his body like a snake, and threw himself over and over. The children watched, quite fascinated.

'What is he doing?' asked Penny, in a whisper.

'He wants to amaze all the birds and animals round about,' whispered back Tammylan. 'He wants them to come nearer and nearer to look at him. Then he will pounce – and get his dinner!'

The weasel went on and on. The birds in the hedgerow stopped their singing to watch. They couldn't take their eyes off the extraordinary weasel. They had never seen such a thing before.

The weasel wriggled and ran round himself. A small vole popped his head out of a hole and watched. A mouse looked on in amazement and went a little nearer to see what was happening. A big blackbird flew down to inspect the performance.

Then two sparrows fluttered down and a chaffinch. They all watched, quite still. The children could not stop watching either – and although they longed to warn the birds and little animals they could not open their mouths to say a word! It seemed as if the weasel was putting a spell on everything and everyone. It was very strange.

The weasel went on and on with his performance – and he got gradually nearer to the fat blackbird. The bird did not move, but looked at the wriggling animal. Penny wanted to call out but she couldn't. Everyone seemed to have their eyes glued on the extraordinary weasel.

And now the weasel was almost within striking distance of the foolish blackbird – and then Tammylan broke the spell. He clapped his hands – and at once the blackbird flew off, sending out his ringing alarm-call! All the other birds flew high into the trees, and every mouse and vole disappeared as if by magic. Even the weasel jumped with fright.

As for the children they jumped even more than the weasel! They all got a real fright when Tammylan so suddenly clapped his hands!

'Oh, Tammylan – you *did* make me jump!' cried Penny crossly.

'Well, I was only just in time,' smiled the wild man. 'Another second and Master Weasel would have pounced on the fascinated blackbird – and you didn't want to see him do that, did you?'

'Oh no!' said Sheila. 'Goodness, what a strange performance! Fancy a weasel doing that, to get his dinner.'

'He doesn't often do it,' said Tammylan. 'But I have seen one do it two or three times before, usually in a place like this, where there is plenty of bird and animal life around. And he nearly always catches somebody!'

'Well, he didn't that time!' said Penny. 'But I know how that blackbird felt, Tammylan – I just couldn't say a word or move a finger. All I wanted to do was to watch and watch and watch!'

The weasel had gone – but it wasn't very long before they heard of him again! A high, shrill squeal came from behind the hedge, and all the children jumped.

'He has caught a rat,' said Tammylan. 'I expect it's the one I saw a few minutes ago, stalking a little vole.'

It *was* a rat. The weasel struggled with the strong animal for a minute or two and then managed to bite it at the back of the neck. That was the end of the fierce rat. The weasel dragged it off to eat.

'Well,' said Penny, who didn't very much like seeing or hearing anything killed, 'I'm glad it was a rat and not a little vole or bird! I just don't like rats!'

When it was time to go home Sheila and Rory proudly carried their antlers. They held them above their heads as they marched into the farmyard and Uncle Tim was most surprised to see them.

'Well!' he said. 'I never know what you are going to bring back with you – squirrels – hedgehogs – antlers! It's a good thing there are no hippos or giraffes in our woods, or Tammylan would make you a present of one of those, I'm sure! And what your Aunt Bess would say to that I really can't think!'

23

Presents – and an Unexpected Visitor

As the days grew shorter and colder, the children saw much less of their friend. He had moved now from his summer tree-house and was in the cave. He had made a big willow-screen to place over the entrance to his cave, to keep out the cold winds when they blew, for the winter days were bitter. It was a cold winter, and Aunt Bess didn't like the children to go wandering over the windy fields too much.

'You look so fat and well, all of you,' she said. 'I don't want you to get colds or coughs just before your parents come home!'

The children were going to spend Christmas at Cherry Tree Farm, for their parents were coming straight there. They thought it would be marvellous to spend Christmas there, and have Aunt Bess's homemade Christmas pudding and mince-pies, tarts, and fruit.

'We'll all help to decorate the house,' said Rory happily. 'We can get berries of all kinds, and I know where there are plenty of holly trees.'

'We simply *must* see Tammylan before Christmas,' said Benjy. 'He will love to see how Scamper has grown, and what a beauty he is.'

'I wish I could take Prickles with me,' said Penny, who

was very fond of her quaint pet. 'But he is asleep now, and I know he won't wake up in time. He sleeps all day and night in this cold weather!'

'We ought to give Tammylan a present,' said Rory. 'He has been such a brick to us, and all we know about the birds and animals is because of him. What shall we give him?'

'He doesn't seem to need much,' said Benjy. 'He lives on so little, and he doesn't think a lot of the things that most people like. It's no use giving him a pipe, or a cigarette case, or ties, like we give Daddy.'

'I know what Penny and I can give him,' said Sheila. 'A blanket that we will knit ourselves! We will make about a hundred little knitted squares, join them all together, work a nice edging round, and give it to Tammylan to cover himself with on a cold frosty night! He loves colourful things, so we will choose the brightest, warmest wools we can find!'

'That *is* a good idea!' said Rory. 'I wish Benjy and I could think of something good too.'

'Couldn't we make him a low wooden stool that he could use either to sit on, or as a small table?' said Benjy. 'He did say once that one day he must make himself a stool.'

'Oh yes! That's a fine idea!' said Rory. The boys were learning woodwork at the vicarage, and so it was easy to set to work on a stool. Benjy meant to carve a little pattern of squirrels all round it, to remind Tammylan of Scamper.

So the children were soon very busy. Sheila and Penny sat at night knitting one square after another. If they made a mistake they undid it and put it right. Whatever they gave Tammylan must be quite perfect.

The boys began the stool. It was low and sturdy, made of

some pieces of old oak that the vicar had given them. They worked hard on it, and when Benjy sat trying to carve tiny squirrels round it, like Scamper, he felt very happy.

'You know, all this sort of thing is much nicer than going out to parties and shows and cinemas,' he said to Rory. 'Things we do here seem to matter, somehow. Oh Rory, shan't you hate having to live in a town again?'

'Yes, I shall,' said Rory gloomily. 'But we'll have to go after Christmas. Penny cries every night when she thinks of it.'

'Well, if I wasn't going to be twelve next birthday I'd howl too,' said Benjy, digging at the wood in his hand. 'Oh well – it's no use grumbling. We've had a glorious time, and it's coming to an end.'

Christmas came nearer and nearer, and at last it was Christmas week. The children's parents were to come the day before Christmas, so there was great excitement. Presents had to be made and bought. The farmhouse was decorated from top to bottom. Aunt Bess made six enormous puddings and a hundred mince-pies, to say nothing of the biggest Christmas cake that the children had ever seen.

'Can we go and give our presents to Tammylan?' asked Penny one day. 'It's a lovely cold frosty day, and the sun's out, and we'd just love a walk to see old Tammylan, Aunt Bess.'

'Very well,' said her aunt. 'Wrap up warmly and go – and you can ask Tammylan to come to Christmas dinner, if you like.'

'Oooh, good!' cried all the children. They packed up the blanket and the stool and set off. The air was cold and crisp, and their cheeks glowed with the frost. It was lovely to be out on such a morning.

Tammylan was in his cave, doing something that he put away quickly when the children came.

'Hallo!' he said. 'I *am* glad to see you! My goodness, Benjy, how Scamper has grown! He's a bonny squirrel now, and I can see you look after him well.'

Scamper jumped to Tammylan's shoulder, and sat there, brushing the wild man's ear with his whiskers. He loved Tammylan.

'We've brought you our presents for Christmas,' said Penny. 'Look – Sheila and I made this for you to keep you warm at night!'

The girls undid their parcel and Tammylan stared at the brilliant blanket, made so lovingly and with such care.

'It is simply beautiful!' he said. 'I love it very much. I shall use it every night, Sheila and Penny. You couldn't have made anything that pleased me better. Thank you more than I can say!'

He caught up the knitted blanket and swung it round his shoulders. It suited him very well.

'You look like an Old Chief or something,' said Sheila. 'Rory, you give your present now.'

So Rory and Benjy undid the stool. Tammylan sat on it at once, and it was just right for him.

'Did you really make it yourselves?' he asked. 'You are more clever than I thought! Who did these squirrels round the edge? You, I suppose, Benjy! You have done them beautifully. It is a lovely present – sturdy to sit on, and beautiful to look at – just what a stool should be! Many many thanks, children!'

They were all pleased at Tammylan's delight. They could

see that he really was overjoyed at their kindness.

'Well, seeing that giving presents seems to be the fashion, I will give you what I have made for *you*,' said Tammylan. 'Here is my present for you – and like you, I have *made* it!'

He took a covering of heather off a little ledge – and there, arranged on the rocky shelf was a whole set of beautifully carved animals! They were made of wood, and Tammylan had carved them carefully and deftly himself, in the long winter evenings, by the light of his candle.

'Tammylan! Oh, Tammylan! They are all the animals you've shown us!' said Penny joyfully. 'Here's the otter with his flattened tail – and the badger – and the weasel we saw in the autumn – and the stoat, with his longer tail.'

'And here's Scamper!' cried Benjy, taking up a carved squirrel the very image of Scamper. 'Oh, how do you carve them all so well, Tammylan? I didn't know you could do this work.'

The children picked up the wooden animals and looked at them carefully. They were all there – the hedgehog, the mole, the shrew, the vole, the otter, the rabbit, the hare – the snakes, the lizard, the toad, the frog – it was marvellous!

'I was just finishing the fox,' said Tammylan. 'He is really the only animal I have never properly shown you. Did you know that the hunters are out today, hunting the fox? I heard the horns this morning.'

'Yes, so did I,' said Rory. 'And I saw the fox-hounds, too, and the hunters in their scarlet coats.'

'*Pink* coats, Rory,' said Sheila.

'Well, they looked scarlet to me,' said Rory. 'Listen – is that the horn?'

'Yes,' said Tammylan. They all went to the cave entrance and looked out. Away in the distant fields they could see the bright coats of the huntsmen, and could hear the baying of the hounds.

'They've found a fox,' said Tammylan. 'I hope it isn't my old friend. He has gone through many a hunt and has always escaped by using one of his tricks – but he is getting old now, and is not so fast on his legs. I wouldn't like the hounds to get him.'

The hunt came nearer. The children could hear the cries of the huntsmen and the excited barking of the dogs even more clearly. Rory began to shiver with excitement. Benjy and Penny hoped the fox would get away.

'*Why* must he be hunted?' said Penny.

'Because he does harm to the farmer's poultry,' said Tammylan. 'Poor old fox – he can't help his nature – look Penny, look Rory, there he is! Coming up our hill!'

The children looked to where Tammylan pointed. They were trembling with excitement. They saw a long red body with a bushy tail running up the hill, keeping beside a row of bushes. As they watched the fox, he doubled back on his tracks, ran to the pond, plunged into it and swam to the other side. Then he climbed out, shook himself, and ran off the other way.

'Now you see how clever a fox is, when his enemies are near,' said Tammylan. 'He ran back on his track, and entered the water to break his scent. Ah – here he comes again – round the hill. He's coming here!'

Sure enough the fox *was* coming to Tammylan. The children stared in excitement. The hunted animal was panting painfully. His tongue hung out, he was wet from head to foot, and his whole body shook with his breathing.

'He's almost done for,' said Tammylan. 'Come on in, friend!'

The fox went into the cave, pushing by the astonished children. He flung himself down at the far end, and panted as if he would burst. Tammylan put the big willow screen across the entrance, and went to the fox.

The children went near too. The fox had laid his head on his front paws. His eyes were swollen and red, and his tongue still hung out. His breathing was terrible to hear, for his body seemed as if it must break with it. The sound filled the whole of the cave. He had run for miles and miles that morning, with the hounds just behind him.

Penny burst into tears. 'I can't bear it!' she sobbed. 'Make him better, Tammylan!'

'I can't do anything for him just now,' said the wild man gently. 'He must just lie and rest. I only hope the hounds will not come here.'

As he spoke there was a terrific baying down the hill, and Rory rushed to peep out of the willow screen at the door. The hounds were smelling round, trying to track the scent of the fox, which had suddenly come to an end where he had doubled back on his tracks. Soon they picked up the scent on the track to the pond. But there the scent was broken.

'I hope they don't go all round the pond and pick it up again,' thought Rory. 'What shall we do if the hounds come here? There is nowhere for the poor fox to go. I won't give him to the hounds, I won't! I know he eats Uncle's hens when he can get them – but who would throw a poor tired creature like that to the dogs? I couldn't, anyway.'

The fox lay panting in the cave, too tired even to raise his head at the sound of the baying. He was with Tammylan and that was enough for him. There was safety wherever the wild man was.

Rory and Sheila watched the hounds sniffing about the hill. The huntsmen had come up now and were talking to one another, wondering where the fox had gone.

'It's no use wasting time here,' said one huntsman to another. 'He's gone to earth. We'll go round Bell Farm and see if we can start up a fox there. Old Henry said there was a young one round there who would give us a good run. Come on. Call the hounds.'

And, to Rory's enormous relief, the hunt moved off down the hill again, to join the rest of the horsemen in the valley. The hounds went too, their tails waving like tree-tops in the wind.

'They've gone!' cried Rory and he went to Tammylan. The fox was better now. His pants were slower, and he lay more easily. He looked at Tammylan with red eyes.

Tammylan put down a drink for him, and the fox lapped eagerly.

'Well,' said Tammylan, 'I said that the fox was the only animal I hadn't yet shown you – and now, here he is! See his lovely bushy tail, and his fine thick red-brown coat! He is a beautiful creature. He has a good burrow – what we call his "earth", not far from here. He will go to it and rest as soon as he feels well enough. I don't believe he could have run a yard more today.'

'What a good thing he knew you and your cave!' said Benjy.

'Yes,' said Tammylan. 'He has often been here and knows

175

me well. Poor old fellow – I am afraid you will be caught when you are hunted the next time.'

'I don't want him to be,' said Penny, daring to stroke the fox. He took no notice at all, so she stroked him again.

'And now I will just finish doing the fox I was carving for you,' said Tammylan. 'Then you shall wrap up all the animals and take them with you.'

He made two or three strokes with the sharp knife he used – and then stood the figure of the fox beside the others he had made.

'It's lovely!' said Penny. 'Bushy tail – sharp ears – just like him! Oh, Tammylan, it's a beautiful present you have made for us. Thank you very, very much.'

Tammylan wrapped up all the wooden animals and gave them to Benjy. 'A very happy Christmas to you all,' he said.

'Oh, Tammylan, I nearly forgot – will you come to Christmas dinner with us?' asked Rory.

Tammylan shook his head. 'Thank you,' he said, 'but I have already asked several of *my* friends here for Christmas! I hope to have the squirrels – and a few rabbits – and maybe the hare!'

The children stared at Tammylan and imagined the cave full of his friends on Christmas Day. They half-wished they could be there with him, too, instead of at Cherry Tree Farm!

'We'll come and say goodbye before we go home,' said Benjy. 'We shall be going back to London after Christmas. It's very sad.'

'It is indeed,' said Tammylan. 'Now look – the fox wants to go. We will go with him. Maybe he will show you his "earth"!'

The fox had staggered to his feet. He stood there, his body

still trembling from his long run. He went to Tammylan and licked the wild man's hand, just as a dog licks a friend.

'He's your wild dog, Tammylan!' said Benjy. 'It's a good thing for him that he knew he would find safety here!'

The fox went to the entrance and tried to push past the willow screen. Tammylan pushed it to one side and the red-coated animal slipped out. The children followed him. He went slowly, stumbling every now and again, for he was worn out. All he wanted now was to lie in his 'earth' and sleep for hours.

Round the hill he went until he came to where dead bracken stood. He pushed through it and disappeared. Tammylan took the children to the middle of the bracken and showed them the entrance to the fox's den. It was a well-hidden hole. Benjy knelt down and peered into it.

'Pooh!' he said. 'It smells!'

'I expect it does,' said Tammylan. 'Sometimes the fox makes his "earth" near the badger's sett – and the badger hates the smell of the fox so much that he leaves his home and makes another one!'

'Well, good luck to the fox!' said Benjy. 'I hope he sleeps well! Goodbye, Tammylan – and a happy Christmas to you!'

'And thank you ever so much for the lovely set of animals!' said Penny. 'We'll often look at them and remember the real live animals we made friends with this year.'

'And I shall sit on my new stool and wrap myself in my colourful blanket – and remember the nice animals who made them for me!' laughed Tammylan. 'Goodbye!'

24

The Best Surprise of All!

Christmas at Cherry Tree Farm was lovely. To begin with, the children's father and mother arrived the day before – and you should have seen how they stared at the children in the greatest surprise!

'But these can't be our children!' cried their mother. 'They are twice the size! And so fat and rosy!'

'We *are* your children!' said Penny, hugging her mother. 'Oh, Mummy, we've had such a glorious time here – but it's lovely to see you and Daddy again.'

That was a very exciting day indeed, for what with welcoming their parents, preparing their presents for one another and wrapping them up, and hanging up their biggest stockings, the time simply flew past.

'I shall never never get to sleep tonight, I know,' said Penny. 'I know I shan't.'

But she did, and so did the others. They all took a last look at their stockings, hanging empty on the ends of their beds, and then they fell asleep.

In the morning, what an excitement! The stockings were full from top to toe, even Rory's, who, big boy as he was, wouldn't stop hanging up his stocking as long as the others wanted to hang up theirs!

Penny had a marvellous doll, that sang a little song when she was wound up at the back. Benjy had a wonderful present – a cage with two blue and green budgerigars in it! They were beautiful birds, and kept rubbing their beaks against one another, and chattering quietly. Benjy could hardly believe his eyes!

'Just what I've always wanted!' he cried. Scamper, the squirrel, was most interested in the budgies and sat on the top of the cage, chattering to them. They didn't seem to mind him at all.

Sheila had a work-basket on a stand, all complete with scissors, needle-case, cottons, silks, wool, buttons, hooks, eyes and fasteners. There was even a silver thimble exactly the size of her middle finger. She was simply delighted.

Rory had an aeroplane – a magnificent one that flew a very long way. Then, of course, there were their presents to each other, and the presents from their uncle and aunt. Really, the bedroom looked like a shop by breakfast-time!

They all had their Christmas dinner in the middle of the day, and Rory had three helpings of plum pudding.

'You'll be ill, Rory,' said his mother anxiously.

Aunt Bess and Uncle Tim laughed. 'What, Rory ill because he has had three helpings of plum pudding!' said Uncle Tim. 'You don't know the Rory of Cherry Tree Farm, my dear – did we tell you of the time that Rory had five helpings of Bess's raspberry tart and cream?'

'Don't tell tales of me, Uncle,' said Rory. 'Really, I'm not greedy, but Aunt Bess does cook so well!'

Everyone admired Tammylan's wooden animals. Daddy thought they were really marvellous.

'That fellow could make a lot of money if he really went in for this sort of thing,' he said, picking up the carving of the badger. 'This is quite perfect.'

'Tammylan doesn't have even a penny in his pocket,' said Benjy. 'He's just a wild man. Golly, wouldn't I love to see him at this very minute – having Christmas dinner in his cave with rabbits round his feet – squirrels on his shoulder – and the hare somewhere about too – and maybe a few mice around!'

When Christmas was over, with all its good food, its gaiety and laughter, its fruit and crackers, a horrid sad feeling settled down inside each of the children.

Now the time was really near when they must leave their beloved farm. Rory and Benjy were to go to boarding-school, and Sheila and Penny were to have a governess. The lovely free days were coming to an end.

But that year of surprises had still one more surprise in store for them! It happened when the children's parents were talking about the boys' schooling.

'I don't see how we can possibly keep up our house in town, with money so scarce, and the children's education so expensive,' said Mother to Aunt Bess. 'And I do wish, too, that we could keep them more in the country, because the life does seem to suit them.'

Then Uncle Tim said an unexpected thing. 'Well,' he said, putting down his paper, 'why don't you and John take up farming, as Bess and I have done? John was brought up on a farm half his boyhood, and if he buys a good farm, he won't do too badly. It's in his blood!'

Mother stared at Uncle Tim, and the children held their breath.

Their father looked up and laughed.

'What, start farming at my age?' he said. 'After being in business for twenty years!'

'Yes, and that business is making less and less money each year!' said Uncle Tim. 'Now listen, John – there's Willow Farm in the market, and a fine farm it is too. Take your money out of that business and put it into the farm. Come down and live there, and work it yourself. I'll help you. It's only five miles from here, and Bess and I would be glad to have you for neighbours.'

There were shouts from the children, squeals and shrieks. Benjy did a sort of war-dance round his father, and Penny jumped up and down as if she were a bouncing ball. Rory and Sheila got all mixed up with one another, and altogether the room sounded rather like the monkey-house at the Zoo.

'Well, really!' said the children's father in amazement. 'Have you gone mad? First Tim bursts this extraordinary idea on me – and then the whole family goes mad!'

Aunt Bess began to laugh. She laughed till the tears ran down her cheeks. The children's father looked so astonished and the children so ridiculous.

'Oh, John!' said Aunt Bess, wiping her eyes. 'It may seem an extraordinary idea to you – but, really, when you come to think of it, it's very sensible. You said yourself that it's only a matter of time till your business fades away – well, you love the country, and you know farming – so why not begin now instead of waiting till your money's all gone? Then there are the children! I never saw such a set of weaklings as they were last April. Look at them now – see what a country life has done for them!'

181

The children's parents looked – and then they looked at one another. Neither of them wanted to go back to London. And after all, there were the children to think of. They had always been ill and pale till now. And Willow Farm was a heavenly place, with wide-set fields, silver streams, fine old barns and a comfortable farmhouse.

'Well – we'll think about it,' promised the children's father. 'The boys will have to go to boarding-school, but it would be good for them to come back to the farm for holidays. Yes – I'll think about it.'

He did think about it – and he bought Willow Farm! The news came the day before the two boys went off to their boarding-school, and they were wild with delight.

'We shall come home to Willow Farm at Easter!' yelled Benjy, hopping about so violently that Scamper was jerked off his shoulder. 'Oh, I don't mind going off to school now – I shall have Willow Farm to look forward to. We'll have our own cows and I shall milk them. We'll ride our own horses! We'll keep our own pigs and I'll have a piglet. We'll have hens and ducks and geese! We'll . . .'

'And oh, what will Tammylan say!' cried Penny. 'We *must* tell him! We *must* tell him!'

'Let's go now, quick!' shouted Rory. 'Goodness, this is the best news we've ever had in our lives!'

So off they rushed to tell Tammylan, their friend. There we will leave them, running over the frosty fields to find the wild man, and to tell him of their wonderful plans for Willow Farm.

'Willow Farm! Willow Farm!' sang Penny. 'Oh, what fun we'll have at Willow Farm!'

They certainly will – but that's another story!

The Children of Willow Farm

Contents

Goodbye to London!

One wild March day four excited children looked down from the windows of a tall London house, and watched three enormous vans draw slowly up in the square outside.

'There they are!' cried Rory. 'They've come at last!'

'The moving has begun!' said Penny, jigging up and down beside the window-sill.

'Won't it be funny to see all our furniture going into those vans!' said Sheila.

'I shouldn't have thought that we would have needed *three* vans!' said Benjy, astonished.

'Oh, there are three more coming after these, too,' said Sheila. 'Oh goodness – isn't it lovely to think we are going down to Willow Farm! A farm of our own! A farm as nice as Cherry Tree Farm.'

'Nicer,' said Benjy. 'Much nicer. It's got more streams. And it's built on a hill so that we get a marvellous view, not down in a hollow like Cherry Tree Farm.'

The four children were very happy indeed. The year before they had all been ill and had been sent for some months to live on their uncle's farm. The life had suited them well at Cherry Tree Farm, and all the children had grown strong and red-cheeked.

Then, when the time had come for them to return to their London home, their father had found that his business was bringing him in very little money – and Uncle Tim had suggested that he should put his money into Willow Farm, five miles away, and take up farming for his living.

The children's father had been brought up on a farm, and knew how to run one. The children, of course, had been mad with delight at the idea – and here it was, really coming true at last! They were all going to move into Willow Farm that very week!

It had taken three months to buy the place and arrange everything. Rory and Benjy, the two boys, had been to boarding-school, and had just returned home in time to move down with the girls, Sheila and Penny. Their mother had been very busy packing, and everyone had helped. It was such fun!

'I like London if we just come up for a pantomime or a circus,' said Rory. 'But the country is best to live in!'

'I'm simply longing to see Tammylan again,' said Penny. 'Oh, won't he be pleased to see us!'

Tammylan was a great friend of theirs. He was a strange man, who lived in a hillside cave in the winter months, and in a tree-house made of willow branches in the summer. He was called the 'wild man' because he lived alone with animals and birds. Most people were afraid of him, but he was the children's greatest friend. He had taught them all about the birds and animals of the countryside, and now they knew more about all the big and small creatures than any other children in the kingdom. It would be marvellous to see Tammylan again.

Mother put her head in at the door. 'It's time for you to put your things on,' she said. 'Daddy will soon be bringing the car round. Say goodbye to all the nooks and crannies here that you have known since you were babies – for you won't be seeing them again!'

The family were going down by car, and the vans were following. Mother wanted to be ready for them when they came. The children looked at one another.

'I'm glad to be leaving here,' said Benjy. 'But we've had some good times in this tall old London house!'

He ran out of the room.

'Benjy's gone to say goodbye to the plane trees he can see from his bedroom window!' said Rory. 'He always loved those.'

It was true. Benjy leaned out of his bedroom window and looked at the trees with their last year's balls hanging from bare boughs.

'Goodbye,' he said. 'I've known you for eleven years, and you are nice all the year round! I like you now, with bare boughs. I like you when you are just leafing, with bright green leaves shining in the sun. I like you in the summer when you are thick and dark green. I like you in the autumn when you turn yellow and throw your leaves away. Goodbye, plane trees! I'm going where there are no plane trees, but willows, willows, willows all around, growing along the banks of silver streams!'

The plane trees rustled in the wind as if they were whispering back to Benjy. He drew in his head and suddenly felt a little sad. He would never forget those London trees – and he would always remember the little grey squirrels that sometimes ran up and down the branches.

Sheila went to say goodbye to every room in turn. 'I don't want to forget anything,' she said to Rory, who was with her. 'I always want to remember our first home, though I am going to love our second home much much better. Goodbye, drawing-room – you look funny now with all the furniture just anyhow! Goodbye, study. I won't forget how often I've slipped down to you to take a book to read out of your bookcases! Goodbye, dining-room, I never liked you very much because you are so dark!'

Eight-year-old Penny stayed up in the nursery. That was the room she knew and loved the best. It was not called the nursery now, but was known as the schoolroom, because it was there that the two girls worked with their governess. Penny loved it.

She ran her fingers over the wallpaper, which showed a pattern of nursery rhymes. It had been repapered for Penny, four years before. She had chosen the paper herself. She knew every single person on it, every animal, every tree. How often she had looked at Jack and Jill always going up the hill, and how often she had wondered how there could possibly be room in the Old Woman's Shoe for all the children that were playing around it!

She opened the built-in toy cupboard and looked inside. It was empty now, for every toy had been packed in boxes. There were shelves there that had held trains and bricks and dolls.

'I wish you were coming with us, toy cupboard!' said Penny. 'I've always loved you. It was always so exciting every morning to open your doors and see my toys looking at me again. And it has always been such fun to creep right inside you and shut the door and pretend I was a toy too!'

Penny was the baby of the family. Rory was a big boy now, fourteen years old, black-haired and brown-eyed. Sheila was thirteen, curly-haired and pretty. Benjy, dreamy old Benjy, who loved and understood all wild creatures so well, was two years younger – and then came Penny, three years behind him! She tried to be grown-up, so that the others would let her into their secrets and take her about with them, but it was sometimes rather difficult.

She looked round. She was quite alone. Rory and Sheila were saying goodbye to each room in turn. She could hear them in the spare-room now. Sheila was talking to Rory.

'Do you remember counting the cracks in the ceiling when we were both in here with measles? There's one crack over in that corner that looks exactly like a bear with horns – look, there it is.'

Penny heard the two of them talking. She stared at the toy cupboard.

Should she just get inside the last time, and pretend she was a toy? Nobody would know.

She squashed herself in. It wasn't so easy now as it used to be, for Penny had grown. She shut the doors and peeped through the crack – and at once it seemed as if she was only three or four years old again!

'I'm a big doll, peeping through the crack in the door at the children playing in the nursery!' she said to herself. 'What a funny feeling it is!'

Before she could get out again, Benjy came into the room.

He looked round. Where were the others?

'Sheila! Rory!' he called. 'Where are you? Penny!'

Penny didn't answer. She was too afraid of being called a baby to come out and show herself. She stayed as quiet as a mouse in the cupboard.

The other two came running in. They carried coats and hats for everyone. 'Mother says we are to come at once,' said Sheila. 'Here are your things, Benjy. Where's Penny? Now wherever has she gone?'

Penny didn't move. She stared out through the crack. It was funny to see the others through the narrow chink. They looked different somehow.

The three children put on their coats. Mother came in.

'Are you ready?' she said. 'Where's Penny?'

Nobody knew. 'Oh dear!' said Mother. 'Wherever can she have got to?'

Penny was suddenly afraid that everyone would go without her. She pushed open the doors of the toy cupboard and looked out. Benjy almost jumped out of his skin with surprise.

'I'm here,' said Penny, in a small voice.

Everyone burst into laughter. They all knew Penny's old trick of getting into the toy cupboard and pretending to be a doll. Sheila was just going to call her a baby when she saw Penny's red face and stopped.

'Come along,' she said, holding out her hand. 'Daddy's waiting for us. Hurry, Penny!'

Penny squeezed herself out and put on her coat in silence. All the children went downstairs, their feet clattering loudly on the bare stairs. The house seemed suddenly strange and unfriendly. It would soon belong to somebody else.

They crowded into the car. Daddy and Mummy looked up at the tall house, remembering many things. They had had happy times there. The children had grown up there. It was sad to leave – but how happy to be going to a lovely farmhouse set on a hill!

The engine of the car started up. They were off!

'Goodbye!' cried the children, waving to the old house. 'We may perhaps call in and see you sometime in the future. Goodbye! We're off to Willow Farm, Willow Farm, Willow Farm!'

And off they went, purring through the London streets on their way to a new life down in the heart of the country.

2

Willow Farm

Nothing is quite so exciting as moving house. Everything is strange and thrilling and upside-down. Stairs sound different. Meals are taken just anywhere, at all kinds of odd times. Furniture stands about in odd places. The windows are like staring eyes with no eye-brows, because the curtains are not yet up.

It was like that at Willow Farm when the family moved in. Penny thought it was too exciting for words. Everything was fun. It was fun rushing through the different counties to get to Willow Farm. It was fun to pass Cherry Tree Farm on the way and stop for a few minutes' chat with Uncle Tim and Auntie Bess.

'Wouldn't you like to get rid of the children for a few days and let them stay with us?' asked Aunt Bess. But for once the children did not smile at the idea of staying at their beloved Cherry Tree Farm.

They looked quite dismayed. Mother laughed. 'Look at their faces!' she said. 'No thank you, Bess dear – they are all looking forward so much to settling in at Willow Farm. It is true that they will get in the way and be under my feet all the time – but . . .'

'Oh Mummy, we won't!' cried Penny. Then she saw the twinkle in her mother's eye and laughed.

'Aunt Bess, we love Cherry Tree Farm, but we wouldn't miss arriving at Willow Farm, our own farm, today, for worlds!' said Benjy.

'Have you seen Tammylan lately?' asked Rory.

'The wild man?' said Aunt Bess. 'Yes – let me see, we saw him last week, didn't we? He wanted to know when you were coming, and said he would love to see you all again.'

'Oh good,' said Benjy, pleased. 'He's got my pet squirrel for me. He's been keeping it for me while I was at school. I shall love to see Scamper again.'

'Well, we mustn't stay longer,' said their father. 'Goodbye, Tim, goodbye, Bess. We'll come over sometime and let you know how things go.'

Off they went through the lanes. The hedges were just beginning to leaf here and there. Celandine turned smiling, polished faces up to the sun. Primroses sat in rosettes of green leaves. Spring was really beginning!

The car turned a corner and came in sight of a rounded hill. Glowing in the afternoon sun was an old farmhouse built of warm red bricks. It had a thatched roof, as had Cherry Tree Farm, and this shone a deep golden-brown colour, for it had been re-thatched for the new owners.

'Willow Farm!' shouted Rory, and he stood up in the car. 'Willow Farm! Our farm!'

Benjy went red with pleasure. Sheila stared in silence. Penny gave little squeaks, one after the other. All the children gazed with pride and delight on their new home.

It was a lovely old place, three hundred years old, long and rambling, with peculiar tall chimneys, and brown beams that showed in the walls.

The windows were leaded, and there were green shutters outside each. The old front door was made of heavy brown oak, and had a curious little thatched porch above it, in which stood an old bench. Not far from the front door was the old well, rather like a Jack and Jill well. The water was not used now, but in the olden days there had been a bucket to let up and down.

Little gabled windows jutted from the thatch. The children stared up at them, wondering which windows belonged to their bedrooms. How lovely to peep out from those little windows in the early morning, and see the green fields and distant woods and silver streams!

Many streams flowed in and about Willow Farm. Along the banks grew the many many willows that gave the farm its pretty name. In the springtime the pussy willows broke into gold when the catkins became the lovely golden palm. Other kinds of willows grew there too, and the bees murmured in them all day long later on in the springtime.

'Daddy! Hurry up!' cried Rory. 'Oh, let's get to the farm quickly!'

The car ran down a winding lane, with high hedges each side – then up on to the hillside beside a gurgling stream. Then into a big gateway, whose great wooden gates always stood open.

And there they were at the farmhouse door! Behind the farmhouse were the farm-buildings – great barns with old old roofs, big sheds, stables and pens. The farmyard lay at the back too, and here the hens pecked about all day long.

The children tumbled out of the car in great excitement. They rushed to the door – but it was shut. Their father came to open it with a very large key. The children laughed to see it.

The door was thrown open and the children gazed into a large hall, with great beams in the rather low ceiling, and red, uneven tiles on the floor. Beyond lay open doors leading to the fine old kitchen and other rooms. How marvellous to explore them all while they were empty, and to arrange everything in them!

Everyone trooped in, chattering and exclaiming in delight. The place was spotless, for two village-women had been in to rub and scrub the whole week. The windows shone. The floors shone. The old oak cupboards, built into the walls, glowed with polish and age.

'Mummy! This farmhouse has such a happy, friendly feeling!' said Benjy, slipping his arm through his mother's. 'People have been happy here. I can feel it.'

So could they all. It was lovely to stand there and feel the happiness of the old house around them. It seemed glad to have them, glad to welcome them.

'Some houses have a horrid feeling in them,' said Sheila. 'I remember once going to see somebody in an old house down at the seaside, Mummy – and I was glad to come away. It made me feel unhappy. But other houses feel so content and friendly – like this one.'

'Yes – I think people have loved Willow Farm very much, and have worked hard and been happy here,' said their mother. 'I hope we shall work hard too and be happy. It takes a lot of time and hard work to make a farm pay, you know, children. We must all do our bit.'

'Of course!' said Rory. 'I'm going to work like anything! I learnt quite a lot on Uncle's farm last year, I can tell you!'

'Let's go all over the house!' said Penny running to the stairs. They ran up to a wide landing. There were seven rooms upstairs, one fine big room that their mother and father were going to have, one big room for the children's own playroom, a small room for Rory, a tiny one for Benjy, a bigger one for the two girls, a spare-room for friends, and a room for Harriet, the cook, who was coming in the next day.

And over the bedrooms was an attic, right under the thatch itself. It was reached by a funny iron ladder that slid up and down. The children went up it in excitement.

'Oooh!' said Penny, when she saw the dark cobwebby loft. 'It smells odd. Oh look – this is the thatch itself. Put your torch on, Rory – have you got it?'

Rory had. He took it out of his pocket and switched it on. The children gazed round the loft. They could only stand upright where the roof arched. They touched the thatch. It was made of straw. There was nothing between them and the sky but the thick straw – no plaster, no tiles – just the straw.

'The thatcher hasn't finished thatching the kitchen end of the house,' said Sheila. 'I heard Daddy say so. We'll be able to see exactly how he does it. Isn't it fun to be going to live in a thatched house? We shall be lovely and warm in the wintertime!'

The children climbed down the loft ladder. Rory slid it back into place.

'I do like all these black beams,' he said, looking round.

'I think they look exciting. Daddy says they came from old wooden ships. When the ships were broken up, the beams were used in houses – so once upon a time all the wooden part of Willow Farm was sailing on the sea!'

'I like to think that,' said Benjy, touching the black oak beam near him. 'Funny old beam – once you knew the fishes in the sea, and you creaked as great waves splashed over you. Now you live in a house, and listen to people's feet going up and down the stairs.'

The others laughed. 'You do say odd things, Benjy,' said Rory. 'Come on – let's go down. I want to see the rooms below too.'

Down they went. The big dark hall they had already seen. There was a large room that Mummy said would be a lounge or living-room. It had an enormous stone fireplace. Rory looked up it. He could stand on the hearth and look right up the chimney, and see the sky at the top. It was really enormous.

'I could climb up this chimney!' said Rory, in surprise.

'Little boys used to,' said Daddy, with a laugh. 'Yes – you may well stare. It's quite true. In the days when most houses had these big fireplaces and chimneys, little boys used to be forced to go up them to sweep them.'

'I do wish I could climb up and sweep it when it needs it,' said Rory, longingly.

'You might want to do it for fun, but you wouldn't want to do it every day of your life!' said his father.

The children went into the next room. It was a long dining-room, panelled with oak. 'I wonder if there are any sliding panels!' said Benjy, at once. He loved reading stories of hidden treasure, and in the last one he had read there had been a most exciting sliding oak panel, behind which a safe had been hidden.

'The one over there by the door looks as if it might slide!' said his father. Benjy stared at it. Yes – it really didn't seem to fit quite as well as the others. It *might* slide back! In great excitement he tried it.

And it did slide back! Very silently, very neatly it slid back behind the next panel. Benjy gave a yell.

'Daddy! Look!'

And then everyone laughed – for behind the sliding panel were four electric light switches! The people who had lived at Willow Farm before had hidden their switches there, rather than spoil the look of the panelling by the door! So poor Benjy didn't find hidden treasure or anything exciting.

The kitchen was a very big room indeed, with plenty of leaded windows, opening on to the farmyard at the back. It had an enormous door that swung open with a creak. The sinking sun streamed through it.

'It's got the biggest fireplace of all!' said Sheila.

'Yes – many a fine meal has been cooked there!' said her father. 'And look here – at the side is a funny bread-oven, going right into the thick wall. Harriet will be able to bake her bread there!'

'I like the uneven floor,' said Penny, dancing about over it. 'All these nice red tiles, higgledy-piggledy. And I like the great old beams across the ceiling. Just look at all the hooks and nails, Mummy!'

Everyone gazed up at the big beams, and saw the rows of hooks and nails there.

'That is where people have hung up hams and onions, herbs and spices,' said Mummy. 'It's a shame to see all the kitchen beams empty and bare – but never mind, soon Harriet will use them, and then our kitchen will look a most exciting place!'

Off the kitchen was a great cool room with stone shelves – the dairy. Here the milk was set for the cream to form, and the eggs were washed, graded and counted. The butter-churn was there too. All the children tried their hands at it.

'Oh Mummy! Won't it be fun to bring in the eggs and sort them, and to make the butter, and see the cream coming on the big bowls of milk!' cried Penny. She danced about again and fell over an uneven tile in the floor.

'Well, it's a good thing you weren't carrying eggs just at that moment!' said Sheila. 'That would have been the end of them!'

There was just one more room downstairs – a tiny cubby-hole of a room, panelled in black oak – and Daddy said that was to be his study and nobody was to use it except himself.

'Here I shall keep my accounts and find out if Willow Farm is paying or not!' he said.

'Of *course* it will pay!' cried Rory.

'Farming isn't so easy as all that,' said his father. 'You wait and see!'

3

A Little Exploring

Just then the children heard a rumbling noise outside and they rushed to the window.

'It's the first van!' yelled Rory. 'Look, there it comes – in at the gates. Goodness, there's only just room!'

'That's good,' said Mummy, pleased. 'Only one van is arriving tonight – this one. It has our beds and bedding in, so that we can make do for the night. The others come first thing tomorrow.'

The great van rumbled up to the door. The back was let down, and soon the children were watching four men carrying their beds, mattresses, pillows and everything into the house.

'You're in the way, children,' their mother said at last, after Penny had nearly been knocked over by the end of somebody's bed. 'Go and explore the farm, there's good children. Surely you want to see what it's like! You've seen the house from top to bottom – now go and see if you like the farmyard and the barns and the sheds!'

'Oh yes!' cried Rory. 'Come on, all of you. Let's explore the back, where the barns are.'

Off they rushed, munching large slices of cake, which their mother had given them. The farmyard at the back was rather exciting. It was a big squarish place, surrounded by sheds and stables. No hens pecked or clucked there. Those were to come. No pigs looked out of the sty. No cattle stamped in the sheds, and no horses looked out of the stable-doors.

'Uncle Tim has promised to buy all we want,' said Rory. 'I say – won't it be gorgeous when we've got hens and ducks all over the place, just like we had at Cherry Tree Farm? I miss the cackling and clucking, don't you? Look – there's the duck-pond over there.'

The children looked. Through a field-gate gleamed a round pond, set with rushes at one end. Willow trees drooped over it. A moorhen swam across the water, its head bobbing to and fro like a clockwork bird's!

The children peeped into the big barn. It was so large that it seemed almost like a church to them. It was dark and peaceful.

Much hard work had been done there. Men and women had laboured from dawn to dusk, had been tired and happy, and the old barn seemed to be dreaming of those long-ago days as the children walked inside.

It was tiled in dark red tiles, and green and yellow moss grew thickly over the roof. Some of the tiles were missing, and the daylight came in through the holes.

'We shall have to see that the roof is mended,' said Rory, solemnly. 'Uncle Tim always said that a good farmer looks every day at his roofs, gates and fences. He said that a nail in time saves nine, and a tile in time saves a hundred!'

'Well, it will be fun to go round each day and look at everything,' said Benjy. 'I say, look – are those our sheep up there on the hill?'

Everyone looked. There were about fifty sheep dotted

about on the hillside – and with them were many little lambs. In a sheltered place, tucked away behind a copse of trees, was the shepherd's hut. The shepherd stood outside, looking up to the sky.

'We've got a shepherd – look!' said Rory. 'I wonder if he's as nice as Uncle Tim's at Cherry Tree Farm? Shall we go and talk to him today – or shall we explore all the rest of the outbuildings?'

'Oh, let's explore,' said Penny. 'I want to see the cowsheds – I always like the smell of those.'

So into the empty sheds they went, where the sweetish smell of cows still hung. They ran into the stables and pulled at the hay still left in the stalls. They went into the little barn, where a wooden ladder ran straight up to lofts above.

They all climbed the ladder. A few husks of wheat blew about the floor. The loft had been used as a storing place for many years. In another loft nearby were a few old rotten apples.

'Oh – this is where they used to put the apples,' said Sheila. 'I say – won't it be fun to pick the apples in the autumn, and the pears too, and bring them up here to store away!'

'Doesn't it smell nice!' said Penny, sniffing the loft. 'Years and years and years of apples I can smell!'

The others laughed.

'Let's go to the orchard now and see what we can find there,' said Sheila. 'Auntie Bess said that Willow Farm had fine fruit trees. Come on!'

Down the steep wooden ladder they went. Rory held out his hand to help Penny, as she scrambled down too – but she would not take his hand.

'I wish you wouldn't think I'm still a baby,' she said crossly. 'I can get up and down ladders just as well as you can!'

She fell over a stick in the yard and Rory laughed. He helped her up. 'You're not a baby,' he said, 'but you're a little goose at times. A gosling! I say – I wonder if we shall keep geese.'

'Aren't they rather hissy?' asked Penny, remembering an alarming walk one day when she had come across a line of hissing geese who had looked at her quite fiercely.

'Very hissy and very cackly,' said Rory, solemnly. 'You'll have to take my hand every time you go past them, little gosling!'

Penny tried to look cross, but she couldn't. She skipped along in front of the others to a big gate that led into the orchard. It was a really lovely place.

Daffodils were in bloom beneath the fruit trees. They nodded and danced in the pale evening sun. Penny picked a bunch to take back to her mother.

'What fruit trees are these?' asked Sheila, looking down the straight rows.

'Apples – pears – plums,' said Rory, who was quite good at telling one tree from another. 'And – oh look – those must be cherries in the next field! They are all bursting into bud! They will be heavenly in a week or two. Golly! What fun we shall have in the fruit-picking season!'

They wandered through the orchard, where hundreds of daffodils danced for them. They came to a little stream, whose banks were set with yellow primroses. A moorhen looked at them from some rushes nearby and then ran away.

'Moorhens always seem to be running away,' said Penny. 'I'd like to see one close. Rory, will the moorhens nest on our farm, do you think? I'd so like to see a whole crowd of black babies going along behind their mother. Do you remember Tammylan showing us a nest once, and we saw all the babies tumbling out into the water to hide themselves?'

The mention of Tammylan made the children remember him and long to see him.

'We *must* see old Tammylan tomorrow!' said Benjy. 'And I *must* get back my squirrel Scamper!'

Tammylan had given Benjy the squirrel for his last birthday. Scamper had been a tiny baby squirrel when Benjy had first had him – now he was full-grown and the boy longed to see him. He had given Scamper back to Tammylan in the New Year, because he had not been allowed to take the squirrel to school with him – and Tammylan had promised to take great care of him.

'We shall be nearer to Tammylan's cave here than we were at Cherry Tree Farm,' said Rory, pleased. 'We can take the short cut over Christmas Common, and then down into the valley where Tammylan lives. That's good. Maybe he will help us a bit with the farm too. He knows such a lot about everything.'

'Dear old Tammylan,' said Benjy. 'We've had some good times with him – we made friends with nearly every creature of the countryside because of him!'

A bell rang loudly from the farmhouse. The children turned. 'That's Mummy,' said Penny. 'She wants us back. Well, that cake was good – but I'm hungry all over again now – and I'm getting cold too. Oh, what a lovely place Willow Farm is – aren't we lucky to come and live here!'

'We jolly well are!' said Benjy. 'Come on – let's go this way. It leads through the farmhouse garden. Mother says she is going to grow her flowers there, and her herbs. And look, through that white gate is the soft fruit – the gooseberry bushes, the currants, raspberries and strawberries. Mummy will be kept busy making jam, won't she?'

'Oooh! I shall help her with that,' said Penny, at once, thinking with joy of great fat red strawberries and sweet raspberries.

'I shouldn't like you to help *me* with jam-making!' said Sheila. 'I know what would happen to all the fruit. There wouldn't be much left for jam!'

Penny laughed. She felt very happy. Her legs were tired now and would not skip.

She walked along beside the others and suddenly yawned loudly.

'Now Penny, for goodness' sake don't start yawning,' said Benjy. 'We shall all be sent off to bed at once if you do. That's just like you!'

'Sorry,' said Penny. 'I promise I won't yawn when I get indoors. It's awful the way grown-ups always seem to think you are tired out as soon as you do even the tiniest yawn. My mouth sometimes really aches with trying not to yawn.'

'Well, you let it ache tonight,' said Rory. 'The first evening in a new home is far too exciting to be spoilt by being sent off to bed because of a yawn!'

They clattered into the farmyard. The big kitchen door stood wide open. A pleasant noise of crackling wood came to the children's ears as soon as they opened the door.

Their mother had decided to use the kitchen that night, and she had lit a fire in the big hearth. She had thrown on heaps of dry wood, and the fire crackled merrily, lighting up the kitchen gaily. Shadows danced and flickered. It was fun to come in and see such a fine fire. The kettle boiled on a stove nearby, and the big old farmhouse table, which had been bought with the house, was spread with a cloth.

The children's father lit some candles, which he stood on the table and on the mantelpiece. The electric current had not yet been switched on. Everyone was to have candles until proper shades and lanterns were bought. The children all thought that candles were much nicer than anything. Even Penny was told she was old enough to have one to take upstairs. She had been rather afraid that her mother would think her too little.

The children looked at the table. There were loaves of white and brown bread, homemade jam given to them by Aunt Bess, a big currant cake, a jar of potted meat, and a big jug for hot cocoa. It looked good to them!

'There are no chairs yet,' said their mother. 'Take what you want and go and eat it sitting on the broad window-sills while I make some cocoa.'

So the children spread their bread with butter, and with potted meat or jam, and then took their slices to eat on the window-seat. It was lovely to sit there, looking out at the darkening fields, or into the big, friendly kitchen, and see the leaping flames of the log-fire. The candles burned steadily, but the shadows jumped about the kitchen as if they were alive.

'This is nice,' said Penny, in a dreamy voice. 'I feel as if I'm asleep and dreaming some lovely dream. I feel . . .'

Rory gave her such a nudge that she nearly fell off the window-seat. She glared at him. 'Why did you . . .' she began.

'You *would* start talking about being asleep and dreaming,

just to make Mummy think we are all tired out!' said Rory, in a low, fierce voice. Then he spoke in his usual loud clear voice. 'May I have a slice of cake, please?'

'Come and get it,' said his mother, cutting him a large slice. 'Aren't you tired, Rory? You've had a long day, all of you.'

'*Tired!*' said Rory, as if he had never in his life heard the word before. '*Tired!* Why should any of us be tired, Mummy? Gracious, I'm so wide awake that I could go and milk the cows or count the sheep or fetch in eggs!'

'Well, we won't ask you to do any of those things, Rory,' said his father, with a chuckle. 'If anyone is tired, it's your mother! She has made all your beds – they are ready for the night.'

'Yes – and I really think I'm just about ready for mine,' said Mummy, unexpectedly. 'I feel as if I've done ten days' work in one. I've loved it all – and tomorrow will be fun, welcoming the other vans and arranging all the furniture. But I do feel I'd better have a long night, or I shan't be able to do a thing tomorrow.'

'Oh Mummy – do you mean to say we've all got to go to bed?' said Penny in dismay. 'And I've been trying so hard not to yawn!'

Everybody laughed at Penny's face. Then Mummy yawned. She put up her hand but there was no hiding it – and at once everyone else yawned too. They were all tired – and it was lovely to be able to yawn and feel that bed-time was not far away after all!

'As a matter of fact I'm really looking forward to going to bed,' said Sheila. 'I keep thinking of that nice room Penny and I are sharing together. It will be so cosy at night.'

'And I keep thinking of my own tiny room, with its slanting ceiling, and jutting-out window,' said Benjy. 'Mummy, can I shut the shutters?'

'Certainly not,' said his mother. 'You must get in all the air you can, silly boy, not shut it out. We shall only use the shutters for show – unless a tremendous storm comes and we put up the shutters to keep the wind out.'

'Oooh – I hope that happens,' said Penny, imagining a most terrific storm battering against the windows. Then she yawned again – so widely that Rory wondered how she could manage to make her small mouth so big! Then all the children yawned loudly at once, and their mother got up.

'Light your candles and off to bed, all of you!' she said. 'I'll just wash up – and then I shall go too.'

The children lit their candles. It was fun. Their mother said she would look in and say good night to them, so they kissed their father good night and went up the old stairs one by one. The candles flickered as they went. The old house seemed peaceful and friendly as they clattered up the stairs. Willow Farm! They were living there at last. It seemed too good to be true.

They went to their rooms. Their beds were put up, and the covers turned down. Their night-dresses and pyjamas were ready. Their tooth-brushes were in the bathroom so one by one they went to wash and clean their teeth.

'After all, I *am* tired,' said Benjy, as he turned in at the door of his own little room. 'I don't believe I could have kept awake very long!'

They all said good night. The two girls went to the room they shared, and each got into her own little bed. Rory had the room next door. They heard his bed creak as he got into it.

'Good night!' he yelled. 'Won't it be fun to wake up at Willow Farm tomorrow morning! I guess I shan't know where I am for a minute or two.'

'Good night!' called Benjy. 'Tomorrow we'll go and see old Tammylan. Good old Tammylan!'

Then there was silence – and when the children's mother came up in ten minutes' time, she couldn't say good night – because every single child was fast asleep!

4

The First Day

Benjy awoke first the next morning. The sun came in at his window, and when he opened his eyes he saw a golden pattern of sunlight on the wall. He remembered at once where he was, and sat up in delight.

'It's our first real day at Willow Farm!' he thought. 'I shall see Tammylan today – and Scamper. I wonder if Rory is awake.'

He slipped into Rory's room, but Rory was still fast asleep. So Benjy put on his clothes and went downstairs all by himself. He let himself out into the farmyard through the big kitchen door. The early morning sun was pale and had little warmth in it, but it was lovely to see it.

'I wish there were hens and ducks clucking and quacking,' thought Benjy. 'But there soon will be. My word, how the birds are singing!'

The early morning chorus sounded loudly about Benjy's ears as he wandered round the farm. The chaffinches carolled merrily – 'chip-chip-chip-cherry-erry-erry, chippy-ooEEEar!' they sang madly. Benjy whistled the song after them.

Blackbirds were sitting at the tops of trees singing slowly and solemnly to themselves, listening to their own tunes.

Thrushes sang joyfully, repeating their musical sentences over and over again.

'Ju-dee, Ju-dee, Ju-dee!' sang one thrush.

'Mind how you do it, mind how you do it!' called another, as Benjy jumped over a puddle and splashed himself. The boy laughed.

'Soon the swallows will be back,' he thought. 'I wonder if they'll build in the barn. It will be lovely if they do. After all, their real name is barn-swallow – and we have lots of barns. I must peep in and see if I can spy any old nests.'

It was too dark in the barn to see if the remains of old swallows' nests were on the rafters high in the roof. But Benjy saw the old nests of house-martins against the walls of the farmhouse. Two or three were just below his own window!

'I say – how lovely if they come back next month and build again there,' thought Benjy, gazing up at his little jutting-out window, tucked so cosily into the thatch. 'I shall hear their pretty twittering, and see the baby martins peeping out of the mud-nests. I hope they come back soon.'

Far in the distance the shepherd moved in the fields. He was doing something to one of the sheep. Nobody else seemed to be about at all. There were no animals or birds to see to, nothing to feed.

But wait – somebody *was* about! Benjy saw the end of a ladder suddenly appearing round the corner of the farmhouse. Who could be carrying it?

A man came round the corner, whistling softly. He saw Benjy and stopped.

'Good morning, young sir,' he said.

'Good morning,' said Benjy. 'Who are you?'

'I'm Bill the thatcher,' said the man. 'I'm just thatching the house for you – and after that I'm going to take a hand on the farm to get you all going!'

'Oh, that's fine!' said Benjy, pleased, for he liked the look of the man very much. His face was burnt as brown as an oak-apple, and his eyes were like bits of blue china in his brown face. They twinkled all the time.

Bill took the ladder to the kitchen end of the farmhouse. Lying on the ground nearby was a great heap of straw.

'I do wish I could thatch a roof,' said Benjy. 'You know, we learn all sorts of things at school, Bill – like what happened at the battle of Crecy and things like that – and yet nobody thinks of teaching us how to do really useful and exciting things like thatching a roof. Think how good it would be if I could say to my father – "Let *me* thatch the roof, Daddy!" or "Let *me* clean out the duck-pond!" Or, "Let *me* sweep the chimney!" '

Bill laughed. 'Well, you come and watch me do a bit of thatching,' he said. 'Then maybe next year when the old summer-house over there wants patching up with straw, you'll be able to do it yourself!'

Bill had a great many willow-sticks that he had cut on his way to Willow Farm that morning. He began to cut them into short strips and to sharpen the ends. Benjy watched him. 'What do you want those for?' he asked.

'To peg down the straw thatch near the edge, young sir,' said Bill. 'Look and see the piece I've finished.'

Benjy looked, and saw that the thatcher had made a very neat edging near the bottom of the thatched roof. 'It looks rather like an embroidered pattern!' he said. 'Do you put it there just to look pretty?'

'Oh no,' said the thatcher. 'The straw would work loose if it wasn't held towards the bottom like that – but the pattern is one used by many thatchers. My father used it, and his father before him. Look at the top of the roof too – see the pattern there? Ah, thatching isn't so easy as it looks – it's a job that goes in families and has to be learnt when you're a boy.'

'Oh good,' said Benjy, glad that he was still a boy and could learn to thatch. 'I say, do you think you could just wait till I call the others? They'd love to see you do the thatching.'

'You go and get the others, but I'll not wait,' said the thatcher, going up the ladder with a heavy load of straw on his shoulder. 'A minute here and a minute there – that's no use when you've work to do. I don't wait about. I'll be at work all day and you'll have plenty of time to see me.'

At that moment the other three came out. They saw Benjy and rushed at him. 'Why didn't you wake us, you mean thing? You've been up ages, haven't you?'

'Ages,' said Benjy. 'Everything's lovely! Look – that's the thatcher. His name's Bill. See those willow-twigs he's been sharpening – they're for making that fine pattern to hold down the straw at the edges of the roof.'

'You *have* been learning a lot!' said Rory, with a laugh. 'Tell us how a roof is thatched, Benjy!'

'Well,' said Benjy, making it all up quickly in his head, 'the thatcher pulls off all the straw first – and then he . . .'

The thatcher gave a shout of laughter. Benjy stared at him. 'What's the matter?' he asked.

215

'I'd just like to set you to work thatching!' he chuckled. 'My, you'd give yourself a job! Now look what I do – I pull out about six or seven inches of this old rotten straw – see – and work in handfuls of the new – about twelve inches thick. That'll work down flatter when the rain comes. You don't need to pull off all the old straw – that would be a real waste. When a roof is re-thatched we just pull out what's no use and pack in the new.'

'Do you mean to say then, that there is straw in our roof that may have been there for years and years and years?' asked Rory, in surprise.

'Maybe,' said the thatcher, with a grin, as he swiftly pulled and pushed with his strong hands, working in the new straw deftly and surely. 'Ah, and you'd be surprised the things I've found hidden in old thatch – boxes of old coins, bits of stolen jewellery, bags of rubbish – a thatched roof was a favourite hiding-place in the old days.'

The children stared at him, open-mouthed. This was marvellous! 'Did you find anything in *our* thatch?' asked Penny hopefully.

'Not a thing,' said Bill. 'It's the third time I've thatched and patched this roof – I don't reckon I'll find anything this time if I didn't find it the first time! Now look – isn't that somebody calling you?'

It was the children's father, looking for them to come to breakfast. They left the thatcher and hurried indoors, full of what Bill had said. Penny thought it must be the most exciting thing in the world to be somebody who might at any moment find treasure in a roof. She made up her mind to go up into the loft above her bedroom and poke about in the thatch there.

She might find something that the thatcher had missed!

'You must get out of our way this morning,' said their mother, as they finished up their breakfast with bread and marmalade. 'The other vans are coming and we shall be very busy.'

'Oh – can't we stay and help?' said Benjy, disappointed. 'I do like seeing the furniture being carried up the stairs, Mummy.'

'Well, the men don't feel quite so excited about that as you,' said Mummy. 'No – I shall make you up a picnic lunch – and you can go and find Tammylan!'

There were loud cheers then! Everyone wanted to see Tammylan.

'Good,' said Benjy, pleased. 'I'd like that better than anything. And it will be fun to come back and see all the rooms with their furniture in, looking so nice and homey.'

'Oh, you won't find that yet!' said his mother, laughing. 'It will be a week or two before we are straight. Now, what would you like for your picnic lunch, I wonder? I'll make you some potted meat sandwiches, and you can take some cake and a packet of biscuits. There is a big bottle of milk between you too, if you like.'

Before they started off to find Tammylan the girls made the beds and the boys helped to wash up and to cut the sandwiches. Just as they were packing the things into two bags for the boys to carry, there came the rumbling of the big removal vans up the lane.

'Just in time,' said their mother, running to the door. 'Now we shall be able to get rid of you children for a while whilst the men unload!'

217

The children got their hats and coats and went outside the big front door. The first van drew up outside and the men jumped down. They opened the doors at the back and the children gazed inside and saw all the furniture they knew so well.

'There's the nursery table!' yelled Penny.

'And there's the old bookcase,' said Rory. 'I suppose Mummy has got to tell the men which room everything's to go into. I half wish we could stop and help.'

'Go along now!' cried his mother. 'Don't wait about there in the cold!'

The children set off, looking behind every now and again. They decided to go over the top of Willow Hill and across Christmas Common to Tammylan's cave. It was about two miles away. When they reached the top of the hill they looked down at Willow Farm. It stood firmly in the hillside, smoke curling up from the kitchen chimney. It looked alive now, with people running about and smoke coming from the chimney.

Then over the hill went the four children on their way to old Tammylan. They sang as they went, for they were happy. It was holiday time. The spring and summer were coming. They had a home in the country instead of in London. And Tammylan could be seen as often as they liked! They had missed him so much.

They rounded a small hill. Bracken and heather grew there, and birch trees waved lacy twigs in the wind. The children made their way to a spot they knew well.

It was a cave in the hillside. In the summertime tall fronds of green bracken hid the entrance, but now only the broken, russet-brown remains of last year's bracken showed. The new bracken had not even begun growing. Heather dropped its big tufts from the top edge of the cave.

The children stood outside and called. 'Tammylan! Tammylan!'

'Let's go inside,' said Rory. 'I'm sure he's not there – but he *might* be fast asleep!'

'Don't be silly!' said Benjy, scornfully. 'Why, old Tammylan wakes if a mouse sits up and washes his whiskers! He would have heard us coming round the hill long ago if he'd been here.'

They went into the cave. It was exciting to be back there again. It opened out widely inside. The ceiling rose high, dark and rocky.

'Here's his bed,' said Rory, sitting down on a rocky ledge, on which Tammylan had put layers of heather and bracken. 'And look – he still keeps his tin plates and things on the same shelf.'

The children looked at the little rocky shelf opposite the bed. On it, clean and neatly arranged, were Tammylan's few possessions.

'There is the stool that Rory and I made for Tammylan for Christmas!' said Benjy, in delight. 'Look – see the squirrels I carved round the edge!'

'And here is the blanket that Sheila and I knitted for him,' said Penny, patting a neatly folded blanket at the foot of the bed of heather and bracken. 'I do hope he found it nice and warm this cold winter!'

'I wonder if the little spring that gives Tammylan his drinking-water still wells up at the back of the cave,' said

Rory. He went to see. He flashed his torch into the darkness there, and then gave a squeal.

'What's the matter?' asked Benjy, in surprise.

'Nothing much – except that one of Tammylan's friends is here!' said Rory, with a laugh. The others came quietly to see. Tammylan had taught them to move silently when they wanted to see animals or birds.

Lying by the tiny spring that welled up from the rocky floor, was a hare. Its enormous eyes looked up patiently at the children. It could not move.

'Look – his back legs have been broken,' said Sheila, sadly. 'Tammylan is trying to mend them. He has put them into splints. Poor hare – he must somehow have been caught in a trap.'

The children gazed down at the patient hare. It dipped its nose into the springing water and lapped a little. Benjy felt sure that it was in pain.

Penny wanted to stroke it but Benjy wouldn't let her. 'No hurt animal likes to be touched,' he said. 'Leave it alone, Penny.'

'Listen!' said Sheila, suddenly. 'I can hear Tammylan I think!'

They listened – and they all knew at once that it was dear old Tammylan. No one else had that sweet clear whistle, no one else in the world could flute like a blackbird, or whistle like a blackcap! The children all rushed to the cave entrance.

'Tammylan!' they shouted. 'Tammylan! We're here!'

Good Old Tammylan!

Tammylan was coming along up the hillside, his arms full of green stuff and roots. He dropped it all when he saw the children, and a broad smile spread across his brown face. His bright eyes twinkled like the sparkles on a stream as the children flung themselves at him and hugged him.

'Well, well, well,' he said, 'What a storm of children breaking over me! Rory, how you've grown! Sheila, let me have a look at you! Benjy – dear old Benjy, I've thought of you so often. And my dear little Penny – not so very little now – quite grown-up!'

Chattering and laughing, the five of them sat down on a heathery bank. They were all delighted to see Tammylan again. He was a person they trusted absolutely. He would always do the right thing, never misunderstand them, always be their trusted friend. He was as natural as the animals he loved so much, as happy as the birds, as wise as the hills around. Oh, it was good to see Tammylan again!

'Tammylan, have you seen Willow Farm?' cried Penny. 'Isn't it lovely?'

'It's a fine place,' said Tammylan. 'And a good farm too. With hard work and a bit of luck you should all do well there. The land's good. The fields are well-sheltered just where they need it, and it has always had a name for doing well with its stock. You'll all help, I suppose?'

'Of course!' said Rory. 'We boys are doing lessons with the vicar again this term – and the girls are going to as well! So we shall have all our spare-time for the farm and Saturdays and Sundays as well. Aren't we lucky, Tammylan?'

'Very,' said their friend. 'Well, if you need any help at any time, come to me. I can work as hard as anybody, you know – and I know many strange medicines to help sick creatures.'

'Oh, Tammylan – we saw that poor hare in your cave,' said Benjy, remembering. 'Will it get better?'

'If it lives till tonight, it will mend,' said Tammylan. 'I have some roots here that I want to pound and mix with something else. If I can get the hare to take the mixture, it will deaden the pain and help it to live. An animal who is badly shocked, or who suffers great pain dies very easily. Poor little hare – it is a great friend of mine. You have seen him before, Benjy.'

'Oh – is it the hare who came so often to your cave last year?' asked Benjy, sadly. 'He was such a dear – so swift-running, and so gentle. I did love him. What happened to hurt him so badly, Tammylan?'

'I don't know,' said the wild man. 'It almost looks as if he had been hit hard with a stick, though I should not have thought anyone could have got near enough to him to do that. I don't know how he dragged himself here to me, poor thing. He only had his front legs to crawl with.'

Penny was almost in tears. She watched the wild man pound up some roots with a heavy stone. He mixed the juice with a fine brown powder and stirred the two together. Then he went into his cave, followed by the children.

The hare gazed up at the wild man with big, pained eyes. Tammylan knelt down and took the soft head gently in his left hand. He opened the slack mouth and deftly thrust in a soft pellet of his curious mixture. He shut the hare's mouth and held it. The creature struggled weakly and then swallowed.

Tammylan let go the hare's mouth, and ran his strong brown fingers down the back of the creature's head. 'You'll feel better in a little while,' he said in his soft voice.

They all went out into the open air again. Benjy asked a question that had been on the tip of his tongue for some time.

'Tammylan – where's Scamper?'

'Well, well – to think I hadn't mentioned your squirrel before!' said the wild man with a laugh. 'Scamper is doing exactly what his name says – scampering about the trees with all the other squirrels. He stayed with me in the cave in the cold weather, hardly stirring – but this last week it has been warm, and the little creature has often gone to play in the trees with his cousins.'

'Oh,' said Benjy, disappointed. 'Isn't he tame any more then?'

'Of course!' said Tammylan. 'You'll see him in a minute or two. I'll whistle him!'

Tammylan gave a curiously piercing whistle, loud and musical.

'It's a bit like an otter's whistle,' said Benjy, remembering a night he had spent with Tammylan when he had heard otters whistling in the river to one another. 'I hope Scamper hears you, Tammylan.'

'He will hear me, no matter in what part of the woods he

223

is!' said Tammylan. The wild man was right! In about half a minute Benjy gave a shout.

'Look! There comes Scamper up the hillside, look!' Sure enough they could all see the little brown squirrel bounding gracefully up the hill, his bushy tail streaming out behind him. He rushed straight up to the little group, gave a snicker of joy and leapt up to Benjy's shoulder!

'Oh you dear little thing, you've remembered me after three months!' said Benjy, joyfully. 'I wondered if you would. Oh, Tammylan, isn't he lovely? He's grown – and his tail is magnificent!'

The squirrel made some funny little chattering noises, and gently bit Benjy's ear. He ran round and round the boy's neck, then up and down his back and then sat on the very top of his head! Everybody laughed.

'He is certainly delighted to see you, Benjy,' said Tammylan. Scamper looked at the wild man, leapt to his shoulder and then back to Benjy again. It was almost as if he said 'I'm pleased to see Benjy, but I'm very fond of you too, Tammylan!'

Do you think he will come back to Willow Farm with me?' asked Benjy. 'I do want him to.'

'Oh yes,' said the wild man. 'But you mustn't mind if he goes off by himself at times, Benjy. He loves his own kind, you know. I will teach you the whistle I keep specially for him, and then he will always come to you when you want him.'

'I'm jolly hungry,' said Penny, suddenly. 'We've brought a picnic lunch, Tammylan. You'll share it with us, won't you?'

'Of course,' said Tammylan. 'Come with me. I know a warm and sheltered spot out of this cold March wind. It will be April next week, and then the sun will really begin to feel hot!'

He took them to a spot above his cave. Here there was a kind of hollow in the hillside, quite out of the wind, where the sun poured down. Primroses grew there by the hundred, and later on the cowslips nodded there. The children sat down on some old bracken and basked like cats in the sun.

'Lovely!' said Benjy. 'Hurry up with the food, Rory.'

They ate a good dinner, and talked nineteen to the dozen all the time to Tammylan, telling him about school and London, and Willow Farm. Then Tammylan in his turn told them his news.

'It's not so exciting as yours,' he said, 'because I have lived quietly here in my cave since you left. I was very glad of your woolly blanket, Sheila and Penny, when that cold snap came – and as for your carved stool, Rory and Benjy, I really don't know what I should have done without it! I have used it as a table, and as a stool every day!'

'Good,' said the children, pleased. 'Now, Tammylan, what animals have you had for company since we saw you last?'

'Well, as you know, a great many of them sleep the winter away,' said Tammylan. 'But the rabbits have been in to see me a great deal, and have skipped round my cave merrily. They soon disappeared when the weasel came though!'

'*Weasel!*' said Benjy, astonished. 'Was a weasel tame enough to visit you?'

'Yes,' said Tammylan. 'I was pleased to see him too, for he was a fine little fellow. He smelt the smell of rabbits and that is how he first came into my cave. You'd have liked him, Benjy. He used to bound about like a little clown.'

225

'Who else came to see you?' asked Penny, wishing that she had lived with Tammylan in his cave for the last three months!

'Plenty of birds,' said Tammylan. 'The moorhens often came. Thrushes, robins, blackbirds, chaffinches – they all hopped in at times, and for a whole month a robin slept here in the cave with me.'

'Did the fox come again?' asked Rory, remembering the hunted fox to whom Tammylan had given shelter one winter's day when they had all been there.

'Yes,' said Tammylan. 'He comes often. He is a most beautiful creature. He always goes straight to the little water-spring at the back of the cave and laps two or three drops from it, almost as if he remembers each time how the waters helped him when he was so weary with being hunted!'

The children stayed talking in the warm hollow until almost teatime. Then they got up and stretched their legs.

'We promised Mummy we would be back at teatime,' said Sheila. 'We must go. Come and see us at Willow Farm, Tammylan, won't you? We'll be awfully busy soon, and may not have time to come and see you every day, though we'd love to. But you can come and see us whenever you like. Daddy and Mummy will love to see you – and we do want to show you everything at Willow Farm.'

The children said goodbye to the wild man and left. Before they went they slipped softly into the cave to have a look at the hare.

Rory shone his torch down on to it.

'Oh, it looks better,' he said, pleased. 'Its eyes haven't got that hurt, glassy look. I believe it will mend. Poor hare – don't look so sad. One day soon you will be bounding over the fields again, as swiftly as the wind.'

'I doubt that,' said Tammylan. 'He will never run fast again. I shall have to keep him as a pet. He will limp for the rest of his life. But he will be happy here with me if I can tame him.'

The children ran home over Christmas Common, came to the top of Willow Hill and ran down it to their home. It was nice to come home to Willow Farm. The vans had gone. Bits of straw blew about in the yard. Smoke came from three chimneys now instead of one. Bill the thatcher was talking to their father in the yard. Somebody was singing in the kitchen.

'It really feels like home,' said Sheila, running in at the kitchen door. She stopped when she saw somebody strange there.

A plump, red-cheeked woman smiled at her. 'Come along in,' she said. 'I'm Harriet. I've been wanting to see you children all day!'

The children all came in. They liked the look of Harriet. A young girl of about fifteen was busy laying a tea-tray. She glanced shyly at the children.

'That's Frannie, my niece,' said Harriet. 'She's coming in daily to help.'

'I'm Sheila, and this is my sister Penny,' said Sheila. 'And that's Rory, the eldest, and this is Benjy. Is that our tea being got ready?'

'It is,' said Harriet. 'Your mother is upstairs putting things to rights, if you want her. She was wondering if you were back.'

The children ran to find their mother. They peeped into

each room downstairs. Oh, how different they looked now, with all the familiar chairs and tables in them!

The children went upstairs. They looked into their bedrooms. Not only were their beds there now but their own chests and chairs and bookcases! Penny's dolls' cot stood beside her own little bed. The big ship that Rory had once made stood proudly on his mantelpiece.

'Oh, it all looks lovely!' said the children. 'Mummy! Where are you?'

'Here,' said Mummy, from the playroom. The children rushed in. The playroom looked fine too with all their own chairs and the two old nursery tables. The old rocking chair was there too, the two dolls' houses, the fort, and a great pile of old toy animals belonging to Penny and Benjy.

'This is going to be a lovely room for us!' said Benjy, staring out of the window down the hill to where the silver streams gleamed in the dying sun. 'Mummy, how quick you've been to get everything ready like this!'

'Well, it may look as if it's ready,' said his mother, with a laugh. 'But it isn't really. We must put the rugs down tomorrow – and the pictures up – and you must sort out your books and put them into your bookcases, and Penny must arrange her toys in the cupboard over there. There's a lot to do yet.'

'Well, we shall love doing it!' said Rory, thinking with joy of arranging all his belongings in his new bedroom. 'Everything's fun at Willow Farm!'

6

A Surprise for Penny

The next few days were great fun. The children arranged all their things to their liking. They made friends with Harriet and Frannie – though Frannie at first was too shy to say a word! Harriet was very jolly, and nearly always had some titbit ready for the children when they trooped into the kitchen.

Bill the thatcher finished the roof, and did not find anything exciting in the thatch at all, much to Penny's disappointment.

'I'm glad that job's finished,' he said. 'Now I can get on to the farm-work. There's a lot of sowing to be done – and I must get the garden ready for your mother. She wants to grow all kinds of things there!'

'Isn't there anything *we* can do?' asked Rory. 'I want to WORK! I wish we could get in our hens and ducks and pigs and cows and things – then we could help to look after them.'

The children asked their parents when the birds and animals of the farm were coming.

'Soon,' said their father. 'Your uncle Tim is bringing over the poultry tomorrow. The hen-houses are ready now. Which of you is going to take care of the hens?'

'I will,' said Sheila at once. 'I like hens – though I like

ducks better. Let me take care of the hens, Daddy.'

'Well, Sheila, if you do, you must really learn about them properly,' said her father. 'It was all very well at Cherry Tree Farm for you and others to throw corn to the hens when you felt like it, and go and find nice warm eggs to carry in to your Aunt Bess – but if you are really and truly going to see to the hens and make them your special care, you will have to know quite a lot.'

'I see, Daddy,' said Sheila. 'Well – have you got a book about them?'

'I've two or three,' said Daddy. 'I'll get them for you.'

'Sheila, could I help with the hens too?' asked Penny. 'I want to do something. The boys say they are going to do the pigs and milk the cows when they come.'

Sheila badly wanted to manage the hens entirely by herself, but when she saw Penny's small, earnest face her heart melted.

'Well,' she said, 'yes, you can. You can read the books too.'

Penny was overjoyed. She felt tremendously important. She was going to read books about poultry-keeping! She longed to tell somebody that. She would tell Tammylan as soon as ever she saw him.

Daddy fetched them the books. They looked very grown-up and rather dull. But Sheila and Penny didn't mind. Now they would know all about hens! Sheila handed Penny the one that looked the easiest. It had pictures of hens inside.

'Daddy, you'll let us see to the pigs when they come, won't you?' asked Benjy. 'And milk the cows too. We can clean out the sheds quite well. I did it once or twice at Cherry Tree Farm.'

'You can try,' said Daddy. 'Soon the farm will be working properly – cows in the fields, pigs in the sty, horses in the stable, hens and ducks running about, butter being made, sheep being dipped – my word, what a busy life we shall lead! And we shall all have breakfast at seven o'clock in the morning!'

'Goodness!' said Sheila, who was a lie-abed. 'That means getting up at half-past six!'

'Yes – and going to bed early too,' said her father. 'Farmers have to be up and about soon after dawn – and they can't be up early if they go to bed late!'

None of the children liked the idea of going to bed early. But still, if they were going to be farmers, they must do as farmers did!

Sheila and Penny went up to the playroom with the hen books. Penny struggled hard with the reading. She could read very well indeed – but oh dear, what long words there were – and what a lot of chapters about things called incubators and brooders. She soon gave it up.

'Sheila,' she said, in a small voice. 'I really can't understand this book. Is yours any easier?'

Sheila was finding her book dreadfully difficult too. It seemed to be written for people who had kept hens for years, not for anybody just beginning. She felt that she wouldn't know how to feed them properly – she wouldn't know when a hen wanted to sit on eggs, she wouldn't know how to tell if they were ill.

But she wasn't going to tell that to Penny! So she looked up and smiled. 'Oh, Penny dear,' she said, 'what a baby you are! *I'll* read the books, if you can't, and I'll tell you what they say. I can tell you in words that you'll understand.'

Penny went red. 'All right,' she said. 'You will just have to tell me.'

The little girl was quite ashamed because she couldn't understand the books. She left the playroom and went downstairs. She thought she would go and talk to the old shepherd up on the hill. So off she went.

The sheep were peacefully grazing on the hillside. Little lambs skipped about, and Penny laughed to see them. She wished and wished that she could have one of her own. She had fed some at Cherry Tree Farm from a baby's bottle, and how she had loved that!

'Really, I think lambs are much nicer than hens,' said Penny to herself. 'I know Sheila likes hens – but I do think they are a bit dull. They all seem exactly alike, somehow. Now, lambs are like people – all different.'

She stood and watched the lambs skipping about. Then she looked at the sheep.

'It's a great pity that lambs grow into sheep,' she thought. 'Sheep are like hens – all exactly the same. I suppose the shepherd can tell one from the other – but I certainly couldn't!'

She looked to see where the shepherd was. He was at the top of the hill, where a rough fold had been made of wattle hurdles. Penny ran to it.

'Hallo,' she said, when she came to the shepherd. 'I've come to see you.'

'Well, little missy,' said the shepherd, leaning on his staff and looking at the little girl with eyes as grey as his hair. 'And what's your name?'

'Penny,' said Penny. 'What's yours?'

'Davey,' said the shepherd. 'That's a funny name you've got. When you were small, I suppose they called you Ha'penny? Now you're Penny. When will you be Tuppence?'

Penny laughed. She liked Davey. 'No, I didn't have those names,' she said. 'My real name is Penelope, but I'm called Penny for short.'

'Well, I shall call you Tuppenny,' said the shepherd. 'A penny is too cheap!'

They both laughed. A big collie-dog came running up to them and licked Penny's hand. She patted him.

'That's my best dog, Rascal,' said Davey. 'He's a wonder with the sheep!'

'Is he really? What does he do to them, then?' asked Penny.

'Oh, you come along one day when I'm moving the sheep from one hill to another,' said Davey. 'Then you'll see what old Rascal does. Do you know, if I were ill and wanted my sheep taken from here to the top of the next hill, I've only got to tell Rascal – and before two hours had gone by, those sheep would all be safely down this hill and up the next!'

'Goodness!' said Penny. 'I'd love to see him do that. Davey, there's another dog over there. What is his name?'

'That's Nancy,' said Davey. 'She's good too, but not so obedient as Rascal. And look, over there is Tinker. He's not a sheep-dog, but he's almost as good as the others.'

'Rascal, Nancy and Tinker,' said Penny, thinking what nice names they were. 'Davey, is it easy to keep sheep?'

'Yes, if you know how,' said Davey. 'I've been doing it all my life, little Tuppenny, and I've made all the mistakes there are to be made – but there's not much I don't know about sheep now!'

'Do you know, I used to feed lambs out of a bottle at Cherry Tree Farm?' said Penny. 'I did love it. I do wish I was like the Mary in the nursery rhyme who had a lamb of her own. I do so love lambs.'

'Well, you come and have a look at this poor little lambie,' said Davey, taking Penny's hand. 'Now, if you'd been here six weeks ago I'd have asked you to take it and care for it, for in the lambing season I've no time for sickly lambs. Still, I've tried to do my best for this one.'

He took Penny to a small fold in which lay one lamb. It was some weeks old, but was tiny, and very weakly.

'It's mother had three lambs,' said the shepherd. 'She liked two of them but she just wouldn't have anything to do with this one. So I took it away and gave it to another ewe whose lamb had died. But I had to skin the dead lamb first and cover this one with the hide.'

'But what a funny thing to do!' cried Penny. 'Why did you do that?'

'Because the mother would only take a lamb that smelt like hers,' said Davey. 'Well, she sniffed at this one, covered with the skin of her dead lamb, and she took to it and mothered it.'

'Oh, I'm glad,' said Penny.

'Ah, but wait a bit,' said Davey. 'She mothered it for a week. Then she took a dislike to it and butted it away with her head every time it came near, poor thing. It was half-starved, and I had to bring it away and try to feed it by hand out of a bottle.'

'Did it wear the skin of the dead lamb all the two weeks?' asked Penny.

'Oh no – as soon as the mother sheep took the lamb, I stripped off the skin,' said Davey. 'But there must be something about this wee thing that the ewes dislike. No one will feed it.'

'Davey, I suppose I couldn't possibly have it for my own, could I?' asked Penny, her eyes sparkling. 'I could get a baby's milk-bottle – and Harriet would let me have milk. Oh, do let me!'

'Well, I'll speak to your father,' said the shepherd. 'It would help me if you took it and cared for it. I've not much time now – and the lamb will die if it doesn't begin to grow a bit soon!'

Penny looked at the long-legged lamb in the fold. It had a little black face, a long wriggly tail, a thin little body, and legs just like her toy lamb at home.

'It's not a very pretty lamb,' she said. 'It looks sort of miserable. Lambs are always so full of spring and leap and frisk, aren't they – but this one isn't.'

'That's because it isn't well,' said Davey. 'I'll talk to your father about it, Tuppenny. Ah – there he is. I'll have a word with him now. See – is that somebody calling you down there?'

It was Penny's mother. Penny rushed down the hill to see what she wanted. 'Mummy, Mummy!' she yelled, as soon as she got near, 'Davey the shepherd says perhaps I may have a lamb of my own to feed. Oh, Mummy, do you suppose I can? Davey is going to talk to Daddy about it. He says the lamb will die if somebody doesn't take care of it properly.'

Sheila overheard what Penny said. 'I thought you were going to help with the hens,' she said.

'So I will,' said Penny. 'But I do feel I shall understand one lamb better than a whole lot of hens, Sheila. Anyway, it won't take long to feed each day.'

Penny's mother had called her in to make her bed. She had forgotten to do it. It was the rule that each of the children should make their own beds and tidy their own rooms.

Penny made her bed quickly and dusted and tidied her room. She looked out of the window to see if Daddy and the shepherd were still talking. No – daddy had left Davey and was now walking down to the farm.

Penny put her head out of the window. 'Daddy!' she yelled. 'Can I have the lamb?'

'Yes, if you'll really care for it properly,' said her father. The little girl gave an enormous yell and rushed downstairs, nearly knocking over poor Frannie as she went. 'I'm going to have a lamb!' she yelled to Frannie.

She tore up the hill as if a hundred dogs were after her. She meant to get that lamb before anybody changed their minds about it!

'What a whirlwind!' said Davey, as Penny raced up to him. 'Well, you're to have the lamb. Mind you bring it up to me sometimes so that I can see how well it is growing.'

'Oh, I will, I will,' said Penny. 'I'm going to buy it a feeding-bottle out of my own money.'

'You needn't do that,' said Davey. 'You can have this one.' He held out a feeding-bottle to Penny. It had a big teat through which the lamb could suck the milk just as a baby sucks from a bottle. 'I've fed him this morning. Give him another bottle of milk at dinner-time, and another at teatime. Just give him as much as Harriet can spare.'

Penny took the bottle. Then Davey undid one of the hurdles of the fold and took up the lamb. He tied a rope loosely round its neck.

'He won't follow you till he knows you,' he said. 'Take him gently down to the farm. Ask your mother if you can keep him in the little orchard till he knows you. Then he'll keep by you and not wander, as you go about the farmyard.'

Penny was most excited and joyful. She had always wanted a lamb of her very own. She wondered what she would call the little creature.

'I'll call it Skippetty,' she said. 'It isn't very skippetty now – but perhaps it soon will be.'

She took hold of the rope and tried to lead the lamb down the hill. At first it held back and tugged at the rope as if it wanted a tug-of-war with Penny. But soon it followed her peacefully enough and once it even ran in front of her.

When she got down to the farm, the other three children came to stare in astonishment.

'What are you doing with that lamb?' asked Benjy. 'What a dear little black-faced creature!'

'It's mine,' said Penny, proudly. 'Its name is Skippetty.'

'Yours!' said Rory, in amazement. 'Who gave it to you!'

'Davey the shepherd,' said Penny. 'He's awfully nice. He's got three dogs, Rascal, Nancy and Tinker – and he says when he moves the sheep, we are to go and watch how well his dogs work for him. He gave me this lamb for my own to look after because it is such a poor little thing and he hasn't got time for it.'

'You *are* lucky!' said Benjy. 'I like it almost as much as I like Scamper.'

Scamper was on his shoulder. The squirrel had not left Benjy once since he had brought it back to the farm. It even slept with Benjy at night!

'I'm going to show Skippetty to Mummy,' said Penny, and off she went. She took the lamb into the lounge and Mummy cried out in surprise.

'Oh no, Penny dear – you really can't bring the lamb into the house! Keep it in the orchard.'

Well, it was all very well for Mummy to say that Penny wasn't to bring Skippetty into the house! The lamb lived in the orchard for a day or two and then Penny set it free to see if it would follow her, like Mary's little lamb. And it did!

It followed her everywhere! It followed her to the barn. It followed her into the kitchen. It even went up the stairs after her to the playroom! It just wouldn't be left without Penny.

The little girl loved it. She fed it as often as Harriet would spare her the milk. It was such fun. Harriet emptied the milk into the bottle and then Penny would take it to the lamb. It ran to her at once, and sometimes even put its funny long legs up on to her waist to get at the milk more quickly. It emptied the bottle in a trice, sucking noisily at the teat.

It grew even in three days! It became frisky and skippetty, and Penny loved it.

The others sang the nursery rhyme whenever they saw Penny coming with her lamb trotting behind her.

'Penny had a little lamb,
Its fleece was white as snow,
And everywhere that Penny went,

The lamb was sure to go!'

Mother grew used to the lamb trotting in and out of the house – but she scolded Penny for letting it go into the bathroom when Penny bathed at night.

'Oh, Penny darling, I really can't have that!' she cried. 'You'll be bathing it in the bath next!'

Penny went red. She had secretly thought that it *would* be great fun to bath the lamb, especially one evening when it had rolled in some mud and got dirty.

'All right, I won't take it into the bathroom again,' she said.

Harriet joined in the conversation. '*Nor* in the larder, *nor* in the dairy, *nor* in the broom-cupboard!' she said, her eyes twinkling.

'I'll make my lamb be good,' promised Penny, laughing. 'I'll make it just as good as I am!'

'Good gracious!' said Harriet, smiling, 'what a monkey of a lamb it will be!'

Sheila Finds a Friend

Penny's lamb had been a great excitement – and something else was too! The hens came. This may not sound a very exciting thing, but to the four children at Willow Farm, it was very thrilling. Hens of their own! Hens that would lay eggs and make money – this was a real bit of farm-life to the children.

Sheila had studied the three books and had learnt very little from them. She hadn't liked to own up that the books were too difficult – but she had found help most unexpectedly.

It came from Frannie, the girl who came in daily to help Harriet. She had come in to clean the playroom when Sheila had been sitting there trying to puzzle out what the poultry books meant.

'Oh, Frannie!' sighed Sheila. 'I wish I knew a lot more about hens. I'm going to look after them, you know, and I really must learn about them, or they won't lay eggs, and won't do well at all. And I do want to help my mother and father to make our farm pay.'

'Well, Miss Sheila, what do you want to know?' asked Frannie, shyly. 'My mother keeps hens, and I've looked after them since I was a tiny thing. You don't need to worry about your hens, surely – you've got a fine hen-house – and plenty of coops – and Harriet will cook the scraps for you – and there's corn in the bins.'

'Frannie, tell me about hens,' begged Sheila. 'From the very beginning. I don't want to make any mistakes.'

Frannie laughed. 'Oh, you learn by making mistakes,' she said. 'First of all, what hens are you going to have? There are a good many kinds you know. Are you going to keep yours for egg-laying or for meat – you know, eating?'

'Oh, egg-laying,' said Sheila. 'I want lots and lots of eggs. Uncle Tim is bringing the hens over tomorrow. They are to be Buff Orpingtons.'

'Oh, those nice fat brown, comfortable-looking hens!' said Frannie, pleased. 'They are like ours. They lay a fine lot of eggs. You know, Miss Sheila, they're the best hens to have in the wintertime anyway, because they'll lay when other kinds won't.'

'Well, that's good,' said Sheila. 'But will they sit on eggs well too?'

'Oh yes,' said Frannie. 'Ours do, anyway. Oh, Miss Sheila, it will be fun to set some eggs, won't it, and see the chicks come out?'

'Goodness, yes!' said Sheila. 'Fancy, Frannie, I don't even know how many eggs to put under a sitting hen!'

'Oh, I can tell you things like that,' said Frannie. 'You put thirteen good fresh eggs. And you'll have to see the hen doesn't leave her eggs for more than twenty minutes!'

'Why, would they get cold?' asked Sheila.

'Freezing cold,' said Frannie. 'Then they wouldn't hatch out. That's why we put a sitting hen into a coop, Miss. So that she can't get out and leave her eggs.'

'But how does she get food and water?' asked Sheila.

Frannie laughed. 'That's easy enough!' she said. 'You just let her out for a feed of corn and a drink and a stretch of her legs each day.'

'What would happen if I forgot to do that?' asked Sheila.

'Well, the poor thing would sit till she got so hungry she'd peck her own eggs and eat them,' said Frannie. 'It's just common sense, Miss, that's all. Did you know that a hen turns her eggs over now and then, to warm them evenly? I've often watched our sitting hens do that. You wouldn't think they were clever enough to do that, would you?'

'How long does the hen sit on her eggs?' asked Sheila. 'Ages and ages, I suppose.'

'Oh no – only for three weeks,' said Frannie. 'Oh, Miss Sheila, it's fun when the eggs hatch and the baby chicks come out! You'll love that.'

'Yes, I shall,' said Sheila, thinking with delight of dozens of tiny cheeping chicks running about the farmyard. 'Oh, Frannie, I've learnt more about hens from you in five minutes than I've learnt from all these difficult books!'

'If I've got time, I'll come and see the hen-house with you this afternoon,' said Frannie. 'You'll want some peat-moss for the floor, you know. That's the best stuff to have – you only need to change it once or twice a year.'

'Oh, Frannie, hurry up with your work then, and we'll go and plan for the hens!' said Sheila. 'I'll tell Daddy we want some peat-moss.'

Frannie was just as pleased as Sheila to make plans for the hens. She had been used to keeping them all her life, but only in a tiny back-yard with a very small hen-house.

Now they would be kept properly, with plenty of room for coops and chicks too. What fun! She flew over her work that morning and her Aunt Harriet was very pleased with her.

'You've earned your time off this afternoon, Frannie,' she said. 'You've been a good girl this morning. You scrubbed my kitchen floor well for me, and that stove shines like glass!'

'I'm going to help Miss Sheila get ready for her hens,' said Frannie. 'Goodness, Aunt Harriet, you wait and see what a lot of eggs and chicks we get!'

'Don't you count your chickens before they are hatched!' said Harriet.

Sheila and Frannie and Penny spent a very happy afternoon indeed. The three of them cleaned out the hen-house. It was not very dirty, and had already been white-washed inside. Frannie got some peat-moss from the village in a small sack and brought it back to the farm. It was lovely stuff, dark brown and velvety. The three girls let it run through their fingers joyfully.

'I should love to tread on this and scratch about in it if I was a hen,' said Penny. 'Do we scatter it over the floor?'

'Yes, like this,' said Frannie. Soon the hen-house floor was strewn with the dark brown peat-moss and looked very nice indeed.

'Do we put it into the nesting-boxes as well?' asked Penny, looking into the row of neat, empty nesting-boxes.

'No. We'll get some straw for those,' said Frannie, happily. She was enjoying herself. She was a real country-girl, liking anything to do with farm-life. The three girls found some straw in a shed and took enough back for the nesting-boxes.

They patted it down flat, and tried to make it comfortable for the hens.

'I wish I was small enough to get right into one of the nesting-boxes, and sit down on the straw to see how it felt,' said Penny.

The others laughed. 'You're funny, Penny,' said Sheila. 'You hate to be treated as if you were little – and yet you are always wanting to be smaller than you are – a toy in a cupboard, or a hen in a nesting-box!'

The hen-house had a hen-run, with wire netting around. It was overgrown with grass.

'That won't matter,' said Frannie. 'The hens will soon peck that up! Anyway, you'll let them free to wander over the yard, won't you, Miss Sheila?'

'Oh yes,' said Sheila. 'But I hope they won't lay their eggs away anywhere – you know, under a hedge or something. It would be a pity.'

'Well, we'll just have to watch out for that,' said Frannie. 'Now, what about food? Look – there is corn in this big bin. We'll give them some of that each day! Corn helps them to lay often, and we shall get bigger eggs if we give them plenty.'

'What else do we give them?' asked Penny.

'Well, my Aunt Harriet will cook up all the household scraps,' said Frannie. 'You know – potato peel, milk-pudding scrapings, crusts of bread – anything we have over. It will all go into the hen-food. Then we will mix it with mash – and give them a good helping early in the morning, and after tea. We'll let them have the corn at midday. They'll like that.'

'It does sound exciting,' said Penny. 'What about water? They want plenty of that, don't they?'

'Yes – a big dishful,' said Frannie. 'Look – that trough will do. We'll fill it full each day. They must have fresh water. And I'll get my aunt to give us all the cabbage stalks and things like that. The hens will love to peck them.'

'We'll clean the house each day,' said Sheila. 'I'll scrape the dropping-board with this little hoe. Oh, I *do* hope my hens do well!'

'They should do,' said Frannie. 'The thing is not to make too much fuss of them; but to be sure to give them a clean house, good food, fresh water and plenty of space to run. Well, they'll have all that. Oh – I've quite forgotten something important! We must give them grit to help them to digest their food – and lime or oyster-shell broken up as well,' said Frannie.

'Broken oyster-shell! Whatever for?' said Penny in surprise. 'Hens won't like sea-shell, will they?'

Frannie laughed. 'They don't like it as food,' she said, 'but they need it to help them to make the shells for their eggs. If they don't get it the eggs will be soft-shelled and no use.'

'I saw some stuff in a bag where we saw the corn,' said Sheila. 'I think it must have been broken oyster shell – and there was some grit there too. Let's get it. We can put it into this wooden box inside the house – then the rain won't spoil it.'

By teatime there was nothing else to be done to prepare for the hens. The boys came in and the girls showed them everything. Scamper leapt down from Benjy's shoulder to examine the hen-house. He went into one of the nesting-boxes and peeped out of it cheekily.

'Are you going to lay a squirrel-egg, Scamper?' laughed Benjy. 'Funny little thing, aren't you?'

'Uncle Tim is bringing the hens tomorrow afternoon,' said Sheila. 'Oh, Rory – won't it be fun if we have some baby chicks? I should so love that.'

'Well, maybe one or two of your hens will go broody and want to sit all day long,' said Benjy. 'Then you can give her some eggs, and she'll hatch them out for you.'

'We can get out the coops then,' said Sheila. 'You know, Benjy, Frannie's been awfully helpful. I couldn't understand a thing in those books – but she's told me everything.'

'Good,' said Benjy. 'Hie, Penny, where are you going? It's teatime.' Penny was tearing off to the little orchard. She climbed over the gate. 'I'm going to fetch Skippetty!' she shouted. 'It's his teatime too. Frannie, ask Harriet if she can let me have another bottle of milk for him. He looks so hungry, poor lamb!'

The lamb came tearing up to Penny. She took it to the farmyard. Benjy was there with Scamper. Scamper leapt from his shoulder and sat on the lamb's back. 'He wants a ride!' laughed Penny. 'Oh, how I wish I could take a picture of them both!'

'Aren't you two ever coming?' called Sheila. 'There are hot scones and honey for tea – and I can tell you there won't be any left if you don't come AT ONCE!'

8

The Coming of the Hens

Next day the hens came. Uncle Tim brought them over in a great big box. Aunt Bess was with him. It was the first time they had visited Willow Farm since the family had settled in. They jumped down from the wagon they had come in, and everyone ran to greet them.

'Uncle Tim! Aunt Bess! Look at my own pet lamb!' yelled Penny.

'Uncle Tim – I've got Scamper again!' cried Benjy.

'Hallo, Tim, hallo, Bess!' cried the children's parents. 'Welcome to Willow Farm! We are getting straight at last! Come along in and have something to eat and drink.'

Everyone went indoors, talking and laughing. After a while Sheila and Penny slipped out. They went to the kitchen. Harriet was there, cleaning the silver and Frannie was helping her.

'Harriet! Could you spare Frannie just a few minutes?' begged Sheila. 'The hens have come! I thought it would be such fun to put them into the hen-house ourselves! I do want to see how they like it.'

Harriet laughed. 'Yes – Frannie can come. Go along, Frannie – but see you finish that silver when you come back!'

'Oh yes, aunt!' said Frannie. She ran out into the drive

with the two children. The hens were still in the big box, strapped on to the back of the wagon.

They were clucking loudly. 'Oh, there's a fine cock too!' cried Sheila, pleased. 'See his beautiful tail-feathers sticking out of the crack in the crate! Frannie, how are we to get the hens to the house?'

'We'll carry them,' said Frannie. 'I'll show you how.'

The three of them undid the rope round the crate, and Frannie forced up the top. She put in her arm and got a hen. It squawked loudly and struggled wildly.

But Frannie knew how to calm it and carry it. She showed the others how to take the hens by the top part of their legs, very firmly, and hold down the wings at the same time. 'Put the bird under your left arm, so,' she said. 'That's right. Now you've got your other hand to hold the legs. We'll take them one at a time.'

The three enjoyed carrying the squawking hens. One by one they were all taken to the big hen-house. There were twenty Buff Orpingtons, and one fine cock.

'Aren't they lovely hens?' said Sheila joyfully. 'They look so brown and shiny, so fat and comfortable. I do like them. Look how straight up their combs are.'

'They are nice young hens,' said Frannie, pleased. 'They should lay well. Twenty is just about the right number for the house and yard. If you have too many and they are overcrowded, they don't keep healthy. My word, your uncle has picked you out some beauties – they look as healthy as can be. It's always best to start with the finest hens you can possibly get.'

The hens clucked about the house. Then they found the

opening that led down the ladder-plank to the run. Down it they went, stepping carefully, their heads bobbing as they walked. 'Cluck-cluck!' they said as they each entered the run. 'Cluck-luck, what-luck!'

'Did you hear that!' said Penny. 'They think they are lucky to come here!'

'Cluck-luck, what-luck!' said the hens again, and they pecked at some cabbage stalks that Frannie had brought from the kitchen.

'We'll give them some corn to scratch for,' said Frannie. The three went to the corn-bin and each got a handful. They scattered the corn in the run. The hens ran to it, clucking and scratching eagerly.

Sheila counted them. 'One cock – and only nineteen hens,' she said. 'Where's the other?'

It was in one of the nesting-boxes, laying an egg. Penny gave a shout of delight.

'It *must* feel at home to do that already! Sheila – let's see if they laid any in the crate on the way over.'

The girls went to look – and sure enough there were two nice big brown eggs on the floor of the crate! How pleased they were!

'I'm going to keep a proper egg-book,' said Sheila. 'I shall put down in it every egg that is laid! Then I shall be able to find out how much money my hens make for me, because I shall know the market-price of eggs each week, and reckon it up. Oh – it will be fun!'

Just then everyone else came out from the farmhouse. Uncle Tim had said that he really must take the hens out of their crate – and lo and behold the crate was empty!

'Oh! The girls have done it all themselves, the mean things!' cried Rory, with a laugh. 'No wonder they slipped out so quietly! Oh, look at all the hens in the run, Uncle. Don't they look fine?'

Everyone went to look at the brown hens. They seemed quite at home already, pecking about for the corn.

'One of them is laying an egg,' said Sheila proudly. 'I shall enter it in my egg-book.'

'Sheila is going to manage the hens for us,' said her father. 'We shall just see how well she can do it!'

'Does she understand everything she has to do?' said Aunt Bess. 'You know, the children only just gave the hens corn at times, and took the eggs in, when they were with us – they didn't really know much about the keeping of them.'

'Have you got grit and oyster-shell, Sheila?' asked Uncle Tim. 'Fresh water? Corn? Mash? Ah – I see you have studied some books!'

'Well,' said Sheila, 'I did try to study the books Daddy gave me – but actually Frannie told me most of what I had to do. Uncle Tim, I shall make my hens do even better than yours. You just see!'

'I hope you do,' said her uncle. 'Then I will come and take a few lessons from you on poultry-farming!'

It really was fun having hens to look after. Sheila said that she knew which was which after a few days, though the others could never tell more than one or two from the rest, and they secretly thought that Sheila couldn't either.

It was lovely to go and look in the nesting-boxes for the eggs. One day Sheila actually got twenty eggs! She was so delighted that she could hardly write it down in her egg-book! She and Penny used to go to the nesting-boxes morning and evening and take the eggs in. If they were to be sold, the children wiped them clean and sorted them into sizes.

'I do like eating the eggs that my own hens lay,' said Sheila, each morning. 'And I must say that the brown eggs always *seem* to taste nicer, though I can't think why they should.'

The hens were soon let loose in the farmyard. Then they were very happy indeed. They scratched about everywhere, and the place was full of their contented clucking. The cock was a fine fellow. He stretched his neck and crowed loudly, and his tail-feathers were really magnificent. They were purple and green and blue.

'He's a real gentleman, you know, Penny,' said Sheila. 'He never helps himself first to anything but always waits till his hens have eaten. And look – when he finds a grain of corn, he doesn't eat it himself. Watch – he's found one – and he's calling to his favourite hen to come and have it. Really, he has most beautiful manners!'

The two girls found that they were quite busy with the hens. The house was cleaned of droppings each day. Fresh water was put into the trough in the run, and into the dish in the house too. The box was kept full of oyster-shell. Harriet cooked the scraps, and gave them to Sheila before breakfast. Then the two girls mixed the smelly stuff with the mash out of the bin and gave a good share to the hungry hens. In the middle of the day they gave them corn, and a helping of mash again in the evening.

At night either Sheila or Penny shut the hens into their

house. They liked seeing the big brown birds perching so solemnly there. They always counted them to make quite sure that every hen was in for the night.

Their parents were pleased with the way they looked after the poultry. 'We'll have ducks later on!' they said. 'Perhaps you will be able to manage those as well!'

The boys were anxious to do their share too. They were glad to hear that the cows were coming at once, and that their father had bought a sow and ten little piglets.

'The farm will really be a farm then!' said Rory. 'How are the cows coming, Daddy? By train?'

'No – they are walking,' said his father. 'It is not far from the market where I have bought them, and they are coming along by the roads and the lanes.'

The cows were to be short-horns. Uncle Tim said that they were excellent milkers, and made good beef.

'What colour will they be?' asked Rory.

'Oh, mostly red and white, I expect,' said his mother. 'I must say it will be nice to look from the window and see cows standing in the pasture. I always like cows standing about the countryside!'

'I'm looking forward to milking them,' said Benjy. 'It's quite easy!'

'I suppose they will feed on the grass?' asked Penny. 'They won't cost much!'

'Oh, the grass won't be good enough yet for them to feed on that alone,' said her father. 'We must give them swedes or mangold wurzels. The boys can cart them each day to the fields and throw them out on the grass.'

The cow-sheds were all clean, and prepared for the cows.

They were to be milked there. The pails were scoured and shining, everything was ready.

'Once we have the cows to give us milk we shall be able to have our own milk, take our own cream, and make our own butter!' said Mother. 'I am looking forward to that.'

'When will the cows come?' asked Benjy. 'I want to watch for them.'

'Sometime tomorrow afternoon, I expect,' said his father. 'It's a good thing we have so many streams on our farm. We shan't have to cart water to the field-troughs – the cows can water themselves at the stream.'

'I wish tomorrow would come!' sighed Penny. 'I want to see our cows. Do you think they'll have names already, Rory? Or can we give them names? I'd like to name them all. I know such pretty cow-names.'

'What names do you know?' said Rory smiling at Penny's earnest face.

'Oh, Daisy and Buttercup and Pimpernel and Kitty and Bluebell,' began Penny.

'Why, those are the names of the cows at Cherry Tree Farm!' said Rory. 'I'd think of a few new ones if I were you.'

So Penny thought of some more. 'Honeysuckle, Rhododendron, Columbine, Snapdragon,' she began, but the others squealed with laughter.

'Fancy standing at the field-gate and shouting "Rhododendron, Rhododendron!"' said Sheila. 'Everybody would think you had gone mad.'

'Well, anyway, I shall name *some* of the cows,' said Penny, firmly. 'I do so want to do that. I shall wait for them tomorrow, and see which looks like one of my names!'

9

Sixteen Cows for Willow Farm

The cows arrived the next day, just before tea. Rory saw them first. He was swinging on the gate, waiting to welcome the cows to their new home. The others had gone to watch Skippetty frisking among the hens in the farmyard. The lamb was now much bigger, and was as springy and as frisky as any other lamb on the farm.

Everyone loved him, for he was a most friendly and affectionate creature. He had even gone into Penny's father's study one morning and pushed his little black face into the farmer's elbow!

'Hie! The cows are coming, the cows are coming!' yelled Rory, almost falling off the gate in his excitement. 'Hurry up, you others – the cows are coming. They're MARVELLOUS!'

Sheila, Benjy and Penny tore to the gate. They saw the cows rounding the corner of the lane. They came slowly, swaying a little from side to side as they walked.

'They're red, and red-and-white!' shouted Rory. 'Just the kind I like. Oh, aren't they nice and fat?'

They certainly looked good cows. They gazed at the children as they went through the field-gate, and whisked their tails. They smelt nice.

They were glad to get into the field and pull at the grass.

'They twist their tongues round the grass when they pick it!' said Penny. 'Oh look – there's Tammylan at the back with the herdsman!'

Sure enough it was Old Tammylan, come to see how the farm was getting on! He smiled at the children.

'So you've got your cows now!' he said. 'And your hens too. And does this lamb belong to *you*, Penny? It seems to follow you close!'

'Yes, Skippetty is mine,' said Penny, giving Tammylan a hug and then a hug to the lamb. 'Tammylan, aren't our cows beautiful?'

'Yes – they look fine creatures,' said Tammylan. 'Have you plenty of names for them, Penny?'

'Oh, don't ask her that!' said Rory. 'She keeps on and on thinking of names! I say, Tammylan, won't it be fun to milk the cows each day?'

'Rather!' said Tammylan. 'Look at them all – how pleased they are to be able to stand and graze, after their long walk. They will soon get all their four stomachs into working order now!'

'*Four* stomachs! Whatever do you mean, Tammylan?' asked Sheila, astonished. 'Has a cow got *four* stomachs!'

'Well – perhaps it would be truer to say that she has four compartments in her stomach!' said Tammylan, with a laugh. 'Watch a cow eating, Sheila. She only bites the grass now and swallows it – she doesn't chew it. Watch one and see.'

The children watched the cows. They saw that each one curled her tongue around the blades of grass, pulled them into her mouth, and then swallowed straightaway.

'And yet I've seen a cow chewing and chewing and

chewing!' said Benjy. 'It's called chewing the cud, isn't it, Tammylan?'

'Yes,' said Tammylan. 'What happens is that when she swallows the grass straightaway it goes down into the first part of her stomach. Then, when she is in her byre, or lying down resting, the swallowed grass comes up again into her mouth in balls all ready for chewing. Then she has a fine time chewing for a while. She enjoys that. You wait and see how she loves it, chewing with half-shut eyes, thinking of the golden sunshine and the fields she loves!'

'Does it go back to the first part of her tummy again?' asked Penny, wishing that she had four stomachs too. 'I'd love to swallow a sweet and then have it back to chew whenever I felt like it.'

Tammylan laughed. 'I expect you would!' he said. 'No – when the cow has finished chewing the cud, the food goes down to the next part of her stomach, and then on to the third and the fourth. Have you ever seen a cow's upper teeth, Penny?'

'No – what are they like?' asked Penny, surprised. The wild man went to a cow and took its nose gently into his hand. He opened her mouth and pushed back the upper lip. 'Tell me what her upper teeth are like!' he said, with a smile.

'Gracious! The cow hasn't any!' said Sheila.

'No – just a sort of bare pad of flesh,' said Rory.

'How funny!' said Penny. 'But a horse has upper teeth. I know, because I once saw a horse put back its lips and it had big teeth at the bottom and at the top too.'

'Yes, a horse is different,' said Tammylan. 'It only has

one stomach. And its hooves are different too. Look at this cow's hoof!'

He lifted up the front foot of the surprised cow. The children saw that it was split in two.

'Why is that?' asked Rory, astonished. 'A horse only has one round bit of hoof – the cow's is split in two.'

'She so often walks on soft, wet ground,' said Tammylan. 'Her split hoof helps her to do that without sticking to it.'

'I like the way cows whisk their tails about,' said Penny. 'This one whisked hers round so far that it hit me. I do wish I had a tail like a cow.'

'So that you could go round whisking people, I suppose?' said Tammylan. 'Now, Penny, I will set you a little problem. I would like to know if a cow and a horse get up from the ground in the same way. Will you please watch and tell me next time you see me?'

'I should have thought they would both have got up exactly the same way!' said the little girl, surprised.

'Well, they don't,' said Tammylan. 'You just see!'

'We've got sixteen cows,' said Rory, who had been counting. 'They are all fat and red and nice. I do think they look funny from behind – sort of wooden.'

'Let's go and ask the herdsman when they have to be milked,' said Sheila. 'I'm just longing to do that!'

The herdsman was talking to their father. He was a tiny little fellow, with very broad shoulders and long arms. Although he was small he was tremendously strong. The children's father was keeping him on the farm, for he was a useful man with cows, and good at many other jobs too. His name was Jim.

'Can we help to milk the cows?' cried Benjy. 'When is it time?'

'Oh, not till well after tea,' said the man, smiling. 'Are you sure you know how to? Milking isn't as easy as it looks, you know!'

'Of *course* I know how to!' said Benjy, scornfully. 'And I get a jolly good froth on top of my pail too!'

'Ah, that's fine,' said Jim. 'A good milker always gets a froth. Well – you shall help if you like. I can do with one or two good milkers! Are you going to be up at five o'clock in the morning to help me, young sir?'

That made Benjy look a little blue. Five o'clock in the morning!

'Well – if I do, shall I have to go to bed very, very early?' he asked his mother.

'I'm afraid so, Benjy,' she said. 'An hour earlier.'

'Oh. Then I'm very sorry, Jim, but I think I'll only help you in the evenings,' said Benjy, who simply couldn't bear the idea of going to bed an hour sooner than the others.

'That's all right,' said Jim. 'I can get someone else, I daresay, to give me a hand in the morning!'

The children were all pleased when milking-time came. They took the cows down to the cow-sheds, and got the shining pails and the little milking-stools.

Penny hadn't milked before. All the others had. Benjy was a fine milker. His hands were strong, yet gentle. Sheila was quite a good milker too, but Rory was poor. He could *not* make a froth come on the top of the milk in his pail as the others could. It was most annoying!

'I only get plain milk!' he said, 'and I don't get my pail full nearly as quickly as you others! Look at Jim – he has milked three cows already and I haven't even done one!'

'You've got rather an awkward cow,' said Jim. 'She doesn't like to give her milk to a stranger. I'll finish her for you. The last milk from a cow is always the richest, you know, so we must be sure to get it. Try the next cow – Daisy, she's called. She's an easy one to milk.'

'I love this warm milk,' said Penny, putting her hand against the warm sides of a pailful of milk. 'Jim, can I try to milk an easy cow?'

'You come over by me and watch me,' said Jim. 'Then you can try.' So Penny stood by Jim and watched. She soon felt sure she could do what he did – but her little fingers were not nearly strong enough for milking and she gave it up. 'Can I have a little milk for my lamb?' she asked. 'It's time for his supper.'

'No – you go and get some of the old milk from the kitchen,' said Jim. 'And keep your lamb by you – look at him nosing into that pail over there! My goodness, we don't want him emptying the pails as fast as we fill them!'

So off went Penny to the kitchen. 'You know, Skippetty,' she said, 'I like lambs much better than cows! But please don't grow up too soon, will you? You won't be nearly so sweet when you are a sheep!'

10

Fun in the Dairy

The days were very busy at Willow Farm now. There was always something to do! The hens had to be fed and looked after, the eggs taken and counted, the cows had to be milked, and swedes had to be carted to and from their field. The milk had to be set in the dairy for cream – and butter had to be made!

The dairy was a lovely place, big, airy and cold. The floor was of stone, the walls and ceiling were white-washed, and all the shelves were of stone too. It was very cold in there when the wind was in the east or the north. In the summer it would be a lovely cool place – the coolest place on the farm!

The children's mother loved the dairy. She was glad when the cows came because now she would be able to make her own butter. The children longed to see exactly how butter was made.

'What is going to be done with all the milk from our cows?' asked Rory. 'There will be gallons each day!'

'Well, some is to be sold, in big churns,' said his father. 'Some we shall keep for ourselves. Some we shall skim for cream, and sell the cream. The skim-milk will be given to the pigs, or the calves when we have any – and the rest we shall make into butter.'

'It all sounds lovely,' said Sheila. 'Do we empty the warm milk straight into the milk-churns, Daddy?'

'Good gracious no!' said her father. 'We can't send warm milk out – it would soon turn sour. It has to be cooled.'

'How can we cool it?' asked Benjy. 'There are all kinds of funny things in the dairy, Daddy – does one of them cool the milk?'

'Come and see, next time the milk is taken to the dairy,' said his father. So all the children trooped into the cool white room to see what happened that evening.

'Do you see that box-like thing fixed to the wall over there?' said their mother. 'That is a kind of refrigerator – a machine for making things cold. See this pipe running to it – it brings cold water to the refrigerator, which has many pipes to carry the ice-cold water.'

Mother poured some milk into a big pan on the top of the machine. The milk ran over the cold pipes and then fell into the big milk-churn standing below. It was quite cool by then!

'That's clever,' said Rory, pleased. 'Now I suppose the cool milk in the churn is ready to be taken to the town to be sold, Mummy?'

'Yes, it is,' said his mother. 'And what we are going to use ourselves has been taken to Harriet in the kitchen.'

'What's going to be done with these big pails full of creamy milk?' asked Penny.

'That milk is going to be made into butter. But alas – our separator hasn't arrived yet – so we must separate our milk and cream in the old-fashioned way, and wait until our separator comes when we can then do it much more quickly,' said her mother.

Mother put the creamy milk into big shallow pans, which were set on the cold stone shelves.

'What will the milk do now?' asked Benjy. 'I suppose the cream will all come up to the top, as it did on our bottles at home.'

'Yes,' said his mother. 'You know that light liquids always rise to the top of heavier ones – and as cream is lighter than milk, it will rise to the surface, if we leave it to do so.'

'How long will it be before the cream has all risen to the top?' asked Penny. 'Ten minutes? I want to make some butter from it!'

Everybody laughed. Penny was always so impatient and expected things to be done at once.

'Penny! Don't be silly!' said Mother. 'It will take twenty-four hours!'

'Gracious! I can't wait and see it come all that time!' said Penny. 'Can't we make the butter today then?'

'Oh no, Penny,' said Rory. 'We've got to get enough cream first, silly. There won't be enough cream from one lot of milk, will there, Mummy? We'll have to store it a bit and wait till we have enough to churn into butter.'

So Penny had to be patient and wait until the next day to see the cream being skimmed and stored for the making of butter. The children loved seeing the rich yellow cream lying smoothly on the top of the pans. Penny dipped her finger in and wrinkled the cream – it was almost as stiff as treacle!

'Don't, Penny!' said Sheila. 'Do keep your fingers out of things!'

Mother skimmed the lovely cream off very carefully. She put it into a big cool crock. It did look fine. Mother put a little into a jug too.

'What's that for?' asked Penny.

'For your porridge tomorrow morning!' said Mother. 'Take it in to Harriet when you go.'

'What's going to be done with the blue-looking milk that's left,' said Sheila.

'That can go to the pigs when they come tomorrow,' said Mother. 'Calves love it too – but we haven't any yet. It is called skim-milk, because we have skimmed the cream off.'

Just then there was a great commotion outside, and Jim appeared, carrying something that looked extremely heavy over his broad shoulder. It was well packed up.

'Goodness! It's our separator!' cried Mother in delight. 'Come and help to unpack it, everybody.'

'Now we shan't have to wait ages for the cream to separate itself from the milk!' said Rory, pleased. 'We can separate it in a few minutes.'

Everyone wanted to see how the separator worked. It looked an extraordinary machine when it was unpacked. The main body of it was painted a bright clean red. On the top was a round pan. A big handle stood out from the side. Two pipes came out from the middle part. It really looked a most business-like machine.

Jim ran some water through the machine to clean it. 'I reckon you can start it straightaway,' he said. 'It's a new machine, quite ready to use.'

'Pour some fresh milk into the pan at the top, Rory,' said Mother. So Rory poured some in, filling the pan full.

Then Sheila was allowed to turn the handle. 'I feel as if I'm turning the handle of a barrel-organ!' she said. 'I wouldn't be surprised if the separator played a tune!'

'Well, *I* would!' said her mother, with a laugh. 'Go on turning, Sheila. Now children, watch these two pipes that come out at the front.'

Everybody watched – and lo and behold, from the top pipe came out good thick yellow cream – and from the bottom pipe flowed the separated milk, free from any cream!

'Goodness – isn't that clever?' said Rory. 'I see now why this machine is called a separator – it really does separate the milk from the cream. I suppose as the cream is the lighter of the two liquids, it always comes out of the higher pipe, and the milk comes out of the lower one because it is heavier.'

'Yes,' said Mother. 'This clever little machine does in a few minutes what it takes us quite a long time to do by hand!'

Rory swung open the front of the machine when all the milk was separated. It was very neat inside. The children loved to see how things worked, and they tried to follow out what happened. It wasn't very difficult.

'Well now,' said Mother, 'that is another lot of cream for us! Pour in some more milk, Rory. Penny, you can have a turn at playing the barrel-organ this time!'

It was lovely to watch the milk and the cream spurting out from the two pipes. The children begged to be allowed to take it in turns to do the separating each day, and their mother said yes, they could.

'It is all part of the work of the farm,' she said. 'So you may certainly do your share. But don't come to me and say you are tired of using the separator in a week's time, because I certainly shan't listen to you!'

The children couldn't imagine being tired of playing about with the separator. They were simply longing to use the butter-churn too, and see the butter being made.

Harriet was to make the butter, with Mother to help her. Harriet had been a dairy-maid before, and she was good at butter-making.

'You know, butter comes well with some folks and it doesn't come at all with others,' she said, solemnly, to the children. 'Now I'm going to make butter on Tuesdays and Saturdays so if anyone wants to help, they can come along to the dairy then.'

'We'll all come!' said the children at once. 'We're not going to miss doing a single thing at Willow Farm!'

11

Butter – and Pigs

On the following Saturday Harriet bustled into the cool dairy. The sun poured down outside, for it was now mid-April, and spring was well on the way. But the dairy was as cool as ever.

In the big cold crock there was a great deal of cream. Harriet was going to turn it into golden butter. Penny peeped into the dairy with Skippetty behind her.

'Are you going to begin, Harriet?' she asked. 'Shall I tell the others?'

'Yes,' said Harriet, turning up her sleeves. 'But just you leave that lamb of yours behind, please, Miss Penny. I never knew such a creature for poking its nose into things! It would gobble up all my precious cream as soon as look at it! You keep it out of the dairy. Do you know that it went into my larder this morning and nibbled the cheese?'

Penny giggled. Skippetty was a marvellous lamb, always doing the most unexpected things. She went to fetch the others. They came crowding into the dairy.

The butter-churn was in the middle. It was a funny-looking thing. 'It's just a strong barrel mounted on a framework of wood to hold it,' said Rory. 'And there's a handle to turn the barrel over and over and over.'

'All hand-churns are like this,' said Harriet. 'This one's

made of beech. The last one I had was made of oak – but I always say butter comes fastest in beech!'

Harriet poured the thick, yellow cream into the barrel-shaped churn. She fixed on the lid firmly. Then she took the handle and turned it strongly and regularly. The barrel at once turned over and over and over, swinging easily as it went.

'What a lovely noise the cream makes, splashing about inside!' said Sheila. They all listened. They could hear the cream being dashed about inside the churn.

'Why do you have to turn the churn over and over like that?' asked Benjy. 'Is that the way to make the cream into butter? I know I once helped our cook to whip some cream for the top of a jelly, and after I had whipped it with a fork for a while it went all solid.'

'Yes – cream goes solid when it is whipped,' said Harriet, still turning the churn by the handle. Her face was red, and she looked hot.

'Let me have a turn,' begged Sheila. 'I could do it just as easily as you, Harriet.'

All the children had a turn, though Penny found the churn heavy for her small arms. Harriet took the handle again, and soon she nodded her head.

'The butter's coming,' she said. 'I can feel it. The churn is heavier to turn.'

'It's taken about twenty minutes,' said Rory, looking at his watch. 'I call that quick. Harriet – please take off the lid and let's look inside. I can't hear so much splashing now!'

So Harriet stopped churning and took off the lid. The children all peered inside. There was no thick cream to be seen! Instead there were lumps of yellow butter floating in some milky-looking liquid.

'That's the buttermilk that the butter is swimming about in,' said Harriet. 'Now a few more turns and I'll get out the butter!'

It was really exciting to see the butter forming like that from the cream. It seemed like magic to Penny. The children watched closely as Harriet poured away the buttermilk and then washed the lumps of butter till it was quite free from the milk.

She took up two flat wooden butter-handles and picked up the butter. She placed it all on a wooden tray, and then took the wooden butter-roller. With clever hands she pressed and rolled the butter till it was quite free of all moisture, and was firm and hard. Then neatly and deftly she made it into pound and half-pound pieces.

'There!' she said, wiping her hands on her apron. 'Good rich butter, yellow and firm! Some to sell, some to eat. You shall have some for breakfast tomorrow morning!'

'Daddy is going to have paper wrapping printed to wrap our butter in when it's sold,' said Sheila. 'It is going to have "Willow Farm Butter" printed on it. Oh dear – I shall feel so grand when I see that. Harriet, can we wrap the butter up when the new wrappings come?'

'If your hands are clean and you can wrap the butter neatly,' said Harriet. 'I'll show you how later on.'

'Now we know how to separate cream from milk, and how to make butter from cream,' said Penny, patting the wooden churn with her hand.

'I do think we are lucky,' said Benjy, as they all left the

cool dairy. 'Our own eggs for breakfast – our own milk to drink – our own cream for porridge – and our own butter for our bread!'

'And I expect we shall have our own cheese too,' said Rory. 'Harriet says she can make cheese. She says she can make it from milk. She puts rennet into the milk and that separates the curds and the whey in the milk. Then she presses the curds, and they make cheese!'

'Gracious! It all sounds very easy,' said Penny. 'I shall help her when she does it.'

The children were very happy. The weather was kind, the sun shone down warmly, and work on the farm went smoothly. The hens laid well, the cows gave splendid milk, and twice a week butter was made in the dairy.

The piglets were the next excitement. They arrived in a cart, squealing loudly! How they squealed! The children could not imagine what the noise was when they heard the cart coming slowly up the lane.

'Oh! It's the piglets!' yelled Benjy, and gave Scamper such a fright that the little squirrel shot up into a tree and would not come down for a long time. The children, with Skippetty the lamb behind them, rushed up the lane to meet the cart.

'The old mother-pig is there too,' said Rory, in delight. 'Gracious, what a giant she is! Oh, look at the piglets – aren't they sweet?'

All the children crowded round the pig-sty when the pig-family were put into it. The old sow grunted and lay down. The piglets scampered about busily.

'I simply *must* catch one and feel what it's like!' said Rory and he jumped down into the sty. He bent down to pick up a piglet – but it slipped away from him. He bent to get another – but that slipped away too. No matter how he tried he could *not* get hold of a piglet.

'They're all soft and silky and slippery!' he called to the others. 'I can't possibly catch hold of one – they all slip off like eels!'

The others went into the sty to see if they could catch a piglet too, but to their surprise they found that it was just as Rory had said – the tiny creatures were far too slippery to hold!

They all went out of the sty a good deal more quickly than they went in! The sow didn't like to see them trying to catch her piglets, and she rose up in anger. She rushed at Rory and he only just got out of the way in time!

'Goodness! I didn't think she would be so fierce!' said Rory, rubbing his legs. 'Isn't she ugly? But I like her all the same. Good old sow!'

'What's a father-pig called?' asked Penny.

'A boar,' said Rory. 'We haven't got a boar. But do you remember there was one at Cherry Tree Farm? He had a ring through his nose.'

'Yes, why did he?' asked Penny. 'I always meant to ask Uncle Tim and I never did.'

'It's because pigs root about so,' said Rory. 'They try to root up the grass to get at any grubs or insects underneath, you know – and Uncle Tim didn't want his grass spoilt so he put a ring through the boar's nose.'

'Well, I don't see how that stopped him from rooting about,' said Penny.

'Well – would *you* like to go rooting up grass if Daddy put a ring through your nose?' asked Rory. 'Wouldn't it hurt you every time you tried to nose up the grass?'

'Oh, I see,' said Penny. 'Yes, of course it would. Well, what about bulls? They have a ring through their noses too because I've seen them. And they don't go rooting up grass, do they?'

'No, they don't,' said Rory. 'But their ring isn't because of that, silly! It's so that they can be led by their nose, and not run away or get fierce, because if they try to pull away, their nose will be dreadfully hurt!'

The little pigs were really sweet. All the children loved them and begged to feed them each day. The big sow fed them herself for a while, but soon they grew big enough to want other food than her milk. Then the big trough was filled with food for them. How they loved it!

'Hie, little piglets, here is the butter-milk for you from our butter-making!' cried Rory. 'And here is some whey from our cheese-making! And here is some separated milk from our cream-making!'

'And here are kitchen scraps!' cried Sheila, putting them into the trough. The little pigs squealed with excitement and rushed to the long wooden trough. There was plenty of room for them all, but they couldn't see that. They tried to push each other away to get at the food and made such a noise that the children laughed with glee.

'Oh look – three of them have got right into the trough itself!' cried Penny. 'Oh you naughty little piglets! Get out of your dinner! Oh, how I would hate to eat dinner I was treading on!'

The pig-wash in the trough soon disappeared. The piglets loved it. They grew fat and round and big. The sow ate well too. She loved little potatoes and the children often brought her a meal of these, or of potato parings.

'I really believe the old sow would eat anything!' said Rory, as he watched her gobble up enormous mouthfuls. 'I don't wonder we have a saying "As greedy as a pig"!'

'What about the saying "As dirty as a pig",' said Sheila. 'People always seem to think that pigs are dirty animals. But our sow is beautifully clean – and so are her dear little piglets.'

'It depends on how they are kept,' said Jim, who was passing by with the cows. 'If pig-sties aren't regularly cleaned out of course the pigs will be dirty. How can they help it, poor creatures? Now, your sty has a good run, and it is cleaned out well – so your pigs are clean and healthy. Maybe you'll let them run on grass a bit later on. They'll love that.'

Jim was right. The piglets and the sow had the run of the orchard, and they were very happy.

Skippetty often went to join them, and once he jumped on the side of the old sow when she was lying down basking in the sun.

But he didn't do it again! The old sow was very angry, and she ran all round the orchard after Skippetty till he was quite frightened!

'Skippetty, you must behave yourself!' said Penny. 'Come with me, and don't worry the sow any more! Keep out of mischief for an hour or two!'

But the lamb couldn't be good for long. He went into the hen-house and began to nibble at the box of broken oyster-shell there! How Penny laughed!

'Look, Benjy! Look, Rory!' she called. 'Skippetty wants to lay eggs with hard shells. He's nibbling the broken oyster-shell in the hen-house! Whatever will he do next!'

Nobody knew – but nobody minded, for who could help
loving a black-faced, skippetty lamb?

12

Out in the Fields

Around the farmhouse lay great fields, sloping gently down the hill. Most of the fields were bordered by little brooks, whose sides were set with willows. The fields all had names, and Penny liked to chant them in a kind of song.

'Long Meadow, Top Field, Green Meadow, Swing Field, Long Bottom, Brook's Lea, Holtspur!'

All these places were fields of different shapes and sizes. The children soon knew every one. They had all been ploughed in the autumn, and Rory wished that he had been able to watch the plough at work.

'I've always wanted to guide a plough,' he said, longingly. 'I wanted to help with the ploughing last autumn when we were at Cherry Tree Farm – but Uncle Tim wouldn't let me.'

'Why do fields have to be ploughed?' asked Penny. 'It seems a waste of time to me to turn up a field and furrow it!'

'We'll ask Tammylan. There he comes!' said Rory, waving to the wild man, who was coming along beside the hedge nearby. He often came to see them, and told them tales about the different animals and birds he knew so well.

'Tammylan! How's the hare?' yelled Penny, as soon as she saw him.

'Much better,' said Tammylan. 'His legs have mended – but he limps now. Still, he can get along quite fast. I think he will live with me in my cave though. He seems to be rather afraid of going along into the fields unless I am with him.'

'I wish I had a hare to live with *me*,' said Penny.

'Well, you've got a lamb,' said Benjy. 'That's more than enough, surely. Do you know, Tammylan, Skippetty ate Jim's lunch yesterday? It was cheese, and Skippetty found it and ate it. Jim was awfully cross. I had to get him some of our homemade cheese from Harriet.'

'That lamb sounds more like a goat to me,' said Tammylan, with a laugh. 'Goats eat everything and anything, you know. I once had one that ate books out of book-shelves!'

'Tammylan – why do fields have to be ploughed?' asked Rory. 'I know that gardens have to be dug – and I suppose ploughing is a quick way of digging a big field.'

'Yes,' said Tammylan. 'We couldn't dig over our enormous fields! We plough up the ground because we want the rain and air and frost to get to it, Rory. Let's come and look at the plough over there in the shed.'

They all went to look at it. Tammylan pointed out the big steel blade or share that was pushed into the earth when the plough was dragged along by the horses.

'That great steel blade cuts a big slice of earth,' he said. 'Then it is turned over. Now look at this smaller blade at the side of the plough. That's called a coulter, and it cuts the straight edge of the furrow.'

'The ploughman holds the handles of the plough, doesn't he?' said Penny, taking hold of them, and pretending to guide the plough. 'Oh, I'm sure I could plough!'

'Yes – you could plough!' said Tammylan, a twinkle in his eye. 'But you wouldn't be able to plough *straight*!'

'I've watched the ploughman often,' said Benjy. 'He keeps the plough awfully straight, so that the furrows lie quite straight too, close to one another. At Uncle Tim's farm a boy sometimes guided the horses – he walked at their heads and led them. Perhaps Jim would let *me* do that this autumn when he ploughs the fields again.'

'Daddy says he isn't going to have his plough drawn by horses this autumn,' said Sheila. 'He is going to have a tractor.'

'What's that?' asked Penny, surprised.

'Oh, it's a kind of little engine driven by petrol or oil,' said Sheila. 'It can be fastened in front of the plough instead of horses, can't it, Tammylan? Daddy says he will get a tractor with caterpillar wheels.'

'Whatever for?' asked Penny. 'It will be like a tank then!'

'Well, our fields are rather soft,' said Sheila, proud that she knew so much about it, 'and Daddy says that caterpillar wheels prevent the tractor from sinking into the soil. I say – won't it be fun to see a tractor going! I do hope we can take turns at driving it!'

'Look!' cried Rory, suddenly. 'What's Jim getting out of the shed over there?'

They all looked. 'It's a cultivator,' said Tammylan. 'Ah now we shall see a little hard work done on this field!'

Jim was dragging out a big iron frame on wheels. Below it were long steel teeth. Jim did not let them touch the ground until he reached the field where he was going to work. Darling, one of the big farm horses, dragged the cultivator for him, and Jim got into the seat of the machine.

Soon he was at work. Darling plodded along the furrowed field steadily, her head well down as she went uphill. Jim let down the steel teeth of the cultivator with a click. They bit into the good soil.

'Look how it's raking it all thoroughly!' cried Sheila, pleased. 'It's breaking up the furrows and smashing up the earth into tiny bits. It will be all ready for seed-sowing when Jim has finished!'

'Ploughed fields have to be harrowed to make them ready for the seeds,' said Tammylan. 'Get out of the way, Penny – Jim will harrow you if you don't look out!'

But Penny wanted to stop Jim. He pulled up Darling with a jerk. 'Jim! Let me sit on the seat and see what it feels like!' shouted Penny. Jim grinned. He had a soft spot in his heart for small Penny. He got down and lifted her up in the big brown seat. He clicked to the horse and the cultivator moved forward. Penny would have been jerked right off the seat if Jim had not been holding her tightly!

'Oh!' she said. 'It's a very hard, jerky seat, isn't it, Jim?'

'I don't notice it!' said Jim, as he climbed back and clicked to Darling.

'Jim! What's going to be planted in this field?' cried Benjy, as the cultivator moved off with a clanking noise.

'Clover!' shouted back Jim. 'I'll be sowing it on Friday if you want to watch! And there'll be wheat in Long Bottom.'

The children remembered seeing pictures of people walking down a field, casting out seed first on one side and then from the other.

'I could help Jim sow the clover,' said Penny. 'I could bring my basket and tie it in front of me and put the seed there. I should like to walk down the field throwing seed first from one hand and then from the other.'

'Well, it won't be quite like that!' said Tammylan. 'Now come along, children – if you want to show me the new piglets, you'll have to show me now. My visit is only a short one this time!'

'Well, will you come again on Friday and watch us all sowing seeds?' begged Penny, slipping her hand in Tammylan's big brown one. 'Do come, Tammylan. It will be such fun.'

'I'll come if you can tell me the answer to the puzzle I set you about horses and cows!' said Tammylan, with a laugh. 'Now Penny – do a horse and a cow get up from the grass in exactly the same way?'

'Oh, I know the answer to *that*!' said Penny. 'I've watched all our cows and horses – and Tammylan, it's so funny, cows get up on their hind-legs first and kneel on their front legs – but horses do it the other way. They throw out their front legs first and then raise themselves on their hind-legs! So I know the answer to that puzzle you see – and you'll have to come on Friday!'

'Good girl,' said Tammylan. 'Yes – I'll come on Friday – and we'll see whether we sow seed or not!'

'Well, of course we shall,' said Penny, puzzled.

But Penny was wrong! When Friday came the children all went to Top Meadow, hoping to meet Jim there and be given seed to sow. But Jim was taking Darling into the field and behind her was a curious affair. It was like a very long narrow box raised on wheels. The children stared.

'What's that, Jim?' asked Sheila, puzzled.

'It's a broadcast sower,' said Jim. 'Watch me put my clover seed into it!'

'Oh – is *that* going to sow the seed instead of you?' asked Benjy, deeply disappointed. 'I thought we could all help to sow the seed. Oh look – there's Tammylan, grinning all over his face. Tammylan! I believe you knew we wouldn't help with the sowing today!'

'Well, I did have a sort of an idea that we should have to watch Jim!' said Tammylan. 'Anyway, it's very interesting. Let's see what happens.'

Jim had emptied half a sack of fine clover seed into the long narrow box. He shut down the lid. Then he set off down the field, with all the children watching carefully.

'Oh look – the seed is falling from holes at the bottom of the long narrow box!' cried Sheila. Sure enough it was – it fell steadily and evenly over the field, and sowed the field in a far quicker way than if the children had done it by hand.

'Are you going to sow the wheat with the broadcast sower too?' asked Rory, when Jim came by again.

'No,' said Jim. 'I'm sowing that with the seed drill this afternoon. You'll like to see that. It's a cleverer thing than this because the drill makes the furrows, sows the seed evenly, and then covers it up with soil!'

Tammylan stayed to lunch with the children that day. He told them about a robin that had built its nest inside one of his old shoes at the back of the cave!

'When the eggs hatch out I shall have plenty of company!' he said. 'The young robins will be very tame. I don't know how they will get on with the hare, but I've no doubt they will all be friends in no time.'

That afternoon they all went to see the seed drill planting the wheat. This was a bigger thing than the broadcast sower. The seed was carried in a kind of tank, and then passed from there into tubes. These pipes entered the soil a little way below the surface and dropped the seeds there.

'That *is* a good idea,' said Rory, as they watched the seed drill start off down Long Bottom Field. 'It sows the seed under the surface, all at the same depth – and then neatly covers it up so that the birds can't get it!'

Jim went halfway down the field with the seed drill and then stopped. He did something to the drill, and then set off again.

'What was the matter, Jim?' asked Penny, as Jim came up the field by the children again.

'The drill was sowing the seed too thickly,' said Jim. 'I adjusted the drill so that the seed didn't come out so fast. It's about right now, I think.'

Penny ran beside him when the other children went off with Tammylan.

'The fields have been ploughed and harrowed and sown!' she panted. 'What else is there to be done, Jim? It seems to me that fields take as much looking after as animals and hens!'

'Oh they do!' said Jim, guiding the drill round a corner. 'But now I can take a rest from working in them for a while, Miss Penny! They've got to look after themselves a bit now – and the sun and the rain will work for me! I must wait now till the clover is grown and the wheat is ready to cut! Ah, then we'll be busy again. Harvesting is as busy a time as spring!'

13

A Little Excitement for Sheila

The weeks went by, and the four children were sad when their holidays came to an end. Then they all went walking across the fields to the rectory, and there, with three other children, they had lessons. But always they looked longingly out of the window, wondering what their hens were doing, what Scamper was doing, if Skippetty was in mischief, and whether the three dogs were helping Davey with the sheep.

How they raced home after school! Saturdays and Sundays were whole holidays, and if they had worked hard they were allowed Wednesday afternoon off as well. So they could still help a good deal, and Sheila could manage her hens very well.

Skippetty hated to see Penny going off each morning without him. He bleated after her most piteously, and the little girl begged to be allowed to take him. But Mother always said no, most firmly.

But Skippetty was determined to be like the lamb in the nursery rhyme, and one day he managed to squeeze through a gap in the hedge and trot after Penny to school. The children were quite a good way off, but Skippetty could hear their voices far ahead and he followed them eagerly.

Just as the children got to the Rectory they turned and saw Skippetty!

'*Oh! Penny had a little lamb*
That followed her to school!'

shouted the children in delight. The rector came to the door
and laughed.

'Well, like Mary's lamb, I'm afraid it's against the rule,' he
smiled. 'Penny, take the lamb to the apple orchard and shut
it in.'

But Penny couldn't have shut the gate properly because
the lamb got out and went to the schoolroom door. The
children saw the door open just a little – and then they saw
Skippetty's black, blunt nose appearing round the edge!

They squealed with laughter, and Skippetty was frightened
and ran back to the orchard. This time Rory was sent to see
that he was safe, and the lamb was seen no more in school
that morning.

Scamper *was* allowed to come, because he was quite
content to wait for Benjy in the trees outside. Scamper was a
little restless now that spring had really come. He sometimes
went off for a day or two to the woods, and Benjy missed him
terribly then. But he always came back. Once he came back
in the middle of the night, and jumped in at Benjy's little
window under the thatch. Benjy got a shock when Scamper
landed on his middle and ran up to his face!

Frannie was a great help with the hens. She always did
them if Sheila was kept late at school, and she and Sheila
kept the egg-book with enormous pride.

'Fancy – over four hundred eggs already!' said Frannie,
proudly, counting them up in the book. 'Miss Sheila, a hen is
supposed to lay about two hundred and twenty eggs a year,

if it is a good layer – but it looks as if ours will each lay far more than that.'

Then there came a week when there were not so many eggs – and one night when Sheila went to shut up her hens she found that there was one missing!

'Frannie!' she called. 'There are only nineteen hens and one cock. What's happened to the other hen?'

'I can't think,' said Frannie. 'She must be somewhere about. Oh, I do hope she's not wandered away too far and been stolen. There have been gypsies in that field over there this week – maybe they've taken her.'

The girls called Benjy, Rory and Penny, and they all began to hunt for the lost hen. It was Penny who found her!

The little girl had hunted all round the orchard and in the hedges of the fields. As a last hope she went into the farm-garden. There was a big clump of rhododendron bushes there, and Penny pushed her way into the middle of them.

And there, sitting quietly down by herself, was the lost brown hen! She looked up at Penny when the little girl came near, and gave a quiet cluck as if to say 'Hallo! Don't disturb me. I'm all right!'

'Oh, Sheila, I've found the hen, I've found her!' yelled Penny. 'Shall I bring her? She's here under the rhododendron bush!'

'No, I'll come and get her, don't you touch her!' shouted back Sheila, who hated anyone to touch her precious hens. She ran into the garden and went to the clump of rhododendrons. She pushed them aside and looked at the hen.

'Oh you naughty Fluffy!' she said. 'Why didn't you come

to bed when I shut up all the rest tonight?'

She lifted up the hen – and then she and Penny gave a yell. 'She's sitting on eggs! Look, she's sitting on eggs!'

Sure enough, in a neat cluster, were eleven nice brown eggs! The hen clucked and struggled as Sheila lifted her off the eggs.

'Oh! No wonder the eggs have been short the last week or so!' said Sheila. 'And I do believe you must have stayed away for three or four nights out here, you bad hen! I haven't been counting you all as I should, because I felt sure you came when you were called. Well, well – what shall we do with you?'

Frannie was pleased and excited. 'We'll put her and her eggs into a coop,' she said. 'We'll give her two more. We'll have our own chicks now, Miss Sheila. Oh, that *will* be fun!'

So the clucking hen was given a nice coop for herself, and her eggs were put neatly under her – thirteen now – and she settled on them happily, near the hen-house. Everyone went to see her every day. She looked out at them from the coop, and gave little clucks.

Each morning Sheila lifted her off the eggs, and gave her a good meal of corn and fresh water.

'Don't let her be off too long,' said Frannie. 'If the eggs get cold they won't hatch and we won't have our chicks.'

So Sheila timed the hen each day, and gave her exactly twenty minutes off her eggs and no more. She felt the eggs just before the hen went back, and they were quite warm.

'Twenty-one days she's got to sit,' said Frannie. 'But of course we don't exactly know when she began.'

'Do you know, Frannie, there's a hen that sits all day in

one of the nesting-boxes, and never lays an egg!' said Sheila, a few days later. 'It is most annoying of her. I keep shooing her out, but she always goes back.'

'Well, that means she wants to sit on a nest of eggs and hatch out chickens just as old Fluffy is doing,' said Frannie. 'Oh, Miss Sheila – my uncle has a clutch of duck's eggs. I wonder if your father would like to buy them, and let the hen sit on them! Then we'd have ducklings!'

'But do hens sit on duck's eggs?' asked Penny, who was listening. 'Won't the hen know they are not hen's eggs?'

'Of course she won't know!' said Sheila. 'How could she? Oh, Frannie, that would be fun! I'll ask Daddy straight-away.'

Sheila's father gave her the money to buy the duck's eggs. She and Frannie went to get them. Sheila liked them very much.

'What a pretty greeny colour they are!' she said. 'They are bigger than hen's eggs too. Frannie, don't ducks sit on their own eggs? Why must we give them to a hen to sit on?'

'Well, ducks aren't very good mothers,' said Frannie. 'They leave their eggs too long – and sometimes they get tired of sitting and desert them. But a hen is a good mother and nearly always hatches out her eggs.'

The thirteen duck's eggs were put into a coop, and the broody hen was put over them. She got up and down a few times, and then settled on them quite happily. All the children watched with interest while she made up her mind.

'Goodness! We'll have twenty-six new birds soon!' said Benjy, pleased.

'Oh no!' said Frannie. 'You hardly ever get thirteen chicks

from thirteen eggs! Maybe one or two are bad, you know, and won't hatch. We'll be lucky if we get twelve out of the thirteen.'

'Will they hatch out at the same time?' asked Penny.

'No,' said Frannie. 'Duck's eggs take twenty-eight days to hatch, you know – a week more than a hen's. I love little ducklings. They waddle so – and my word, when they first go into the water, you should see how upset the hen is! She thinks they are her own chicks, not somebody else's ducklings, you see! And she knows that water's not good for chicks, so she gets into an awful state when they waddle off to the pond!'

'Oh, I shall like to see that!' said Penny.

The two hens were very contented and happy sitting on their eggs. Each day they were lifted off and given a good meal and fresh water. Penny told the others that she had seen the hens turning their eggs over so that they were warmed evenly on both sides. She thought that was very clever of them.

Then there came the exciting day when the first chicks hatched out! Penny heard the hen clucking and she ran across to the coop. She saw a bit of broken egg-shell – and then she saw a yellow chick peeping out from beneath the mother hen. She ran squealing to the house in excitement.

'Come quickly! The chicks are hatching out!'

The others ran to see. But only one chick had hatched out so far. The hen kept putting her head on one side as if she could hear more chicks getting ready to break their shell. The children were so thrilled.

One more chick hatched out before they had to go off to

school. That was a yellow one too. They begged to be allowed to stay and see all the eggs hatching out but their mother shook her head.

'No,' she said. 'The eggs were not all set at the same time, because the hen laid them herself. It may be tomorrow or the next day when they all hatch out.'

So the children had to wait in patience – but at last all but two of the egg-shells were empty, and eleven little chicks scampered about the coop.

'These two won't hatch,' said Frannie, picking up the last two eggs. 'They are addled. Well – eleven isn't bad – and good healthy chicks they look!'

The chicks were given nothing at all to eat for the first twenty-four hours – then Frannie showed Sheila what to give them – a scattering of bread and oatmeal crumbs, and a tiny saucer of water. They soon pecked up the food and cheeped in little high voices for more.

Everybody loved them. Some were all yellow, as bright as buttercups. Some were yellow and black, and one was all black. The mother-hen took them about the yard and showed them how to scratch for food.

When she found a titbit she called loudly to her chicks and they all came running at once. She shared it with them, which the children thought was very nice of her.

'She's a real proper mother,' said Penny. 'Just like ours!'

When one of the stable cats came into the yard the hen called to her chicks in quite a different voice. They heard the warning in her clucks and ran to her at once. If she was in the coop they got under her wings and breast-feathers, and not one could be seen! Then, when the danger was past and the cat had gone, first one little yellow head, then another and another would poke up from the hen's feathers and look out with bright beady eyes.

That made the children laugh.

The duck's eggs hatched out some time later. The children were glad because it was a Saturday and they could watch everything from beginning to end.

The little ducks uncurled themselves from the egg-shells and stood on unsteady feet. They fluffed themselves out and the children looked at them in amazement.

'How *could* those ducks ever have got into the eggs?' cried Sheila. 'They look twice as big already!'

The children liked the ducks even better than the chicks. They were so funny as they waddled about the yard. They were not so obedient as the chicks, and the mother hen had a lot of trouble with them.

Then the day came when they all wanted to go to the duck-pond! They had wandered quite near the edge of it, and suddenly one little duck felt that it simply MUST splash in that lovely water! So it waddled off, while the mother hen clucked for it to come back.

But to her annoyance the other ducklings also ran off to join the first one – and then, with little splashes and cheeps of delight every duckling slid or fell into the water and sailed off in excitement on the pond!

The mother hen went nearly mad with worry. She rushed about beside the pond, clucking and calling, while the other hen with her chicks stood looking on in horror. The ducklings had a wonderful time on the water and took no notice at all of their mother hen's scolding when they came out.

'Cheep, cheep,' they said to one another. 'That was fine! We'll do it again! Cheep, cheep!'

'Don't you worry so much, old mother-hen,' said Sheila, sorry for the fluffy brown bird. 'Your chicks are not chicks – they are ducklings! Can't you see the difference?' But the hen couldn't! She worried herself dreadfully every time that the ducklings took to the water – and then she grew tired of them and left them to themselves. She joined the hens in the yard, and scratched about contentedly, laying eggs again, and forgetting all about the naughty family of chicks that had so unexpectedly turned into ducklings!

The other mother-hen taught her chicks all that they should know, and then she too left them to themselves. They were quite content to run about together, scratching in the ground, and pecking at the cabbage stalks with the bigger hens. But the children did not like them nearly so much as they grew.

'They're leggy and skinny!' said Benjy. 'They're not so pretty. I like hens to be either hens or chicks. I don't like them in-between!' But Sheila and Frannie were proud of their young chickens, and entered them in the eggbook. 'Eleven chicks, twelve ducklings.' That was a real feather in their caps, to have twenty-three birds more than they had started with!

14

The Wonderful Sheep-dogs

Penny often went to see Davey the shepherd. She took Skippetty with her and the lamb was very funny with the other sheep. It seemed to turn up its little black nose at them, and to think itself much too grand to frisk about with the lambs!

'It nibbles the grass now, Davey,' said Penny. 'It doesn't want nearly so much milk. And oh, it does eat such a lot of things it shouldn't!'

'It's like its mistress then!' said Davey, with a laugh, for he knew that Penny loved picking off the unripe gooseberries, and liked sucking the tubes out of the clover heads. 'Now, Tuppenny, you've come at the right moment this afternoon! I'm going to take the sheep from this hill to the next – and you can see Rascal, Nancy and Tinker at work if you like!'

'Oh, I *would* like!' cried Penny in delight. 'May I go and tell the others? They'd so like to watch too.'

'Well, hurry then,' said Davey. 'I'll give you ten minutes – then I must set the dogs to work.'

It was Wednesday afternoon, and the four children had a half-holiday. Sheila had meant to give the hen-house a good clean. Rory had said he would work in the fields and Benjy had meant to help his mother in her farm-garden, where lettuces and onions, carrots and beans were all coming up well.

But when they heard that the sheep-dogs were to be set to work to help the shepherd, they all of them changed their minds at once!

'Golly! We *must* go and see that,' said Rory, and he rushed to tell Jim that he would finish his work in the fields after tea. In ten minutes' time all four children were up on the hill with Davey.

He smiled at them, his grey eyes twinkling. 'It's marvellous how quick children can be when they want to do anything!' he said, 'and wonderful how slow they are when they have to do something they don't like. Now look – I want my sheep taken to the sheltered slope you can see on the next hill. They've got to cross over three of your streams, two of which only have narrow plank bridges – but my dogs will take them all safely without any help from me!'

'But Davey – aren't you going with them?' asked Penny, in surprise.

'No, little Tuppenny, I'm not!' said Davey. 'I just want you to see how clever my dogs can be. Ah, you should see old Rascal at the sheep-dog trials! My word, he's a wonder! He can round up strange sheep and take them anywhere quicker than any other dog. I tell you, he's worth his weight in gold, that dog!'

The four children stood on the sunny hillside, eager to see what was going to happen. Davey whistled to his dogs. They came running up, two of them beautiful collies, the third a mongrel.

'Round them up, boys,' said Davey, and he waved his arms towards the sheep grazing peacefully on the hillside.

'Take them yonder!' He waved his arms towards the next hill.

The dogs stared at him with wagging tails. Then they bounded off swiftly. They ran to the sheep and made them leave their grazing. The sheep, half-frightened, closed in together. One or two took no notice of the dogs, but Rascal ran so close to their heels that they too had to join the others.

'Sheep always flock when anything troubles them,' said Davey. 'Now watch those silly little lambs!'

Some of the lambs, instead of joining the sheep, had run away down the hillside. Tinker went after them, and very cleverly headed them back. As soon as a lamb seemed to be running away again, Tinker was there, close beside it, and it found that it had to go with the others!

'Goodness! I wish I was a sheep-dog!' said Penny. 'I'd like to make the sheep do what I told them!'

Soon the sheep were in a bunch together, with the three dogs running round them. Davey waved his arms. That was the signal for the dogs to begin guiding the sheep to the next hill.

In a trice the sheep were set running downhill. Rascal ran round and round the flock, keeping it together. He didn't bark once. Nancy helped him. Tinker kept in front, making the leading sheep go the right way. It was marvellous to see how he made them keep to the path he wanted.

They came to a stream, too broad for the sheep to jump and too deep to wade. A narrow plank bridge ran from side to side. The leading sheep did not want to cross it. They ran along the bank, bleating.

It took Rascal half a minute to get them back to the bridge. But still they wouldn't cross.

'He can't make them!' cried Benjy, excited. 'The sheep are too stupid!'

'Oh, the stupider they are, the easier,' said Davey. 'It's the ones that try to think for themselves that are the most difficult to manage. The ones that don't think, but just blindly follow the others, are very easy indeed. But watch Rascal – he can't be beaten by a few silly sheep! There – look – he's got one on to the bridge!'

How Rascal had got the first sheep there nobody quite knew. The dog seemed to go in and out and round about the sheep till it found itself on the bridge! It couldn't go backwards, because Rascal was just behind it – so it had to go forward!

Once one sheep had crossed the others felt they must follow! Rascal leapt off the bridge and stood close beside it. Tinker stood the other side. Nancy kept the sheep together behind, forcing them forwards to the bridge.

It was marvellous to watch. The dogs worked together beautifully, never letting a sheep get away, and making them all go over the bridge as quickly as possible.

The sheep were sure-footed, and trotted easily over the narrow plank. Penny was afraid that one of the lambs might fall in, but of course not one lost its footing.

'Sheep are really mountain animals,' said Davey. 'I used to keep them in Wales on the mountainside. Some of the hills there were so rocky and steep that I couldn't get near the sheep – but they leapt from rock to rock and didn't slip once. So a narrow bridge like that means nothing to them!'

All the sheep passed over the bridge. Rascal leapt ahead of the flock and turned them to the left instead of to the right. Nancy brought up the stragglers. Tinker ran round the flock. They all went on to the next stream, where a little stone bridge was built across.

The sheep went over without any difficulty. 'They know by now that the dogs are taking them somewhere,' said Davey. 'They don't like leaving the hill where they have been for many weeks, but they will soon get used to new grazing.'

Just then the dogs paused and looked back to the hillside they had left. They had come to a forking of the hillpaths, and were not sure which one to take – to the east or to the west.

Davey knew what they wanted. He waved his arm and gave a shrill whistle. 'That means I want the sheep taken to the west side of the hill,' he told the children. 'Watch how the dogs understand me!'

The dogs had hardly seen Davey wave and heard his whistle before they headed the sheep towards the West! The children were amazed.

'Why, it's as if they were men,' said Rory. 'Though men couldn't run around the sheep as quickly as the dogs. But they understand just as we do. Oh Davey, you couldn't do without your dogs, could you?'

'No shepherd could,' said Davey. 'We depend on our dogs more than on anything else. Why, once when I was ill for two days, those dogs of mine looked after the sheep for me just as if I was out on the hills with them. Sharp as needles they are, and think for themselves just as much as you do!'

'Are they born as clever as all that?' asked Rory.

'Oh, sheep-dogs are always clever,' said Davey, 'but they have to be trained. I train them a little, but the other dogs teach a pup much more than I can by just letting him run around with them and see what they do. Some sheep-dogs are more clever than others, just as some children are sharp and others are not. I can tell in a few months if a pup is going to be a good sheep-dog or not.'

The sheep were made to cross another stream and then they were allowed to scatter on the western side of the hill. The dogs lay down, panting and tired. They had run many miles, because they had had to tear round and round the flock so many times! The sheep dropped their heads and began pulling at the short grass with enjoyment. It was good to be out there on the hillside in the sun, with new grass to eat!

'The dogs will stay with them till I come,' said Davey. 'Well – what do you think of them? Pretty sharp, aren't they?'

The shepherd was very proud of his dogs, and the children were too. 'I think they're marvellous,' said Rory. 'I wish I had a flock of sheep and dogs like that!'

'Do you know, one winter's day two sheep got lost in a snowstorm,' said Davey. 'I reckoned I'd never get them again – but old Rascal there, he went out in the snow – and he brought back those sheep six hours later!'

'Did he really?' said Benjy, astonished. 'But how could he find them in the snow? Was it deep?'

'Yes,' said the shepherd. 'I counted the sheep and told Rascal that two were gone – and off he went. He must have hunted all up the hills and down before he found them. He was so tired when he got here that he couldn't even eat his supper! He just lay down with his head on my foot and fell fast asleep! Ah, he's a good dog that!'

'Well, thank you Davey, for letting us watch what your

dogs can do,' said Sheila. 'Please tell us when they do anything else exciting!'

'You must come and watch the sheep-shearing in a fortnight's time,' said Davey. 'And when we dip the sheep you'll like to see that too. I'll let you know when to come!'

The children ran off down the hill. 'Aren't there exciting things to do on a farm!' cried Penny, as she skipped along just like Skippetty the lamb. 'Oh, how glad I am that we've left London and come to Willow Farm, Willow Farm, Willow Farm!'

15

The Shearers Arrive

One day three strange men appeared at the farm. The children looked at them in surprise, for they met them just as they were going off to school.

'Is your father about?' asked one of the men. 'Well, tell him we're the shearers, will you?'

'I say! The sheep are going to be sheared!' cried Rory. 'Oh golly – if only we could stay home today and watch!'

'You'll see plenty, young sir,' said the shearer, with a smile. 'We'll be at work all day long, till night falls. We don't stop – once we're on the job!'

Rory flew off to tell his father. The four children watched the men being taken to one of the big open sheds.

'So that's where the sheep are to be sheared!' said Benjy. 'I saw the shed being cleared yesterday, and I wondered why. I shall simply *tear* home from school today to watch.'

'Do the shearers cut off all the poor sheep's wool?' asked Penny, feeling quite sad for the sheep. 'Poor things – they *will* be cold!'

'Well, they're jolly hot now, in this sunny weather!' said Rory. 'How would you like to wear a heavy woolly coat to go to school in this morning, Penny? I guess you'd be begging and begging us to let you take it off!'

Penny looked down at her short cotton frock. 'Well, I'm hot even in this,' she said, 'and I'm sure I should *melt* if I wore a woolly coat like the sheep. I expect they will be glad, after all.'

'Of course they will!' said Sheila. 'But they *will* look funny afterwards! I expect they feel funny too – all sort of undressed.'

When the children came back from school they found the air full of the noise of bleating! The mother sheep had been separated from their lambs, and each was bleating for the other! What a noise it was!

'Look – they have driven the sheep into hurdles in the field near the shearing-shed,' said Rory. 'Last year's lambs are with them – but not this year's babies. So Skippetty won't lose his nice little woolly coat, Penny!'

'I'm glad,' said Penny. 'I don't want him all shaven and shorn! He's sweet as he is.'

The dogs had had a busy morning bringing in the sheep for the shearers. They had had to collect them from the hills, and bring them all back to the farm. They had worked hard and well, and Davey was pleased with them.

The shearers sat in the open shed. The sheep that had already been sheared had been set free and stood in a small flock, with Tinker on guard. He was to take them to the hills to graze as soon as another dozen or so sheep were ready.

The children ran to see exactly what happened. The farm felt busy that day – men hurried here and there with sheep, and the children's father gave loud orders. It was fun!

Rory watched the first shearer. A big sheep was taken up to him. Very deftly the sheep's legs were tied together so that it could not move. It might hurt itself if it struggled and got cut by the clippers.

Then the shearer got to work with his clippers. The children thought he was marvellous. He clipped the sheep's wool so that it came off like a big coat! Snip, snip, snip, went the clippers, and the wool was sheared off swiftly and cleanly. How odd the sheep began to look as its wool fell away from its skin!

The shearer looked up and smiled at the watching children.

'Are you my next customers?' he asked. 'I've done nineteen sheep already today. One of you going to be the twentieth?'

'We're not sheep!' said Penny, indignantly.

'Dear me, so you're not!' said the shearer. He twisted the sheep he was doing so that he could shear the wool from its back. The wool fell away neatly.

'The wool's dirty,' said Rory. 'And it smells!'

'Well, these sheep haven't been made to swim through water,' said the shearer. 'If they are sent swimming a week or two before they are sheared, their fleeces are cleaner. Washed wool is worth more money. On the other hand, it doesn't weigh so much as unwashed, so there's not much in it!'

'What's the biggest number of sheep you have sheared in a day?' asked Benjy, who was longing to try his hand at clipping too.

'Sixty-eight,' said the shearer. 'But they were small ones. The bigger the sheep the longer it takes to shear it. I like shearing fat sheep the best – they are easiest of all to shear.'

'Why?' asked Rory, surprised. 'I should have thought it would have been difficult to get round them!'

'Well, you see,' said the shearer, 'a fat sheep's wool rises

299

up well from the skin and makes it easier to shear. It's skin is oilier than a lean sheep's, and the oil makes the wool rise nicely. Wait till the shepherd brings along a really fat sheep and you'll see what I mean.'

The shearer nearby was shearing the year-old lambs. They hated the shearing and bleated piteously.

'Are they being hurt?' asked Penny, anxiously.

'Not a bit!' said the shearer. 'Sheep hate two things – one is being sheared, and the other is being dipped.'

'*Dipped!*' said Rory. 'What do you mean, dipped?'

'Oh, you'll see soon enough,' said the man. 'Davey here will show you one day soon!' He finished his lamb and sent it away with a smack. 'These shearlings are quick to do,' he said. 'Their coats are not so thick as the big sheep's.'

'Is a shearling a yearling!' asked Benjy.

'That's right,' said the man, and took another shearling to clip. It was wonderful to see how quickly he clipped away the wool.

As each sheep was finished, and stood up, bare and frightened, Jim daubed its back with tar, and then sent it off to Tinker.

'What are you doing that for?' asked Benjy.

'Marking the sheep with your father's mark,' said Jim. 'Then if the sheep happen to wander, the mark is known and the sheep are sent back.'

The children looked at the mark. It was a big crooked letter W. 'W for Willow Farm,' said Penny. 'Oh – now we shall always know our own sheep!'

Jim rolled each fleece up tightly and tied it together. He threw it into a corner of the shed.

'They will all be packed into sacks and sold,' he said. 'It looks as if your father will do well this year with his wool. It's good wool, and weighs very heavy.'

'Oh, I'm glad,' said Rory. 'I know he wants to buy some new farm-machinery, and he said if the sheep did well he would be able to. We've had lots of lambs, and not one of them has died. Skippetty was the only weakly one, and as soon as Penny took him for a pet, he began to grow big and fat.'

'I notice he doesn't come into the shearing shed!' said Jim, with a grin. 'I reckon he's afraid he will lose his nice little coat if he does!'

Skippetty was keeping well out of the way. He didn't like all the noise of bleating and crying. When the clipped sheep came out from the shed Skippetty looked at them in amazement. What were these curious-looking creatures? He didn't like them at all!

The sheep certainly did look different when they ran back to the fields, shaven and shorn. They looked so small without their thick woolly coats. They felt cold too, but the month was warm, and they would take no harm. The shearing was never done when the winds were cold – only when it seemed as if the weather was going to hold fine and sunny and warm.

'Another day's work and we'll be finished,' said the first shearer, busy with a fat sheep. He showed the children how easily he could clip the wool. 'Your father hasn't a very big flock. If he had, he wouldn't get *us* to do his shearing!'

'Why not?' asked Rory.

'Well, he'd buy a clipping-machine,' said the man. 'You should see one at work – it's marvellous! Clips the sheep in no time. And it's better than hand-shearing too, in some ways; a machine can clip a sheep more closely than our hands can, so the fleece weighs more heavily, and brings in more money.'

'Perhaps we shall have a clipping-machine next year!' said Rory. 'I'd love to work one.'

'How much does a fleece weigh?' asked Sheila, looking at the grey fleeces thrown at the back of the shed.

'These fleeces are good,' said the shearer. 'I reckon they weigh about nine pounds apiece. The shearlings don't weigh so much of course. That shepherd of yours knows how to look after his sheep. These are fine and healthy!'

The shearers did not stop their work till dusk. Then, tired and thirsty they went to the farm kitchen for food and drink. Harriet made them wash under the pump before they came in.

'You smell like sheep yourselves!' she said. 'And my, you're covered with fluff!'

'That was fun!' said Rory, as he and the others went indoors. 'Next year we'll get a clipping-machine, and *I* shall work it! My word, I *shall* enjoy that!'

16

Down to the Smithy

Each of the children had their own favourite animals or birds on the farm. Sheila, of course, thought the world of her hens, ducklings and chicks. Penny loved her lamb, and all the other little lambs. Benjy and Rory liked the horses best of all.

The farm-horses were enormous. They were shire horses, large and heavy, slow-moving and tremendously strong. As the children's father had not very much machinery for working his farm, he used his horses a good deal. Benjy and Rory really loved them.

They liked Darling the best, a great dark-brown horse with patient brown eyes and long sweeping eyelashes. Darling was a wonderful worker. She never got tired, and could plod up and down fields for miles from dawn to dusk. All the men on the farm were fond of her, and would bring her a lump of sugar from their tea.

'She's a good horse, that,' Bill would say, as he stood leaning over a gate looking at her.

'Ay, she's a fine horse, that,' Jim would agree, and the listening children thought so too. Darling's broad back had often carried them home from a distant field, and they loved the regular clip-clop, clip-clop of her big hoofs.

'It's lovely to wake up in the morning and hear Darling's

big feet clip-clopping along the yard,' said Benjy.

'And I love to lie in bed and hear the hens clucking and the ducks quacking,' said Sheila.

'And I like to think of Skippetty frisking out there waiting for me,' said Penny.

'And I like to hear the cows mooing and the other horses neighing,' said Rory. 'I say, Benjy – Darling will need shoeing today. Don't you think we could ask Daddy if we could take her down to the smithy? I know the men are going to be busy in the fields.'

'Oh, let me go too!' begged Penny. 'I do so want to see a horse being shoed. I never have. Does it have to have lots of shoes fitted to see which is the right size?'

'Listen to Penny! Isn't she a baby!' said Rory. 'No, silly! Horses have shoes *nailed* on to their hoofs.'

'Oh – poor things! Doesn't it hurt them dreadfully?' said Penny, almost in tears at the thought of nails being driven into a horse's feet. 'Oh, I don't think I want to see a horse shoed after all!'

'Well, you'd better,' said Benjy. 'Then you'll see just what happens!'

Daddy said that Rory might take Darling down to be shod. It was Saturday so all the children were free. Of course every one of them wanted to come.

'Well, you can all come – but *I* am going to lead the horse!' said Rory, firmly. He had never taken a horse down to the village smithy before, and it seemed rather a grand thing to do. He didn't want to share it with the others!

'Well, can I ride on Darling's back?' asked Penny.

'Yes, you can do that,' said Rory.

They went off to tell Jim that they were to take Darling down to be shod. Just as they were starting off they saw Tammylan. He had brought some special flower-seeds for their mother. He gave them to Sheila, and said he would come with them to the smithy. Scamper leapt to his shoulder as soon as he saw the wild man, and nibbled gently at his hair.

'Can Skippetty come too?' asked Penny. 'I shall be on Darling's back – but Skippetty could go with you, Tammylan.' The lamb was quite willing to follow behind Tammylan. Like all animals it adored him. It skipped round him in delight whenever he came.

Jim led Darling up to Rory. The boy proudly took the horse, and led it out of the gate into the lane.

'You're going to have new shoes!' he said. 'Get up, Penny. We're going.'

Tammylan lifted the little girl up on to the broad back of the horse. 'It's like sitting on an enormous sofa!' she said. 'Only a sofa doesn't usually go bump-bump-bump like Darling's back!'

They set off down to the village along the lane where fool's parsley waved its lacy whiteness in every hedgerow. The buttercups were showing in the fields. The distant hills were blue and the countryside was at its very best.

'I wonder what all these flowers are called!' said Sheila, as she bent to pick a bunch from below the hedges. 'There is such a lot to learn if you live in the country – the names of flowers and trees and animals and birds – and yet most country folk hardly know any names at all.'

'You are right there,' said Tammylan. 'It is strange that so many people living all their lives in the country know so little about these things! Well, Sheila, make up your mind to know as much as you can! It's fun – as you are so found of saying!'

Rory was leading Darling on the left-hand side of the lane. Tammylan called to him.

'Rory – take Darling to the right side of the road. A led horse should always be walked on the right.'

'Oh, goodness, yes – I forgot that,' said Rory. 'Jim has told me that before.'

He took Darling to the right-hand side of the road. The horse was on his left hand, and again Tammylan called to him.

'Go to the other side of the horse, Rory. Take the rope with your right hand, close to its head. Hold the loose end in your left. That's right, old son. Now, if anything startles the horse you have full control of it.'

'Thanks, Tammylan,' said Rory, who never minded learning anything fresh. 'Suppose I was leading a horse and cart – do I keep on the right still?'

'No, left,' said Tammylan, 'but if you meet a led horse then, you must go to the right. Watch this horse and wagon coming. You are both on the same side of the lane. See what the carter does.'

A carter was leading a horse yoked to a farm-wagon. As soon as he saw Rory leading Darling the man took his horse across to the other side of the road, and then back again when he had passed Rory.

'There!' said Tammylan. 'That's the rule of the road where horses are concerned, Rory. My goodness me, Skippetty, it's time you learnt the rules of the road too! You nearly ran into the wagon just then!'

They soon came to the smithy. It was an exciting place

with a big fire burning at the back. The smith was a great big man with a beard and a brown face. His black curly hair was damp with the heat of the smithy.

'Good morning, young sir,' he said to Rory. 'So you have brought old Darling for shoes. Ah, she's a fine horse, that one!'

'Everybody says that!' said Penny, slipping down from Darling's broad back. 'Are you going to take her old shoes off first, Mr Smith?'

'Of course!' said the smith, with a laugh. 'You watch and see what I do, Missy. Hup, there, Darling, hup you go!'

'Tammylan, why do horses have to wear shoes?' said Penny, slipping her hand into the wild man's big brown one. 'Cows don't, do they – or sheep – or cats or dogs.'

Tammylan laughed. 'Well, Penny,' he said, 'a horse wouldn't need shoes if he just ran over the soft grass – but he has to walk on our hard roads, and his hoof would break then, if he wore no shoes. His hoof is made of the same kind of stuff as our fingernails, you know – it is a kind of horny case for his foot.'

Penny and the others watched the smith. He wore an old leather apron. He lifted Darling's hind foot and looked at it. He took his pincers and pulled away the old shoe from the hoof, and then, with his paring knife, he pared away part of the new-grown hoof.

'What's that raised part in the middle of the horse's hoof?' asked Sheila.

'That is called the frog,' said Tammylan. The children laughed.

'What a funny name to give to part of a horse's foot!' said Penny. 'Does it croak?'

'Funny joke!' said Rory. 'I suppose, Tammylan, that the frog is the bit the horse would walk on if he hadn't a shoe?'

'Yes,' said Tammylan. 'Now watch the smith make a new shoe for Darling. He is very clever at his job.'

All the children watched while the smith took up a straight bar of cold iron. He heated it until it was so hot that it looked white. Then it was easy to bend into the shape of a horse-shoe. The smith hammered it hard. He put it into his fire again and made it hot once more.

'Now he's making the holes for the nails to go through!' said Benjy. 'Look at him punching them!'

While the shoe was still hot the smith laid it up against Darling's hoof. 'He wants to see if it is pressing evenly all over the hoof,' said Tammylan. 'No – it isn't quite. Now watch him paring away the bits that the shoe burnt.'

The shoe fitted Darling when the smith once again pressed it against her hoof. The smith put the shoe into cold water and then placed it once more over the hoof. Darling patiently lifted up her foot. She knew exactly what was being done and stood perfectly still.

'He is nailing the shoe to Darling's hoof!' cried Penny. 'Oh Tammylan, he's not hurting Darling, is he?'

'Of course not!' said Tammylan. 'Does it hurt when your nails are cut, Penny, or when they are filed? Darling doesn't mind a bit! Look – do you see how the nails are bent a little at their points. That is so that they will turn outwards as they are hammered in – otherwise they might go into the fleshy piece of the hoof and hurt Darling. Then she would be lame.'

The smith dealt swiftly with the nails in the shoe. Then

he rubbed the edges of the hoof well with a rasp – and that was one shoe done! Darling put down her hoof and stamped a little.

'That's to see if it fits!' said Penny. 'I stamp in new shoes too!'

The smith took Darling's other hind foot and fitted that with a hot shoe too. 'You want to notice that the hind shoes are more pointed than the shoes I'll be making for the fore-feet,' he said, in his deep voice. 'When you pick up a horse-shoe in the road, you'll be able to tell if it's from the fore foot of a horse or the hind foot.'

Penny didn't like the smell of burning hoof. She went outside with Skippetty. The others stayed with Tammylan and watched. Benjy wished he could be a smith. He thought it would be a fine life to have a smithy of his own, with a big fire going and all kinds of horses coming in morning, noon and night to be shod.

'I expect you are very busy, aren't you?' he asked the smith.

'Not one quarter so busy as my father was, and not a tenth so busy as my grandfather!' said the smith. 'Ah, in the old days, before motor-cars came along and before farmers got this new machinery to work their farms, there were more horses than we could handle. My trade is all going. There are no carriage horses nowadays, and very few horses on farms! Don't you be a smith, young sir! You'll not make any money at that!'

'Well, I'll see,' said Benjy. 'One day I may have a farm of my own – then I'll work it with horses and have my own smithy! That would be fine!'

'There – she's finished!' said the smith, giving Darling a smack on her shining back. 'Go along, old girl – back to your work!'

Penny mounted on his back again, and the five of them went slowly back up the lane. Tammylan was coming to tea. That was fine. Afterwards they would all go for a walk – and once again the wild man would tell them all he knew about the animals and birds they met.

'When are you coming again?' asked Benjy, when Tammylan said goodbye much later in the day.

'I'll come for the sheep-dipping!' said Tammylan. 'I can give a hand there. The sheep do hate it so – and I can quiet them a little. Expect me at the sheep-dipping, Benjy. I think it will have to be done soon!'

17

A Bad Day for the Sheep

Tammylan was right. Davey had wanted to dip the sheep a week or two back, because he said the flies were getting at them, and laying eggs in the wool. But things kept happening to prevent the dipping, and then Davey found that one or two of the sheep were really in a bad way.

'If we don't dip the sheep as soon as possible, we'll be sorry,' he told the children's father.

The children went to look at the dipping-trough. 'It looks like a funny kind of bath, sunk into the ground,' said Penny. 'Isn't it deep – the sheep will have to swim through it, won't they, Rory?'

'Yes, I should think so,' said Rory. 'It's about eighteen or twenty feet long – goodness, by the time they've swum through that, their wool will be soaked! That's just what we want, of course.'

'What's put into the bath?' asked Sheila.

'A very strong disinfectant!' said Rory, proud that he knew so much about it. 'The men are going to dip the sheep tomorrow. We'll see all that happens then. How the sheep will hate it, poor things!'

Rory was right! The sheep hated the dipping even more than they hated their shearing. Jim and Bill got the bath ready. They filled it full of water, into which they emptied a big tin of something.

'Pooh, it smells!' said Penny, and she went away a little. She always hated smells. The men stirred up the bath with sticks. It became cloudy.

Rascal, Tinker and Nancy had got the sheep in from the hills that morning. The flock were in a fold nearby. They bleated, for they knew that something unpleasant was about to happen to them!

'There's Tammylan!' said Rory, pleased. 'He said he'd come. Hallo, Tammylan – you're just in time!'

Davey was pleased to see Tammylan. The wild man was so good with animals, and he would be a help in dipping the sheep, who were always very difficult when being dipped in the trough.

'Hallo, children,' said Tammylan. 'I'm glad your sheep are being dipped today. I reckon it's only just in time to save some of them from illness, Davey.'

'How would they be ill?' asked Sheila.

'Well, in this hot weather the flies' eggs hatch out in a few hours in their wool,' said Tammylan. 'The maggots eat away hungrily and do the sheep a lot of harm. There's a few in your flock that are in a bad way.'

'Look!' said Rory. 'The first sheep is being driven down the passage-way to the trough!'

Hurdles made a narrow passage from the fold to the swimming-trough. The sheep was made to run down the passage-way and came to the dipping-trough. It stood there, not at all wanting to go in. A farm-hand seized it – and into the bath it went! It bleated piteously as it found itself in the water and struck out with all its legs.

'It's swimming!' cried Penny. 'I've never seen a sheep swim before! Look – it's going quite fast!'

The sheep swam through the trough. It seemed a very long way to the panting animal. It was afraid of the water, and afraid of the men who shouted at it. It only wanted to get out and run away!

'Why does the poor sheep have to swim such a long way?' asked Penny, indignantly. 'It's a shame! Why couldn't they make the bath much shorter?'

'Well, Penny, the disinfectant *must* soak in to every single part of the sheep's wool and skin,' said Tammylan. 'If the bath were very short, then the sheep might not be thoroughly soaked, and the eggs and maggots might still be alive to work their harm. By making the sheep swim a long way, we make sure that it is soaked to the skin!'

The sheep at last reached the other end of the bath. It went up a slope and stood still in a little enclosed place, shaking itself now and again.

'That place is called the "dripper",' said Tammylan. 'The sheep stand there and let the disinfectant drip off them. See it falling in drops and rivulets off that sheep, Penny? Look how it runs back into the bath, so that very little is wasted!'

The children saw that the disinfectant dripping off the sheep ran back into the trough. They felt sorry for the dripping sheep and hoped that it would soon be allowed to go back to the field.

'Can it soon go back to eat grass on the hills?' asked Penny. 'I wish it would.'

'Not till it is dry,' said Tammylan. 'You see, if the liquid drips from the sheep on to the grass, it taints the grass, Penny – and then, if the sheep eat it, they might become ill. So they have to wait a little, and get dry before Davey lets the dogs take them back to the hills to graze.'

'Another sheep is going into the dipping-trough!' cried Rory. A second sheep was being driven down – and then a third and a fourth – and soon the air was full of frightened bleatings as the sheep struggled in the water, and swam pantingly to the other end.

The cries of the sheep in the trough made the waiting sheep feel afraid. They ran round the fold and bleated too. Davey looked at Tammylan.

'Can you say a few words to them?' said the old shepherd with a smile.

Tammylan went into the fold. He spoke to the sheep in the deep low voice he kept for animals, and the sheep stood still and listened. It was curious to see Tammylan with animals or birds. They *had* to listen to him. They had to be still. His voice always quietened any animal at once, even if it was in great pain. He had a wonderful way with him.

Benjy watched him. The sheep crowded round the wild man, comforted. They were no longer frightened by the wild bleatings of the sheep being dipped in the trough.

'How I wish I could handle animals as Tammylan does,' thought Benjy. 'My goodness, if I could, I'd try to tame animals like lions and tigers, bears and elephants! What fun that would be!'

One by one all the sheep had to go down the slope into the trough. They did not make such a fuss now. The men were pleased, because the job was over more quickly when the sheep were docile. It was always a messy job, and they were glad when it was over.

Each sheep stood for a while in the dripper. When half of them were done the water was very dirty indeed. The men emptied it and put in fresh water.

'That's good,' said Tammylan, pleased. 'That gives the rest of the sheep a good chance to be thoroughly disinfected now. It's a mistake to use the water too much before changing it.'

As soon as the sheep left the dripper they went into a big fold and there they had to stay until they were dry and there was no fear of drippings spoiling their grass.

Rascal, Tinker and Nancy lay down, patiently waiting until the sheep were ready. Then they would take them off to the hills again, at a wave of the hand from old Davey. They kept well away from the trough! They had no wish to be bathed there too!

Penny suddenly missed Skippetty. Where could he be? Had he been frightened by the bleatings and gone running away by himself somewhere? The little girl called him.

'Skippetty! Skippetty! Where are you? Come here, Skippetty!'

A pitiful bleating answered her – and to Penny's horror she saw Skippetty running down into the dipping-trough with some other sheep! He had got into the fold and had to take his turn.

'Oh, stop Skippetty, stop him!' cried Penny. 'Oh, he'll be drowned! Davey, save him!'

But it was too late to stop the lamb from going into the

trough. In he went with the others, and scrambled through, bleating at the top of his loud voice. He climbed out, with everyone laughing at him.

Penny rushed to get him. 'No, Tuppenny, no!' cried Davey. 'Don't you touch him while he's fresh from the bath. You'll get yourself all messed. Let him stand in the dripper with the others. That lamb of yours is always up to something!'

So poor Skippetty had to stand in the dripper with the others, and then he went into the fold to dry. Penny was dreadfully upset, but the others laughed loudly.

'You *are* horrid to laugh at poor Skippetty!' said Penny, almost in tears. 'What would you feel like if your squirrel went into that horrid dipping-trough, Benjy?'

'Oh, he wouldn't be so silly,' said Benjy, putting his hand up to caress Scamper, who, as usual, was on his shoulder. 'You must teach Skippetty a little common sense, Penny – though you could do with some yourself sometimes!'

Penny said that Skippetty smelt, after he had dried himself. She wanted to pet the lamb and comfort him after his horrid bath – and yet she could not bear to have her hands smell horrid. So she went and put on her old gloves, which made everyone laugh still more loudly!

'Don't you worry, Tuppenny!' cried Davey. 'Your lamb hasn't come to any harm. It has probably done him good. You watch and see how much better my sheep are, after their bath!'

So they were. They were much livelier and happier, and Davey was pleased with them. 'You see, all the eggs and grubs are gone now,' he said. 'If I can keep my sheep healthy and fit, the flies are not so likely to go to them, and I shan't have to keep dipping them. One year I had to dip sheep so many times that they almost got used to it!'

'Was there ever a year when you didn't dip them at all?' asked Penny.

'Well, there's a law that says we *must* dip our sheep so many times each year,' said Davey. 'It's a good law. It stops disease from spreading among the flocks. One careless farmer can do a lot of harm to others, you know. We should take as much care of our animals as we do of ourselves.'

'I never knew there were so many things to be done on a farm,' said Rory, seriously. 'As I mean to be a farmer when I grow up I'm glad I'm learning now. Farming's fine, isn't it, Davey?'

'It's a man's job!' said Davey. 'Ay, young sir, it's a man's job!'

18

Everybody has a Job!

The weeks went happily by. The children went off to their lessons on week-days, and enjoyed their Saturdays and Sundays immensely. There was always something fresh to do on the farm. The weather was fine and sunny, and the children became as brown as acorns.

The dairy was doing well. Mother was delighted, because her cream and butter sold well. Everybody praised the butter and said how delicious it was. Harriet was very deft in the way she put it up into half-pound and pound pats, and Sheila had learnt to wrap them up very neatly.

Sheila felt happy those summer days, as she worked in the cool dairy with her mother and Harriet. It was such fun to separate the cream from the milk, and to churn the butter from the cream. It was lovely to be allowed to pat and squeeze the butter till it was just right to be cut up and wrapped. Sheila felt proud when she saw the neat piles of yellow butter sitting on the dairy shelves, wrapped in 'WILLOW FARM' paper.

She and Frannie had been very good indeed with the hens. They had set two more clutches of eggs under two broody hens, and had brought off twenty-four chicks, much to their pride and delight. Now the farmyard was full of hens, half-grown pullets and chicks – to say nothing of the fine batch of ducks that swam gaily on the pond from dawn to dusk.

The two girls had sold a great many eggs, and had made quite a lot of money. They still kept their egg-book most carefully, and Sheila felt quite grown-up when she showed her parents all that was in it.

The piglets had grown marvellously too, and were big and fat and round. They rooted about in the orchard all day long. The sow was a contented old thing, and the children couldn't help liking her, though she was no beauty.

Rory and Benjy had been taught how to groom the horses. Their father said that it would be a help in the busy summertime, if the boys could sometimes groom the horses for Jim in the mornings. Then Jim could get on with something else.

Of course Rory and Benjy were simply delighted, for they both adored the big shire horses. Captain, Blossom and Darling were their favourites.

Jim showed the boys how to groom them. 'You stand on the near side of the horse first,' he said. 'The near side is the left side, of course. Now, take the brush in your left hand and the curry-comb in your right. That's the way, Rory.'

'What a funny comb!' said Penny, who was watching in great interest. 'I shouldn't like to comb *my* hair with that.'

'It's got iron teeth,' said Rory. 'What do I do next, Jim?'

'Begin at the head, Rory,' said Jim. 'Comb and brush in turn. Now the neck – then the shoulder – the fore-leg. Go on – that's right. Work vigorously – the horse likes it.'

Rory combed and brushed hard. It made him hot, but he didn't mind. It was lovely to work with horses like this. It was a real job, Rory thought.

'Knock your comb hard against the stall to get out the dirt and hair,' said Jim. So Rory tapped the comb to clean it. The others watched him, wishing they could curry-comb a horse too. Benjy meant to have his turn the next day!

'When you've finished this side of the horse, get on with the other side,' said Jim. 'I'll leave you to it now. Feed Darling when you've finished her – then I'll come back and help you to harness her.'

In a week or two both Rory and Benjy could manage the horses beautifully. They were really almost as good as the men, and their father was proud of them. Benjy was really better than Rory because he was very good with all animals, and they loved him to handle them.

Penny was always interested to see the bit being put into a horse's mouth. 'How does it go in so nicely?' she asked. 'It seems to fit beautifully.'

Jim opened Darling's mouth and showed the little girl the horse's strong teeth. 'Look,' he said, 'there is a space between Darling's front and back teeth – just there, see – and that is where the bit goes, quite comfortably.'

'Oh,' said Penny, looking sad, 'did you pull out those teeth to make room for the bit, Jim? How unkind!'

Jim laughed loudly. Penny always said such funny things.

'No, no,' he said. 'We don't do things like that! A horse always has that space – teeth never grow there – so we just put the bit in that space and the horse is quite comfortable.'

'Oh,' said Penny, 'I'm so glad you don't have to pull teeth out to make room for it. Isn't it a good thing that the horse's teeth are made like that?'

One of the things that made Penny very happy that

summer was the coming of the three calves. They were born on the farm. The cows who had the calves were called Buttercup, Clover and Daisy, and were lovely red and white creatures, with soft brown eyes.

The calves were like their mothers, and were really adorable. Penny went to see them twenty times a day at the very least. They sucked at her little hand, and she liked that. They were playful little things, not a bit staid like the big fat cows.

'Daddy, I want to look after the calves,' said Penny seriously, when she heard that the calves were born. 'I really do. Sheila and Frannie manage the hens by themselves now – they don't want me to help at all. Rory and Benjy are doing the horses. I've only got Skippetty to see to, and now that he eats the grass, I don't even have to feed him out of the bottle.'

'But Penny dear, you're too little to be of any *real* help!' said her father, who still thought of Penny as a very small girl. 'You're only eight.'

'Well, I can't help that,' said Penny, almost crying. 'I want to be nine as soon as possible, but a year takes such a long time to go. I do think you might let me have the calves, Daddy. Tammylan said he felt sure I could manage them well. He says they are awfully easy, if they are healthy from the beginning – and ours are.'

In the end Penny got her way, though Harriet was to help her at first. The little girl was overjoyed.

'Ah, Skippetty, I shall be doing real work now, like the others!' she said to her lamb, who, as usual, followed her everywhere. 'You'll be quite jealous when you see me feeding the calves, Skippetty – but I shan't feed them out of a bottle as I did you!'

Harriett put milk in pails for the three calves. They were out in the fields all day long, but at night they were brought back to the sheds. Penny went with Harriet to feed the calves.

'Now you look what I do,' said Harriet, setting down the pails in front of the calves. 'They don't know how to drink yet, bless them – they're so new-born! Well, we have to teach them. They know how to suck, as all little creatures do – but these calves have to learn drinking, not sucking. We must teach them.'

'How?' asked Penny. 'Skippetty sucked out of a bottle – but the calves can't do that, they're too big.'

'Now watch me,' said Harriet. She dipped her fingers into a pail of milk till they were dripping with the white liquid. She held out her hand to the nearest calf. It took no notice. Harriet put her milky fingers against its mouth. The calf at once smelt the milk and opened its mouth. In half a second it was sucking Harriet's hand.

'Oh, but Harriet, it will take ages and ages to feed the calves that way!' said Penny, looking with dismay at the big pails of milk.

Harriet laughed. 'Watch, Penny, watch,' she said. She drew her hand slowly away towards the pail of milk. The calf, eager to suck her hand, followed it down with its mouth. Harriet quickly dipped her hand in the milk again and held it out to the calf. Then, as it sucked hard, she drew her hand away once more, and put it slowly into the milk. The calf followed her hand hungrily – and put its nose right into the pail!

It sucked at Harriet's fingers busily, and as its mouth was now in the milk, it sucked and drank at the same time!

'Oh, that's clever of you, Harriet!' said Penny. 'Take your hand away and see if the calf will drink by itself.'

But it wouldn't. It wanted Harriet's fingers to suck, even though it could drink the milk as well! So Harriet kept her hand in the milk, and the calf sucked and drank hungrily.

'Please let me do that for the second calf,' begged Penny. 'I know I can.'

So Harriet let her, and to Penny's enormous delight, the little creature sucked at her small hand and followed it greedily down to the milk, just as the first calf had done with Harriet.

'Good,' said Harriet. 'Well, Penny, that's the first step! It won't be long before the calves come running at the smallest clink of a pail!'

Harriet was quite right. The calves soon learnt to drink the milk, and when Penny carried out the pails one by one, she had to be careful that the hungry calves did not knock them over!

She had to feed them three times a day – before breakfast, at midday, and before she went to bed. It was lovely work and the little girl enjoyed it. It made her feel important and grown-up to have something of her very own to manage.

For nine weeks Penny fed the calves three times a day. They were given the separated milk, which had no cream, and Harriet taught Penny to put a few drops of cod-liver-oil into the pails, to make up for the lack of cream. The little girl always measured it out very carefully, and never once forgot.

The piglets had the buttermilk and loved it. Penny was glad that her calves had better milk than the pigs! When they were just over two months old she only had to feed them morning and night. Then very soon they would be put on to solid food – hay, turnips, things like that. Penny asked all kinds of questions and was sure she could manage the calves even when they grew older.

The calves grew well. They loved Penny, and as soon as she appeared at the gate of their field with Skippetty, they ran to her, flinging their long tails into the air. Whether she brought them food or not, they were always pleased to see her.

At night she fetched them from the field and put them into a big well-aired shed. She saw that they had plenty of clean straw, and looked after them so well that the other children were quite astonished.

'Penny, you're growing up!' said Rory, solemnly. 'You really are!'

'Oh, am I!' said Penny, delighted. 'How lovely! I always seem so small to myself, when I'm with you others. But I really feel big and important when I'm managing the calves. So perhaps I really am growing up now!'

'Don't grow up too fast, little Penny!' said Tammylan, who was watching her take the calves to their field. 'Calves are nicer than cows – lambs are sweeter than sheep – chicks are prettier than hens – and children are nicer than grown-ups! So don't grow up *just* yet!'

'Oh, I won't,' said Penny, slipping her hand into the wild man's. 'Not really for years and years. But I do like to *feel* grown-up even if I'm not, Tammylan.'

'Well, you're doing your bit on the farm,' said Tammylan. 'You all are. You're children to be proud of. I really don't know what the farm would do without you now!'

19

A Visit to Tammylan – and a Storm

In June the hayfields at Willow Farm were a lovely sight. The grass waved in them, and all kinds of flowers peeped here and there. The children loved to walk beside the hedges that ran round the fields. They were not allowed to wander in the grass, of course, for fear of spoiling the hay – and Skippetty had to be kept out too.

'The hay crop is good this year,' said the children's father, pleased. 'That means that we shall have plenty of hay for the cattle in the winter – good feeding for them. Well – when haymaking time comes I am going to get you four children a holiday, because we shall want your help!'

'Oh good!' cried everyone, delighted at the idea of an unexpected holiday.

'We'll work jolly hard,' said Rory. 'Feel the muscles in my arm, Daddy – aren't they getting hard?'

His father felt them. 'My word, they are!' he said, surprised. He looked at Rory closely. 'Who would have thought you were the same boy as the ill-grown, pale, weedy Rory of last year!' he said. 'Well, we work hard – but it's worth it when I look at you all, and see how bonny and rosy you are. Now about this haymaking – we shall begin on Monday, because the weather is beautiful at present.'

'Can we only make hay properly when the weather is nice, then?' asked Penny.

'Well, you surely know the old saying "Make hay while the sun shines!" ' said her father. 'Yes – we have to cut and cart the hay while the weather is dry and warm. Wet hay isn't much good, and needs a lot more labour.'

'It has to be cut, and turned, carted away and stacked, hasn't it?' said Rory, remembering what had happened at Cherry Tree Farm the year before. 'Daddy, what happens if hay is stacked before it is quite dry?'

'It becomes very hot,' said his father. 'So hot that the hay actually gets blackened by the heart – and it may even get on fire. I remember one summer helping your Uncle Tim with his hay, and it was such wet weather that it was impossible to get it really dry.'

'What did you do, then?' asked Rory.

'We had to put thick layers of straw into the haystack as we built it,' said his father. 'That prevented the hay from becoming too hot because the straw sucked up the moisture. The straw made splendid fodder for the winter, I remember.'

'I do like hearing all these things,' said Rory. 'I shall remember them when I have a farm of my own.'

The children went to find Tammylan on Sunday, to tell him that haymaking would begin the next day. Tammylan was not in his cave, so they guessed that he must be in his tree-house by the river. They went to see.

Tammylan's tree-house was a lovely place. It was built of willows which, although cut from the trees, still grew green leaves – so that it looked almost as if Tammylan lived in a growing house! The children loved it. The wild man had a bed of heather and bracken. It was there in the house, but Tammylan was nowhere to be seen.

'I wonder where he is,' said Benjy, looking all round. 'Oh look – there's the hare! It's come to the tree-house with Tammylan!'

The hare was crouching in a corner, half-afraid of the children. But when Benjy went towards it, it did not run away. It knew he was a friend and heard in the boy's voice the same gentle, friendly tones that it knew in Tammylan's. It allowed Benjy to stroke it, and then, with a few swift bounds it fled out of the tree-house into the woods.

'It does limp a bit,' said Benjy, watching. 'But it's wonderful the way its poor leg's mended. How can we find Tammylan, I wonder?'

'Send Scamper to look for him!' said Penny.

'Good idea!' said Benjy. 'Where *is* Scamper?'

The squirrel was bounding about the tree-house, sniffing for his friend, Tammylan. Benjy spoke to him. 'Scamper – find Tammylan, find him!'

Scamper was very sharp. He understood what Benjy meant, because he himself wanted to find the wild man too! So off he went into the tree, keeping a sharp look-out for Tammylan from the branches.

And before very long the four children saw their friend coming from the river-bank with Scamper on his shoulder!

'Hallo, Tammylan!' they shouted. 'So Scamper found you!'

'Yes, he made me jump!' said the wild man. 'I was lying down on the bank, watching a kingfisher catching fish, when suddenly this rascal landed right in the middle of my back! I knew that you must be somewhere about so I came to see.'

The children went with the wild man to watch the brilliant kingfisher fishing. It was marvellous to see how he sat on a low branch, watching for fish in the water below.

'There he goes!' cried Penny, as the blue and green bird flashed down to the water. He was back again in a second, with a small fish in his mouth. He banged it against the bough and killed it. Then he flew off with it.

'Isn't he going to eat it?' asked Penny.

'He would have liked to!' said Tammylan. 'But he has a nest at the end of a tunnel in a bank nearby – and no doubt his wife is sitting on a nest of fish-bones, warming her white eggs, hoping that her mate will soon bring her something to eat. Well – she will have fish for dinner!'

'Tammylan, we came to tell you something,' said Benjy, lying on his back and looking up into the brilliant blue sky. 'I say – isn't it gorgeous weather!'

'Is that what you came to tell me?' asked Tammylan, looking astonished.

'No, of course not!' said Benjy, laughing. 'We came to tell you that we are having a holiday for a few days – so will you come and see us?'

'But why the holiday?' asked Tammylan. 'Have you been specially good at your lessons lately? I can't believe it!'

The children laughed. 'No,' said Rory, 'but we are going to begin haymaking tomorrow. Won't that be fun, Tammylan?'

But Tammylan did not smile. He looked worried.

'What's the matter, Tammylan?' asked Penny.

'I hope you *won't* begin haymaking tomorrow,' said Tammylan. 'There will be a great thunderstorm tomorrow night – with a good deal of rain. It would be best to put off your haymaking until the end of the week, although I know the hay is ready now.'

'Tammylan! How can you possibly know that a thunder-storm is coming?' said Benjy, sitting up. 'Why, it feels simply lovely today – not a bit thundery.'

'To you, perhaps,' said Tammylan, 'but you must remember that I live out of doors all the time, and I know the weather as well as you know your tables! You can't live as I do, looking at the sky and the hills day and night, feeling the wind on my cheek, seeing how the trees blow, without knowing exactly what the weather is going to be. And I am quite sure that there will be a storm tomorrow night, and your hay will be spoilt if it is cut tomorrow. The weather will clear again on Tuesday, the wind will be fresh, the days warm, and the hay will be perfect for cutting by Thursday or Friday.'

'We must tell Daddy,' said Rory, at once. 'Oh, Tammylan, I hope he believes what you say! Bother! We shan't have a holiday tomorrow!'

'Well, that doesn't matter, surely, if you save your hay-crop, does it?' said Tammylan.

'Of course not,' said Rory. 'Well, we'd better get back and tell Daddy at once, or he will be making all kinds of arrangements for the haymaking.'

The children said goodbye and went quickly home. They ran to find their father. He was in the fields, looking at the cattle. They ran to him.

'Daddy! Don't cut the hay tomorrow! There will be a storm and heaps of rain tomorrow night!' cried Benjy. 'Tammylan says so.'

'Oh, Tammylan says so, does he?' said his father, looking thoughtful. 'Well, well – I don't know what to do. I've made all arrangements to start tomorrow – but Tammylan has a strange way of foretelling the weather. Look, there's old Davey the shepherd. Call him here and we'll see if he thinks there will be a storm too.'

The children yelled to Davey. He came up with Tinker close at his heels. The other dogs were guarding the sheep.

'Davey, what do you think about the haymaking tomorrow?' asked the children's father.

'The grass is in fine fettle,' said the old shepherd. 'And the weather's right. But I doubt you'll get caught by a storm tomorrow.'

'That's just what Tammylan said!' cried Penny.

Davey's grey eyes twinkled at her. 'Did he, Tuppenny?' he said. 'Well now, that's not surprising, seeing that he and I spend our days watching the things that make the weather! The clouds tell us many things, the way the trees turn to the wind, the feel of the air, the look of the far-away hills. And I say there's thunder coming, and a mighty storm. So, sir, if I were you, I'd put off the haymaking tomorrow, and wait for a day or two till the rain's dried out, and you can cut in safety. 'Twould be a pity to spoil a fine crop like yours!'

'Thanks, Davey,' said the farmer, and the old shepherd went on his way, his dog at his heels. The four children looked at their father.

'Well, haymaking is off!' he said. 'We'll see if the storm comes. If it does, we'll be glad the hay wasn't cut – if it doesn't, there's no harm done. We can cut the next day!'

So the children went to school after all on Monday. They

looked up at the sky. It was brilliant blue, without a single cloud to be seen.

'Perfect for cutting hay,' said Rory. 'Oh goodness – I wonder if that storm will come tonight.'

When the children went to bed that night the sky was still clear. But Mother said she had a thunder-headache, and Harriet said that some of the milk had gone sour.

'There's a storm coming,' she said. And sure enough there was! The children awoke at two o'clock in the morning to the sound of an enormous crash of thunder! Then the lightning flashed vividly and lighted up the room. The children leapt out of bed and ran to their windows. They all loved a good thunderstorm.

The wind blew through the trees with a curious swishing noise. Then the rain came down. It fell first in a few big drops, and then it pelted down savagely, slashing at the trees and the flowers, the corn and the grass as if it wanted to lay them to the ground.

Crash after crash of thunder came and rolled around the sky. The lightning lit up the whole of the countryside and the children were quite silent, marvelling at the magnificent sight. Frannie crept into their room, trembling.

'Oh please, Miss Sheila, can I come in here with you?' she asked, in a quivering voice. 'I can't wake Aunt Harriet, and I'm so frightened.'

'*Frightened!*' said Sheila and Penny together, in astonishment. 'What are you frightened of?'

'The storm!' said poor Frannie.

'But why?' asked Penny. 'It won't hurt you! It's grand and beautiful. Come and watch it!'

'Oh no, thank you,' said Frannie, crouching behind the wardrobe. 'I can't think how you dare to stand at the window.'

'Have you ever been hurt by a storm?' asked Sheila. 'You haven't? Well, then, why are you frightened, Frannie?'

'Oh, my mother always used to hide under a bed when there was a storm,' said Frannie. 'And that used to frighten me terribly. So I always knew there was something dreadful about a storm!'

'How funny you are!' said Sheila, going to Frannie. 'You're not frightened of the storm itself – but only because your mother showed you *she* was frightened. Don't be silly! Come and watch.'

So Frannie went to watch – and when she saw how marvellous the countryside looked when it was lit up so vividly by the lightning, she forgot her fear and marvelled at it just as the others did.

'My word, it's a good thing we didn't cut the hay today!' she said. 'That would have been out in the field, lying cut – and the rain would have soaked it so much that we'd have had to turn it time and time again! Now if we get sunny weather and a fresh wind tomorrow, it will dry standing and be quite all right in a day or two.'

'Tammylan was quite right,' said Rory. 'He always is! I *am* glad we took his advice. Good old Tammylan!'

20

Making Hay While the Sun Shines

THE weather cleared up again on Tuesday, and the sky shone brilliant blue.

'I can't see a single cloud,' said Sheila to Frannie, when she went to feed the hens. 'Not one! But look at the puddles everywhere underfoot! We must have had torrents of rain last night.'

'We did,' said Frannie. 'The duck-pond is almost over-flowing this morning – and the ducks are as pleased as can be to find puddles everywhere. Wouldn't it be nice to have webbed feet and to go splashing through every puddle we came to!'

Sheila laughed. 'That's the sort of thing Penny would say!' she said. 'Look – there she is, taking the calves to their field. Penny! Penny! Isn't everywhere wet this morning?'

'Yes,' shouted back Penny. 'The grass is soaking my shoes. They're as wet as can be. What a good thing we didn't cut the hay yesterday – it would be terribly wet today.'

By the end of the day the hot sun had dried the grass well. A fresh wind sprang up that night and finished the drying, so that the children's father felt sure that it would be safe to cut the hay on Thursday.

'We've got a holiday till Monday!' cried Rory, joyfully,

when he heard the news. 'Isn't that marvellous! Daddy says we've to be up at dawn tomorrow to start the hay-making. Everyone's going to help this week, even Mother and Harriet.'

Darling and Blossom dragged along the machine that cut the grass. It fell in swathes behind them, and soon the hay-fields looked as shaven and shorn as the sheep had looked after their shearing. In a very short while the cut hay turned to a grey-green colour, and a sweet smell rose on the air.

'I love the smell of the hay!' said Sheila, sniffing it. 'No wonder the cattle like to have it to eat in the winter. I feel as if I wouldn't mind it myself!'

The new-mown hay did smell lovely, especially in the evening. It was so beautifully dry that the farmer said it need only be turned once.

The hay lay in long rows. The children played about in it to their heart's content, flinging handfuls at one another, and burying themselves under the delicious-smelling hay.

'It doesn't matter us messing about in the hayfields like this, does it?' said Penny.

'Not a bit,' said her father. 'The more the hay is flung about the better I shall like it! You are helping to dry it. Tomorrow it must be properly turned.'

'How was hay cut before machines were invented?' asked Rory. 'Was it cut by hand?'

'Yes,' said his father. 'And a long job it must have been too! The big hayfields were all cut down by men using scythes – sharp curved blades, set in a large handle – and it took them days to mow it. Our modern machines help us a great deal. I wish I had more of them – but when the farm begins to pay

I shall buy what I can, and you shall learn how to use the machines on Willow Farm.'

'Good,' said Rory, pleased.

The next day everyone worked hard in the hayfields, turning the hay over with hand-rakes, so that the moist bits underneath could be exposed to the sun and well-dried. The hay was in fine condition and the farmer was pleased. He looked up at the sky.

'This hot dry weather is just right for the hay,' he said. 'I'm glad we took Tammylan's advice and waited a few days.'

Tammylan was helping to make hay too. He and the children had great fun together, especially when they found Penny and Skippetty fast asleep in a corner, and buried them both very carefully under a pile of the sweet-smelling hay. Penny couldn't *think* where she was when she awoke, and found the hay all on top of her!

'We must get the hay into windrows,' said the farmer. 'Big long rows all down the field.'

'Oh,' said Sheila, in dismay. 'What a lot of hard work that will mean!'

'Not for you!' said her father. 'We will let Captain do that work for us! He will pull the horse-rake that rakes the hay into windrows.'

Rory helped Jim to get out the big horse-rake. It was twelve or fourteen feet wide, and had two strong wheels and a number of hinged steel teeth. Captain was harnessed to it and was soon set to work. The big horse was guided up and down the hayfields by Rory.

Penny went to watch, running along beside the machine.

'Rory, it's clever!' she cried. 'The big steel teeth slide along under the hay and collect it all.'

'Yes,' said Rory, proudly. 'Now watch what happens. The rake is full of hay – so I pull this handle – and that lifts up the row of steel teeth – and the big load of hay is dropped in a long row on the field. That's more clever still, isn't it, Penny?'

The horse-rake did the work of six or seven men. Jim and Rory worked it by turns, and soon the hayfields were beautiful with long windrows of turned hay.

The next thing was to build it up into haycocks – small stacks of hay down the field. The children helped with this, and when they left the field one evening, tired out but happy, they thought that the haycocks looked simply lovely, standing so peacefully in the fields as if they were dreaming about the sun and wind and rain that had helped them to grow when they were grass.

'What else has to be done to the hay?' asked Penny.

'It's got to be built into haystacks,' said Tammylan, picking up the tired little girl and carrying her on his shoulder. 'You'll find that Bill is the best man at that! He knows how to thatch, and can build the best haystack for miles around.'

'I shouldn't have thought that it was very difficult to build a hay-stack,' said Penny, sleepily. 'Just piling the hay higher and higher.'

Tammylan laughed at her. 'You wait till you see one being built,' he said. 'Then you won't think it is quite such an easy job!'

The hay was carted to the rick-yard on the old hay-wagon. The children liked that. They climbed on the top of every wagon-load and rode there, while Darling went clip-clop, clip-clop down the lanes that smelt of honeysuckle. The hedges reached out greedy fingers and clutched at the hay as it passed.

'You can see the way we go by the bits of hay on the hedges!' said Sheila. 'Oh, isn't it fun to lie here on the top of the haywagon, with the soft hay under us, and the blue summer sky above. I hope Darling doesn't mind our extra weight!'

Darling certainly didn't. It made no difference at all to her whether she had four, six or twelve children on the hay-wagon. She plodded down the lanes to the rick-yard, strong, slow and patient.

Some of the hay was stored in a shed, but the farmer hadn't enough room for it all, so most of it was to be built into stacks. Bill took command at once.

The first stack was begun. The children watched with great interest. It was a big stack, and was to be oblong. When it was fairly high, Bill and two other men stood up on the top.

'We've got to press the hay down as much as we can,' he told the children. 'Ah, here comes another wagon-load.'

The haywagon was pulled up close to the stack. Rory was allowed to climb up on top of the hay and use a pitchfork. He had to toss the hay from the wagon to where Bill stood waiting for it on the half-built stack.

'You watch your pitch-fork well, the first few times you use it,' Jim warned Rory. 'It's a dangerous thing till you're well used to it.'

Rory was very careful indeed. He turned away from the man helping him, so that his fork would not jab him at all, and threw the hay quite cleverly from the wagon to the stack.

The men there worked hard and well, tramping down the hay and stacking it firmly and neatly. The stack rose higher and higher.

Benjy was told to go round the stack with a rake. 'Rake out the loose bits of hay,' said Jim. 'You can keep the stack for us and make the sides neat. Is your father down there? Good. He'll tell us if the stack gets a bit lopsided and will prop it up till we put it right.'

'I'll get an elevator next year if I can,' said the farmer. 'That sends the hay up by machinery and saves a lot of labour.'

Rory thought that an elevator would be a very good thing, for he was tired out by the time that the stack was finished! His arms ached with throwing the hay!

Bill thatched the stack beautifully to keep the rain out. He had made the centre of the top of the thatch higher than the surrounding sides, so that the rain could run down and drop off the eaves, just as it runs down the roof of a house.

'And now to give the finishing touch!' said the thatcher. The children watched him. He twisted up some hay together and began to make something at the very top of the stack in the middle. The children saw that it was a crown!

'There!' said Bill. 'Now anyone coming this way will know that I've built and thatched this stack, for the crown at the top is my mark.'

'It does look fine,' said Penny, admiringly. 'It's such a big fat stack, and smells so nice. How the animals will love to eat the hay from it, when it is cut in the winter from the big stack!'

Haymaking time was over when the last stack was built and finished. Three fine stacks then stood in the rick-yard and the farmer and his men were pleased. They liked to think that there was such good fodder for their animals in the winter. The children liked the stacks too, and often remembered the waving grass, so beautiful in the wind, that had gone to make the sturdy stacks on the farm.

'I'm sorry haymaking time is over,' said Penny. 'That's really been most exciting. I'm sure there won't be anything *quite* so exciting on Willow Farm this year.'

'Wait till harvest-time!' said Rory. 'That's the big event of the year! You wait till then, Penny!'

21

Harvest Home

The summer was very fine and warm that year. The four children grew browner and browner, and Penny grew so plump that Rory said he was sure he would one day mistake her for one of the fat piglets!

Everything grew, just as the children did! The wheat and the clover were strong and sturdy, the potato fields were a sight to see, and the other crops looked healthy and well-grown.

'Well, it may be beginner's luck,' said Uncle Tim, one day when he came over, 'but your farm is certainly flourishing this year! It's doing a good deal better than mine. I've got four cows ill of some mysterious disease, and my wheat is very poor.'

'Well, the children have been a great help to me, bless them,' said the farmer. 'Sheila really manages wonderfully with the poultry, and helps in the dairy too, and little Penny has looked after the calves just as well as Jim or Bill might have. As for my two boys, I don't know what I should do without them – they see to the horses for me, and work as hard in the fields as anyone.'

'Well, you'll need all the help you can get at harvest-time,' said Uncle Tim. 'You've a fine grain crop, no doubt about that! My word, you'll make some money this year – and be able to buy all the machinery I've been longing for myself for years! Lucky man!'

When the summer was full, the farmer went to look at his wheat fields with the children. They looked lovely.

'The corn is such a beautiful golden colour!' said Sheila, 'and I do love to see it bend and make waves of itself when the wind blows.'

'I like the whispering noise it makes,' said Penny.

'It always seems to me as if every stalk of wheat is whispering a secret to the next one – and the next one is listening with its ear!'

Everybody laughed. 'An ear of corn can't hear, silly!' said Rory.

'Well, the ears always bend to one another as if they *are* listening,' said Penny.

'First the corn was like a green mist over the brown field,' said Sheila. 'Then it grew thicker and greener and taller. Then it was tall enough to wave itself about, and looked rather like the sea. Then it grew taller still and turned this lovely golden colour. Is it ripe, yet, Daddy?'

'Yes,' said her father, picking an ear of corn and rubbing it between his hands. 'Beautifully ripe. Just ready for reaping.'

'How are we going to reap it?' asked Rory. 'With sickles or scythes? I've always wanted to use one – swish, swish, swish – and down goes the corn!'

'I've no doubt that this is the way the corn in this field was cut many years ago,' said his father. 'And it still is cut that way on some very small farms. But not on this one! I'm going to borrow your uncle's reaping-machine. It's a very old-fashioned one but it will reap our fields all right! Then next year maybe I can buy a really modern machine – one called a tractor-binder – a really marvellous machine.'

'When are you going to begin the reaping?' asked Penny, eagerly. 'We've got our summer holidays now and we can help.'

'We'll begin it this week,' said her father. 'I'll telephone to Uncle Tim tonight and see if he can lend us his machine. He won't be reaping just yet because his crops are rather later than ours this year.'

The next excitement was the arrival of the reaping-machine. It came clanking up the lane to Willow Farm drawn by two horses. They were Boy and Beauty, two of Uncle Tim's strongest horses. Rory unharnessed them, and the carter who had come with the machine led back the two horses to Cherry Tree Farm.

The children looked at the reaping-machine. Jim explained it to them. 'See this long bar that rides a few inches from the ground?' he said. 'That's the cutter bar. Look at its steel fingers. And now see this bar – it's the knife bar – look at the sharp knives it is fitted with. Now when the reaper goes along, the knives pass between the teeth of the cutter bar – and the corn is cut just as if big scissors were snipping it down!'

'Oh, isn't that clever!' said Rory. 'What happens to the corn when it is cut like that? Does it fall to the ground?'

'It falls on to this little platform,' said Jim. 'It has to be raked off by hand by the man who sits on the seat here. Then the cut corn is gathered up by the people following behind – we call them lifters, because they lift up the corn – and they bind it into sheaves.'

'I'm longing to see the reaper at work,' said Benjy. 'Is it starting today, Jim?'

'Right now,' said Jim. 'I'm just going to get Darling and Blossom to pull it. You get them for me, Rory, will you, then I can have a word with your father about which field he wants reaping first.'

Rory and Benjy went proudly off to get the two big horses, who were in the nearby field, waiting to be set to work. The boys led them back to the reaper and harnessed the patient animals to it.

The reaper was taken to the glowing field of yellow corn. The children gathered round, watching. Bill took the reins to guide the horses. Jim sat on the reaping-machine with a wooden rake. The machine was started, and the two horses pulled with all their might.

How the corn fell! It was cut as neatly and as quickly as if somebody with an enormous pair of scissors had snipped off great patches of it! Jim pushed off the cut corn as it fell on the little platform or tilting-board as he called it, and it tumbled to the ground.

Behind the reaper worked the other men of the farm – and Mother, Harriet and Frannie as well! Yes, everyone had to help at harvest-time, and how they loved it, although it was not easy. But it was so lovely out there in the golden sunshine, working together, laughing and chattering in the corn.

The children watched to see what the 'lifters' did. They gathered up a bundle of the cut corn, and tied each one round with wisps of straw.

'I've made a sheaf!' said Penny, suddenly. The others

looked. Sure enough, the little girl had managed to tie up a bundle of corn very neatly with some stalks, and there was her sheaf – a bit smaller than the sheaves that the other lifters had made, it was true – but still, a very neat and presentable one!

'You others can try your hands at making the sheaves!' called Mother. 'It's just a knack. The more we do, the better for the corn. Once it is in sheaves, we can stand it up in shocks.'

So all the children tried their hand at being lifters too. Very soon they had become quite good at gathering and binding the corn into sheaves – though Penny was rather slower than the others. Soon they had made enough sheaves to build up into a nice shock.

'Sixteen sheaves to a shock!' called out Jim, as he went by with the reaper. 'Set up the sheaves in pairs – lean them against one another – that's right, Rory. See how many shocks you children can make!'

Penny got tired of gathering up the corn and binding it, so the others let her stand up the sheaves and make shocks for them. She liked doing that. 'Don't the shocks look fine?' she said, as she finished a very neat one. 'This is as good as building castles on the sea-shore!'

The reaping and binding went on all day long. The farmer was pleased with the way the work went.

'Next year, when I buy a self-binder,' he said, 'you will not have nearly so much work to do!'

'Why?' asked Sheila. 'Does it do even more work than our reaper does?'

'Oh yes!' said her father. 'It not only cuts the corn, but it gathers it into sheaves, ties each one neatly round with strong string, and then throws each sheaf out on to the ground! It's like magic! It goes through the field of waving corn leaving rows of sheaves behind it. So all you will have to do next year is to pick up the sheaves and place them in shocks, ready to be carted away!'

When all the corn-fields were reaped, and lay quiet and still with rows of shocks in the evening sun, everyone was glad.

Tammylan came down to see the fields and nodded his head as he saw the fine shocks. 'It's a good crop,' he said to the farmer. 'You've had luck this year. It won't be long before you can cart the corn to the rick-yard, for it's already as dry as can be.'

The wild man slipped his brown hand into the middle of a nearby sheaf. He felt about and then withdrew his hand. 'The corn's in rattling order!' he said. Penny laughed.

'Why do you say that?' she asked. 'Does it rattle?'

'Put your hand into the middle of the sheaf,' said Tammylan. 'Then you will feel how crisp and light and dry it is – and if you move your hand about you will hear a whispery, rattly noise. Yes – the corn's in rattling order!'

Tammylan and the farmer, followed by the four children, moved to other sheaves here and there in the field and felt to see if the corn was ready to be carted.

'We'll cart it tomorrow,' said the farmer. 'It is lovely weather – my word what a summer we've had!'

So the next day the wagons were sent into the corn-fields to cart the corn away. Jim and Bill took their pitchforks and threw the sheaves deftly into the wagons. It was good to watch them, for they worked easily and well. A sheaf was picked up by a fork, lifted and thrown into the wagon – then down it went again for another sheaf. Another man stood in the wagon to arrange the sheaves properly inside. If they were not stacked well there, the whole thing might topple over, once the cart began moving.

It was easy work as long as there was not much corn in the wagon – but as it got full, and the sheaves were built up higher and higher in the cart, Jim and Bill had to throw more strongly, right above their heads. Soon the wagon was groaning with the weight of the corn, which had been built up neatly in the cart, and was not likely to topple out.

'Come along, Benjy!' shouted Jim. 'The wagon's ready. You can take it to the rick-yard.'

Benjy and Rory ran to the horses harnessed to the loaded wagon. Sheila and Penny climbed up on to the load. It was not so soft as the hay had been, but was very pleasant to sit on as the creaking wagon rumbled slowly down the lanes.

The corn was pitched out of the wagon into the rick-yard, ready for the building of corn-stacks – then back to the corn-field went the two horses with the empty wagon. By that time the second wagon had been filled with corn-sheaves by the men, and Rory and Benjy had to unharness the two horses and take the second wagon to the yard, leaving the first one in the field to be filled again.

It was glorious fun. Each time the girls rode home on the corn, high up in the air. Their mother saw them and smiled.

'Harvest home!' she said, when the last load was safely in. 'Harvest home! Come along in – and you shall have a very special harvest-home supper, for I'm sure you are all hungry and thoroughly deserve it!'

So in they went – and the farm-hands went too, tired but

happy because the harvest was in safely. What a lot they ate and drank, for they were all hungry and thirsty and tired!

The children fell asleep as soon as their heads touched their pillows that night. 'It was the nicest day of the year,' said Sheila to Penny, as she closed her eyes. 'Harvest home! The very nicest day of all the year!'

22

Summer Goes By

Jim and Bill built the corn into fine fat stacks. The children helped, of course! Nothing could go on in the farm without their help, Jim said!

It was fun to watch the men build the corn-stacks. They first made the bottom of the stack, arranging the sheaves neatly in the right shape for the stack. Then Bill stood in the middle and caught the sheaves as Jim forked them to him. He stood them upright in a ring, but, as he worked to the outside, he stood them less and less upright till at the edge they were lying down.

Then Bill knelt down to his work, and he and Jim together soon had the corn-stack mounting higher and higher. 'I suppose you children think you could build a stack easily enough?' called Bill.

'No,' said Rory, doubtfully. 'It looks rather difficult. You have to place the sheaves just so – the ends downwards at a certain slope – and Bill, do you know that you've got the centre of the stack higher than the outside edge?'

'Oh yes, I'm doing that on purpose,' said Jim. 'That's what's called keeping the heart full in a stack. If I don't do that, the rain will get in when the stack settles down.'

Jim and Bill brought the head of the stack to a point,

and tied the top sheaves firmly to one another.

'Is it finished now?' asked Penny.

'Oh no – it has to be thatched and roped,' said Bill. 'We'll not be finished for some time yet!'

Bill thatched the stack firmly, just as he had thatched the farmhouse itself. He began at the eaves of the stack and worked up to the top. He got Jim to hand him up water every now and again to damp the straw, for it was too dry to work with comfortably. He stroked the thatch down with a stick as he worked, and soon it began to look very neat indeed.

Then he and Jim roped the stack firmly. First they tied a rope round the body of the stack just below the eaves. Then they roped the thatched top firmly, running the rope round and round in a curious pattern and then tying it to the rope below the eaves.

'The stack looks simply lovely!' said Benjy, admiringly. 'I'm sure the rain won't get into it.'

'That it won't!' said Bill. 'Now we'll get on to the next stack.'

'Aren't you going to make your nice straw crown at the top of the stack?' asked Penny, disappointed.

'There's no time just now,' said Bill. 'I must start on the next stack – but when I've time to spare in the evenings I'll put my mark on each stack, Penny! Ah, you'll see golden crowns on the top of every one!'

Bill kept his word, and when the stacks were all finished, and stood solid and golden in the rick-yard Bill put his mark on them – a neat crown of twisted straw right at the very top of the stacks!

'I'd like to do that,' said Penny. 'It must be so nice to

sign your name on a beautiful stack, like that!'

'I wouldn't put my mark on a stack unless I'd done it well,' said Bill. He had trimmed his stacks with his shears and was really proud of them.

Sheila's hens were thrilled to be loose in the rick-yard after the stacks had been made. There was so much corn to peck at, so many grains to scratch for. They filled the air with contented clucks, and laid more eggs than ever.

'Good corn always makes hens lay well,' said Frannie, as she counted the eggs and entered them in the egg-book.

Penny's three calves were big by now. They were in the field with the cows, and had a lovely time there, chasing one another and sometimes butting their little heads against the sides of the staid cows. They always came running when they saw Penny, who was very fond of them.

Skippetty had grown into a small sheep! He was no longer so frolicsome, but seemed to think himself rather important and grown-up. Jim said it would be better for him to go into the sheep-field now, so Penny sadly gave him up.

'It was so nice having him follow me about everywhere,' she said. 'He was such a darling when he was a skippetty lamb, feeding out of a bottle. Animals grow up far too quickly – much more quickly than children. Why, in a few months they have grown up – and yet it seems to me as if I've been little for ages and ages. Animals are lucky!'

'Don't you believe it!' said Tammylan. 'It's good to be young for a long time. You can learn so much more!'

But the children didn't agree with that at all! They thought it would be nice to be like the animals and not have to do so many lessons.

Although Skippetty was now almost a sheep in his looks, he always looked out for Penny when she came by. Then he would bleat for joy and run to her, frisking round her in his old joyful way. Penny was glad that he had remembered her.

'But it makes me sad to think he will be so like the sheep next year that I shan't know him,' she said to Davey. 'I shall miss my dear little Skippetty then.'

'No, you won't, Tuppenny,' said Davey, comfortingly. 'And do you know why?'

'No. Why?' asked Penny.

'Well, because you'll have more new-born lambs to look after!' said Davey, smiling at her. 'I shall give you one or two to see to for me, because you are so good with them. So don't look sad and sigh for last spring and Skippetty – but look forward to next spring and new lambs to feed from a bottle!'

'Oh, I will!' said Penny, joyfully. 'That's a good idea, Davey. It's much nicer to look forward than to look back!'

'That's the best of farm-life,' said old Davey. 'We're always looking forward – wondering what our crops are going to be like – hoping that our young creatures will do well – planning all kinds of things.'

The four children loved the summer months, especially when the fruit was ripening. They helped to harvest the fruit crop, and Penny ate so many plums that she made herself quite ill for a day or two.

The apple harvest was the most important fruit crop for Willow Farm. The orchards had many fine apple trees, and these were bearing well, though not as well as they sometimes did.

'They bore marvellously last year,' said Jim. 'You don't

often get fruit trees bearing wonderfully well for two years running. But you'll have plenty to eat, plenty to set by in the apple-loft for the winter, and plenty to sell!'

The children felt certain that they could manage the apple-harvesting by themselves. The orchards were not very large, and as it was still holiday time, the boys said that they would like to spend a week in the apple trees, picking and storing the apples.

'We can help too,' said Sheila, at once. 'You boys can have the tree-climbing to do, and Penny and I will stay below and take the apples from you.'

The farmer said that the four children could pick the fruit. 'But remember this,' he said. 'The whole secret of having good clean fruit that keeps well and doesn't go bad is not to bruise it. Will you remember that? Handle the apples gently and if you drop any, put them on one side so that we may eat those first. I don't want to store any that are likely to go bad.'

The children remembered his advice. The boys picked carefully, standing on the ladders, and putting the fruit into big baskets swung on the branches with hooks. When they were filled the girls took them down to the ground.

Sheila and Penny picked over the apples carefully. Any that were at all pecked by the birds or bitten by wasps they put on one side for Harriet to use in the near future. Any that they dropped they put on one side also.

'Now these are the quite perfect ones,' said Sheila, looking at a pile of beautiful smooth red apples. 'We must take them to the loft in baskets. Put them in very carefully, Penny. Oh – you've dropped one, butter-fingers! That must go to the bruised pile!'

Soon the apple-loft was smelling very sweet indeed. The girls laid out the apples very carefully in long rows.

'Don't let them touch each other if you can help it, Penny,' said Sheila. 'If you do, one bad one will turn all the others rotten.'

Their father came to see their work. He was very pleased. 'My word, you are neat and tidy!' he said. 'And how well you have picked out the apples! Not one pecked one among them! We shall be having apple-pie next May at this rate, for the apples will keep beautifully.'

The children worked very hard at picking and storing the apples, and for payment they were allowed to have as many as they liked.

Penny ate so many that the others told her she would turn into an apple herself. 'Your cheeks are already like two rosy apples,' said Rory, solemnly.

Penny went to look in her mirror. She saw two plump cheeks, as red as the apples she had picked. 'Oh goodness!' she said. 'I really must be careful!'

So poor Penny didn't eat as many apples as before – but still, as Mother said, six or seven apples was quite enough for anyone, and that was the number that Penny still got through every day!

23

Good Luck for Willow Farm!

The year went on. September came and lessons began again. All the crops had been gathered in and stored. The potatoes had been harvested, and the farmer was pleased with them. The mangold wurzels had not done so well, because so many of the seeds had not come up. But the farmer said that was quite usual with mangolds.

'We must get them in before the frosts come,' he said, when the autumn came. So the big mangold wurzels were gathered and stored in pits, covered with earth and straw.

'The sheep and cattle will be glad of these in the winter,' said Bill, as he stored the big roots in their pits. 'The turnips will give them good eating too. I've stored them in a pit in the field. We've plenty for all the animals.'

When the early days of December came a large machine arrived at Willow Farm. It was drawn by a traction engine which made an enormous noise coming up the narrow lanes. 'Whatever is it?' asked Rory.

'Oh good – it's the threshing-machine coming,' said the farmer, pleased. 'I hired it for the beginning of December, and here it is! It has come to thresh our corn and get the wheat for us!'

'Why didn't you borrow it from Uncle Tim?' asked Sheila.

'He hasn't got one,' said her father. 'Farmers don't usually own threshing-machines – it is easier and cheaper to hire them when we want them. They go from farm to farm. Now it is our turn to have it.'

'But why do we want it?' asked Penny. 'We've got our corn in!'

'Ah, but the grain has to be beaten from the ears!' said her father. 'We can't eat it straight from the corn-stack, Penny – or would you like to try it?'

'No, thank you,' said Penny. 'But we don't eat corn either, Daddy, do we? The hens do that.'

'Well, we shall sell our corn to the miller,' said her father. 'He will grind it into flour – and we shall buy it to bake our bread and to make our cakes and puddings.'

Soon the air was full of a deep, booming sound. 'That's the thresher at work,' said the farmer. 'You can go and see it when you come back from school.'

The children raced home from their lessons. They went to the rick-yard, where the corn-stacks stood, and there they saw the big threshing-machine. Nearby stood the traction-engine that had brought it, and that set it to work.

When Scamper heard the noise nearby he leapt from Benjy's shoulder and bounded into the bare trees. He was really frightened of it. Penny felt a little bit scared too, but she soon became brave enough to go near and see what was happening.

It was very interesting. Bill was up on a stack, forking out the sheaves that he had so carefully arranged there. He threw them to Jim, who quickly cut the bands that bound the sheaves together. Then he put the loose cornstalks into the mill just below him – and they fell into a swiftly revolving drum in which were six long arms or 'beaters' that struck the corn and beat out the grain from the ears.

The grain fell through into another kind of machine called a winnowing machine, where the chaff was blown away from the grain. Then the wheat fell out into sacks held ready by the farmer himself. He was pleased to see such yellow grain filling his sacks! As soon as one sack was full he heaved it away and put another empty one to be filled. Rory and Benjy helped him. It was great fun.

The straw tumbled out loose, and was stacked in a shed. 'It will make fine bedding for the cattle in the winter,' said Rory.

'Yes, and we'll chop it up and put it into their food too,' said Jim. 'There's not much wasted from the corn!'

'What about the chaff?' asked Sheila, as she watched the light chaff being put into sacks too.

'Ah, my wife will be along for some of that,' said Bill. 'Our mattresses are filled with chaff, you know – and we like good new chaff each year. We shall have fine bedding now!'

'Goodness!' said Benjy, 'what a lot of good the corn is! Wheat for making flour – straw for animal bedding and for thatching – and chaff for mattresses!'

All that day and the next the threshing-mill boomed on the farm, as it worked in the rick-yard. Soon all the farmer's corn was turned into grain, straw and chaff, and the farmer and his men looked with pride at their full sacks.

'It's a good harvest,' said the farmer, as he dipped his fingers into a full sack and let the grain trickle through them. 'Our fields have done well this year.'

When the threshing-mill had rumbled away again down the lanes, pulled by the heavy traction engine, the weather changed from cold and sunny, to damp and grey. Rain-mists hid the countryside and the children could no longer go over the fields to their lessons. Instead they had to go down the lanes and along the main road. This was very much farther, and they had to start out earlier and get back later.

Penny was tired. She didn't like trudging so far in bad weather, and was very glad when the Christmas holidays came and she had no longer to get up early and walk three miles to school.

'Do you think we had better send the children to boarding-school?' said their father one day. 'They can't walk all that way all the winter through. Penny looks quite tired out. It's impossible to spare a horse and wagon four times a day. I almost think they had better go away to school.'

But when the children heard this idea they were really horrified. 'What!' cried Rory, 'leave Willow Farm for nine months every year, just when things are beginning to be exciting! Oh Daddy, how can you think of such a thing!'

The four children were so worried about this idea that they went to tell Tammylan. It was five days before Christmas. They set out over the damp fields, and came to his cave. He had left his tree-house, of course, and was now living cosily in the cave. His friend the hare was, as usual, beside him.

'Hallo!' called the children, and ran to meet their friend. 'How are you, Tammylan? We haven't seen you for ages.'

Tammylan told them his news, and then he asked for theirs.

'Tammylan, we've bad news,' said Rory. 'Do you know, Mummy and Daddy are actually thinking of sending us all away to boarding-school, because we have such a long way to walk to our lessons now that the winter has come and we can't go across the wet fields!'

'Oh, that would be dreadful!' said the wild man. 'I should miss you all terribly.'

'Tammylan, go and talk to Daddy and Mummy about it,' said Penny, slipping her hand into Tammylan's. She thought that the wild man could do anything. She could not bear the thought of leaving Willow Farm to go to school. What, leave the calves and Skippetty – and not be able to have new lambs to feed in the spring – and not see the new chicks and ducklings! It was too dreadful to think of!

'Well, I'm going over to Willow Farm tomorrow to take your father something,' said Tammylan. 'I'll have a word with him – but I don't think that anything I can say will make any difference! After all, it *is* a long way for you all to walk, especially little Penny.'

The children were out Christmas shopping when Tammylan went over to the farm the next day, so they did not see him or hear if he had said anything to their parents. Indeed, they were so excited over their shopping that they even forgot to worry about going to school after the Christmas holidays!

'Can Tammylan come for Christmas Day?' asked Penny. 'Do ask him, Mummy!'

'Oh, he's coming,' said her mother. 'He'll be along after breakfast.'

Christmas Day dawned cold and sunny and bright. The children woke early and found their stockings full of exciting things. Even Rory and Sheila had stockings, for that was the one day of the year when they felt as childish as Penny and begged for stockings too!

Mummy had given them a watch each. Rory and Sheila had had watches before, but Rory had lost his and Sheila had broken hers. Now each child had a neat silver watch and they were overjoyed. They all strapped them proudly on their wrists.

They went down to the kitchen and gave presents to Harriet and Frannie. Frannie was delighted to have so many presents. Her face beamed with joy as she opened her parcels and found a smart pencil from Rory, a book from Sheila, a thimble from Benjy and some sweets from Penny.

'And thank you, Frannie, for being such a help with the hens,' said Sheila. 'Won't it be fun to have chicks again in the spring!'

The children left the kitchen and then Rory said something that had been in everyone's mind.

'How funny! Everyone has given us a present, except Daddy!'

Their father overheard him. He smiled.

'My present is coming along soon,' he said. 'I couldn't find room in your stockings for it! Watch out of the window and you'll see it arriving soon!'

The children squealed with joy and ran to the window. They simply could not imagine what their father was giving them.

But they soon found out! Tammylan appeared – but he was not alone! With him were four grey donkeys, plump and lively. The children could hardly believe their eyes.

'Daddy! Are the donkeys your present?' shouted Rory. 'One for each of us?'

'Yes – one for each of you!' said his father with a smile. 'Tammylan came along the other day and begged so hard for you to stay on at Willow Farm instead of going to school – and he suggested giving you a donkey each to ride over the fields, so that you might still stay on here. Your mother and I thought it would be a splendid idea, and Tammylan said he would go to the market and buy the donkeys in time for Christmas. He knew someone who was selling six. So he chose four and here they are!'

The children tore out of the door and rushed to Tammylan! They were so pleased and excited that they could hardly wish him a happy Christmas!

'Which is my donkey?' cried Rory. 'Oh, aren't they beauties!'

Tammylan gave each child a donkey. The two biggest went to the boys, and the other two to the girls. Each child mounted at once and galloped off round the farm. They were so happy that they sang as they went.

'Now we shan't have to leave Willow Farm, Willow Farm, Willow Farm!' they all sang. 'Gee-up, donkeys, gee-up! Oh, what a fine life you'll have here!'

The children's parents watched with Tammylan, laughing as they saw the happy children galloping all over the place.

When they came back at last, their father spoke to them. 'You have all worked so well this year,' he said. 'You have been such a help. You haven't grumbled or complained, you have been cheerful and happy, and you have helped to make our farm a great success. So it is only fair that you should share in that success, and that is why I have spent part of the farm's money on each of you. What are you going to call your donkeys?'

'Mine shall be Neddy!' said Rory.

'Mine's Bray!' said Benjy.

'Mine's Canter!' said Sheila.

'And mine's Hee-Haw!' said Penny. And just as she said that her donkey threw up his head and brayed loudly. 'Hee-haw! Hee-haw! Hee-haw!'

'There! He's saying his name to me!' said Penny, with a laugh. 'Oh Daddy – what a lovely present! And to think we don't need to go away to school now! How lovely! Oh, what fun it will be to ride to lessons on four grey donkeys every morning and afternoon!'

And there we will leave them all, galloping in delight over the fields of Willow Farm. 'Our dear, dear farm!' said Penny. 'Oh, I wonder what will happen next year – there's always something exciting on a farm. I'm sure next year will be greater fun than ever!'

But that, of course, is another story.

More Adventures on Willow Tree Farm

Contents

1

Christmas Holidays at the Farm

Four children sat looking out of a farmhouse window at the whirling snow. It was January, and a cold spell had set in. Today the snow had come, and the sky was leaden and heavy.

Rory was the biggest of the children. He was fourteen, tall and well made, and even stronger than he looked. A year's hard work on his father's farm was making him a fine youth. Then came Sheila, a year younger, who managed the hens and ducks so well that she had made quite a large sum of money out of them since the Easter before.

Benjy pressed his nose hard against the leaded panes of the old farmhouse windows. He loved the snow. 'I wonder where Scamper is,' he said.

Scamper was his pet squirrel, always to be found on his shoulder when they were together. But Scamper had been missing for a day or two.

'He's curled himself up somewhere to sleep, I expect,' said Penny, the youngest. 'Squirrels are supposed to sleep away the winter, aren't they? I'm sure you won't see him again till this cold spell has gone, Benjy.'

Penny was eight, three years younger than Benjy, so she was the baby of the family. She didn't like this at all, and was always wishing she was bigger.

'Do you think Mark will come, if it keeps snowing like this?' she asked.

Mark was a friend of theirs. He took lessons with them at the vicarage away over the fields, and the children's mother had said he might come to stay for few days. He had never been to Willow Farm, and the children were longing to show him everything.

'Won't he be surprised to see our donkeys?' said Benjy. 'My word, mine did gallop fast this morning!'

Each of the children had a donkey, a Christmas present from their father. They had worked well on the farm, and deserved a reward – and when the four donkeys arrived on Christmas morning there had been wild excitement. The children were looking forward to riding on them when school began again. The fields had been too muddy to walk across, and they had had to go a long way round by the roads. Now they would be able to gallop there on their donkeys!

'I'm longing to show Mark over our farm,' said Rory. 'I hope this snow doesn't last too long.'

'Everywhere is beginning to look rather strange,' said Sheila. 'Snow is rather magic – it changes everything almost at once. I hope my hens are all right. I wonder what they think of the snow.'

Sheila felt sure her hens would not lay many eggs in the snowy weather. She made up her mind to give them a little extra hot mash morning and night to keep them warm. She slipped out into the kitchen to talk to Frannie about it. Frannie was the cook's niece and helped Sheila willingly with the poultry.

The snow went on falling. Soon all the farm-buildings

were outlined in soft white. When their father came in to tea he shook the snow from his broad shoulders and took off his boots at the door.

'Well,' he said, 'we can't do much this weather, except tend the beasts and see they have plenty to eat and drink. Aren't you going to help milk the cows, Benjy?'

'Gracious, yes!' said Benjy, who was still dreaming at the window. He rushed to get his old mack and sou'-wester, and pulled on his rubber boots. Then he disappeared into the flurrying snow and made his way to the sweet-smelling cow-sheds.

Only Rory and Penny, the eldest and the youngest, were left at the window. Rory put his arm round Penny. 'Have you seen Skippetty lately?' he asked.

Skippetty was the pet lamb that Penny had had the spring and summer before. The little girl had been very fond of him, and he had followed her all over the place. But now he had grown into a sheep, and had gone to live in the fields with the others. Penny shook her head sadly.

'I don't know Skippetty when I see him!' she said. 'He's just exactly like all the others. I wish he didn't have to grow up. I miss him very much. Wasn't it fun when he used to trot at my heels everywhere?'

'Well, you'll have another pet lamb this spring, so don't worry,' said Rory. 'Won't it be lovely when the winter is over and the sun is warm again – and all the fields are green, and there are young things everywhere?'

'Yes,' said Penny happily. 'Oh, Rory, don't you love Willow Farm? Aren't you glad it's ours? Wasn't it lucky that it did so well last year?'

Her father came into the room and heard what she said. He laughed. 'Beginner's luck!' he said. 'You look out this year – maybe we shan't have such an easy time!'

Harriet the cook came bustling in. Frannie was out collecting the eggs with Sheila, and Harriet had come to lay the tea. She put down a dish of golden butter, and a dish of homemade cheese. Then came scones and cakes and a home-cured ham. A big jug of cream appeared, and a dish of stewed apple. Penny's eyes gleamed. This was the sort of high-tea she liked!

'Everything grown on our own farm,' she said. 'Doesn't it look good? Are you hungry, Daddy?'

'Famished!' said her father. 'Where's your mother? Ah, there she is.'

Mother had been in the icy-cold dairy and she was frozen! 'My goodness, I'm cold!' she said. 'Our dairy is wonderfully cool in the hot summer months – but I wish it was wonderfully hot in the cold winter months! I've been helping Harriet to wrap up the butter for sale. Daddy, we've done very well out of our butter-sales, you know. I feel I'd like to try my hand at something else now, as well.'

'Well, for instance?' said Daddy, pulling his chair up to the table. 'We have hens, ducks, cows, sheep, pigs, dogs and goodness knows what else! There doesn't seem much else to have.'

'Well, we haven't got bees,' said Mother, beginning to pour out the tea. 'I'd like to keep bees. I love their friendly humming – and I love their sweet yellow honey, too!'

'Oooh – bees would be fun,' said Penny. 'Oh, Mother – let's keep them this year. And we haven't got a goat. Couldn't we keep one? And what about some white pigeons? And we could have . . .'

'We could have a bull!' said Rory. 'Fancy, we haven't got a bull, Daddy. Aren't you going to get one?'

'One thing at a time,' said his father, cutting the ham. 'After all, we haven't had our farm a year yet. I dare say we'll have everything before the second year is out! Now, where are Sheila and Benjy?'

The two soon appeared, rosy of cheek. Benjy was pleased with his milking. He always got a wonderful froth in his pail, the sign of a good milker. He was tremendously hungry.

Sheila had good news about the hens too. 'Four more eggs today than we had yesterday,' she announced. 'Mother, the hens don't like the snow at all. They all huddle in the house together, and stare out as if they simply couldn't imagine what's happening.'

'Silly creatures, hens,' said Rory. 'Give me ducks any day! Pass the scones, Sheila.'

All the children discussed the farm-happenings with their parents. They knew all the animals and birds, they knew each field and what had been grown in each, they even knew what the sowing and manuring had cost, and what profits had been made. Each child was a keen little farmer, and not one of them was afraid of hard work. Benjy was the dreamy one, but he could work hard enough when he wanted to.

'Mark's coming tomorrow,' said Rory to his mother. 'He'd better sleep with me, hadn't he, Mother? He's never been to stay on a farm before. He lives in an ordinary house with an ordinary garden – and they don't even grow easy things like lettuces and beans. They buy everything.'

'Won't he like the things *we* grow?' said Penny. 'You know – this cheese – and that butter – and this jam – and that ham?'

'He'll like the live things better,' said Rory. 'I bet he'll like a ride on old Darling. Listen – she's coming into the yard now.'

Everyone heard the slow clip-clop of Darling's great hooves, biting through the snow on to the yard below. Everyone pictured the big, patient brown horse with her lovely brown eyes and sweeping eyelashes. They all loved Darling.

'One thing I like about farm-life,' said Benjy, cutting himself a big slab of Harriet's cream-cheese, 'is that there are so many things to love. You know, all the animals seem friends. I'd hate to live in London now, as we used to do – no great horses to rub down and talk to – no cows to milk – no lambs to watch – no hens to hear clucking – no tiny chicks and ducklings to laugh at. Golly, wouldn't I miss all our farmyard friends.'

'I wonder what Tammylan is doing this snowy weather,' said Penny. Tammylan, the wild man, was their firm friend. He lived in a cave in the hillside, and looked after himself. All the animals of the countryside came to him, and he knew each one. The children loved visiting him, for he always had something to tell them, and something new to show them.

'We shan't be able to go and see him if the snow gets thick,' said Sheila. 'And I did want to tell him how we love our four donkeys.'

Tammylan had got the donkeys for their father to give them. He had arrived on Christmas Day, leading the four fat little creatures, and had stayed for the day and then gone back to his cave.

'Won't you be lonely tonight?' Penny had asked him. But Tammylan had shaken his head.

'I've no doubt some of my animal-friends will come and sit with me this Christmas night,' he had said, and the children had pictured him sitting in his cave, lighted by a flickering candle, with perhaps a hare at his feet, a rabbit near by, and one or two birds perched up on the shelf behind his head! No animal was ever afraid of Tammylan.

Darkness came, and the children's mother lighted the big lamp. The children felt lazy and comfortable. There were no lessons to do because it was holiday-time. There was no farm-work to do because it was dark outside and snowy. They could do what they liked.

'Let's have a game of cards,' said Penny.

'No – let's read,' said Benjy.

'I'd like to sew a bit,' said Sheila.

'Well – I vote we have the radio on,' said Rory. He turned it on. There was a short silence and then a voice announced:

'This evening we are going to devote half an hour to "Work on the Farm."'

'Oh, no, we're not!' laughed Daddy, and he switched the radio off. 'This evening we're all going to play Snap! Now then – where are the cards?'

And play Snap they did, even Mother. It was good for them to forget the farm and its work for one short evening!

2

The Visitor

Mark arrived the next day. Rory went to meet him at the bus-stop, a mile or two away. The snow was now thick, but would soon melt, for the wind had changed. Then everywhere would be terribly muddy.

'Will you lend me Bray?' asked Rory of Benjy. 'I thought I'd ride on Neddy to meet Mark, and if you'd lend me your donkey, I could take it along for Mark to ride back on.'

'Yes, you can have him,' said Benjy. So Rory went off on Neddy, his own donkey, and Bray trotted willingly beside him. They came to the bus-stop and waited patiently for Mark. The bus came in sight after a while, and Mark jumped down carrying a small bag. He was astonished to see Rory on a grey donkey.

'Hallo, Rory,' he said. 'I didn't know you had donkeys. You never told me.'

'Well, we didn't have them till Christmas Day,' said Rory. 'Did you have a good Christmas? We did! We each got a donkey for our own. This is Neddy, the one I'm riding on. And this is Bray. He belongs to Benjy. You can ride him home.'

'Well, I've never really ridden a donkey before, except once at the seaside,' said Mark, who was smaller and fatter than Rory. 'I fell off then. Is Benjy's donkey well behaved?'

Rory laughed. 'Of course! Don't be silly, Mark! Gracious, wait till you've been on the farm a few days. You'll have ridden all the horses, and all our donkeys, too. And Buttercup the cow if you like. She doesn't mind.'

Mark had no wish to ride horses or cows. He looked doubtfully at Bray, and then tried to mount him. Bray stood quite still. Soon Mark was on his back holding tightly to the reins.

'Give me your bag,' said Rory, trying not to laugh at Mark. 'That's right. Now off we go.'

But Bray did not seem to want to move. He stood there, his ears back, flicking his tail a little. Mark yelled after Rory, who was cantering off.

'Hie! This donkey's stuck. He won't move!'

Rory cantered back. He gave Bray a push in the back with Mark's bag. 'Get up!' he said. 'You know the way home! Get up, then!'

Bray moved so suddenly that Mark nearly fell off. The donkey cantered quickly down the road, and Rory cantered after him. Soon Mark got used to the bumpity motion of the little donkey, and quite enjoyed the ride. Once he had got over his fear of falling off, he felt rather grand riding on the little donkey.

'We'll soon see the farm,' said Rory. 'It's a jolly good one. It's a mixed farm, you know.'

Mark didn't know. He wondered what a mixed farm was. 'Why is it mixed?' he said.

'Well – a mixed farm is one that keeps animals and hens and things, and grows things in the fields too,' explained Rory. 'It's the most paying sort of farm. You see, if you have a bad year with the sheep, well, you probably have a good year with the wheat. Or if you have a bad year with the potatoes, you may make it up by doing well with the poultry. We love a mixed farm, because there's always such a lot of different things to do.'

'It does sound fun,' said Mark, wishing his donkey didn't bump him quite so much. 'I shall love to see everything. I say – is that Willow Farm?'

It was. They had rounded a corner, and the farmhouse now lay before them. It was built of warm red bricks. Its thatched roof was now covered with white snow. Tall chimneys stood up from the roof. Leaded windows with green shutters were set in the walls, and Rory pointed out which belonged to his bedroom.

'You're to sleep with me,' he said. 'I've a lovely view from my room. I can see five different streams from it. All the streams have willow trees growing beside them – they are what give the farm its name.'

Mark gazed at the farmhouse and at all the old farm-buildings around – the barns and sheds, the hen-houses and other outbuildings, now white with snow. It seemed a big place to him.

'Come on,' said Rory. 'We'll put our donkeys into their shed, and go and see the others.'

Soon the five children were gathered together in Rory's bedroom, hearing Mark's news and telling him theirs. Then they took him to see the farm and all its animals.

'Come and see the horses first,' said Rory. 'I and Benjy look after them. We groom them just as well as the men could, Daddy says.'

Mark was taken to the stables and gazed rather nervously at three enormous shire horses there.

'This is Darling, the best of the lot,' said Benjy, rubbing a big brown horse. 'And that's Captain. He's immensely strong. Stronger than any horse Daddy's ever known. And that's Blossom.'

Then Mark had to see the cows. He liked these even less than the horses because they had horns!

'See this one?' said Benjy, pointing to a soft-eyed red and white cow. 'We hope she'll have a calf this spring. We want her to have a she-calf that we can keep and rear ourselves. If she has a bull-calf we'll have to sell it. Jonquil, you'll have a little she-calf, won't you?'

'We may be going to have a big fierce bull of our own this year,' said Penny, twinkling at Mark. She guessed he wouldn't like the sound of bulls at all! He didn't. He looked round nervously as if he half expected to see a bull coming towards him, snorting fiercely!

'Well – I hope I shan't be here when the bull arrives,' he said. 'I say – what a horrid smell! What is it?'

'It's only Jim cleaning out the pig-sties,' said Sheila. 'Come and see our old sow. She had ever so many piglets in the summer – but they've all grown now. We hope she'll have some more soon. You've no idea how sweet they are!'

'*Sweet?*' said Mark in amazement. 'Surely pigs aren't sweet? I should have thought that was the last thing they were.'

'*Piglets* are sweet,' said Penny. 'They really are.'

'Well, your old sow is simply hideous,' said Mark. The five children stared at the enormous creature. The four farm children had thought she was very ugly indeed when they first saw her – but now that they were used to her and knew her so well, they thought she was nice. They felt quite cross with Mark for calling her hideous.

She grunted as she rooted round in the big sty. Mark wrinkled up his nose as he smelt the horrid smell again. 'Let's come and see something else,' he said. So they all moved off over the snowy ground to the hen-houses. Mark saw the hens sitting side by side on the perches. They did not like walking about in the snowy run.

'I manage the hens, with Frannie, our little maid,' said Sheila proudly. 'I made a lot of money through selling the eggs last year. I put some hens on ducks' eggs as well as on hens' eggs, and Frannie and I brought off heaps and heaps of chicks and ducklings.'

'Cluck-luck-luck,' said a hen.

'Yes, you did bring us luck,' said Sheila, laughing. 'Luck-luck-luck-luck!'

In the fields were big folds in which Davey the shepherd had put the sheep. He did not want them to roam too far in the snowy hills in case they got lost. Penny stood on the fence and called loudly.

'Skippetty, Skippetty, Skippetty!'

'She's calling the pet lamb she had last year,' explained Rory. 'Oh, Mark, do you remember when it followed her to school, like Mary's lamb in the rhyme? Wasn't that funny?'

Mark did remember. He looked to see if a little lamb was coming. But no lamb came. Instead, Davey the shepherd let a fat sheep out of the fold. It came trotting across the snowy grass to Penny.

'Penny! This isn't your lamb, is it?' cried Mark, in surprise. 'Gracious! It's a big heavy sheep now.'

'I know,' said Penny regretfully. 'When I remember that dear little frisky, long-leggitty creature that drank out of a baby's milk-bottle, I can hardly believe this sheep was once that lamb. I think it's very sad.'

'Yes, it is,' said Mark. Skippetty put his nose through the fence and nuzzled against Penny's legs. To him Penny was still the dear little girl who had been his companion all through the spring and summer before. She hadn't changed as he had.

'I wish I could show you my tame squirrel,' said Benjy. 'He's been missing the last few days. We think he may be sleeping the cold spell away.'

'Oh, I've seen Scamper, you know,' said Mark, remembering the times when Benjy had brought him to school on his shoulder. 'Whistle to him as you used to do. Maybe he'll come. Even if he's asleep somewhere surely he will hear your whistle and wake!'

'Well, I've whistled lots of times,' said Benjy. 'But I'll whistle again if you like.'

So the boy stood in the farmyard and whistled. He had a very special whistle for Scamper the squirrel, low and piercing, and very musical. Tammylan the wild man had taught him the whistle. The five children stood still and waited.

Benjy whistled again – and then, over the snow, his tail spread out behind him, scampered the tame squirrel. He had been sleeping in a hole in a nearby willow tree – but not very soundly. Squirrels rarely sleep all the winter through. They wake up at intervals to find their hidden stores of food, and have a feed. Scamper had heard Benjy's whistle in his dreams, and had awakened.

Then down the tree he came with a flying leap, and made his way to the farmyard, bounding along as light as a feather.

'Oh, here he is!' yelled Benjy in delight. The squirrel sprang to his shoulder with a little chattering noise and nibbled the bottom of Benjy's right ear. He adored the boy. Mark gazed at him in envy. How he wished he had a pet wild creature who would go to him like that. 'Would he come to me?' he asked.

'Yes,' said Benjy, and patted Mark's shoulder. The squirrel leapt to it, brushed against Mark's hair, and sprang back to Benjy's shoulder again.

'Lovely!' said Mark. 'I wish he was mine.'

A bell rang down at the farmhouse. 'That's Harriet ringing to tell us dinner's ready,' said Rory. 'Come on. I'm jolly hungry.'

'So am I,' said Mark. 'I could eat as much as that old sow there!'

'Well, I hope you won't make such a noise when you're eating as *she* does!' said Benjy. 'Listen to her! We've never been able to teach her table-manners – have we, Penny?'

3

An Exciting Time

It was thrilling to Mark to wake up in Rory's bedroom the next morning and hear all the farmyard sounds, though they were somewhat muffled by the snow. He heard the sound of the horses, the far-off mooing of the cows, and the clucking of the hens. The ducks quacked sadly because their pond was frozen.

'I wish I lived on a farm always,' thought Mark. He looked across to Rory's bed. The boy was awake and sat up. He looked at his watch. 'Time to get up,' he said.

'What, so early!' said Mark, in dismay. 'It's quite dark.'

'Ah, you have to be up and about early on a farm,' said Rory, leaping out of bed. 'Jim and Bill have been up ages already – and as for Davey the shepherd, I guess he's been awake for hours!'

Mark dressed with Rory and they went down to join the others, who were already at the breakfast table. Rory's father had had his breakfast and gone out. The children sat and ate and chattered.

'What would Mark like to do today?' said Sheila politely, looking at Rory. 'It's too cold for a picnic. One day we'll take him to see Tammylan, the wild man. But not today.'

'Oh, I don't want you to plan anything special for me at

all,' said Mark hastily. 'I don't want to be treated as a visitor. Just let me do things you all do. That would be much more fun for me.'

'All right,' said Rory. 'I dare say you are right. I remember when we all went from London to stay for a while at our uncle's farm, the year before last, we simply loved doing the ordinary little things – feeding the hens and things like that. You shall do just the same as we do. Sheila, you take him with you after breakfast.'

'He can help me to scrape all the perches,' said Sheila. 'And he can wash the eggs too.'

'I want to do that,' said Penny. 'Since the calves that I looked after have grown up, there isn't much for me to do.'

'Davey the shepherd will let you have another lamb soon,' said Mother. 'Then you can hand-feed it and look after it as you looked after Skippetty last year. You will soon be busy.'

'And you can come and milk a cow this afternoon, Mark,' promised Benjy. 'We'll see if you are a good milker or not.'

Mark wasn't sure he wanted to milk a cow. He thought all animals with horns looked dangerous. But he didn't like to seem a coward, so he nodded his head.

'Have you finished your breakfast?' asked Sheila. 'Have another bit of toast? You've only had four. We've all had about six.'

'No, thanks,' said Mark, whose appetite was not quite so enormous as that of the other children. 'Are you going to do the hens now, Sheila? Shall I get ready?'

'Have you brought some old things?' asked Sheila. 'Good. Well, put on an old coat and your rubber boots and a scarf. I'll go and get ready too.'

It wasn't long before both children were on their way to the hen-house, each carrying a pailful of hot mash that Harriet the cook had given them. The snow was now melting and the yard was in a fearful state of slush. The children slithered about in it.

'Oh, isn't this awful?' said Sheila. 'Snow is lovely when it's white and clean – but when it goes into slush it's simply horrid. MARK – be careful, you silly!'

At Sheila's shout, Mark looked where he was going. He had turned his head to watch Jim the farm-hand, taking a cart full of mangels out of the yard – and he walked straight into an enormous, slushy puddle near the pig-sty. He tried to leap aside, and the pail of mash caught his legs and sent him over. In a trice he was in the puddle, and the pail of mash emptied itself over his legs.

'MARK! What a mess you're in!' cried Sheila in dismay. Mark scrambled up and looked down at himself. His coat was soaked with horrid-smelling dampness, and his rubber boots were full of hot hen-mash. He was almost ready to cry!

'Don't worry,' said Sheila. 'Your coat will dry.'

'I'm not bothering about that,' said Mark. 'I'm bothering about the waste of that hot mash. Just look at it, all over the place.'

'You go in and ask Mother to lend you some old clothes of Rory's,' said Sheila comfortingly. 'I'll get a spade out of the shed and just get most of the spilt mash back into the pail. It will be dirty, but I don't expect the hens will mind very much.'

Mark disappeared into the house. Sheila shovelled up most of the spilt mash. She took it to the hen-houses and the hens came down from their houses into the slushy rain, clucking hungrily.

'I'll let you out into the farmyard to scratch about there as you usually do,' said Sheila, who had always talked to her hens as if they were children. 'Your yard is nothing but mud – but so is everywhere else. Now then, greedy – take your head out of the bucket!'

Sheila put the mash into the big bowls, and then broke the ice on the water-bowls. There had been a frost in the night, and the ice had not yet melted. She went to get a can to put in fresh water. The hens clucked round it.

'I know that your water must always be clean and fresh,' said Sheila to her hens. 'Look – there's the cock calling to you. He's found something for you!'

The cock was a beautiful bird, with an enormous, drooping tail of purple-green feathers, and a fine comb. He had a very loud voice, and always awoke all his hens in the morning when it was time to get up. Now he had found a grain of corn or some other titbit on the ground and he was telling the hens to come and eat it.

Mark arrived again, wearing an old brown coat of Rory's, and somebody else's boots. 'Look at the cock,' said Sheila. 'He's a perfect gentleman, Mark – he never eats a titbit himself – he always calls his hens to have it.'

'Cock-a-doodle-doo!' said the cock to Mark.

'He's saying "Good morning, how do you do?"' said Sheila, with a laugh. She always amused the others because whenever her hens or ducks clucked or quacked, she always made it seem as if they were really saying something. Penny honestly thought that they said the things Sheila made up, and she felt that they were really very clever.

'Come and scrape the perches for me,' said Sheila. 'The hens haven't very good manners, you know, and they make their perches in an awful mess.'

Mark had the job of scraping the perches clean. He wasn't sure that he liked it much, but he was a sensible boy and knew that there were dirty jobs to do as well as nice ones. You can't pick your jobs on a farm. You have to be ready to do everything!

Sheila looked to see if there was enough grit in the little box she kept for that purpose. She told Mark what it was for. 'It's to help the hens digest their food properly,' she told him. 'And that broken oyster-shell over there is to help them to make good shells for their eggs. Take this basket of eggs indoors into the kitchen, Mark. You can begin to wash them for me. Some of them are awfully dirty.'

Poor Mark broke one of the eggs as he washed it! It just slipped out of his fingers. He was upset about it, but Sheila said, 'Never mind! We brought in twenty-three eggs, and that's very good for a day like this.'

Mark soon began to enjoy the life on the farm very much. The days slipped by, and he was sad when Saturday came and he packed to go home. Then, quite unexpectedly, his mother telephoned to ask if he could be kept there a little longer as his grandmother was ill, and she wanted to go and look after her.

'Oh,' said Mark, in delight, 'oh, do you think I *can* stay? If I can, I promise I'll do my best to help on the farm. I'll even clean out the pig-sties!'

Everyone laughed at that, for they knew how Mark hated

the smell. 'Of course you can stay,' said Mother, who liked the quiet but rather awkward little boy. 'You are really quite useful, especially since you have learnt how to milk.'

It was a very funny thing, but Mark had been most successful at milking the cows. He had been terrified at first, and had gone quite pale when he had sat down on a milking-stool, and had watched whilst Benjy showed him how to squeeze the big teats and make the milk squirt down into the great clean pails.

He couldn't get a drop of milk at first – and then suddenly it had come, and Mark had jumped when he heard the milk go splash-splash into the pail. The boy's hands were strong, and he just seemed to have the right knack for milking. Jim the farm-hand had praised him, and Mark had felt proud.

'Milking is quite hard work,' he said to Penny. 'And what a lot you get! Isn't it creamy too? No wonder you are able to make a lot of butter.'

All the children worked during the holidays, and they disliked the slush and wet very much. Rain had come after the snow, and everywhere was squelchy, so that it was no pleasure to go round the farm and do anything. The farm-hands were splashed with mud from head to foot, and the old shire horses had to be cleaned well every day, for they too were covered with mud.

'I shall be quite glad when it's time to go to school again,' said Rory, coming in one day with his coat soaked, and his hair dripping. 'Farming really isn't much fun in this weather. I've been cleaning out our donkey-stable. Mark's been helping me. He kept holding his nose till he found the smell wasn't bad after all. Daddy says the manure will be marvellous for the kitchen-garden, where Mother grows her lettuces and things.'

'Nothing's wasted on a farm, is it?' said Mark. 'Jim told me yesterday that he takes all the woodash for that field called Long Bottom. He says it's just what the soil wants there. And Bill is piling the soot from the chimneys into sacks in that shed behind the donkeys. He says you will use that somewhere on the farm too.'

Mark was learning a great deal, and liked airing what he had learnt. He had ridden all the donkeys now, and all the horses too – though that wasn't very difficult, for the shire horses had backs like sofas! He wouldn't ride on Buttercup the cow. The children themselves were not supposed to, but actually Buttercup didn't mind at all. She was a placid old lady, and loved having children round her.

The Christmas holidays only had a day or two more to go. The children began to look out their pencil-boxes and pile together their books. All of them went to the vicarage for lessons, but later on, perhaps in the autumn, the two boys were going to boarding-school again. They hated to think of this, and never talked about it.

Mark was to go home after the first day at school. The others were sorry, for it had been fun to show him all round Willow Farm. Mark was sad too. He knew all the animals there by now, and it was such a nice friendly feeling to go out and talk to a horse or a cow, or to Rascal, the shepherd's clever dog.

'If only holidays lasted for always!' he sighed. But alas, they never do!

The New Horses

'You know, I *must* get a couple of strong horses for light work,' said the farmer, one morning at breakfast, as the children were hurrying to get off to school. Rory had gone out to get the donkeys, so he was not there. 'It's silly to use our big shire horses for light cart-work. We really could do with a couple of smaller horses.'

"Oooh, how lovely!' said Penny, who always welcomed any addition to the farm's livestock. 'Oh, Daddy, do let me go with you.'

'I shall go on Wednesday afternoon,' said her father. 'It's market-day then. You'll be at school, little Penny.'

'I shan't, I shan't!' squeaked Penny. 'It's a half-holiday this week. I shall come with you. I do love market-day. Will you use one of the new horses for the milk-round, Daddy?'

'Yes, I shall,' said her father. The children were all very interested in the sale of their milk. Some of it was cooled, and put into big churns to be sent away to the large towns – and some of it was delivered to people nearby who were willing to buy the good creamy milk of the farm.

Sometimes their father grumbled and sighed because he had so many papers to fill in about his cows and their milk. He had inspectors to examine his cow-sheds, and other men to examine and test his cows to make sure they were healthy.

'You see,' he explained to the children, 'I want my milk to be as perfect as it can be, free from any bad germs that might make people ill. Well, you can only get milk like that if you buy the right cows who come of a good stock, and are healthy and strong, and good milkers. Our cows are fine, but our cow-sheds could be made much better.'

'How could they, Daddy?' asked Benjy, in surprise. He always liked the old, rather dark cow-sheds. They smelt of cow, and it was cosy in there, milking on a winter's day, whilst the cows munched away happily.

'I'd like to take them down and put up clean, airy sheds,' said his father. 'I'd like cow-sheds where you could eat your dinner off the floor, it would be so clean! Well – maybe if I get a good price for the potatoes I've got stored, I can think about the cow-sheds. And you can help me then, Benjy and Rory! We'll think out some lovely sheds, and get books to see what kind are the best.'

'Oooh yes,' said Benjy. 'We'd have more cows then, wouldn't we, Daddy? Sixteen isn't very many, really, though it seemed a lot at first. Daddy, I wish you'd let me and Rory do the milk-round on Saturdays once or twice. It would be such fun.'

'Oh no – Jim has time enough for that,' said his father. 'But if he's ever too busy, as he may be when the spring comes again, I'll let you try. You had better go with him once or twice to see what he does.'

'Can we all go to the market with you to buy our new horses?' asked Sheila eagerly.

'Yes, if you like,' said their father. 'I shall go in the car. You can go on your donkeys. Look – there they are at the door, waiting for you.'

'Sheila! Benjy! Penny!' shouted Rory impatiently. 'Aren't you ever coming? We shall be late.'

The children tore out to their donkeys. 'Hallo, Canter!' said Sheila, giving him a lump of sugar. 'Did you sleep well?'

'Frrrrumph!' said the donkey, nuzzling against Sheila's shoulder.

'He said yes, he had an awfully good night,' said Sheila to the others.

Penny turned to her donkey too. 'Did you sleep well, darling Hee-Haw?' she asked.

'Frrrrrumph!' said her donkey too, and tried to nibble at her sleeve.

'Oh, Hee-Haw didn't have at all a good night,' said Penny solemnly, turning to the others. 'He says a mouse ran over his back all night long.'

The others laughed. 'Now don't *you* begin making up things like Sheila!' said Rory. 'Do come on, Sheila. What's the matter? Is your saddle loose?'

'A bit,' said Sheila, tightening it. 'Rory, Daddy's going to the market on Wednesday to buy two new light horses – not carthorses – and we can go with him!'

'Good!' said Rory, galloping off in front. 'I love the market. Get up, Neddy, get up – you're not as fast as you usually are, this morning!'

The children were glad when they galloped home after morning school on Wednesday. A half-holiday was always nice – but going to the market made it even nicer. They ate a hurried lunch, and then went out to get their donkeys again. Their father set off in his car and told them where to meet him.

The donkeys were ready for a run, and a run they had, for it was quite a long way to the town where the market was held. The little fat grey creatures were glad to be tethered to a post when the children arrived at the market. Rory went round them to make sure they were safely tethered, for it would not be easy to trace a lost donkey in a big crowded market.

They soon found their father, who was talking to a man about the horses he needed. He went to the part of the market where patient horses were standing ready for sale. The boys went with him and the girls went to look at some fat geese cackling near by. There were no geese at Willow Farm, and Sheila longed to have some to add to her hens and ducks.

'They only eat things like grass, you know,' said Sheila. 'They are awfully cheap to keep.'

'They're very hissy, aren't they?' said Penny, who wasn't quite sure about the big birds.

'You are a baby, Penny!' laughed Sheila. 'You always say that when you see geese. Why shouldn't they hiss and cackle? It's their way of talking.'

'What are they saying?' asked Penny, looking at the big birds.

'They're saying, 'Ss-ss-sss-it's funny Penny's frightened of us-ss-ss-sss!'' said Sheila solemnly.

Meanwhile the boys were looking at horses with their father and his farmer friend. Horses of all colours and size were paraded up and down in front of them. Benjy liked a little brown one with gentle eyes. She had good legs and he was sure she was just the right horse for the milk-round.

'She'd be good for the milk-round, Daddy,' he said. 'I'm sure she'd soon learn what houses to stop at without being told!'

'Oh, it's for a milk-round you want her, is it?' said the man.

'Among other things,' answered the farmer.

'You can't do better than have that little brown horse then,' said the man. 'She's been used to a milk-round already. She's strong and healthy, and as gentle as a lamb.'

So little Brownie was chosen, and Benjy was delighted. He mounted her at once and she put her head round and looked at him inquiringly out of her large brown eyes, as if to say, 'Hallo! I'm yours now, am I?'

The other horse chosen was an ugly fellow, but healthy and good-tempered. He was brown and white in patches, and had long legs and bony hindquarters. He moved in an ungainly manner, but it was plain that he had great strength.

'He's a good stayer,' said the man who owned him. 'He'll work till he drops. He's done more work on my farm than any other horse, and that's saying something. I wish I hadn't to let him go – but I need carthorses, not light horses.'

So Patchy was bought too, at a fair price, and the man promised to take them both back to the farm that evening. Rory paused to look at a magnificently-built horse in a near-by stall. The horse looked at him and then rolled his eyes so that the whites showed.

'Daddy, this is the finest-looking horse in the market,' said Rory. 'I wonder he isn't sold!'

'He's bad-tempered,' said his father. 'Look how he rolls his eyes at you. Keep out of the way of his hind-feet! Nobody wants a bad-tempered horse, because so often he is stupid, though he may be strong and healthy. I'd rather work a horse like Patchy, ugly though he is, than this magnificent creature.'

The children wandered round the market before they went back to their donkeys. It was such an exciting place, and so noisy at times that they had to shout to one another to make themselves heard!

Sheep baaed loudly and continuously. Cows mooed and bellowed. A great strong bull, safely roped to his stall, stamped impatiently. The children watched him from a safe distance.

'I do wish we had a bull,' said Rory. 'I'm sure a farm isn't a proper farm without a bull.'

'I'll get one in the spring,' said his father. 'He can live in the orchard. My word, look at those beautiful goats!'

In a pen by themselves were three beautiful milk-white goats. Penny immediately longed for one.

'I don't think a farm is a farm unless it has goats, too,' she announced. 'Daddy, do buy me a goat when I have a birthday.'

'I'll buy you a baby-goat, a kid, when it's your birthday,' said her father. 'Yes, I promise I will. Now, don't go quite mad, Penny – you may be sorry you've got a goat when it grows up. They can be a great nuisance.'

Penny flung her arms round her father's waist and hugged him. The thought of the kid filled her with joy for the rest of the day. She tried to think out all kinds of names for it, and the others became impatient when she recited them.

'Penny, do wait till you get the kid,' said Sheila. 'What *is* the good of thinking of a name like Blackie when the kid may be as white as snow? Don't be silly.'

When they had seen everything in the market and had looked at the big sows there and wondered if their own sow at home was as big, the children made their way back to their donkeys.

'Well, it's been a lovely afternoon,' said Penny. 'Goodness, it's cold now. Gee-up, Hee-Haw. Gallop along and bump me and get me warm!'

Whilst the children were sitting eating their high-tea, there came the noise of hooves, and a knock at the back door.

'The new horses!' squealed Penny and rushed out to see. 'I'm going to give them each a carrot to let them know they've come to a nice farm. Harriet, can I take two carrots? Oh, thank you. Here you are, Patchy; here you are, Brownie. Crunch them up. Welcome to Willow Farm!'

'Well, Missy, if that's the sort of welcome you give horses, they'll work well for you!' said the man who had brought them. Jim appeared at that moment and took the horses off to their stable. They both looked round at Penny as they went, and said, 'Hrrrrumph!'

'They told me they were *awfully* pleased to come here!' Penny told the others. 'They really did!'

5

Darling in Trouble

The two new horses settled down well. They put their noses to the muzzles of the big plough horses and seemed to talk to one another.

'I suppose that's their way of shaking hands,' said Penny, watching them. 'I do like the way animals nose one another. I wish we could do that too.'

'Our noses aren't big enough,' said Benjy. 'Besides, we'd always be catching colds from one another if we did that.'

'Animals don't,' said Penny. 'I don't think I've ever seen an animal with a cold now I come to think of it.'

'Well, I have,' said Benjy. 'I've seen dogs and cats with colds – and I've seen Rascal when he had a tummy-ache too.'

'It's a good thing horses don't get the tummy-ache,' said Penny. 'They've such big tummies, haven't they?'

Her father overheard what she said and laughed. 'Oh, horses do get ill,' he said. 'It's tiresome when they do, though – they're such big creatures, and kick about so. Thank goodness none of mine have ever been ill.'

It was a funny thing that the farmer said that, because that very night Darling, the biggest horse, was taken ill in her stable.

It was Benjy who found out that Darling was ill.

He had rubbed her down with Rory, when the three plough horses came in from the field, and had watched them eat their meal.

'Isn't Darling hungry?' he said to Rory. 'She always gobbles, but tonight she is eating twice as fast as the others. Darling, don't gobble!'

Darling twitched back a big brown ear, but went on gobbling. She really was very hungry indeed, for she had been working hard in the wet fields all day. The boys gave each horse a slap behind and a kind word and went out. They had rubbed down the two new horses too. Patchy and Brownie liked the children very much, especially little Penny, who was always talking to them and bringing them tit-bits.

As usual the family went to bed early, even the grown-ups being in bed and asleep by ten o'clock. Nobody heard the noise from the stables – except Benjy. He suddenly awoke, hearing some unusual sound.

He lay for a little while in his small bedroom, wondering what had awakened him. Then the sound came again – a sound he had never in his life heard before! He couldn't imagine what it was like.

'What *is* it?' thought the boy, sitting up in alarm. 'It's somebody – or something – groaning – but who can it be? It's such a funny deep groan.'

Then he heard another noise – the sound of hooves against wood, and he leapt out of bed.

'I must see what it is,' he thought. He put on a thick coat, took his torch, found his shoes, and slipped out down the stairs. He undid the big front door and ran into the wet yard. The noise of groans was now much more clearly heard. The boy ran to the stables and opened the door. He switched on his torch, and saw a sight that shocked him.

The great plough horse, Darling, was lying on the floor of the stable, groaning terribly, and gasping as if for breath. She moved her hooves as she groaned and these struck the wooden partition between her stall and the next. The other horses were standing quietly in their own stalls, puzzled by the sounds that came from Darling.

'Oh, Darling, whatever's the matter?' cried Benjy. The big horse took no notice of the boy, but lay with her hooves twitching curiously. Benjy sensed at once that the horse was really ill. He tore out of the stable and went to wake his father.

In two minutes the farmer was in the stable, bending over Darling. 'She's got colic,' he said.

'What's colic?' asked Benjy.

'Just what I said my horses had never had!' said the farmer, with a groan. 'Tummy-ache! And Penny was right when she said it must be dreadful for horses to have that. It is! Very dreadful.'

'Will Darling die?' asked Benjy, in a whisper. It really seemed to him as if the horse was dying under his eyes.

'She will if we don't save her,' said his father. 'Go and get Jim and Bill. Quick now. We've got to get Darling on her feet. She'll die if she lies there. We've GOT to get her up. I can't do it by myself.'

Very frightened, Benjy sped to the cottages where the two farm-hands lived. It wasn't long before they were in the stable with the farmer.

'We must get Darling on to her feet,' said the farmer. 'Come on, Jim, you get to her head. Bill, slap her on the rump – hard. Go on, hard! I'll help Jim. Come on now, old girl – up you get!'

But Darling didn't get up. Instead she began to groan and pant again, and the awful noises made poor Benjy feel quite sick. The three men heaved and hauled, and the great horse made no attempt to help them at all. She felt too ill to stand and she just wasn't *going* to stand. The men gave up after a while and stood exhausted by the horse, panting almost as loudly as the great animal.

'Go and telephone to the vet, Benjy,' said his father, wiping the perspiration off his forehead. 'Tell him Darling has colic and ask him to come as quickly as possible. Good heavens, this horse is worth a lot of money – we can't afford to lose her!'

'Oh, Daddy, who cares about the money!' cried Benjy, almost in tears. 'If she was only worth a penny, we'd have to save her because we love her!'

'Of course, silly boy,' said his father. 'Now go quickly and tell the vet to come. Jim – Bill – let's try again to get Darling up.'

'She's that heavy and obstinate,' grunted Jim. He was a tiny fellow, with immensely broad shoulders and long strong arms. He began to try and get Darling up, helped by the others. The horse seemed to realise what the men were doing this time, and herself tried to rise. She fell back again with a thud and put her great patient head to the ground, groaning deeply.

'Poor creature,' said Bill. 'She's in a bad way, sure enough.'

'I hope the vet comes quickly,' said the farmer, leaning exhausted against the stall. 'Ah – here's Benjy back again. What did the vet say, lad?'

'Oh, Daddy, he's out to a farm twenty miles the other way,' said Benjy, his eyes full of tears. 'So I rang up the other man who came here once – but he's ill in bed and can't possibly come. He said we were to keep the horse on her feet and walk her up and down, up and down till we got someone to come and give her what he called a "drench".'

'Get her on her feet!' growled Jim, looking at the poor horse lying flat down, her hooves twitching. 'That's easier said than done. Come on – we must try again. She's getting worse.'

Bill had an idea that pulling her up with ropes would be a good plan, so the three men between them tried that next – and with a terrifying groan Darling was at last got to her feet. She stood there, swaying as if she was going to fall down the next moment.

'Get her out of the stable and walk her round a bit,' gasped the farmer. 'We mustn't let her get down again. Open the door wide, Benjy.'

Benjy opened it, and the great plough horse staggered out, swaying, her head hanging down in a pathetic manner.

'Daddy, what's made her like this?' asked Benjy. 'It's awful.'

'She eats too fast,' said his father. 'It doesn't sound anything much, I know, to say she has eaten too fast – but a horse can die of the colic brought on by that. And Darling's pretty bad. Hold up there, my pretty – hold up. Jim, go the other side. She's swaying over.'

It was a terrible business to keep the great horse on her feet. Whenever it seemed as if Darling was going to fall over again, or appeared to want to lie down because she really wasn't going to stand or walk about any more, the farmer shouted loud words of command at her, and the well-trained horse tried to obey them. Jim and Bill slapped her smartly too, and the poor old horse somehow managed to keep on her feet and stagger round the farmyard, making a great noise with her feet. The sounds awoke everyone in the house, and one by one, Harriet, Frannie, Mother, and the other children came out to see whatever was the matter.

'Go back to bed,' ordered the farmer. 'You can none of you do anything. You go too, Benjy.'

'I can't, Daddy, I can't,' said Benjy. 'I love Darling so much. I can't go back to bed till I know she won't die. I can't.'

'When is that vet coming?' said Jim, who by now was getting very tired. 'You left a message for him, didn't you, Benjy?'

'Of course,' said Benjy. 'But goodness knows when he'd be back and get my message.'

'Horse'll be dead by that time!' said Bill gloomily. 'Whoa there, my lady. Oh – down she goes again!'

With a terrific thud the horse half fell and half lay down. She lay there in the mud of the yard, her hooves kicking feebly by the light of the big lantern.

'And now we've got to get her up again,' groaned the farmer. 'Benjy, is that you still there? I told you to go to bed. Go on now – you can't do anything to help, and it's only making you miserable to watch us.'

'Please, Daddy,' began Benjy. But his father cut him short angrily, for he was tired and worried.

'Do as you're told – and at once!'

Benjy fled away into the darkness, very unhappy. He went up to his bedroom, thinking of the great horse that he and Rory loved to brush and comb each day. He remembered her soft brown eyes and long eyelashes. She was the dearest horse in the world – and she might not get better if the vet didn't come quickly and cure her.

No sooner had Benjy got into bed, as cold as ice, than a thought came to him that made him sit up and shiver with excitement. Why, oh why hadn't he thought of it before? He would go and fetch Tammylan, the wild man. Tammylan knew how to handle all animals – he knew how to cure them – he knew everything about them. Tammylan, oh, Tammylan, you must come and help old Darling.

Benjy put on a coat again, and his rubber boots. He wound a scarf round his head and neck, for the night really was very cold. He took his torch and slipped down the stairs for the second time that night. Then out into the yard and away up the lane as fast as he could!

'I hope I don't lose the way in the dark,' thought the boy desperately. 'Everything looks so different when it's night-time.'

Tammylan's cave was about two miles away. Benjy ran panting up to the top of Willow Hill, and then across Christmas Common, which looked strange and puzzling in the starlight. If only Tammylan was in his cave! If only he would come! Then Darling would be saved and wouldn't die. Oh, Tammylan, do be in your cave, do be in your cave!

6

Tammylan Comes

It was difficult to find exactly where the wild man's cave was at night. It was always well hidden in the hillside, for Tammylan did not like his dwelling-place to be easily seen. He liked to live alone in peace and happiness with his friends, the wild animals and birds. Benjy flashed his torch over the dead heather and lank grass growing on the hillside, trying to find the entrance to the cave.

'There it is!' said the boy thankfully, at last, and he made his way to it, calling as he went. 'Tammylan! Oh, Tammylan! Are you there?'

There was no answer. Tammylan must be asleep. Benjy didn't dare to think he might not be there. He stumbled into the dark cave and flashed his torch around. There was the wild man's rough couch of dead bracken and heather, with a colourful, knitted blanket thrown over it. Sheila and Penny had made that for him. And there was the little carved stool that the two boys had made for him – and Tammylan's small collection of dishes and tin plates.

But no Tammylan. The couch was empty. The cave had nobody there except a small mouse who sat up and looked at Benjy with brown eyes.

'If only you could tell me where Tammylan is!' said Benjy

desperately to the mouse. 'What bad luck to find him away just this one night!'

He went out of the cave and stood in the starlight. He called loudly and despairingly.

'Tammylan! Tammy-lan! TAMMYLAN!'

He listened, but there was no answer anywhere. 'This is like a bad dream,' thought the boy. 'A dream where something horrid happens, and everything goes wrong, and you can't put it right, no matter what you do. I wonder if I *am* dreaming!'

But he wasn't. The stars twinkled down. An owl called somewhere. Sheep baaed on the hillside far away. Benjy felt very much alone and very sad.

'I must go home,' he thought. 'I can't stay here all night waiting for the wild man. I'll just give one long whistle first – the way he taught me – and then go.'

He pursed up his lips, took in a deep breath, and gave the piercing, musical whistle that Tammylan had taught him, the same whistle he used when he wanted to call Scamper, his squirrel. And oh, how wonderful – an answering whistle came back through the night – Tammylan's whistle!

Benjy almost wept for joy. He whistled again, trying to put as much urgency into it as possible, and once more the answering call came back, fluting through the starlit night.

Then Benjy had a shock. Something ran up his body and jumped to his shoulder, chattering softly. For a moment the boy stiffened in fright – and then he cried out in joy and relief. 'Scamper! Where were you? You've been missing again, and now you've come back. You heard my whistle, didn't you – but I was really whistling for Tammylan, not for you. And Tammylan's coming! He's coming!'

The squirrel chattered softly against Benjy's ear and his warmth was very comforting to the boy. He suddenly felt happy and called loudly,

'Tammylan! Is it you?'

And a voice answered from a distance. 'I'm coming, Benjy, I'm coming!' In two minutes the wild man was standing beside the boy, his arm round his shoulders, questioning him anxiously.

'What's the matter? Why have you come to me at this hour of the night?'

'Oh, Tammylan, it's poor Darling,' said Benjy, and he poured out the whole story. Tammylan listened without a word to the end.

'If the vet doesn't come till the morning Darling will certainly die,' he said. 'I'll come with you and bring her some medicine of my own making.'

'The vet said she wanted a "drench", Tammylan,' said Benjy. 'What did he mean? Did he mean a bath?'

'No – medicine to put her tummy right,' said Tammylan, and he disappeared into his cave. 'I've got what she needs – not quite what the vet would give her, perhaps – but it will set her right in no time!'

He took down a tin, whose lid was very tightly screwed on. He opened it and took down another tin. He shook some powder from one tin into the other, and then swiftly made up some concoction that smelt rather strong. 'Now come along,' he said to Benjy. 'Every minute may count. Hurry!'

They hurried. It was much easier to go with Tammylan than to go alone. It seemed hardly any time before the lights of Willow Farm showed below them, as they went over the top of Willow Hill.

'I can see the light of the big lantern in the yard,' panted Benjy. 'That means that Darling is still there. I wonder if they got her on her feet again. Oh, Tammylan – I hope we're not too late.'

'I can hear her groaning,' said Tammylan, who had ears as sharp as a hare's. They hurried down to the farm and went into the yard where the three men were still struggling to keep Darling walking about. They had managed to get her on her feet once more.

'Who's that?' called the farmer sharply, as he saw the two figures by the light of the lantern. 'Is it the vet?'

'No. It's Tammylan,' said the wild man, and he stepped up to the gasping, groaning horse. 'She's bad, isn't she? I've got something to give her. You can't wait till the vet comes. You must trust me to give her what she needs.'

Bill and Jim looked at Tammylan rather suspiciously. But the farmer knew him well and heaved a sigh of relief. 'Well, I don't know that you'll be able to do anything, Tammylan – she's pretty well exhausted now.'

The horse was so enormous that the wild man could not give her the 'drench' from where he stood on the ground. The men had to lead the horse to a nearby cart and Tammylan mounted the wagon and waited for the horse's head to be swung round to him.

Darling did not want anything more done to her – but Tammylan's voice reached her half-fainting mind. She pricked her ears feebly and turned towards the wild man. All animals heeded his voice, wild or tame. In a trice Tammylan had given her the medicine, helped by Jim, Bill and the farmer, who held on valiantly to the struggling horse. She swallowed with a great deal of noise, and jerked her head hard.

'Now keep her walking,' said Tammylan. 'Here – let me take her for a while. You must all be tired out. I'll see she doesn't lie down again.'

Harriet came out with a can of hot tea. The three tired men turned to her eagerly. Tammylan took the horse by the bridle and firmly walked her round the yard, talking to her in his low voice.

'Could I have some tea too, Daddy?' said a small voice, and Benjy came out of the shadows.

'So *you* fetched Tammylan, did you?' said his father, pouring out some tea for the small boy. 'Well, it was a good idea – a very good idea indeed. Here you are – drink this up. My word, it took three of us to keep that horse on her feet this last hour or two – and there's Tammylan handling her all by himself. He's a marvel, no doubt about that.'

Benjy sat contentedly by his father, sipping his hot tea. He listened to the men talking and felt very grown-up. To be out here in the yard, long past midnight, having tea with three men was marvellous – and he felt happy now that Tammylan was there. Tammylan could put things right – he could put – things—

Benjy's head fell forward and he was asleep. He was awakened by a laugh. Then he heard a curious sound. 'It's rather like the band tuning up before it plays,' thought the boy drowsily. 'I wonder if the band is going to play.' Then he sat up straight, wide awake. 'But there isn't a band, of course. How silly I am. Well, what's that noise then?'

He said these last words out loud and his father laughed again.

'The medicine is working inside old Darling,' he said.

'That's her innards making music,' said Jim, with a chuckle. 'She'll be all right now, so she will.'

It was simply amazing to hear the strange musical noises that came from inside the enormous horse as Tammylan walked her firmly round the yard. Darling groaned once or twice more, but not so deeply as before.

'She'll be all right now,' said the farmer. 'And this time you really *must* go to bed, Benjy. That's definite. If you don't, I'll give you some of the medicine that Tammylan's brought for Darling!'

Benjy stood up, laughing. He felt very contented and happy. Darling was safe. She wouldn't die. He had saved her by getting Tammylan. He ran across to the wild man and put his hand in his. Scamper was on Tammylan's shoulder, and leapt to Benjy with a little cry of delight.

'I'm going to bed,' he said. 'Oh, Tammylan, I'm so glad you came. Thank you ever so much.'

'I'm glad I could help,' said the wild man, still firmly walking Darling about, whilst strange noises gurgled and sang inside her. 'You go off now, Benjy – and don't you dare to get up early tomorrow morning. You can't have had any sleep tonight.'

Benjy went back to bed again. He was so tired that he didn't think of taking off his old coat and scarf, though he managed to remove his boots. He fell asleep half dressed, intending to be down bright and early for breakfast, to tell all the others what had happened in the night.

But he didn't awake in time – and nobody dreamt of waking the tired boy. Mother told Harriet to keep his breakfast hot till he awoke.

Benjy didn't wake up until ten o'clock! It was the clock downstairs striking that awoke him. He stretched himself lazily and rubbed his eyes. The early sunshine came into his room, lighting up everything, and he sat up, puzzled.

Usually it was dark, these winter mornings, when he woke up. How was it that the sun was in the room? He looked at his watch. Golly! Ten o'clock! Then, in a flood, he remembered the happenings of the night before, threw off the old coat, and was out of bed in a twink, and downstairs, in his pyjamas.

'Mother! Mother! Where are you? Is Darling all right? MOTHER! Where are you?'

And then he caught sight of something that pleased and relieved him enormously. It was Darling herself, looking rather sad and sorry, but walking quite steadily with Jim the herdsman out of the farmyard gate.

'She's all right again!' shouted Benjy, overjoyed. 'Darling! How do you feel?'

Benjy actually went out into the cold farmyard in his pyjamas and bare feet, yelling to the horse. Darling turned her big patient head.

And then an astonished voice called to him from the house. 'Benjy! What in the world do you think you are doing out there in nothing but pyjamas and bare feet! You must be mad. Come in at once! BENJY!'

It was his mother – and by the tone in her voice Benjy knew she must be obeyed at once. He was in the house in a moment, grinning all over his face. 'I couldn't help it, Mother. I just had to speak to Darling. Oh, isn't it marvellous that she's better?'

'Wonderful,' said his mother. 'Everyone is as pleased as can be. Now dress quickly and see if you can eat the enormous breakfast that Harriet is keeping hot for you.'

Benjy could – and did – and when the others came home from school, what a story he had to tell them of the night before! It was just as good as a chapter out of a book.

7

Penny is Busy Again

February was a lovely month that year, and the four children enjoyed riding to school and back on their donkeys, doing their jobs on the farm, petting all the animals, and sometimes going joyfully off to find Tammylan, their friend.

Tammylan knew every bird and creature of the countryside, so it was marvellous to be with him. He had taught all the children to move and talk quietly when they went along the lanes, through the woods and over the hills.

'If you can learn to move as quietly as the animals do, you'll see far more and make friends with them much more easily,' he told them.

Tammylan nearly always had some animal or bird living with him in his cave. Sometimes they came to him when they were hurt, and he healed them when he could. Benjy remembered a robin with a broken leg, and a hare whose hind legs were so badly damaged that he could no longer run.

The hare had never forgotten Tammylan's kindness, and came to see the wild man almost every day. Sometimes when the children were sitting with him in his cave, they would look up to see the hare sitting at the entrance, looking inquiringly inside, his large eyes wide open, and his big ears standing straight up. At a word from Tammylan he would come inside, and the children would sit as still as mice, watching him. He would go to Benjy sometimes, but not to any other of the children.

'Well, Penny,' said Tammylan one day when the little girl had come to see him with Benjy, 'how are Davey's lambs getting along? Are you helping him with them?'

'Oh, Tammylan, isn't it bad luck for me – not one of the mother-sheep has had three lambs this year,' said Penny. 'You know, Davey the shepherd *promised* I could have another lamb for my own as soon as a sheep had three, instead of one or two. He says three is too much for a mother to manage properly. But not a single sheep has had more than two lambs. I do feel upset. I haven't any pet of my own at all now – and nothing to look after.'

'You could help Sheila with her hens and ducks,' said the wild man.

'No,' said Penny. 'She has Frannie to help her. I just stand round and watch, and I don't like that. I like to *do* something!'

Penny soon had her wish granted. When the two of them went back home, they found a great disturbance going on. Something had happened!

'What is it?' shouted Benjy, as he saw Jim running up on to the hillside where the sheep were grazing. 'Has anything happened?'

'Sheep got caught in the barbed wire up yonder!' yelled back Jim. 'Sort of hanged itself, I reckon. We're trying to save it.'

Benjy and Penny ran to join the men, who were doing their best to disentangle the sheep from the twisted strands of barbed wire. It had evidently tried to jump the ditch to join its two little lambs on the far side, and had got caught in the wire. It had struggled and struggled, and had got the wire all round its neck. It was baaing piteously.

Its two little lambs stood near by, bleating in fright. Rascal was there, preventing them from jumping into the ditch. The men worked hard with wire-clippers, cutting the wire here and there to help the sheep. One strand sprang back and cut a long, deep scratch down Jim's arm. The red blood flowed at once – but Jim did not seem even to notice it.

'Oh, poor Jim!' said Penny, in distress. She never could bear to see anyone hurt. But Jim gave her a cheerful grin.

'Never felt it!' he said. 'Don't you worry!'

At last the poor sheep was free from the cruel wire that had torn her and cut her even through her thick wool, for she had struggled so much. She tried to run a few steps over the grass, but fell down. Rascal ran to her and gently nosed her towards the waiting shepherd. Her two lambs ran up to her, bleating, for they wanted her milk – but she butted them away angrily. She was too frightened and hurt to want her lambs just then.

'I reckon she won't want to feed her lambs again,' said Jim, and Davey the shepherd nodded gloomily.

'That's so,' he said. 'She'll not have any milk for them after this scare. I'll have to try and put them to another ewe.' Then he felt a warm little hand in his and turned to see Penny's bright eyes looking up at him pleadingly.

'Davey,' she said, 'Davey! Why can't *I* have them? You promised me a lamb to feed and I haven't had one. Can't I have these two? They are so miserable – listen how they bleat. They are saying, "We want Penny to look after us! We want Penny!"'

Davey laughed. He patted Penny on the head. 'Now, now, Tuppenny,' he said, 'don't get all excited till we see what the old ewe is going to do. Maybe she'll want her lambs after all. But if she doesn't – why, then, you shall have them!'

'Oh, thank you!' cried Penny, skipping about like a lamb herself. 'I'm sure I shall have them. What shall I call them? Let me see – Frisky – Frolicky – Wriggly—'

Benjy laughed just as Davey had done. 'Oh, Penny, you and your names! Come and tell Mother. We'll have to hunt out a couple of feeding-bottles if you are going to have the lambs.'

Penny went off with him happily, and Mother found two feeding-bottles, just in case they were needed in a hurry. Lambs needed many feeds when they were small, and it would not do to let the two little lambs go too long without milk.

Penny had her way. The mother-sheep would not even try to feed her little lambs again, and Davey brought them down to Penny that afternoon. Rascal ran round them when the shepherd set them down outside the kitchen door. He had carried them under his arms from the hillside, little, sad, bleating creatures, their whole world changed because their mother butted them away from her. Poor thing, she had had a terrible shock, and it would take her a week or two to get over it.

'It's a good thing Rascal found her when he did, and came to fetch me,' said Davey to Penny's mother, who had come out to see the lambs. 'She would have died if we hadn't cut her free, and we can't afford to lose a good ewe like that. Now, little Tuppenny – you'll be happy to have lambs again, won't you?'

Davey always called Penny Tuppenny, because he said a

penny was too cheap for her. The little girl was fond of the big shepherd, with his wise blue eyes and weather-beaten face. He knew so much about his sheep – but he always said that his dogs knew even more!

Harriet filled the feeding-bottles with milk and gave them to Penny. The little girl put on the teats firmly. 'They're exactly as if they were to feed a baby, not a lamb,' said Frannie, whose mother had a new baby at home, often fed by Frannie from its bottle. 'But, my word – those lambs suck the milk more quickly than a baby does!'

The lambs were terribly hungry, poor little things. Penny went to them, and offered the smaller one the first bottle. She squeezed the teat a little so that milk came into it and the smell reached the lamb's nose. It turned towards the little girl, and it was not long before it was sucking noisily! The other one came nosing round at once, and soon Penny had the joy of feeding both the tiny creatures, a bottle in each hand.

'You won't be able to feed both at once in a few days' time!' said Benjy, watching. 'They will come rushing at you then as soon as they see you, Penny – and you'll have to feed them one at a time, and keep the other lamb off as best you can!'

What Benjy said was true. The lambs soon grew to know Penny, and even if she had no feeding-bottles full of milk with her, they would come rushing up to her eagerly, almost knocking her over. They even put their front legs up against her waist almost as if they thought they were puppies!

Penny loved them. 'You are just every bit as sweet as the lamb I had last year,' she told the two little creatures. 'He was called Skippetty – and he *was* skippetty too! He skipped about all over the place. I shall call you Jumpity and Hoppitty, because you jump and hop all round me. Jumpity, you're the one with the black nose. Hoppitty, you're the one without.'

Soon the lambs followed Penny everywhere, and she was very happy. 'If only my birthday would hurry up and I could have the little kid that Daddy promised me!' she thought. 'Then I would have three dear little creatures of my very own. I wish lambs didn't grow into sheep and kids into goats. It does seem such a pity.'

Penny's birthday came at the beginning of March, and she was very excited. 'I'm going to be nine,' she told everyone. 'Then next year I shall be ten, and be in double figures. But I shall never catch up Benjy or the others.'

'Of course not,' said Mother. 'Now I wonder what I can give you for your birthday!'

When Penny's birthday came at last, she had a lovely day. Mother gave her a new mirror for her bedroom, with flowers all round it. It looked beautiful on her chest-of-drawers. Benjy gave her a pencil-box with two lambs on it that he said were exactly like Hoppitty and Jumpity. Sheila gave her a work-box made of shells, and Rory gave her a fat little walking-stick. This pleased her very much, for she had always wanted a proper stick of her own.

Harriet made her a wonderful birthday cake with nine candles on it, and pink roses all round. It had 'A happy birthday to Penny' on it, written in pink icing in Harriet's best icing-handwriting.

Tammylan came to tea and brought Penny a very curious stone. It shone a dull blue, and in the middle of it was a twisted line in yellow, almost exactly like the letter P.

415

'P for Penny,' said Tammylan solemnly. 'I found it at the back of my cave, in that little spring there that wells up. Perhaps the hare brought it for you. Anyway, it's very strange and unusual, but it *must* be meant for you, because it has P on it.'

Penny was thrilled. She felt quite certain that the stone was magic, and she slipped it into her pocket at once, keeping her hand on it till it grew warm. 'It's a magic stone,' she told everyone. 'Very magic. If I want anything very badly I shall hold it in my hand till it gets warm, and then I shall wish – and my wish might come true!'

The present that Penny liked best of all was from her father. He kept his promise to her – and brought her a little kid! It was snow-white with a black mark in the middle of its back. It bleated in a little high voice, and Penny loved it the moment she saw it.

'Oh!' she squealed in delight. 'Daddy, what a darling little kid! It can run about with my two lambs, can't it? Oh, I do love it. Thank you, Daddy, ever so much. Oh, what shall I call it?'

'Squealer,' said Rory.

'Sniffy,' said Sheila.

'Sooty,' said Benjy, with a laugh, fondling the kid's snow-white head. Penny looked at the others with scorn.

'You're all silly,' she said. 'I shall think of dozens of names much, much better than any you could think of!'

Penny did. She went round the house and farmyard saying strings of names, trying to find one that would suit the little kid. The two lambs ran beside the little white creature, butting it gently with their noses. It was funny to see them.

'Snowy, Snowball, Snowdrop, Snow-white,' chanted Penny, as she went. 'No – somehow none of these names suits you, little kid. Oh, come away from those hens! They don't like you a bit!'

A hen turned on the kid and pecked him. The little thing bleated and jumped straight on to the top of a bin. The lid was half balanced on it and slipped off. The kid disappeared inside the bin, and Penny had to rescue him from the corn inside.

'Really!' she said. 'Whatever will you do next?'

The next thing he did was to run under Blossom, one of the carthorses, and give her such a start that she reared up. The kid leapt out from under her and fell into the duck-pond.

'There's only one name for that kid of yours, Penny,' said Frannie, with a laugh. She had come out to feed the hens. 'Call him Dopey. He's quite mad, and always will be. You can tell it from his eyes. He'll be a darling – but quite, quite mad – just like the dear little dwarf Dopey in the story of Snow-white.'

'Yes – Dopey is a nice name,' said Penny. 'You shall be called Dopey, little kid. Now I've got Hoppitty, Jumpity and Dopey. I *am* lucky! I really am!'

Penny had a wonderful time with her three pets. She fed them herself, and, as Frannie had said, little Dopey was quite, quite mad. He was maddest of all when he tried to eat things he shouldn't – from muddy shoes left out in the yard, to barbed wire round the gaps in the hedges! There was just no stopping him.

'You'll get a dreadful tummy-ache, just like Darling did once,' Penny warned him. But somehow he never did!

8

The Coming of the Bull

The children's father sold his store of potatoes at top prices. They were wonderful potatoes, quite untouched by the frost, and he had had a marvellous crop. He was very pleased indeed.

'I've made quite a heap of money,' he told the children. 'Now – what would be the best thing to do with it?'

That was the nice part about their father – he always told the children what was happening, and they listened and learnt a tremendous lot about profits and prices, as well as about the animals and crops themselves. As they all meant to be farmers or farmers' wives when they grew up, they took the greatest interest in what was told them.

'Daddy – what about a bull?' said Rory at once. 'We ought to have a bull. Let's buy a good one.'

'And what about new cow-sheds?' asked Benjy. 'I like our old ones – but since you said you'd like to have new ones, Daddy, I've been reading up about them. And ours really *are* old-fashioned. It would be lovely to have proper ones. Do you know, Daddy, that in some cow-sheds the cows can actually turn on their own water-tap in their drinking bowls so as to get perfectly fresh water when they want it? And, Daddy, we must have curved mangers, so that they don't get corners full of dust like ours. And . . .'

'Half a minute, half a minute!' laughed his father. 'My word, I've only just got to mention a thing and you've got it all at your finger-ends at once. Cow-sheds cost an awful lot of money – we'd better wait a while for those – but a bull I *could* get. Yes – I think we'll go off to market and get a bull this very week!'

This was a great thrill. The children talked of nothing else but bulls, and when Mark came to spend the day with them, they talked to him about it too.

Mark was not at all thrilled. He had hardly got over his dislike of the horns on cows, and to him a bull was a creature that ran at you and tossed you whenever you came by! He secretly hoped that there would be no bull at the market to buy. He felt that he would not enjoy coming to Willow Farm nearly so much if it had a bull.

The children were going to market with their father to get the bull that very day – so Mark went with them. They all set off on their donkeys, but Mark went with the farmer in his car, feeling rather grand – though really he would have preferred the fun of riding on a donkey.

There were three bulls at the market that day. One was a youngster, big and strong, dark brown all over. The other two were older, enormous creatures that bellowed loudly enough to set all the sheep baaing, hens clucking, ducks quacking, and cows mooing. It was astonishing to hear them.

The price of the young bull was low. The children's father liked the look of him, and thought that he would live for many years as master of the herd of quiet cows. Perhaps he would be the father of many good milking-cows. Benjy was the only one of them who didn't like the bull, and he couldn't say why. Sometimes, like Tammylan, the boy sensed something and didn't know why. He just felt that the bull wasn't going to be a success.

'Well, I can't afford to pay the price of either of the other two,' said his father. 'It's a pity Tammylan isn't here. He might be able to tell me if this bull is really a good bargain. Everyone seems to think he is – so I'll risk it and buy him.'

So the bull was bought. Penny couldn't name him, for he already had a name that he knew. He was called Stamper – a good name for him because he stamped a great deal in his narrow pen, and roared to be let out.

'I should think his second name is Roarer,' said Penny, looking at him. 'Look at the ring through his nose. Mark, do you know what he wears that for?'

'So that he can be led by it, of course!' said Mark, who already knew this from Benjy. 'A bull can't do anything much if someone puts a stick through his ring – it hurts him too much if he tries to be silly and run away – or chase anyone. I say – I hope your bull doesn't chase any of *you*.'

'Of course not,' said Rory. 'It's only bulls in story-books that do that. You'll see our bull will soon settle down – and I expect Penny will try to take him lumps of sugar, just like she does Darling. I believe she would give sugar to the ducks if they'd have it!'

The bull was brought to Willow Farm that evening by the man who had reared him from a calf. He was a little man with a most enormous voice and hands as big as hams. His face was red-brown as an autumn apple, and his eyes were so blue that you simply had to look at them in astonishment.

He spoke to the bull in his enormous voice, and bade him behave himself in his new home.

'Now don't you disgrace me,' boomed the little man fiercely, and he gave the bull a smack on its big head. 'You behave yourself. No monkey-tricks! No nonsense – or I'll be after you, so I will.'

The bull backed a little away from the fierce little man, and blinked at him. The man gave the ring in the bull's nose a little pull by way of farewell.

'I hope the next I hear of you is that you are the proud father of many beautiful calves!' he said. 'Well – goodbye, Stamper. I'm right sorry to part with you!'

He was paid his price and went away, calling back to the bull as he went.

'Now see you behave yourself, Stamper – I'll be after you if you don't!'

The children thought all this was very funny indeed. Jim took the bull to the little paddock where he was to live. He led him in and shut the stout gate. The bull gave a mild roar, and stamped round a bit. Penny sat on the gate watching him.

'You come down from there, Missy,' said Jim. 'That bull feels strange tonight, in a new home. He might tip you off.'

'Oh, do come down, Penny,' begged Mark, who was still with the children. 'You'd just hate to be tossed.'

Penny didn't get down. She really didn't feel afraid of the bull, and she felt sure he liked her. But he didn't. He didn't like anything that night. He hadn't liked the strange market. He hadn't liked walking to Willow Farm. And now he didn't like that little girl on his gate.

'Wooooooorrrrrrr!' he roared suddenly and stamped

loudly. He lowered his head and looked under his eyelids at Penny. Then he made a rush for the gate, his horns lowered ready to toss.

Rory just managed to pull Penny down in time. The bull crashed into the gate and got such a shock that he stood still, glaring round him.

'Penny, you really are a little idiot!' said Rory, angry and frightened. 'Daddy will forbid us all to go near the bull if you behave in this silly, foolish way. You might have been gored by his horns.'

Penny looked a bit white. She had got so used to farm life and to all the creatures, big and little, welcoming her, that it was a shock to her to find that the bull had been about to hurt her.

'I won't be silly again, Rory,' she said quickly. 'Don't tell tales of me. I promise not to sit on the bull's gate again.'

'He looked quite mad when he rushed at you,' said Benjy. 'Really, I don't like him a bit. I hope he soon settles down and gets used to us. Some bulls get quite tame.'

Stamper did settle down after a few days. He seemed to like his paddock, and curiously enough he always welcomed Hoppitty, Jumpity and Dopey when they squeezed through a little hole and came to visit him. He would trot up to them and make a curious noise in his throat to welcome them. They would all three frisk round him madly, and he would pretend to chase them, his great powerful head lowered. But he never did them any harm at all, and Penny soon stopped being afraid that he would toss them over the gate.

The only time he ever got annoyed with the two lambs and little kid was when they came into his paddock one day when he was lying down, and Dopey actually began to nibble his tail. Dopey, of course, would eat anything he came across, but he should have thought twice before he tried to eat the tail of a bull. Stamper leapt up with a bellow and chased the three swiftly round the paddock. They squeezed out in fright and didn't go near Stamper for two days. But when they did go he had quite forgotten his annoyance and gave them a great welcome.

Everyone grew used to Stamper. Nobody bothered about his roaring. He seemed to like the cows, and was just about as good and sensible a bull as could be. He grazed peacefully in the orchard, on the watch for the two lambs and the kid, and he no longer minded if any of the children climbed up on the gate.

'He isn't the tiniest *bit* fierce,' said Penny. 'Honestly, Benjy, I believe I could teach him to nibble a carrot or a lump of sugar.'

'Well, don't you try,' said Benjy, who still did not trust Stamper, though he felt rather silly about this, and could not imagine why he did not like the bull. Usually Benjy liked every animal, and because they felt that, they trusted him and came to him. But Stamper would never come to Benjy.

'He was a good bargain,' said the farmer, when he passed Stamper's paddock. 'We did well to choose him. He's settling down fine.'

But he spoke too soon. When the warmer days came,

Stamper became very restless. He roared a great deal and galloped savagely round his paddock. The men soon began to dislike to go in there.

'He's going mad!' said Jim. 'Look at the whites of his eyes showing. He's going mad! We'll have to look out.'

9

A Nasty Accident

That springtime there came some very heavy gales. The children awoke in the mornings and saw the trees outside bending their heads in the wind, and at night they heard the howling of the gale round the old farmhouse.

At first they all liked the wind and the sound it made. 'It's a bit like the sea, really,' said Rory.

'It's exciting, I think,' said Penny. 'I like to run out in the wind and feel it pulling my hair back almost as if it had fingers!'

But after the wind had howled without stopping for three or four days, everyone became very tired of it. 'It gets inside my head,' complained Sheila.

'I shall go mad if someone doesn't keep the dairy door shut, to stop it banging,' said Mother.

'Look at my ankle,' said Rory, pulling down his stocking. 'The lid blew off the corn-bin this morning and it simply *raced* across the yard, and met me just round a corner. Look at the bruise I got!'

'Scamper's tired of the wind too,' said Benjy, putting up his hand to stroke his squirrel, who was nestling on his shoulder. 'It blew him over sideways yesterday when he went across that windswept bit of ground up by the orchard.'

The wind grew wilder that night. It seemed to grow a voice of its own. It bellowed down the big chimneys and shook and rattled every door and window in the house.

Nobody could sleep. They lay in their beds and listened to the howling of the gale. The farmer was worried. He wondered if the roof of the cow-shed was safe. He wondered if any trees would fall.

And then, in the middle of the night, there came a curious sound. It was like a very large creaking at first, mixed with a kind of sighing. Then there came an extra large creak and a long-drawn-out crash. Then silence.

Everyone sat up in bed. 'What's that?' asked Penny in fright.

'Don't know,' said Sheila. She pattered across to Rory's room. He was awake too. 'Rory, did you hear that? What was it?'

'A tree falling,' said Rory. He and Sheila went to the window and looked out into the dark, wind-blown night. But they could see nothing at all. They couldn't imagine which tree it was. It must have been a big one, that was certain.

In the morning Jim came knocking early at the farmhouse door. The farmer opened it. He was having his early morning cup of tea.

'There's a tree down, sir,' said Jim. 'It's the big elm over beyond the cow-sheds. It's caught itself in the next tree, so the sheds are safe. But I reckon we'd better do something about it soon, in case it slips and knocks in the shed roof. It's a mercy it didn't hit the sheds. It would have given the cows a nasty shock, if it had.'

The farmer hurried to see the damage. It looked a sad sight. A big elm, rotten at the roots, had not been able to stand against the gale. It had not been broken in half, but had simply been uprooted and had fallen. Instead of falling on to the cow-sheds, which were near, it had crashed into another elm, which had just saved it from breaking down the sheds with its topmost branches.

'We'd better get Bill here and he and I must get to work to lop up the old tree before it does any more damage,' said Jim. 'I can climb up into the second elm, there, and saw the topmost branches of the fallen tree out of it. Then Bill and I can tackle the rest of the tree between us. It will mean a waste of time, and we're busy enough in the fields just now – but anyway, there'll be plenty of logs this winter.'

The children all went to look at the half-fallen tree, on their way to school. They danced their donkeys round and round it, exclaiming at the sight.

'It might have smashed in the sheds!'

'It might have killed half the cows!'

'No wonder it made a noise. It's a simply enormous tree, the biggest on the farm I should think!'

The farmer came up, rubbing his cheek as he always did when he was troubled. 'If that other tree hadn't been there, things might have been serious,' he said. 'As it is, we'll lose a few days' work, have some extra trouble – but plenty of good wood for the winter fires!'

The children hurried home that day to see how Bill and Jim had got on with the fallen tree. Both men were up in the tree next to it, sawing away hard. They had already managed to saw off many of the topmost branches, and these lay on the ground. Scamper ran along them inquisitively.

The children stood and watched. The fallen tree had

broken many of the branches of the tree next to it. It seemed to Rory as if that tree had been pushed a little sideways!

He stood looking at it. Yes – it really did seem as if it was leaning over a little. He was sure it had been quite straight up before.

'Don't you think the fallen tree has pushed its neighbour over a bit?' he said to Benjy. Benjy looked too. Then he looked again.

'Rory,' he said, 'I think it's moving now, this very minute! I think it's going to fall!'

The children stared, their eyes wide. Surely it wasn't moving. But then it gave a slight creak.

Rory yelled to the men in the tree. 'Your tree's going to fall! The other one's pushing it over. Get out, quick!'

'It won't fall,' said Bill, still busy sawing. 'It would have fallen before, if it was going to.'

There came another creak. Rory jumped violently. He was very anxious. 'Bill! Jim! You *must* come down! I know your tree is going to fall, I know it is!'

Scamper took a look up at the tree and then fled away, his tail streaming out behind him. He smelt danger.

Bill stopped sawing. Another creak came, and he scratched his head. He didn't for one moment think there was any danger, but he reckoned he'd better go down and see what was worrying Rory. There might be danger for the children.

So down he swung, slipping easily from bough to bough, landing with a jump on to the ground. 'Now,' he said, with a grin, 'let's see what all the fuss is about!'

There came such a creak that it sounded almost like a groan – and before everyone's eyes the tree that Bill had just left slipped a good bit sideways. Half its roots came out of the ground. Bill gave a terrified yell.

'Jim! Come on down! The tree's going to fall. Get out of the way, children. Run! Run! Quick!'

The four children ran. Rory caught hold of Penny's hand and pulled her along fast. She almost fell over. Behind them came enormous creaks and groans as the tree heaved itself out of the ground.

'Oh, is Jim all right, is Jim all right?' cried Penny. She was very fond of Jim, who was never too busy to talk to her. 'Is he out of the tree?'

The children stopped and turned, when they were well away from the tree. It was a strange sight they saw. The fallen elm's weight had been too much for its neighbour and now the second tree was falling too. Over it went, as the children watched in terror. It fell slowly, so slowly – and caught in its big branches was poor Jim, who had had no time to save himself!

Everyone watched in fear, trying to see where Jim was. He gave a shout as the tree fell. It reached the ground with a terrific crash and then settled itself there as if it meant to go to sleep. Its neighbour lay on top of it, and their branches were tangled and mixed so that one could not be told from the other. The trees seemed enormous as they lay there on the ground. They just missed the cow-sheds, though some of the lighter branches struck the roof, doing no damage.

'Jim! Where are you, Jim?' cried Bill, and he ran at once to the tree. The children's father and mother came running up too, for they had heard the crash. Harriet came and Frannie, and even Davey the shepherd hurried down from the hillside.

There was no answering cry from Jim. There was no movement of someone scrambling out of the tree. The farmer waved the children back, as they ran up to the trees.

'You're not to come near,' he said. He was afraid that Jim might have been killed, and he did not want the children to see the poor fellow.

All the grown-ups began to scramble over the spreading, fallen branches, trying to get into the middle of the tree, where Jim had been. The farmer shouted to Sheila.

'Sheila! Better go and ring up the doctor and tell him to come at once. We'll need him when we get Jim.'

Sheila sped off, and Penny went with her, crying from fright and anxiety. It had all happened so suddenly. She could hardly believe it!

The farmer soon found Jim. He was lying in the middle of the tree, his eyes closed, and a great, bleeding bruise on his head.

'Careful now,' said the farmer, as he and the others gently lifted poor Jim out. 'Careful! He may have a leg or arm broken.'

Jim was laid on the ground, and the children's mother examined him anxiously. 'He doesn't seem to have any limbs broken,' she said. 'I think it's just his head. He must have been knocked unconscious when the tree fell. Get some water, Harriet, and I'll see how bad this bruise is.'

The doctor was in when Sheila telephoned, and as soon as he heard what the matter was he jumped into his car and came round at once. He was soon bending over Jim, feeling his body here and there.

'Will he be all right?' asked the farmer.

'There's not much wrong,' said the doctor cheerfully. 'He

got a knock on the head from the trunk or a branch. That knocked him out properly. He's got concussion, and he'll have to be kept quiet for a bit. Put him off work for a week or ten days, then he'll be as right as rain!'

Everyone was glad to know that Jim was not seriously hurt. Davey and Bill carried him back to his cottage, and his wife put him to bed. He had not opened his eyes.

'He may not come to himself for a while,' said the doctor. 'Let him be. He's a strong fellow and it won't be long before he's himself again.'

'I wish I hadn't let him go up into that tree,' said the farmer that evening. 'Elms are dangerous trees. They go rotten at the roots, and then, in a storm, they suddenly get top-heavy and fall. I might have guessed that that second elm was rotten too.'

'I shall go and see Jim every day and take him one of my books to read,' said Penny. 'It will be quite a holiday for him, won't it, Daddy?'

'Yes,' said her father. 'But unluckily this has come at one of our busiest times of year, when I need Jim out in the fields all day long. And there's the milk-round too. I can't see how I can possibly spare Bill for that. He's not good at things like that, either. He'll probably get into a frightful muddle, and charge all the bills wrong.'

'Daddy! Oh, Daddy! Can't Rory and I do the milk-round whilst Jim is ill?' cried Benjy eagerly. 'Brownie's so good, Jim says she already knows half the houses she has to stop at.'

'You can't do the milk-round,' said the farmer, half laughing. 'There's more in it than simply taking bottles of milk and standing them on door-steps! You have to keep the

431

milk-book very carefully too, and enter up everything in it.'

'Well, Rory is awfully good at that sort of thing,' said Benjy earnestly. 'He's the best at maths in our little school. I could give out the milk and drive, and Rory could do the money part.'

'I don't see why they shouldn't try,' said Mother suddenly. 'It would save you a good deal if they could do that, wouldn't it? You wouldn't need to take Bill from his field-work then. Let them try just once. If they don't do it properly, *I'll* do it!'

'No, you won't, Mother!' cried Rory. 'Benjy and I will manage beautifully. We shall have to be late for school each day, that's all.'

'All right – you can try,' said their father, with a laugh. 'Begin tomorrow. You'll have to harness Brownie into the cart, get the milk and everything. Bill can give you a hand tomorrow, and then we'll see how you get on!'

10

The Two New Milkmen

The boys were really excited about their milk-round. They felt very grown up. They fetched Jim's books and had a look at them. In the books were entered the name and address of every customer, the amount of milk they took each day, and what was paid. There were some 'standing orders' – that meant that the same amount of milk was to be left each day. Those would be easy to do.

'I know what we'll do tonight,' said Benjy. 'I'll copy out the names and addresses on a big sheet of paper, and we'll pin it in the cart, so that we don't have to keep on and on looking up the books. Jim knows everyone by heart, because he does the round so often, but we don't. We shall waste an awful lot of time if we keep having to look up the names.'

So that was done, and a big sheet was soon ready for the next day. Then Rory made out a list of the 'Standing orders' so that those could be dealt with easily in the same way. It was fun. They felt important.

'We'd better begin at this street,' said Rory, pointing to an address on the list.

'No,' said Benjy. 'We'll begin here, look. We don't want to overlap the streets at all. We want to deliver the milk and go the shortest distance to do it.'

But it wasn't any good planning *that*! Brownie had her own ideas about which was the best way to go! She took charge of the milk-round, as the boys soon found out.

They were up early the next morning. They went out to the sheds, where Bill, Harriet and Frannie were already milking the cows. It was cooled, and put into the waiting bottles, which had been cleaned and sterilised the day before.

'Well, roundsmen?' said Harriet, a twinkle in her eye. 'Ready for your work?'

'We're going straightaway, as soon as the milk's in the bottles,' said Rory.

'Not going to stop for anything?' said Frannie.

'No,' said Rory.

'Dear me, what a pity!' said Harriet. 'Jim always stopped for a cup of cocoa and a slice of cake before he set off.'

'Oh, well – we could stop for *that*,' said Rory, with a laugh. So, when the bottles were all ready, and the boys were setting them carefully in the racks in their milk-cart, Frannie was sent off to the kitchen for the cocoa and the cake. The two roundsmen ate and drank quickly, for they were anxious to be off.

'We shan't be so quick as Jim was, at first,' said Rory. 'He knew everyone to go to and we don't. But we shall soon learn. Now – let's get Brownie. You fetch her, Benjy.'

Benjy went off to get the little horse. Brownie looked at him out of her gentle eyes, rather astonished to see Benjy, instead of Jim. But, like all the horses, she loved Benjy, and whinnied softly as he took her out to the cart. He harnessed her and then rubbed her soft nose.

'Now, Brownie! *We're* the milkmen today! So off you go,

and show us the right houses to call at!'

The milk was sold to four or five villages around. Brownie set off at a canter, dragging the little milk-cart easily behind her. Benjy drove, his lean brown hands holding the leather reins loosely.

'Let's go to Tittleton first,' said Rory, looking up from the list he was studying.

'Right,' said Benjy, and when he came to the road that forked to Tittleton, he pulled on the rein to make Brownie go the right way.

Brownie took no notice at all! She just tossed her brown head, and took the other way, cantering steadily along!

'Brownie!' yelled Benjy, pulling at the rein. 'You're going the wrong way!'

The little horse stopped. She looked round inquiringly, gazed at the milk-bottles, said 'Hrrrumph' softly and set off down the road again, taking her own way!

Benjy began to laugh. He let her go the way she wanted. 'Rory, isn't she funny?' he said. 'Did you see how she stopped and looked round at the milk-bottles? Then she thought to herself, "Well, there the bottles are, as usual, so I must be right. Off I go!" And off she went!'

'Better let her go the way she wants to,' said Rory, with a grin. 'We'll see where she takes us to. She's a clever little thing.' She was! She cantered smartly into the nearest village and came to a stop outside a house called 'Green Gates.'

'Quite right, Brownie,' said Rory, laughing. 'Green Gates. Standing order, two pints of milk. Here you are, Benjy. Leave it on the door-step.'

Benjy jumped down, took the quart of milk, sped in with

it, dumped it down on the step and ran out again. Almost before he was in the cart, Brownie was cantering down the quiet street, coming to a stop before a row of little houses.

A woman came out. She was surprised to see two boys instead of Jim. 'Pint, please,' she said, 'and here's the money.'

'Are you Mrs Jones?' asked Rory, and he put a tick against the woman's name and wrote down the money she had given him. Benjy gave her the milk. Brownie took a few steps on, and stopped again, at No. 10.

'Standing order, one pint,' said Rory, and Benjy hopped out again. Whilst he was out, Brownie moved on again, missing out three houses and stopping at the fourth. It was No. 18.

'Golly, isn't Brownie clever?' said Rory, looking at the list. 'You're right, Brownie. No. 18 is the next customer!'

The little horse knew the milk-round just as well as Jim did. She knew where to stop, and Benjy felt certain that if she could speak she would tell him whether to leave a pint of milk, or two or three! She turned her head each time to watch the boys take the bottles.

'Just as if she was watching to see if we were taking the right amount!' said Rory.

Then off to the next village they went at a canter. Brownie was just as good there. Once the boys could not see where a house called 'Top Wood' was. Brownie stood outside a gate, but when the boys went through it, they could see no house.

Brownie whinnied to them as if she wanted to tell them something. They came back to the gate. Brownie suddenly left the roadway and walked up to the gate with the cart. She went through it and then went a little way up a small dark path the boys had not noticed.

'Oh. That must be the way, not the other path, I suppose,' said Benjy. And he was right. The first path, the wrong one, led to a workshop belonging to the little house, which was built among trees and hard to see. It was reached by the little path that Brownie had shown the boys.

The milk-round was easy with Brownie to help them so much. The horse really seemed to think. She seemed to know that the boys were new at the job and wanted help. It was difficult sometimes when a house had only a name, not a number, to know exactly where it was. But Brownie always knew.

'Oh dear – where's Cherry Trees?' sighed Benjy. 'It's got no number, and not even a street. It must be one of those houses standing by itself.'

'Cherry Trees, Brownie!' called Rory. And, as if she quite understood, Brownie would trot over to a house, and there on the gate would be the right name – Cherry Trees! It did make things easy.

'We shall know much better tomorrow,' said Rory, marking down the money he had been given at Cherry Trees. 'It is really rather fun, isn't it, Benjy? Now we know the history of our milk from when it leaves the cow to when it reaches the people who make it into custards and puddings!'

They were tired when the round was finished. Brownie cantered home at a smart pace, and the boys waved to their father when they met him in the road beyond the farm.

'How did you get on?' he called.

'Fine!' cried Rory. 'Brownie knows everything. *She* did the milk-round, not us! How's Jim, do you know?'

'He's much better,' said their father. 'I've been in to see him. He's come out of that faint he was in. He says he's got an awful headache, but that will pass. Nobody is to see him till tomorrow, except me. Then tomorrow you can go and tell him how you got on with the milk-round!'

The boys gave their mother the lists of money they had taken, and told her about Brownie. She gave them a good breakfast and then told them to get their donkeys and hurry off to school. 'You'll be tired at the end of the morning!' she said. 'You'll be wanting *me* to do the milk-round tomorrow.'

'We shan't!' said Benjy stoutly. Mother was right when she said they would be tired. They were. But it made no difference to their feelings about the milk-round. They were going to do it just as long as Jim was ill. And they were going to do it properly too.

So they were up early again the next morning, seeing about the milk, harnessing Brownie to the cart, and setting off in the early morning sunshine. But it rained before they got back and they were wet through. That wasn't so pleasant. The wind was cold, and the boys were chilled when they got back to their breakfast, very hungry and wet.

'Change your wet things,' said Mother. 'Yes, at once, before you have your breakfast, please. I don't want to have you in bed as well as Jim! We'd have to get Penny and Scamper to do the milk-round then.'

It was pouring with rain the next day too when the boys set off. The milk-round did not seem quite so jolly. The boys said very little as they set off in the cart.

'This is beastly, isn't it?' said Benny, pulling his collar up to

438

stop the rain falling down his neck. 'I don't feel at all excited about the milk-round today!'

'Nor do I,' said Rory honestly. 'But we've got to stick it, and stick it without grumbling, Benjy. We took it on and we've got to keep it going all right.'

'Of course!' said Benjy. 'Get on, Brownie! We'll be as quick as we can today.'

For a whole week the two boys did the milk-round between them. They soon knew almost as well as Brownie did what customers to serve and what houses to stop at. The little horse worked in very well with the boys, and enjoyed their company.

Jim got rapidly better. The great lump on his head went down, and healed beautifully. Penny kept her word and took one of her books for him to read each day. Sheila and the others laughed at her.

'Fancy taking Jim books like yours!' they said. 'He doesn't want to read books about dolls and toys and things, Penny!'

But Jim thanked Penny solemnly, and said he enjoyed the books immensely, and certainly when the children went in to see him he always had one of the books open on his bed.

'It's real kind of you to do the milk-round for me and save Bill the trouble,' Jim said to the two boys. 'It means he can get on in the fields, and there's a mighty lot to do there now!'

'Oh, we like doing it!' said Rory. 'And as a matter of fact, Brownie does most of it! We never bother to guide her to the customers – she always knows them and goes there by herself. She's wonderful!'

'Yes, she was a good bargain,' said Jim. 'I'll be glad to handle the little thing again tomorrow. I miss my milk-round!

I lie here thinking of all the things I ought to be doing, and it worries me.'

'Did you say you were going to do the round tomorrow?' asked Rory. He couldn't help feeling a little bit glad! 'Are you sure you'll be well enough?'

'Doctor says so,' said Jim. 'And I'm just spoiling to be at my work again. But I don't want to rob you of any pleasure – if you want to go on with my milk-round, you just say so, and I'll speak the word to your father. Though I reckon he wouldn't want you to be missing an hour's school each morning, as you've had to do!'

But Rory and Benjy did not ask Jim to speak to their father! They were glad to have had the chance of doing the round, and had enjoyed the change – but they were quite ready to give it up now Jim was better!

'Thanks, boys,' said their father that day. 'You've helped a lot. It hasn't been pleasant, I know, when the rain poured down on your open cart – but you've stuck it well, and I'm proud of you! I shall know who to turn to, another time!'

The boys glowed with pride. They went to give Brownie some lumps of sugar. 'You did most of it!' said Benjy, patting the big brown head. 'Thanks, Brownie! You're a very good sort!'

'Hrrrrumph!' said Brownie, and crunched up the sugar lumps in delight.

11

What Can be Done with Stamper?

Jim went to complain about the bull to the farmer. 'You should come and see him today,' he told him. 'He's just as mad as can be. There's no doing anything with him. None of us dares to go into the orchard – only those three little things of Miss Penny's go in and out still – and I'm afraid for them too.'

'Well, you'd better wire up the gap they squeeze through,' said the farmer. 'I'll go and see Stamper for myself.'

The children's father was not afraid of any animal at all. He went to the bull's paddock and had a look at him. Stamper was lying down quietly in the far corner. He did not even turn his head to look at the farmer. Wandering beside him were Hoppitty, Jumpity and Dopey, butting one another and playing touch-you-last in the funny way they had.

The farmer felt certain that Jim was exaggerating. Stamper looked as peaceful as any old cow.

'I'll go in and speak to him,' the farmer thought. 'I don't believe he'll even get up!'

So he sprang over the gate and went into the paddock – but as he approached the bull, Stamper rose slowly to his feet. He turned to face the farmer, and showed the whites of his eyes in a curious fashion. Then he gave a bellow, lowered his head, and rushed straight at the startled man. The farmer only just had time to dodge. The bull's horns ripped a little bit out of the edge of his coat. The farmer knew then that he was in grave danger. He glanced at the gate – if only he were nearer!

Jim was passing by and he caught sight of the farmer in the paddock with the roaring bull. He ran at once to the gate.

'He's mad, sir, he's mad!' he yelled. 'Yes, he's roaring mad. You come on out, sir, or he'll toss you!'

The bull saw Jim and turned to bellow at him. The farmer edged round nearer to the gate. The bull turned again at once and pounded over the grass. He would most certainly have gored the farmer and tossed him, if something had not happened.

Little Dopey, the kid, thinking that the bull was having a kind of game, ran between his legs with an excited bleat. The bull stumbled and almost fell. That one moment gave the farmer a chance to get to the gate. He was over it and safe on the other side even as the bull was tearing up to the gate, landing against it with a crash.

The farmer fell off the gate and rolled on the ground. Jim helped him up. 'He hasn't hurt you, sir, has he?' he asked anxiously. 'What did I tell you? He's mad! He's just gone right off his head. He'll be no use to us at all. Nobody will dare to tend him now.'

'Oh, look!' said the farmer, and Jim turned to look at the bull. Poor little Dopey hadn't known that the bull was in a raging temper and he had run around him once more, bleating playfully. Stamper, furiously bellowing, lowered his huge head, got the little kid on his horns and tossed him high over the hedge.

The two men saw the snow-white kid sailing through the air, bleating in the greatest surprise. He landed in a big blackberry bush, and scrambled out as best he could.

'He's not been gored,' said Jim, looking at the frightened little creature. 'He's been scared out of his wits – not that he's got many! But he's not hurt. Those little things are like cats – they always fall on their feet. I wish the lambs would come out. They'll get tossed next.'

The lambs heard Dopey's frightened bleating and decided that it was time to escape from the paddock before they were sent flying through the air too. So they squeezed out and joined Dopey, who, with many high bleats, told them exactly what he thought of bulls.

The two men stood and looked at the mad bull. Stamper was now rushing round the paddock, tossing any old bough or log that was in his way. What was to be done with him?

'Hallo, Daddy!' came a voice behind them. 'What's happened to Stamper? He's in a fine old rage, isn't he?'

The farmer turned and saw Benjy, with Tammylan beside him. The wild man was looking intently at the bull, a troubled expression on his face.

'Why, Tammylan!' cried Benjy's father, delighted to see the wild man. 'Can you do anything with our new bull? He seems to have gone completely mad.'

'You'll never do anything with him,' said Tammylan. 'He's a bad bargain.'

'Well, I'll have to get rid of him then,' said the farmer. 'Can't keep him here with all these children about. And anyway, the men wouldn't handle him. He'll be no use. But who *can* handle him? And what can I do with him?'

'Where did you buy him? Who sold him to you?' asked Tammylan. The farmer told him.

'Well, there is only one man who will be able to handle that bull and make him come to heel,' said Tammylan. 'And that's the man who brought him up from a calf. The bull will still remember him, and how he had to obey him – and maybe he'll go off with him like a lamb. You know, great fully-grown lions can be handled perfectly easily by a trainer who has had them as cubs. They remember the words of command and the smacks they had as cubs, and even when they are fully grown they still remember and have a respect for that man.'

'Well – I'd better telephone to Farley then,' said the farmer. 'That's the man who sold him to me. Maybe he can tell me who had the bull as a calf, and I could get him along here. But goodness knows if I can ever sell the bull now.'

The farmer went indoors to telephone. He was feeling rather miserable to think he had wasted so much money on a bull who was no good.

'Still, that's the way of farming,' he thought to himself, as he looked up the number he wanted to ring. 'You have to take the good with the bad!'

Mr Farley was in. He listened to the tale of the mad bull, and was sorry to hear it. 'Well, sir,' he said, 'I'm right sorry he was a bad bargain. But I'll tell you what I'll do for you. I'll take him back again – and give you half the price you paid for him. I can manage him all right and maybe he'll behave with me. He's of good stock, and I'll find some use for him.'

'Did you handle him as a calf?' asked the farmer.

'I did so!' answered Mr Farley. 'Ah, he'll remember me all right, the rascal. Many's the slap I've given him for cheeking me! My, I'll take it out of him when I come. Well – will you take half-price for him, sir?'

'I'll be glad to,' said the farmer, pleased to think that he need not lose all the money he had paid. 'Thanks, Mr Farley. When shall we see you?'

'I'll be along after tea,' said Mr Farley. 'I'll come on my bike, and maybe one of your lads can bring it back for me later. I'll walk the bull home.'

The farmer was amazed. Walk the bull home! Walk mad, roaring, furious Stamper along the road, home! Why, surely no one could do that? Wouldn't it be too dangerous to allow Mr Farley to take the bull out? He would surely be tossed high into the air.

Mr Farley arrived on his bike after tea, his blue eyes twinkling in his red-brown face. He shouted as soon as he arrived, and his enormous voice boomed round the farmyard.

'Where's that bull?'

Everyone came hurrying out to him. Penny thought he must be the bravest man in the world. She had heard how poor Dopey had been tossed over the hedge, and had made such a fuss of the little kid that he would now hardly leave her side.

'The bull's in the paddock over there,' said the farmer. Everyone went up to the paddock. Stamper was lying down but he got up and bellowed as soon as he saw the little company coming.

'You children are to stand right away,' ordered their father. 'Rory, take Penny's hand, and don't let her go.'

445

'No, don't, Rory,' said Penny, trying to pull her hand away. 'I'm nine now. Don't hold my hand.'

But Rory did. He had an idea that if Dopey or the lambs went too near the bull, Penny would go after them to rescue them – and he wasn't going to have her leave his side. So Penny had to be content to leave her small hand inside Rory's big one.

Mr Farley swung himself lightly over the gate. Stamper stared in surprise at this daring fellow. He bellowed loudly.

Mr Farley had a voice that bellowed too! He yelled at the bull. 'STAMPER! You wicked fellow! How dare you behave like this? I'm ashamed of you, right down ashamed of you! Don't you remember how I clouted you when you weren't as high as my shoulder? Now just you listen to me – and don't you roar at me, either!'

The bull had run a few steps towards Mr Farley, his head lowered as if to toss him. But at the sound of the man's voice something stirred in his memory. Yes – that was the voice of the man he had known when he was a little bull-calf. He had respected that man. He had had to do as he was told with that man. He had been slapped and smacked if he hadn't obeyed. Stamper paused, remembering.

'You be careful, sir,' called Jim, who felt perfectly certain that Mr Farley was as mad as the bull. To go into that paddock without even a pitchfork in his hands – well, well, a man was mad to do that!

Mr Farley took not the slightest notice. He actually went right up to the bull! Stamper couldn't make it out at all. He stood looking at Mr Farley, his eyes rolling.

'Yes, you roll your eyes at me!' roared Mr Farley, shaking

his fist at the enormous creature. 'That won't do you any good. I'm going to take you back home again. Ashamed of you, I am!'

The bull made as if he would butt Mr Farley. But the man did not budge. Instead, he caught the bull's horns in his enormous hands and shook hard. It was a tussle between the man and the bull, with Mr Farley doing the bellowing!

'Look at that now, look at that!' cried Jim beside himself with admiration and delight. 'I never saw such a sight before! Go it, Mr Farley, sir, go it!'

Everyone was thrilled, but Mr Farley took not the slightest notice. All his attention was on his bull. He had no fear at all, and to him the big bull was simply the obstinate little bull-calf he had trained from babyhood. And, to the bull, Mr Farley was the man who had seen to him, fed him, scolded him, fussed him – and punished him.

'Now, don't you dare to struggle with me, Stamper!' cried Mr Farley, and he gave the bull a resounding slap on his tough head. The bull hardly felt it, but it made him remember that he had feared slaps when he was small He shook his head slightly and stopped rolling his eyes.

Mr Farley slipped a stick through the ring in the bull's nose. He gave him another slap for luck, and then spoke to him firmly. 'Now we're going to walk back home. And ashamed I am to be taking you, you great unruly creature! If you so much as bellow at me I'll give you a smack you'll remember to your dying day! Do you hear me?'

The bull heard. He looked meekly at Mr Farley. The man walked him to the gate, and everyone scattered at once. Rory dragged Penny into the barn and shut the door. She was very much annoyed.

'You can look out of the window, Penny,' said Rory. So she did, and saw the amazing sight of Mr Farley and the bull walking through the farmyard together; Mr Farley holding the big bull firmly by the ring in his nose, talking to him at the top of his enormous voice.

Even when they got to the lane everyone could still hear Mr Farley. 'A great bull like you behaving like that! What do you think you're up to? Bringing you home in disgrace like this! Sure, it's right down ashamed of you I am!'

The noise of the big voice died away. The children, their father, and the farm-hands rejoined one another. They were all smiling.

'As good as a play!' said the farmer. 'Well, we were lucky to get rid of a mad bull so easily. Thank goodness, Tammylan gave me the tip to get the man who'd reared Stamper from a calf! Well – that was a bit of bad luck, choosing a bull like that. Never mind – we'll know better another time.'

Everyone was glad that Stamper was gone. Nobody missed him except Dopey and the lambs. They wandered in and out of the bull's paddock quite unhappy, seeking their lost friend.

'Dopey's very forgiving,' said Penny. 'If Stamper was still there, he'd go and play with him.'

'That's because he's stupid,' said Benjy, with a laugh, and ran off before Penny could catch him and pummel him with her small fists!

12

Rory Wants a Dog

'You know,' said Rory, one day, 'we've none of us ever had a dog of our own. Isn't that strange? To think how fond we all are of animals – and yet we've never had a dog! I know Davey's got three – but they're not really ours, though they come to the farmyard often enough.'

'Well, let's ask Daddy if we can have a dog,' said Penny eagerly. 'A nice little puppy-dog called – called – let me see – called . . .'

'Oh, Penny, let's get the dog before you find a name for it,' said Rory. So they asked their father at breakfast-time the next day. But he shook his head.

'Three dogs are enough,' he said. 'We don't need any more. Anyway, we've enough cats to make up for any amount of dogs!'

That was true. There were dozens of cats about – or so it seemed! At first Penny had been sure she knew them all, but now she felt she didn't. Kittens appeared in the stables and in the barns, and she loved them and tried to pet them. But they were wild little things, and spat and scratched. Harriet had a cat of her own who lived sedately in the kitchen. He was called Mr By-Himself, because he wouldn't mix with the stable cats.

'But, Daddy, a dog is worth a dozen cats,' said Rory. 'I'd so love a dog of my own.'

'Well, we'll see,' said Daddy. 'If I hear of a good puppy, I'll perhaps get it for you.'

But Daddy didn't seem to hear of one – and it was Benjy who produced a dog after all for Rory! He was going down the lane one day, whistling softly to himself, Scamper on his shoulder, when he thought he heard a little whine from somewhere. Benjy stopped. Scamper leapt down from his shoulder and went to hunt around in the ditch. He found something there and leapt back to Benjy's shoulder, making tiny barking noises in his ear, as if to say, 'Come and see, come and see!'

Benjy went to the ditch and parted the nettles there. Lying among them was a dog, his brown eyes looking beseechingly up at the boy.

'What's the matter?' said Benjy. 'Are you hurt?'

The dog whined. Benjy stamped down the nettles that stung his hands and legs, and tried to lift up the dog. It was a mongrel dog, rather like a rough-haired terrier.

'You've been run over!' said Benjy pityingly. 'Poor creature! I'll carry you home.'

Benjy knew that it was dangerous to touch hurt animals, for they will turn on anyone, even their owner. But animals always loved the boy, and he was never afraid of them. The dog allowed him to carry it in his arms, and he went down the lane with it, Scamper on his shoulder, peering down at the hurt animal in his bright, inquisitive way.

Benjy took the dog to Rory. 'Rory! Look at this poor hurt

dog! Wouldn't you like to have it for your own? I'm sure Daddy wouldn't say no.'

'But it must already belong to someone!' said Rory. 'Oh, Benjy – it's bleeding. I'll get a bowl of water and a rag.'

Rory bathed the dog, which allowed him to do everything, though once or twice it bared its teeth when Rory accidentally hurt it. Rory liked the dog immensely. It licked his hands, and the boy's heart warmed to it. Benjy liked the dog too, but he wanted Rory to have it. He knew how much his brother longed for a pet of his own. After all, he had Scamper.

Their mother and father were out. The two boys made the dog as comfortable as they could, and gave it water to drink. Penny, Sheila and Frannie came to look at it, and they all thought it was a darling.

'Its eyes look at you so gratefully, Rory,' said Penny. 'It keeps on and on looking at you. I'm sure it loves you.'

Rory was sure it did too. When he went to bed that night he put the hurt dog in a basket in his bedroom. His father and mother had still not come back, and he felt that he really must have the dog near him. He hoped his mother wouldn't mind.

Next day he showed the dog to his mother. 'Oh, Rory,' she said, 'it's badly hurt, poor creature. I don't think it will live! I wonder who it belongs to.'

Nobody knew who the dog belonged to. It hadn't a collar on, and the police said that no dog had been reported to them as lost. Rory looked after it all the next day which was Saturday, and tried to make it eat. But it wouldn't.

'Do you think we'd better ask Tammylan to make it

better?' said Rory at last. He could no longer bear the pain in the poor dog's eyes.

'I'll fetch him,' said Benjy. Off he sped, and came to Tammylan's cave in about half an hour. He poured out the tale of the dog, and Tammylan nodded his head and said yes, he would come with him.

But when the two of them arrived at the farmhouse, they found Rory almost in tears, big boy though he was. The dog was in his arms, breathing heavily. Its eyes were looking glazed and its paws were limp.

'It's dying,' said Rory, in a trembling voice. 'I can't bear it, Tammylan. I did everything I could. I do like it so much, and it looked at me so gratefully.'

'Don't fret so, Rory,' said Tammylan, putting a gentle hand on the dog's head. 'This dog would never be any use to itself or to others if it lived. Its back is hurt too badly. But it has had a long life and a healthy one. It is an old dog. It would have died in a year or two, anyhow. It must be happy to die in the arms of someone who loves it.'

The dog gave a heavy sigh and then stopped breathing. 'Poor thing,' said Tammylan. 'It is at rest now – no more pain. You could not wish it to live if it could no longer run or hunt, Rory. Give it a good funeral, and put up a little post of wood with its name on.'

'I don't know its name,' said Rory. 'We'll have to put "Here lies a poor dog without a name."'

Everyone was sad because the dog had died. 'I shan't ever want a dog again,' said Rory sadly. 'Not ever. It's spoilt me for having a dog. I only had that dog for a day or two, but it seemed as if I'd loved it for years.'

About a week after that Tammylan came again to the farm. 'Where's Rory?' he asked Sheila, who was busy with the hens.

'Oh, hallo, Tammylan,' said Sheila, looking out of the hen-house at the wild man. 'Rory's in the barn. He's gone all mopey this week, poor Rory – since the dog died, you know.'

Tammylan went swiftly to the barn. He peeped inside. Rory was getting seeds out of a bin. He had lost his usual cheerful expression. He was a boy who, when he felt things, felt them very deeply.

Tammylan went up to Rory. 'I've brought you a present, Rory,' he said. 'Hold out your arms.'

And into Rory's arms he put a fat, round, wriggling little puppy! Rory looked down at it in surprise. His arms tightened over the tiny creature in pleasure.

'Oh, Tammylan – but I don't want a dog now,' he said. 'I don't really. I couldn't love it. This is sweet, but I just don't want it.'

'Well – if you feel like that, of course, you don't need to have it,' said Tammylan, at once. 'But would you mind looking after it for me, just for a day or two, Rory? Then I can take it back to the man who let me have it.'

'Yes – of course I'll mind it for a day or two,' said Rory. 'What sort of dog will it grow into?'

'A collie-dog – like Rascal,' said Tammylan. 'A clever sheep-dog. He'll be a fine fellow.'

Tammylan left the puppy with Rory. Rory ran to show it to the others. Penny squeaked over it in delight, and the puppy frisked round Dopey and the lambs in a most comical way.

'Oh, where did you get it from?' cried Penny. 'Oh, Rory,

it's the darlingest puppy I ever saw. What shall we call it? Don't you think Dumpy would be a good name? It *is* such a dumpling.'

'Well – Tammylan brought it to give to me for my own,' said Rory, 'but I said I didn't want another dog – I'd just mind this one for a day or two for him. So we'd better not name it. Anyway Dumpy's a silly name for a dog that's going to grow into a collie! Fancy calling a collie *Dumpy*!'

Rory took the puppy to bed with him that night. It was supposed to sleep in a small cat-basket on the floor – but although it began the night there, it ended it curled up on Rory's toes, a warm little weight. It awoke Rory by licking him on the nose.

It was such a playful little thing. It capered about, and gambolled like a lamb. It had the most ridiculous little bark in the world. It found one of Rory's slippers under the bed and dragged it out in delight. Then it grew tired, curled itself up inside the slipper and went to sleep.

'I'll look after it for you today, if you like,' said Penny. But Rory didn't want anyone else to do that. He took the puppy with him wherever he went. Davey the shepherd saw it and he approved of it.

'That's a fine pup of yours,' he said. 'I can tell he'll be clever. He's got a look of my Rascal about him. You are lucky to have him, Rory.'

'Well,' said Rory, 'I'm not keeping him, you know. I'm just minding him for Tammylan for a day or two.'

The puppy slept on Rory's toes again that night, and once or twice when the boy awoke he stretched out his hand to the pup and patted him. A sleepy pink tongue licked him.

There was no doubt about it – the puppy was fine company.

'Rory, if you're not going to keep the puppy, couldn't *I* have him instead?' begged Penny. 'I do love him so. And he would be company for Dopey, Hoppitty and Jumpity. Do let me have him.'

'No,' said Rory, picking up the pup and fondling him. 'He wouldn't love you. He only loves me. He would follow me about all over the place, and then you wouldn't like that.'

The next day Tammylan came to fetch the puppy. He found him capering about Rory's heels as the boy groomed Darling. Rory was talking to him.

'That's right – you bite my heels off! Yes, now go and nibble Darling's great hoof! *She* won't hurt you! Oh, you monkey, you've pulled my shoe-lace undone again!'

'Hallo, Rory,' said Tammylan. 'Thanks so much for looking after the little pup for me. I hope he wasn't any bother.'

Rory looked round at Tammylan. He went rather red. 'No bother at all,' he said. 'He's – he's perfect!'

'Yes, he is,' agreed the wild man, looking down at the fat little puppy who was now careering round Tammylan's feet. 'Well – come on, little fellow! Back you go again!' He picked up the puppy. 'Want to say goodbye to him, Rory?' he asked.

'No,' said the boy, in a funny sort of voice, and went on brushing Darling, his back to Tammylan.

'Right,' said the wild man, and went out of the stable, talking to the pup, who was struggling wildly to get out of his arms and go to Rory. 'Now, now, you rascal – you'll have to forget Rory, and come with me. You must have a new little master, who will love you very much.'

Suddenly Rory threw down his brush and ran after

Tammylan. 'Tammylan! Don't take him! *I* love him. He's mine, you know he's mine. He wants *me* for his master. Give him to me!'

'Well, well, now, how you do change your mind!' said the wild man, giving the puppy back to the boy at once. 'Of course you shall have him – didn't I bring him for you? Didn't I choose the best pup out of the litter especially for you?'

Rory took the puppy and squeezed him till the little creature yelped. 'I was silly,' he said. 'I want him awfully. I feel he's just *meant* to be my dog. Oh, Tammylan, I simply couldn't bear it when you said he must forget me and have a new master. I don't want him to forget me.'

'He never will,' said Tammylan gently. 'He knows he is your dog and no one else's. You must feed him and train him and love him, and he will be your constant companion and friend till you grow to be a man, and have a farm of your own.'

'Yes,' said Rory. 'He'll be a true friend to me, I know. And I shall be a true friend to him. Oh, Tammylan – don't you think that would be a wonderful name for him – True? It would be quite good to call, True! True! True! It sounds all right, doesn't it?'

'Quite all right,' said Tammylan, smiling. 'Well – as you won't let me have the pup back, I'll go. Oh, I'll just go and see Penny and her three pets first. Has the kid been eating anything else it shouldn't?'

'Gracious, yes,' said Rory, looking very happy again now. 'I should just think so! It ate Daddy's newspaper yesterday, and we *couldn't* think where it had gone till we saw a bit sticking out of the corner of Dopey's mouth. And it ate my rubber too – my best one. I was cross about that. I just dropped it on the floor, and before I could pick it up, Dopey had eaten it. What it will be like when it's a goat I can't think. It will be a walking dust-bin!'

Tammylan went across to where Penny was playing with Dopey, Jumpity and Hoppitty. She had just fed her lambs from the bottles, and Dopey had tried his best to push them away and take the milk himself. She looked up as Tammylan came to her.

'Oh, Tammylan – have you come to fetch that darling little puppy?' she cried.

'Well – Rory won't let me take it,' said Tammylan, with a smile. Penny gave such a squeal that Dopey jumped two feet in the air with fright, and the lambs darted under a nearby cart.

'Oh, Tammylan, is Rory going to keep it? Oh, I shall think of a name for it. Rory, let's call the puppy Tubby – or Roundy – or . . .'

'He's already got a name,' said Rory. 'I've called him True.'

'Oh – I like that,' said Penny. 'Let's come and tell Mother. There she is!'

Mother was pleased about the puppy. She patted the little thing and smiled at Rory.

'Wasn't it a good thing Tammylan asked me to take care of him for a day or two!' said Rory.

Mother laughed. 'Oh – I expect he knew that if he left the pup with you for even a short while, you wouldn't be able to part with it!' she said. 'Tammylan did that on purpose!'

'*Well!*' said Rory, with a delighted chuckle. 'I'll pull old Tammylan's nose for that. Just see if I don't.'

13

A Little about Dopey and True

Everyone was pleased about the puppy-dog, True. The farmer said he would grow into a fine collie-dog, who would be useful with the sheep.

'But, Daddy, I want him for my companion, not to be with Davey all the time,' said Rory, in dismay.

'Well, my boy, you plan to have a farm of your own when you are grown up,' said his father, 'and maybe you'll keep sheep, just as I do, and will want a good sheep-dog. You could let Davey train True for you whilst he's young, and sometimes help Rascal and the others. Then you will find him of great use to you on your farm, as well as a companion.'

'Oh yes – I hadn't thought of that,' said Rory, pleased at the idea of True guarding his sheep for him one day in the future. 'Do you hear that, True? You're going to get a good training. *Two* trainings. One from me to make you into a good farm-dog and companion – and one from Davey and Rascal to make you into a good sheep-dog. Aren't you lucky?'

'Wuff!' answered True, capering round Rory's feet as if he was quite as mad as Dopey the kid. He was so small and fat that it seemed impossible he would ever grow up into a long, graceful collie-dog. Penny wished he would stay a puppy. It always seemed to her such a pity that young animals grew up in a few months. It took children years to grow up. Animals were quite different.

True was a great success. Even Harriet, who would not put up with any creatures in her kitchen except her cat, Mr By-Himself, liked True running in and out. Mr By-Himself didn't like it at all, however, and made such alarming noises when the puppy dashed into the kitchen, that True set back his ears in fright.

Dopey loved True. Rory said that Dopey had a very bad influence on the puppy. 'The pup is quite mad enough as it is without having Dopey for a friend,' he said. 'Honestly, Penny, I've never seen any creature quite so silly as Dopey.'

Dopey certainly was completely mad. When he was tired of playing with the two lambs, he would caper off by himself, making ridiculous little leaps into the air. He would go into the kitchen and eat the cushion in Harriet's chair. Then when she shooed him out he would go into the dairy and see if he could find a pan of cream to lick. He was able to leap up on to any table with the greatest ease.

Once he even went upstairs into Rory's room and ate all his homework, which Rory had put on the low window-shelf.

Rory was very angry about this and gave Dopey some hard smacks, after he had tried to rescue half a page of French verbs from the kid's mouth. The kid bleated piteously and Penny came running upstairs in fright, wondering what was the matter. She heard Rory smack Dopey and flew into a temper with him.

'Rory! You cruel boy! How *can* you hit a little creature like Dopey? Oh, I do think you're mean.'

'Look here, Penny – I spent a whole hour over my French

today,' said Rory, exasperated. 'And that kid of yours has eaten all the pages I wrote. He deserves much harder smacks than I've given him. And he'll get some too, if you don't stop him doing this kind of thing. Little wretch!'

'You're horrid,' said Penny, with tears in her eyes. 'As if he could help it! He doesn't know what he's doing. He's only a baby.'

'Penny! He'll go round eating the house down if you don't train him,' said Rory. 'Go away. You're both silly.'

Penny went downstairs, crying. Rory felt rather ashamed of himself, after a time. But he still thought Dopey should be punished. He looked round for the puppy-dog, True. But True was not there.

He went downstairs to look for him. His mother was in the dairy, wrapping up the butter with Sheila.

'Rory! Why have you made Penny cry?' said his mother. 'It's not like you to be unkind.'

'Mother, I *wasn't* unkind,' said Rory. 'It's that tiresome kid of hers. It will keep doing things it shouldn't, so I punished it. That's all. Penny should make it behave better.'

Suddenly there came a wail from the sitting-room, and Rory's mother looked up in dismay. 'Rory! That's Penny. She sounds as if she's hurt herself.'

Rory and Sheila rushed into the sitting-room at once. Penny's wails were so dreadful that both of them thought she must have burnt herself or something. The little girl was holding up her knitting. The needles were out, and all the stitches were coming loose. True, the puppy, was sitting near by, a strand of wool sticking out of his mouth.

Penny looked at him, wailing. She stamped her foot at

him. 'You horrid puppy! I don't like you any more! You've spoilt my knitting. Come here!'

Before Rory could stop her she had got hold of True and given him a hard smack. The puppy fled away, howling, his tail between his legs.

'Penny! How dare you smack True!' cried Rory.

'Well, he's spoilt my knitting. He's a bad dog, and you ought to train him better!' sobbed Penny.

Mother appeared at the door. She burst out into such hearty laughter that the three children stared at her in amazement.

'Mother! What's the joke?' asked Rory, rather indignantly. '*I* don't think it's funny that True should be smacked when he really didn't mean to do harm.'

'And *I* don't think it's funny that my knitting should all be spoilt. It was a scarf for you, Mother,' wept Penny.

'My dear, stupid darlings, I'm not laughing at either of those things,' said Mother, with a chuckle. 'I'm laughing at *you*. First Dopey spoils your homework, Rory, and you smack him and make Penny angry. Then True spoils Penny's knitting, and *she* smacks him, and makes *you* angry. You're quits, aren't you? You have both got naughty little creatures to train, and you must both make allowances for them. Stop crying, Penny. I can easily pick up your stitches for you. And Rory need not do his homework again. I'll write a note to explain things.'

Rory and Penny looked rather ashamed of themselves. 'Thank you, Mother,' said Penny, and ran out of the room with a red face.

'You're right, Mother – we deserve to be laughed at,'

said Rory. 'It's very funny. I see that now.'

'Well, what annoyed each of you was that you punished the animal belonging to the other,' said Mother. 'You felt just as I would do if I saw another woman smacking *my* children. Make an arrangement between you that if your pets do wrong, no one shall punish them but yourselves. Then things will be quite all right.'

'Mother, you're so sensible,' said Rory, and gave her a hug. 'I love True and I did hate to see Penny smacking him, though I knew I would have punished him myself if I'd discovered what he was doing. And I expect Penny felt the same when I whacked Dopey. I'll go and find Penny.'

'Mother, you're the wisest person in the world!' said Sheila, as they went back to the dairy. She looked out of the window and saw Rory running after Penny. The little girl had her kid in her arms. Rory had True in his.

'Sorry, Penny darling,' said Rory, putting his arm round his little sister and squeezing her. 'Mother says we'd better each punish our own pets, and I think she's right. So if True annoys you, tell me and *I'll* smack him. And if Dopey gets into trouble with me, I'll tell you and *you* shall punish him. See?'

'Yes, Rory,' said Penny, smiling at her big brother through her half-dried tears. 'I do love True, you know that. Do you think he'll hate me for slapping him?'

True licked Penny's nose. Dopey nibbled Rory's sleeve. Both children laughed. 'They've made it up with us,' said Penny happily. 'They don't like quarrelling with us any more than we like it!'

So after that it was an understood thing that pets should

only be punished by their owners. True soon learnt what things were considered bad and what things were good, and became a very adorable little puppy, answering eagerly to his name, or to Rory's loud whistle. He lay curled up on Rory's bed at night, and the boy loved him with all his heart. The puppy adored Rory and was always on the look-out for him when he came home from school. Harriet said she was sure he could tell the time from the big kitchen clock!

'That puppy-dog comes into the kitchen regular as clockwork at just a quarter-to-one,' she said. 'And why does he come there? Because he knows my clock is the only one in this house that's kept exactly right! He's a cunning fellow, he is!'

Benjy loved the puppy very much, but he was careful not to pet him a great deal. All animals preferred Benjy to any of the other children, and sometimes True begged to be allowed to go with Benjy when he was going for a walk. But Benjy knew that Rory wanted him all for his very own, and he would shake his head.

'No, True!' he would say. 'I'm taking Scamper. You wait till Rory can take you. Go and find him!'

Dopey the kid never learnt the difference between right and wrong, no matter how hard Penny tried to teach him. She tried scolding him, reasoning with him, slapping him. He simply did not remember a single thing he was told, and he did the maddest, most stupid things that could be imagined.

'You'll be quite mad when you're a grown-up goat, Dopey, I'm afraid,' Penny would say sadly to him. And she was right. Little Dopey grew from a silly, mad little kid into a silly, mad big goat, and though everyone loved him and laughed at him, he did get into more trouble than all the other animals on the farm put together. He just couldn't help it. His appetite was his biggest trouble. He ate everything and anything, from small nails to big posts.

'One day he'll start eating his own tail and he won't be able to stop himself till he's eaten up to his head,' said Benjy solemnly. 'Then that will be the end of poor old Dopey!'

14

Mark Makes a Lot of Trouble

Mark loved coming to Willow Farm to spend the day and all the children liked him, because, although he knew very little really about farm-life, he was so willing to learn that it was a pleasure to teach him.

He came about once a fortnight, and then he nearly stopped coming because Harriet scolded him for letting the big sow out of the pig-sty. Mark hadn't meant to. He stood on the gate and jiggled it, and it suddenly swung open. It was a nice feeling to stand on it whilst it swung back, and Mark began to swing on the gate, to and fro, to and fro.

In the middle of this, the sow, astonished at the sight of the gate opening and shutting so regularly, had the idea that it would be good fun to walk out. So she walked out, her great, fat, round body hardly able to squeeze out between the posts!

'Hie, hie! Don't do that!' shouted Mark, in a panic, and he tried to shut the gate hurriedly. But the sow took no notice of that. She just went on walking, and her great body forced the gate wide open.

It was quite impossible for Mark to make her go back, and he was really rather afraid of her. He ran round her in circles, begging her to return to her sty. She walked on with her nose in the air, taking not the slightest notice of the anxious boy.

Mark felt most uncomfortable about it. What should he do? Go and tell someone? No – he'd wait till somebody came by. After all, the sow couldn't come to any harm, just taking a walk round the farm.

The sow certainly did not come to any harm – but Harriet's washing did! The sow walked straight into the end-post of the washing-line, and broke it clean in half with her great weight. Down went the clean washing into the dirt!

Out came Harriet, and scolded the sow soundly, picking up her washing as she talked. Then she turned on Mark. 'What did you let that sow out for? You know she mustn't stir from her sty unless Jim takes her. You're a bad boy to make trouble like that, and I've a good mind to tell the farmer. You take that sow back at once.'

'She won't come,' said poor Mark.

'Ho! Won't she!' said Harriet, and picked up a stick. The sow got a thwack on her back and she turned round promptly, made for her sty and got herself inside in half a minute! Mark shut the gate tight.

'Now, don't you do a thing like that again,' scolded Harriet. Mark was very red. He hated being scolded, and did not take it in good part as the farm-children did. He almost made up his mind not to come again. But when the children asked him to join them in a picnic the next Sunday, to go and visit Tammylan, he felt he really must go. He wouldn't need to see Harriet!

So at twelve o'clock he was at the farm, ready to set off. Penny popped her head out of the window and called to him.

'We're not quite ready, Mark. Would you mind doing something for me? Would you go to the field where the horses are, and see if the lambs are there? Harriet's going to feed them for me today.'

'Right,' said Mark, and set off to the field. He knew it well. It was a pleasant field, almost a water-meadow, with streams running on three sides, where the horses loved to go and water. He opened the gate, and looked into the field.

'There they are – and Dopey too,' said Mark. He called them in the same high voice that Penny always used to call her pets. 'Come along, come along, come along!'

The three little creatures heard his voice and tore at top speed towards him. They shot out of the gate, capering and gambolling, and Dopey did his best to butt him with his hard little head.

'You rascal!' said Mark, and tried to catch Dopey. But the kid leapt away from him, his tail wriggling and jumped right over Hoppitty. They rushed off to the kitchen, where they could hear Harriet clinking a pail.

Mark followed, laughing. He didn't know that he had forgotten to shut the gate. He had always been told very solemnly and earnestly that every gate must always be shut, and the lesson with the sow should have taught him the importance of this on a farm. But Mark was not so responsible as the other children, and he didn't even think of the open gate, once he had left the field.

Nobody knew that the gate had been left open. It was Sunday, and except for the ordinary everyday work of the farm, such as milking the cows, and feeding the animals and poultry, nothing else was done. The horses had a rest too, and how they enjoyed the quietness and peace of a day in the fields!

The children set off for their picnic, chattering to one another at the tops of their voices. True went with them, and Scamper. Penny badly wanted to take Dopey, but nobody would let her.

'He'll eat all our lunch,' said Rory.

'He'd be under our feet the whole way,' said Sheila.

'He'd do something silly and mad,' said Benjy. So Dopey was left behind with the lambs, bleating in anger, and trying to eat the padlock on the gate that shut him into the orchard.

Tammylan was in his cave, waiting for them all. Mark loved the wild man. He was so kind and wise, he could tell such marvellous tales of animals and birds, he made the children laugh so much, and often he had some wild animal to show them.

Today he took them to a sun-warmed, wind-sheltered copse, where primroses were flowering by the thousand. They shone pale and beautiful in their rosettes of green, crinkled leaves, and on the tiny breeze came their faint, sweet scent.

The children sat down among the primroses and undid their lunch packets. Scamper darted up a nearby tree and leapt from branch to branch. Mark picked a primrose leaf and looked at it.

'I wonder why primrose leaves are always so crinkled,' he said.

'So that the rain may trickle down the crinkles and fall to the outside of the plant, not down into the centre, where the flower-buds are,' said Tammylan.

Mark looked with a new interest at the curious wrinkled leaves. That was the best of Tammylan. He always knew the reasons for everything, and that made the whole out-of-door world so interesting. He knew why sparrows hopped and pigeons walked. He knew why cats could draw back their claws and dogs couldn't.

'Have you any animal to show us today, Tammylan?' asked Penny. Tammylan nodded.

'You wait a moment and you'll see him,' he said. The children ate their lunch and waited. In a little while they heard a scrabbling noise in the hedge near by and saw a big prickly brown hedgehog hurrying towards them, his bright little eyes hunting for the wild man.

'Here he is,' said Tammylan, and reached out his hand to the hedgehog. The prickly creature touched it with his nose, then ran all round the wild man, as if to make sure there was every bit of him there!

'Tammylan! Do you remember once you gave me a baby hedgehog for a pet?' said Penny eagerly. 'It went away into the countryside when it grew big. Do you possibly think this could be my hedgehog grown up?'

'It might be, little Penny!' said Tammylan, with a laugh. 'Call it and see!'

'Prickles, Prickles!' called Penny, in excitement. To her intense delight the hedgehog, which had curled itself up by the wild man, uncurled itself and looked at Penny inquiringly. She felt perfectly certain that it was her old hedgehog.

'Oh, Prickles, I do hope it's really you,' said the little girl.

'Do you remember how I squirted milk into your mouth with a fountain-pen filler?'

The hedgehog curled itself up again and made no reply. After a moment it gave a tiny little snore.

'I do love the way hedgehogs snore,' said Penny. 'I do really think it's the funniest sound.'

It was fun to be with Tammylan. The rabbits always came out of their holes and sat around when Tammylan was with them. Birds came much nearer. A bog moorhen came stalking by, and said 'Krek, krek,' politely to the wild man.

'Don't they jerk their heads funnily to and fro?' said Benjy, watching the bird slip into a nearby stream and swim away, its head bobbing like clockwork. 'Oh, Tammylan, what a lot of things people miss if they don't know the countryside well!'

'Yes,' said the wild man dreamily. 'They miss the sound of the wind in the grasses – the way a cloud sails over a hill – the sight of bright brown eyes peering from a hedgerow – the call of an otter at night – the faint scent of the first wild rose . . .'

The children listened. They liked to hear the wild man talking like this. 'It isn't poetry, but it's awfully like it,' thought Benjy to himself.

It was just at this moment that Mark remembered, with a terrible shock, that he hadn't shut the gate of the horses' field! What made him think of it he couldn't imagine, but he did. The thought slid into his mind. 'I didn't shut that gate when I fetched the lambs! I know I didn't.'

He sat bolt upright, his face scarlet. Tammylan looked at him in surprise.

'What's the matter?' he asked.

'I've just remembered something perfectly awful,' said Mark, in rather a loud voice. Everyone stared at him. 'I – I didn't shut the gate of the horses' field when I went to get Dopey and the lambs,' said Mark. 'Do you suppose the horses are all right?'

'You *are* an idiot, Mark,' said Rory, sitting up too. 'How many times have you got to be told to shut gates, before you remember it? All the horses may have got out and be wandering goodness knows where!'

'Wouldn't someone see the gate was open and shut it?' said Mark hopefully.

'No. It's Sunday,' said Benjy. 'Look here – we'd better get back and see if the horses are all right. We can't have them wandering half over the country. Daddy wants them for work tomorrow.'

The picnic was broken up at once. The wild man was sorry, but he said of course the children must go back and see. 'And you had better *all* go,' he said, 'because if the horses have wandered away, you'll want everyone giving a hand in the search. Come again another day.'

The children set off home. They said no more to Mark about the open gate, and did not grumble at him – but he felt most uncomfortable because by his silly carelessness he had spoilt a lovely picnic.

Their father and mother saw them trooping down over Willow Hill, above the farm, and were most astonished.

'You've soon finished your picnic!' cried their mother. 'Why are you home so early? It isn't nearly teatime.'

'I left the gate of the horses' field open,' said Mark. 'We've come to see if the horses are still there all right. I'm most terribly sorry.'

The children ran to the big field where the horses lived. They saw Darling near by. Then Rory saw Captain and Blossom drinking from the stream. Good – the three cart-horses were safe.

But where were Patchy and Brownie, the two new horses? The children slipped into the field, and shut the gate behind them.

They looked carefully all round the big field – but there was no doubt about it, the two new horses had gone.

'The shire horses would be too sensible to wander off, even if they saw the gate was open,' said Rory. 'Oh dear – where can the other two have got to?'

They went to tell their father. He looked grave. 'I'd better get the car out and see if I can see them anywhere down the lanes,' he said. 'You children scout about a bit and see if you can find out if anyone has seen stray horses.'

Then began such a hunt. The five children separated and searched all over the farm to find the missing horses. It was a serious thing to lose horses, because, although they were certain to be found again some time or other, some days might pass before they were traced – and that meant so many hours' work on a farm left undone for lack of the horses to do it. Loss of labour was loss of money on a farm.

Mark hunted harder than anyone, for he felt guilty and was ready to search till he dropped, if only he could find the missing horses in the end. Suddenly he gave a loud shout and pointed to something on the ground. The others came up, one at a time, panting to see what he had found.

'Look – hoof-marks! That's the way they went,' said Mark excitedly, pointing away from the farm, up Willow Hill. 'We must follow these prints until we find the horses. Come on!'

15

Where Can the Horses Have Gone?

The children ran to tell their parents that they had found hoof-marks and were going to track them. 'We'll bring back Patchy and Brownie, *you'll* see!' said Benjy. 'Even if we have to follow them for miles.'

'You may quite well have to,' said the farmer. 'I can't come with you, because I've got a man coming to see me about a new bull. I'll go hunting in the car after that.'

'Penny's not to go,' said the children's mother firmly. 'I'm not going to let her rush for miles. She's too little.'

'*Mother!* I'm *not* little any more!' cried Penny indignantly. 'It isn't fair. When you want me to do anything you tell me I'm a great big girl, big enough to do what you want. And when you don't want me to do anything, you say I'm too little. Which am I, little or big?'

'Both!' said her mother, with a laugh. 'A dear little girl who does what she's told – and a great big girl who never makes a fuss about it!'

Everyone laughed – even Penny. 'Mother's too clever for you, Penny,' said Rory. 'Stay behind and look after True for me, will you, there's a dear. I can't take him with me.'

The idea of looking after True was so nice that Penny at once gave up the pleasure of going to hunt for lost horses.

She held out her arms eagerly for the fat little pup. He snuggled up to her and she took him indoors to play with.

The others set off up the hill after the hoof-marks. They could see them easily. They followed them right to the top of the hill and then down to the east.

Rory stood on the top of the hill, shaded his eyes and looked down into the next valley, and over the common that lay to the east.

'I can't see a sign of the horses,' he said. 'Not a sign.'

'Well, come on, we've got the hoof-marks to guide us,' said Benjy, and the four set off down the hill.

They followed the marks for two or three miles. It was tiring. The prints went on and on, often very difficult to see. Sometimes the children lost them for a while and then found them again after a ten minutes' hunt to the right and left.

'Bother these horses!' said Rory. 'Why couldn't they have stayed somewhere near instead of taking a ten-mile walk!'

'Surely we'll come up to them soon,' said Mark.

They went on. After another hour they came to the common – and here, alas, the hoof-marks disappeared entirely. Not a sign of them was to be seen. The children stared hopelessly over the wide expanse of common.

'It's no good hunting over the common,' said Benjy. 'We might hunt all day and night and never see the horses. We'd better go back.'

'I'm so hungry,' said Rory. 'It's long past teatime. Come on.'

The four children were disappointed, hungry, and miserable, especially Mark. He didn't say a single word all the way home. Sheila was sorry for him and walked beside him. She guessed how he was feeling.

When they got back Penny rushed out to meet them. 'Have you got the horses? Where were they?'

Rory shook his head. 'The hoof-marks led to the common, Penny – and there we had to stop and turn back – because there were no more marks to follow. We couldn't hunt the common. It's too big.'

'Poor children,' said Mother, coming out too. 'Go and wash. I've a lovely Sunday tea for you. Hurry now.'

They couldn't hurry, even for a lovely tea, hungry though they were! But they felt much better after eating slices of ham, new-boiled eggs, hot scones and butter, and one of Harriet's current cakes. True darted under the table, pulling everyone's laces undone. There was no stopping him doing that! He seemed to think that shoe-laces were tied up merely for him to pull undone.

After a while the farmer came in and sat down to a late tea too. He had been scouring the countryside in his car, looking far and wide for the horses. He had notified the police of their loss and was hoping that at any moment he might hear where they were and go and fetch them.

But nothing was heard of the horses that evening and Mark felt so dreadful that he was near to bursting into tears.

'It looks as if we'll have to let one of the carthorses do the milk-round tomorrow morning,' said the farmer. 'That's a nuisance, because I wanted him in the fields. Such a waste of time!'

'I'm very sorry, sir, for leaving the gate open,' said Mark, stammering over his words, and feeling rather frightened of the worried farmer.

'I bet you won't do it again,' said Rory.

'Leaving a gate open is a very small thing,' said the farmer, 'but unfortunately small things have a way of leading to bigger things. An open gate – wandering cattle or horses – maybe damage done by them to be paid for – loss of hours of their labour – loss of our time looking for them. It all means a pretty big bill when you add it up. But we all make mistakes, Mark – and providing we learn our lessons and don't make the same mistakes twice, we shan't do so badly. Don't worry too much about it. You can't afford to be careless on a farm. Those horses will turn up sooner or later, so cheer up!'

Mark went home, not at all cheerful. The others went to bed, tired out. Rory was asleep almost before True had settled down on his feet.

In the morning there was still no sign of the missing horses, and Darling had to be harnessed to the milk-cart for the milk-round. Jim grumbled at this because he wanted her for heavy field-work. Blossom was put to the farm-wagon to take root-crops to the field where the sheep were grazing. This was usually work that one of the light horses did. The children went off to school.

Frannie and Harriet were just as upset about the missing horses as everyone else. 'I wish I could find those horses,' Frannie said, a dozen times that morning.

And then, when she went into the yard to fetch a broom, she heard a faint sound that made her turn her head.

'That's a horse's whinny, sure as I'm standing here!' said the girl, and she listened again. She heard the noise once more, borne on the wind. It seemed to come from the next

477

farm, whose fields adjoined Willow Farm. She rushed in to Harriet.

'Aunt Harriet! I believe those horses are in Marlow's Field!' she cried. 'I heard them whinnying, and Farmer Marlow hasn't any horses in his field, has he?'

'Not that I know of,' said Harriet. 'Well – you'd better go and look, that's all. You can sweep out the kitchen when you come back.'

Frannie sped off to the next farm. She went across one of the Willow Farm fields, splashed through a stream for a short cut, and then made her way into the field belonging to Farmer Marlow. He only had a small farm, and went in for crops, not livestock.

The girl looked about the big field she had come into – and, to her enormous delight, she saw Patchy and Brownie standing at the far end! To think they had been there, all the time, within five minutes' walk, and not miles and miles away!

The girl called to them. 'Patchy! Come here! Brownie, come along. Come along!'

The horses cantered over to her. They knew her for one of the people belonging to Willow Farm. She took hold of their manes and pulled them gently.

'Bad creatures! You've had everyone worrying about you and hunting for you for hours! Now you come along with me, and don't you wander away again, even if your gate *is* left open!'

The horses came along willingly enough. They had wandered out of the open gate and had made their way slowly to Farmer Marlow's deserted field. No one had noticed them there at all. They had not had the sense to find their way back again, but had stayed there together all the night, waiting for someone to find them.

Frannie proudly marched them back to the farmhouse. To think of everyone hunting away for them – and she, Frannie, had found them! Her aunt, the cook, heard the clip-clop of the hoofs in the farmyard outside, and came out.

'Good girl!' she said. 'Well, well – I'm right glad they're back again. They look a bit ashamed of themselves, don't they? You give a call to Jim and tell him you've got them. Then come back and sweep out the kitchen.'

Frannie went off with the horses and shouted to Jim. He was amazed when he turned round and saw Frannie with the horses.

'Where did they come from?' he asked, staring.

'Oh, I got them from Farmer Marlow's field,' said Frannie, feeling quite a heroine. 'They must have been there all the time, and nobody noticed them.'

Jim took Patchy and Brownie, and soon they were at their work, happy to be back again with the others. They whinnied to the big carthorses, and seemed to be telling them all that had happened.

That morning, when he got to school, Mark asked Rory anxiously about the horses, and was very upset when he heard that they had not yet returned. All the children were gloomy, and they did not expect for one moment that Patchy and Brownie would have been found by the time they returned on their donkeys to their dinner.

But what a surprise for them! When they got near to Willow Farm, Rory gave a shout.

'I say! There's old Patchy – look! And there's Brownie –

see, in that wagon with Bill. Hie, Bill! Hie! Where did the horses turn up from after all?'

'You ask Frannie,' said Bill, with a grin. 'She's the clever one!'

So Frannie had the delight of telling and re-telling her little story to four admiring children. They crowded round her, listening. It was a great moment for the little kitchen-girl.

'Well, to think of us following those hoof-marks all those miles!' said Rory, with a groan. 'Miles and miles! What idiots we were!'

'They must have been old marks,' said Benjy. 'Now, if only Tammylan had been here, he would have told us at once that those marks had been made ages ago, and we'd have known they were no good to follow. I say – won't old Mark be pleased?'

He was! His round, red face was one beam of joy when the children told him, at afternoon school, how the horses had been found.

'They were just four or five minutes' walk away from us all the time we were at the farm, and we never knew it,' said Rory.

'I shall never be careless again,' said Mark. 'That *has* taught me a lesson.'

It certainly had. Poor Mark got into such a habit of shutting gates and doors behind him that he couldn't leave them open when he was told to! 'I think all this ought to be put into a book, to warn other children,' he said solemnly to his mother.

'Maybe one day it will,' she answered.

And so it has.

16

Willow Farm Grows Larger!

The Easter holidays came and went. The summer term began, and the children galloped their donkeys across the fields to school. It was lovely to canter over the emerald green meadows, and to see the trees putting out green fingers everywhere.

Penny liked the beech leaves best. She had discovered that each leaf inside its pointed bud was pleated just like a tiny fan, and she had been amazed and delighted.

'Who pleats them?' she asked Sheila. But Sheila didn't know.

'I suppose they just grow like that,' she said.

'Yes, but *some*body must have pleated each leaf into those tiny folds,' said Penny, puzzled. 'I shall ask Tammylan.'

Penny was very busy before and after school hours with Dopey and the lambs. She fed them and played with them and they followed her around as if they were dogs. They had all grown very fast indeed, and looked strong and healthy. Davey was delighted with the two lambs. 'My word, Tuppenny, you made a better mother to my lambs than the ewes do themselves!' he said, with a laugh.

'Davey, is that poor mother-sheep all right that got caught in the wire?' said Penny.

'Quite all right,' said Davey. 'I believe she would have had her lambs back again in a week's time – but I hadn't the heart to take them away from you!'

'I wouldn't have let you!' cried Penny. 'I just *love* Hoppitty and Jumpity. But I wish they weren't getting so big.'

'Oh, it doesn't matter your lambs growing,' said Davey, 'but it's that kid of yours I'm sorry to see getting big! He'll be the wildest goat we ever had on the farm. He came up here yesterday, and bless me if he didn't find my old hat in my hut and chew it to bits.'

'Oh, Davey – I'll give you a new one for your birthday!' cried Penny. 'Isn't Dopey bad? I just can't teach him to be any better. He nearly drives Harriet mad. He *will* jump in through the low kitchen window and chase Mr By-Himself.'

'Ho!' said Davey, with a chuckle, 'that won't do that sulky old cat any harm. I'll give Dopey a good mark for that!'

'Isn't our flock of sheep getting big?' said Penny as she looked down the hillside at the sheep and lambs grazing together. 'Willow Farm is getting larger and larger, Davey. Sheila and Frannie have heaps of young chicks and ducklings again, so we'll soon have hundreds of hens and ducks! And you know we've got lots of new piglets? They *are* so sweet!'

'Ah, the springtime brings new life everywhere,' said Davey. 'I reckon we'll soon be having little calves, too.'

'Oh! Is Daddy going to buy some?' cried Penny, skipping for joy. 'Oh, last year we had some dear little calves and I fed them out of the milk-pail. It was lovely to feel them sucking my fingers, Davey.'

Mark came to spend the day, and Penny ran to show him all the new creatures that had arrived since he had last been to the farm. He was very interested in the piglets.

'Did you buy them?' he asked. 'I do like them.'

'No, the sow bore them,' said Penny. Mark stared at her. 'We didn't buy them. They belong to the old sow.'

Mark didn't understand. Penny thought he was very silly. She wondered how to explain to him about kittens and puppies and calves and lambs and piglets.

'Listen, Mark,' she said. 'You know hens lay eggs, don't you?'

'Yes,' said Mark.

'Well, silly, cats lay kittens, and dogs lay puppies, and pigs lay piglets, and cows lay calves, and hens lay eggs with chicks in them, and ducks lay eggs with ducklings in them and turkeys lay eggs with baby turkeys in, and geese lay eggs with goslings in them, and – and – and –'

'Well, of course!' said Mark, thinking what a silly he had been. 'Of course – how lovely! Let's go and ask Jonquil the cow what she thinks her little calf will be like when it's born.'

They went to the big field where the cows were kept and looked for Jonquil. She was a red and white cow, with big soft eyes, a great favourite with the children. Cows rarely look for caresses, but Jonquil was different from most cows. If the children came near, she would turn her big head and ask for a pat or stroke on her nose.

'Wherever is Jonquil?' wondered Penny. The two children counted the cows. They had sixteen at Willow Farm – but now they could only count fifteen.

'We'd better look for her,' said Penny. 'Come on, Mark.'

They went round the big field, which had many old willow trees here and there – and behind one big hollow tree, its long branches springing high into the air, they found the red and white cow.

She was standing in the tall grass there, looking lovingly down at a little red and white heap on the grass. Penny and Mark ran up to see what it was. Then Penny gave one of her piercing squeals.

'Oh! Oʜ! It's Jonquil's calf! It's born! Oh, look at the dear, darling little thing! It's *exactly* like Jonquil. Isn't it, Mark? Oh, Jonquil, it's lovely, it's lovely!'

Jonquil gazed at the two children. She was very proud of her little long-legged calf, which had been born only a little while before. She bent her head down and licked it. The calf raised its head and looked at its mother.

'Isn't it sweet?' said Mark. 'I do think baby things are lovely. I wish you'd let me help you to feed the calf, Penny.'

'Well, you can if you come to see it,' promised Penny generously. 'I do, do hope it's a girl-calf. Daddy says the boy-calves have to be sold when they are three weeks old. But we are going to keep the girl-calves this year because they grow up into cows, which give milk and are valuable.'

'Oh,' said Mark, who felt that he was learning a great deal that afternoon. 'I say – why do you have to feed this calf, Penny? Surely its mother can give it all the milk it wants, because she's a cow!'

'Ah, but Daddy says that when a cow has a calf, she has such wonderful rich milk that it's good for children and grown-ups,' said Penny, looking very wise. 'So we take the calf from its mother after a little while, and feed it on separated milk . . .'

'Whatever's that?' asked Mark.

'It's the milk that's had the cream taken away, Mark,' said Penny, feeling quite clever as she related all this to the big boy. 'Last year I put a few drops of cod-liver oil into the milk to make up for the cream that wasn't there.'

'I do think you know a lot, Penny,' said Mark, looking admiringly at the little girl. She felt pleased. It was so tiresome always to be the youngest and smallest and to have to ask the others things she wanted to know – and here she was, telling a big boy all kinds of things he didn't seem to know at all. It was marvellous. Penny felt quite swollen with importance.

'Let's go and tell Daddy about Jonquil's calf,' said Penny. She took Mark's hand and they went to find the farmer. He was two fields away, hard at work.

'Daddy! Jonquil's got a lovely little new-born calf!' shouted Penny. The farmer looked up at once.

'Where is it?' he asked anxiously.

'Come and see,' said Penny. 'Oh, Daddy, I hope it's a girl-calf, then we can keep it. We had three last year, and they were all girl-calves. I was sorry when you sold them – but we kept them a long time, didn't we?'

The farmer went to see Jonquil's calf. It certainly was a pretty little thing.

'But it's a boy-calf!' he told Penny. 'Yes – a little bull-calf. So you must make up your mind to lose it in three or four weeks' time, Penny.'

Penny looked ready to cry. She had so badly wanted the calf to be a girl. 'Cheer up,' said her father. 'Daisy is having a calf, too – so maybe she will present you with a girl that you can feed for months! Now – what are you going to call this one? He's a fine little fellow.'

Penny cheered up when she had to think of a name. She turned to Mark. 'What shall we call him? Let's think hard.'

'Radish, because he's red,' said Mark.

'Don't be silly,' said Penny. 'Nobody ever heard of a cow called Radish.'

'Well, *I've* never heard of a cow called Jonquil before,' said Mark.

'That's because you haven't known many cows,' said Penny. 'You ought to know that most cows are called by the names of flowers.'

'Well – let's call the calf Peony, then,' said Mark. 'That's red too.'

'It's the wrong red,' said Penny, who didn't really mean to let Mark choose the name himself. 'And besides, this is a boy-calf. Peony sounds like a name for a girl-calf. Let *me* think.'

But before she could think of a good name, the other three children came running up, with Frannie behind them, to see the new calf. It was always such a thrill when any new animal arrived – especially one born on the farm itself. Jonquil stood patiently by whilst everyone admired her new-born.

'It's beautiful, Jonquil,' said Sheila, giving the tiny calf her fingers to suck. 'You ought to call your boy-calf Johnnie, after you, Jonquil!'

'Oh *yes*!' said Penny. 'That's lovely. Jonquil, your calf is christened Johnnie.'

And Johnnie he was, and Johnnie he remained even after he was sold at the market, three or four weeks later. Penny went with her father when he took him to market, and she told the buyer that the calf was called Johnnie.

'So please go on calling him that,' she said. 'He's nice. I've been feeding him out of a pail, and he's really very good.'

'I'll look after Johnnie, Missy,' said the man, with a smile.

Daisy had her calf not long afterwards, and to Penny's joy it was a girl-calf, so it was allowed to live on at the farm. 'I shall have you for months and months,' said Penny to the soft-eyed little creature, as she and Mark took turns at feeding it, dipping their fingers into the pail of milk and then letting the calf suck. 'Perhaps Daddy might even let you stay with us for always till you grow into a cow. That would be lovely.'

It was fun to be on the farm in the late spring and early summer, when the whole place was full of young new things. And how they grew! The little lambs grew big and no longer frisked quite so madly. The calves grew. The chicks turned into young hens and the ducklings into ducks. The piglets grew as fat as butter. In the hedges new young wild birds were seen, and tiny baby rabbits scampered on the hillside among the sheep.

'It's lovely to see so many things growing up,' said Sheila. 'They're all growing as fast as the corn in the fields – but it's a pity they stop being funny and get solemn and proper.'

There was one little creature that grew too – but he didn't become solemn and proper. No – Dopey remained as funny and as mad as ever. He just simply *couldn't* grow up!

17

Good Dog True

One of the animals that grew the fastest of all was Rory's puppy, True. For a few weeks he was a round ball of a pup, his short legs hardly seeming able to carry his fat little body.

'Now he's sort of got *longer*,' said Penny, looking at him one day. 'Hasn't he, Rory? He's not so fat. It's a good thing we didn't call him Dumpy.'

Everyone looked at True. He was sitting in his basket, his head on one side, his bright eyes looking at Rory. Rory's heart warmed with love towards him. He thought secretly that never since the world began could there have been such a wonderful puppy as True.

True wagged his tail as he saw the boy's eyes on him. He leapt out of the basket and ran to his master. He put his paws up on his knee.

'Yes – he *is* growing,' said Benjy. 'His nose is getting longer too – not so snubby. I believe he will be awfully like Rascal. I should think he'll be every bit as clever too.'

'Oh, much cleverer,' said Rory, at once. 'Why, he already walks to heel whenever I tell him, and do you know, yesterday I made him sit on my school satchel and guard it, whilst I walked on for a quarter of a mile!'

'And did he guard it?' asked Penny, with great interest.

'Didn't he run after you and leave it?'

'Of course not!' said Rory scornfully. 'He knows better than that! He just sat on that satchel, looking after me as I went off, and he didn't stir from it till I suddenly turned round and whistled to him!'

'How clever of him!' said Sheila.

'He was even cleverer than that,' said Rory. 'He tried to bring the satchel with him! He pulled and pulled at it with his baby teeth, and in the end everything spilt out of it, and when it was empty it was light enough for him to drag along to me. You should just have seen him, dragging it along, falling over the strap, trying to get to me. I did laugh.'

'Aren't you going to let Davey have a hand in his training soon?' asked Daddy. 'Or rather – let Rascal teach him a few things. After all, he's a sheep-dog, you know, and ought to use his fine, quick brain for good work.'

'Oh, I know, Daddy,' said Rory. 'I'm taking him up to Davey tomorrow. It's Saturday, and I can watch him having his first lesson.'

'I'll come too,' said Penny.

'Well, don't bring Dopey,' said Rory. 'I don't feel very kindly towards him at the moment. He's eaten my best handkerchief.'

'I won't bring him,' promised Penny. So the next day, when Rory yelled to Penny that he was going up the hill to find Davey, Penny hurriedly shut Dopey into a shed, and ran to join Rory and True.

Dopey was most annoyed at being shut up. He was mad and silly, but he always had brains enough to try and outwit anyone who wanted to shut him up. He scrambled up on a bin that stood beneath a window. He butted the window with his small, tough head and it opened a little way. He butted it again, bleating at it. It opened wide enough for him to jump out. With a flying leap the kid was out into the yard, startling the hens there enormously. They fled away, clucking.

Dopey ran at them, just for fun. Then he went to say a few rude words to the piglets who lived with their big sow-mother in the sty. Then he looked around for Penny.

The little girl was half-way up the hill with Rory and True. Her clear high voice came floating to Dopey's sharp ears. With bounds, leaps and jumps he was off after her, only pausing to leap at a scared rabbit that shot into its hole in fright.

'Penny! There's Dopey!' said Rory, in disgust. 'I asked you to shut him up.'

'Well, I *did*!' said Penny, in astonishment. 'I put him into the shed. How did he get out?'

Only Dopey knew, and he wasn't going to tell. He frisked round True and tried to bite his tail. Then he butted him with his head. True snapped at him playfully. He liked Dopey and the lambs.

'Catch the kid and shut him up in that little old sheep-hut there,' said Rory. But that was easier said than done! Dopey had brains enough to know that Penny meant to shut him up again, and he skipped out of her way whenever she went near him. He could be most exasperating. Penny gave it up at last.

'Oh well, I dare say it won't make any difference, him being here when True gets his first lesson,' said Rory at last. 'Come on. Hallo, Davey!'

'Good morning, young sir! Good morning, Tuppenny!'

490

said the old shepherd, his eyes wrinkling in the sun as he turned to look at them both. 'You've brought little True for his lesson, I see.'

'Yes,' said Rory proudly. 'He's as clever as can be, Davey. Where's Rascal?'

'Over there, with Nancy and Tinker,' said Davey. He whistled, and the three dogs came running up to him. The shepherd turned to Rory.

'I'll get the dogs to take the sheep down the hill, and then bring them up again,' he said. 'True must run with Rascal. Tell him.'

'True! Rascal!' called Rory. The dogs came up, True wagging his tail so fast that it could hardly be seen. 'Now listen, True. You're to keep with Rascal. See?' said Rory. 'Rascal, see that True is by your side!'

Rascal understood perfectly. He had taught Tinker and Nancy, and he knew that this young pup was to be trained too. He liked the look of him!

Davey gave a few sharp orders to the dogs. He used as few words as possible, and pointed with his stick. Each of the grown dogs knew exactly what he meant. They were, for some reason, to take the sheep down the hill, and then to bring them up again. Rascal nosed True gently to make him start off with them.

The three dogs and the puppy set off together. At first True thought it was just a run, and he enjoyed scurrying along. Then he found that the sheep were running too. Ah – that was even more fun. Were they chasing the sheep? That was really rather strange, thought True, because Rory had already taught him not to chase the hens, ducks or cats.

He made up his mind that they *were* chasing the sheep, and he ran at one, trying to snap at its hind legs. But that was quite the wrong thing to do! Rascal was beside him in a moment, pushing him away, talking to him in dog-language.

'Silly pup! You should never frighten a sheep. We are running them down the hill, that's all, not chasing them. Help to keep them together in a bunch!'

True felt ashamed of himself. His quick mind saw that the dogs were now bunching the sheep together, and taking them somewhere. He must help.

So, when he saw a sheep leaving the flock, he ran to it. He nosed it back again into the flock.

'Good dog True!' shouted Rory proudly. 'Did you see that, Davey? Did you see that, Penny? He's learning already!'

The dogs took the sheep down to the bottom of the hill. Rascal looked back at the shepherd to make quite sure that he still wanted them brought back again. Davey waved his stick. Rascal understood. He *was* to take them up again. The dog was a little puzzled, because there did not seem much sense to him in this order, but he was used to obeying.

True was running with him now, trying to do all that Rascal was doing. He ran round the flock to keep them together.

'He's learning to bunch them already!' said Rory.

It was more difficult to get the sheep back up the hill again than it had been to run them down. They did not want to go. They wanted to stay there and graze. The three grown dogs did their best to send them up the hill, but it took time. True grew tired of this new game. He ran off by himself and put his nose in a rabbit hole.

'Hie, True! Hie, hie!' yelled Rory. 'Back to your work again at once.'

'Rascal! Fetch True!' ordered Davey. The amazingly wise sheep-dog understood. He ran off at once to the puppy and pushed him smartly back to work again. True was not too pleased, for he felt sure he could go down a hole and get a rabbit just then. But he ran round the sheep once more and they began to move slowly back up the hill, trying to stop and nibble the grass every now and again, but driven steadily onwards by the three dogs and the puppy.

Then Dopey chose that moment to try and behave like a sheep-dog too. He began to run round the sheep and to butt them with his hard little head. But the sheep were not standing any nonsense of that sort from a kid! They didn't mind obeying the dogs, whom they sensed to be their guardians and friends – but to be told what to do by a silly little kid! No – that was too much!

With one accord all the nearby sheep turned on Dopey and ran at him. He found himself enclosed in the flock, and could not get out! He was squeezed by the fat woolly bodies of the sheep. He was lost. He bleated pitifully.

Rory and Davey laughed till the tears came into their eyes. 'It serves him right,' said Rory.

'Oh, poor little Dopey!' said Penny, half laughing too. 'Let me go and rescue him.'

'No, you stay where you are,' said Rory. 'It will do Dopey good to be squashed by the sheep. He thinks far too much of himself! Look – there he is!'

Dopey had managed to get free from the sheep when the dogs moved them on again, and he came leaping out from the flock, looking really scared. He sprang right over True and Rascal and leapt up the hill to Penny faster than he had ever moved before!

'Little silly!' said Penny, picking him up. He was still small enough to be carried, though he wouldn't be much longer. 'Did you think you were a sheep-dog, then?'

The sheep were brought right back to the shepherd and he told the dogs to lie down. They lay down, panting, their watchful eyes turning to their flock every now and again. True lay down with them too, feeling most important.

'He's done some work for the first time in his life, and he's feeling good,' said Davey. 'Well done, little True. We'll make a fine sheep-dog of you yet, so we will. You'll be as good as my Rascal.'

'He'll be better,' said Rory.

Davey laughed. 'Maybe,' he said. 'We'll see. I'd trust Rascal to look after my sheep for me if I had to go away for a week! He can count them more quickly than I can, because if one is missing he knows it sooner than I do, and is off to find it. What I'd do without my dogs I don't know.'

'And I don't know what I'd do without True now,' said Rory, picking up the puppy and fondling his ears. 'Come on, True – back home we go! You shall have an extra good feed as a reward for working hard at your first real lesson!'

So back they went and True certainly did have a good meal. Dopey came to share it with him. The little kid thought he had worked as hard as the puppy, and he didn't see why he shouldn't have a reward too!

18

The Coming of the Bees

'Mother, don't you want to keep bees?' asked Sheila, one day, as she helped herself to some golden honey out of the pot. 'You said you were going to.'

'So I did,' said Mother. 'Well – I'll talk to the bee-man about them today. I've got to go into the village and I'll really see if we can't get a hive or two and keep bees.'

'Oooh!' said Penny. 'Lovely! I shall like bees. I think they are such happy things.'

'Why happy?' asked Rory in surprise.

'Well, I hum when I'm happy, and bees are always humming, so they must always be very happy,' said Penny. Everyone laughed. Penny did have such funny ideas.

Mother went down to the village to talk to the bee-man. When the children came back from school that day she told them that she had arranged for two hives of bees. Everyone was thrilled.

'Will there be enough nectar in the flowers we've got to keep two hives going?' asked Rory. 'We haven't really got a great many flowers in our garden, have we, Mother? The farm-garden mostly grows salads and things like sage and thyme that Harriet uses for seasoning things.'

'Oh, bees love thyme,' said Mother. 'But we have plenty

of other nearby flowers growing by the thousand – by the million – that bees love, and can make honey from.'

'What flowers?' asked Penny in surprise.

'Well – what about Daddy's clover-field?' said Mother. 'Haven't you walked by that and seen and heard the bees humming there by the hundred? Clover is full of nectar for them. You know that, Penny darling, because I have often seen you pull a clover flower head, and pick out the little white or pink tubes from the head and suck them to taste the sweet nectar inside!'

'Yes, I have,' said Penny, remembering. 'It tastes as sweet as this honey!'

'And then there is the heather on the nearby common,' said Mother. 'When that is in flower, the bees swarm there in their thousands! Heather honey is most delicious. Oh, our bees will be able to fill the combs in their hives with any amount of sweet honey for us!'

'Do they have brushes as well as combs?' asked Penny. Everyone roared with laughter.

'Idiot!' said Rory. 'Mother, you wouldn't possibly think Penny was nine, would you?'

'Don't tease her,' said Mother, looking at the red-faced girl. 'Yes – they do have brushes, funnily enough! You know, they collect pollen from the flowers too, and put it into tiny pockets in their legs. Well, they have brushes on their legs to brush the powder! So they *do* have brushes and combs! But the combs are for holding the honey. I'll show you some empty ones when the hives come.'

One evening the bee-man came. The two white-painted hives had already arrived, and were set up in Mother's own piece of garden, just behind the farmhouse. The children were on the look-out for the bee-man. He was a funny little fellow, with a wrinkled face like an old, old apple, and eyes as black as ripe pear-pips. He had a funny high voice that squeaked.

'Good evening to you, Mam,' he said to Mother. 'Now, where are the hives? Ah, we'll have to move them from there, so we will. I'll tell you where to put them.'

'Does it matter where we have them?' asked Mother. 'I rather thought I'd like to have them there on the lawn so that I could see them from my window.'

'We'll put them over the other side,' said the bee-man. 'You can still see them from the window then. You see, Mam, there's a gap in the hedge just behind where you've put the hives, and the wind will blow cold on them when it's in that quarter. Ah, bees don't like a draught. Never did. Over there will be splendid.'

So the hives were moved. Then the bee-man dressed himself up in a most peculiar way. He put on a funny broad-brimmed hat, and then put on some puffed white sleeves. Then he pulled a black veil out of his bag, and put that over his head and tucked it in at his waist.

'What's all that for?' asked Rory. 'Are you afraid of getting stung?'

'No,' said the bee-man. 'But I want to be sure that no bee gets up my sleeve, or down my neck, because if one does, it will get squashed and will sting me – not that I mind that overmuch but I don't want to kill any of these bees. A bee will always sting if it's squeezed or squashed!'

Penny was not quite sure if she liked having so many bees

close to her. The bee-man had brought them with him, and was going to put them into the hives. Clouds of them flew about, and the children began to move away.

One buzzed round Penny's head and she gave a squeal. Then she turned and ran.

'Now what's the use of running from bees?' said the bee-man scornfully. 'Don't you know they can out-fly even the fastest train! You stand your ground, Missy. They won't sting you if you don't interfere with them.'

'You've got some on your belt,' said Sheila.

The bee-man flicked them away as if they were bits of dust. He didn't mind them at all. Some crawled over his hands and he shook them off.

'Did they sting you?' asked Rory.

'Not they!' said the bee-man. 'Look – you've a couple of bees on your arm, my boy. You flick them away as I do!'

So Rory did and the bees flew off into the air.

Mother showed Penny the comb full of holes in which the bees would store their honey. 'They will seal each hole up when it is full,' she said. 'You shall have honey-in-the-comb to eat later on in the season. You will like that.'

The bees soon settled into the hives. It was fun to see them each day, sailing up into the air, getting their bearings as it were, and then flying straight off to the clover-fields. There was such a coming and going all day long!

'It must be hot in the hives today,' said Sheila, one very hot morning. 'Mother has put an electric fan into the dairy to make it even cooler. I guess the bees wish they could have an electric fan in their hives too.'

'They cool their hives quite well themselves,' said Daddy.

'If you could look inside the hive you would see that many of the bees have been given the job of standing still and whirring their wings to make a cool draught. They are the electric fans of the hive!'

'Well – that's marvellous!' said Penny, only half believing this. But Daddy spoke the truth, and the inside of the hives was kept cool in this way by the bees themselves on very hot days.

Harriet liked the bees. She could hear their humming from the kitchen window, and it was very pleasant. Penny liked sitting on the low kitchen window-sill, listening to the bees outside, whilst she ate a scone hot out of the oven.

'Harriet, did you know that we've got another calf born today?' she said, as she ate. 'It belongs to Pimpernel.'

'There now!' exclaimed Harriet, pleased. 'We shall have some wonderful rich milk from Pimpernel, and be able to make the finest butter you ever saw. Be sure you tell the bees about it, Penny dear.'

'Tell the bees?' said Penny in great astonishment. 'Why should I tell the bees?'

'Oh, don't you know you should tell the bees whenever anything happens in a household?' said Harriet, who was full of country customs. 'You should always tell them when there is a death in the household, or any change – and they like to hear of such happenings as a new calf being born. It brings good luck to the household if you tell the bees the news. You go and tell them, Penny.'

Penny went first to tell her mother what Harriet had said. Mother laughed. 'Oh, I don't expect the bees mind whether they know our news or not,' she said. 'It's a very old custom that country people follow, Penny dear. You needn't bother.'

'But I'm a country person, and I like to do things like that,' said Penny. She felt certain that if she was a bee hard at work all day, she would simply love to hear any bits of news there were. 'I shall tell the bees everything, Mother!'

So Penny went solemnly out to tell the bees about Pimpernel's calf. 'Bees, I have to tell you something,' she announced. 'Pimpernel's calf is born, and it's a dear little girl-calf. But I'm sorry to say that Pimpernel isn't very well. Isn't it a pity?'

The bees hummed round her head, and Penny felt sure they were listening. 'Please bring us good luck because I've told you the news,' finished Penny.

And the funny thing was that Pimpernel was very much better that evening, and Jim couldn't think why!

'It's because I told the bees,' said Penny solemnly. 'It is, really, Jim. I shall always tell them things in future. They like it.'

'You do so, Missy, then,' said Jim, who had as great a belief as Harriet in the old country customs. 'And you look out for swarms too – maybe one of the hives will swarm in the hot weather.'

'Why do bees swarm?' asked Penny.

'Well, you see, each hive has a queen bee,' said Jim. 'But sometimes in the season there's another queen bee born, and there can't be two in a hive. So some of the bees fly off with the second queen to found a hive of their own. And you have to go after it and take it, or you'll lose half your bees!'

'Bees seem to be just as exciting as everything else,' said Penny. 'But what I'm really looking forward to is tasting their honey. Won't it be lovely to have our own?'

It *was* lovely. When the time came for the honey to be taken, there were so many pounds of it that Mother was able to put it away in store to use the whole winter through! She sent a large pot to Tammylan, who was very fond of honey. The children gave it to him the next time they visited him. They had brought him a fine lot of things, for besides honey each child had a present.

'I've brought you six of my hens' best brown eggs,' said Sheila.

'And I've brought you some of Mother's finest butter,' said Rory.

'And here's some homemade currant jelly,' said Benjy.

'And I've got you the biggest lettuce I've ever grown in my bit of garden,' said Penny. 'It has a wonderful big heart. You feel it, Tammylan.'

'As big a heart as you have, Penny!' said Tammylan, with a laugh. 'My word, I'm lucky to have four friends like you. By the way, tell your father I've heard of a bullock that wants fattening up. If he'll take it, I'll bring it along tomorrow.'

The first thing Penny did when she got home was to go the bees and tell them about the bullock!

'Bees, there's a bullock coming!' she announced.

And when she went in, the little girl was quite certain that the bees were talking over her news as they flew to get the heather-honey from the common.

'A new bullock is coming, he's coming, yes, he's coming!' she thought she heard the bees humming. And maybe she was right!

19

Rory is Too Big for His Boots

That summer was a very dry one. The children revelled in the heat, and grew as brown as the old oak-apples on the trees. Haymaking time came and went. The hay was not as good as the year before, because the rain held off whilst the grass was growing. So it was not as lush as it should have been.

'Well, let's hope the rain keeps off when we cut the hay and turn it,' said the farmer. It did, and the children had a wonderful time helping with the haymaking. They were allowed a holiday from school, and they made the most of it. True helped too, galloping and scrabbling in the mown hay, sending it flying into the air.

Dopey, of course, joined the haymakers. He was now growing into a goat, and was completely mad. He still seemed to think he was a silly young kid, and played the most ridiculous tricks. He loved to spring out at the sheep and the cows, and leap around and about them so that they stared at him in the greatest amazement.

'I wouldn't mind his being such a clown,' said the farmer, 'but I do wish he wouldn't eat anything and everything. It was a mistake to give you Dopey for your birthday, Penny.'

'Oh *no*, Daddy!' said the little girl. 'I know he's silly and mad – but he does love us all.'

'Hmm!' said the farmer. 'I think I could manage quite well without Dopey's love and affection. I'm always very suspicious when that goat comes along with me.'

Penny's lambs were in the field with the other sheep now, because they ate grass. Penny always let them out when she was free from school, and they wandered around after her, baaing in their high voices. They were not allowed in the hayfield. Scamper the squirrel was allowed there, though, and he enjoyed himself very much, bounding about among the haymakers, and frisking up and down Benjy. Those days were fun, and the children were sorry when the haymaking was over.

'Daddy, will you have enough hay to feed all our cattle this winter?' asked Sheila, when she watched the haystacks being built. 'We've more cattle now, you know – and Paul Pry, the bullock, will eat an awful lot.'

The bullock had been called Paul Pry by Penny because he always appeared whenever anything was going on. He was rather a pet, very tame and very affectionate for a bullock. He simply adored joining the children when they watched such things as the ducklings going into the water for the first time, or the piglets being set free to run about the yard, squealing for joy.

'Well, we may have enough this year, but we ought to plant another field with hay next year,' said the farmer to Sheila. 'Willow Farm is growing! There's that field we haven't used yet – the one right away up there – we might burn the bad grass and weeds in it, and then plough it up next season.

503

The field would burn quickly enough this weather.'

But soon after that the rain came and it was impossible to burn the rubbishy field. The children thought the idea of burning it was very exciting.

'It's a quick way of getting rid of the rubbishy grass there,' said Rory. 'I hope Daddy will do it as soon as the hot weather sets in again. Won't it be fun to set light to it?'

Rory was feeling rather big these days. He had done well on the farm that summer, because he was now very strong, and could do almost a man's work. The farmer was proud of him and praised him often. A little too often! Rory was getting 'too big for his boots,' Jim said.

'Why don't you ask Mother to buy you some new boots, Rory?' said Penny, looking at her brother's feet. 'Jim says you are getting too big for your boots – you'll get sore feet, if you're not careful.'

'You *are* a little silly, Penny!' said Rory crossly. He went out and banged the door.

'What's the matter with Rory?' asked Penny in astonishment.

'Well, don't you know what "getting too big for your boots" means?' said Sheila, with a laugh. 'It means getting vain or conceited or swollen headed – having too high an opinion of yourself!'

'Oh,' said Penny in dismay, 'what a silly I am!'

Rory had gone out into the fields. He was hailed by his father. 'Rory! I've got to go over to Headley's farm to look at some things they've got to sell. Keep an eye on things for me, will you?'

'Yes, Dad!' called back Rory, feeling all important again.

He saw Mark coming along, and hoped he had heard what his father had said. Mark had. He looked rather impressed.

'It's a good thing Dad has got me to see to things for him whilst he's away here and there, isn't it?' said Rory to Mark. 'Come on. Let's look how the wheat's coming along. We'll be harvesting it soon.'

The two boys went through the fields. Mark listened to Rory talking about this crop and that crop. He was not so old as the bigger boy, and he thought Rory was really very clever and grown-up.

They came to the field that had lain waste since the farmer had taken over Willow Farm the year before. It was the one that was going to be burnt.

'This is an awful field, isn't it?' said Mark. 'It's not like Willow Farm, somehow.'

'We're going to burn it up,' said Rory. 'It's no good as it is. We must set it on fire, and then the rubbishy grass and weeds will go up in smoke, and we can put the field under the plough. Maybe next year it will be yielding a fine crop of hay, or potatoes, or something like that. Potatoes clean up a field well, you know.'

'Do they really?' said Mark, thinking that Rory knew almost as much as the farmer himself. 'I say – what fun to burn up a field? It looks about ready to burn now, doesn't it? All dry and tindery.'

'It does,' agreed Rory. He looked at the big four-acre field. He wished he could burn it then and there. It would be fun!

'You'll have to wait till your father gives orders for that, I suppose,' said Mark. 'He wouldn't allow you to start a thing like that unless he said so, would he?'

505

'Well – you heard what he said – I was to keep an eye on things for him,' said Rory. 'I don't see why I shouldn't burn up this field today. It looks about right for it. Which way is the wind blowing? We mustn't fire it if the wind is blowing in the wrong direction. We don't want those sheds to go up in smoke!'

The boys wetted their hands and held them out to the breeze. It seemed to be blowing the right way, away from the sheds, and towards the open country.

'Well – what about it?' said Mark, his eyes gleaming. 'Do you really dare to without your father telling you?'

'Of course,' said Rory grandly. 'I'll go and get some matches. It's easy. You just set light to a patch of grass, and then let the breeze take it over the field. We shall see the grass and everything flaring up, and by the time Daddy comes back, the field will be done.'

The two boys went to get some matches. 'What do you want them for?' asked Harriet.

'We're going to fire that rubbishy field away up above the horses' field,' said Rory.

Harriet thought that the farmer was going to be there too. She handed over some matches. 'Well, see you don't burn yourselves,' she said. 'It's easy enough to light a fire, but not so easy to put it out!'

'Oh, a bit of stamping soon puts out a field fire,' said Rory grandly, as if he knew everything about it. He took the matches and he and Mark set off back to the field. Penny joined them, Dopey skipping about behind her.

'Where are you going?' she asked. She jumped in

excitement when she heard what they were going to do. 'I'll come with you!' she said.

So they all of them came to the field. Rory struck a match, bent down and laid the flame to a few tall dry grasses. In a trice they flared up, and the flame jumped to other grasses near by. The fire ran as if by magic!

'Look at it, look at it!' cried Penny, jumping about in excitement. 'Isn't it grand?'

It might have been grand for a minute or two – but it very soon ceased to be grand and became terrifying! Rory had started something that was impossible to stop!

20

An Unpleasant Adventure

'Oooh!' said Penny in surprise. 'I never thought flames could go so fast!'

Mark and Rory hadn't known that either. It was simply amazing to see the fire spread over the field. The weeds and grass were very dry from a long hot spell, and they crackled up at once. The fire grew a loud voice, and a long mane of smoky hair.

'It's alive!' said Penny, dancing about. 'It's a dragon with a mane of smoke. It's eating the field.'

Mark was excited too. He didn't dance about like Penny, but he watched the fire with shining eyes. This was much better than an ordinary bonfire.

The breeze blew a little, and the fire crackled more loudly and grew a bigger mane of smoke. Rory looked a little worried. He hadn't guessed that the flames would rush along like this. They tore over the field, leaving a blackened track behind them.

As the fire burned, the sun went in, and a pall of clouds gathered. The children hardly noticed, they were so intent on the field-fire. But then Rory saw something peculiar.

'Look!' he said. 'The wind must be changing! The flames are blowing the other way now.'

So they were. Instead of blowing straight down the field towards the open country, they were blowing sideways, eating up all the grass towards the east. The crackling grew louder, the smoke grew thicker.

'Rory! Won't those sheds be burnt!' cried Penny suddenly. 'Oh, Rory! Make the fire stop!'

'Stamp it out, quick!' cried Rory, and ran to where the edge of the fire began. But it was quite impossible to stamp it out. Soon the soles of their shoes were so hot that their feet felt as if they were on fire. Rory pushed Penny back. He was afraid the flames would burn her. Dopey, the kid, was the only one who seemed quite unafraid. He danced around the fire-edge, bleating at it.

'Mark! Run and tell Jim what's happened, and you, Penny, go and find Bill,' said Rory. They sped off, fear making them run even faster than usual. Mark soon found Jim, who was already staring in puzzled amazement at the stream of smoke coming from the field up the hill. In a few words he told him what had happened.

Penny found Bill and before she had half told him what had happened, he had guessed and was rushing towards the out-building where empty sacks were kept. He yelled for Harriet as he ran.

'Harriet! Come and soak these sacks. The old field is afire. Those sheds will be burnt down!'

Harriet and Frannie came tearing out in surprise. The three of them dragged the sacks down to the duck-pond and soaked them well. Then they ran as fast as they could with the heavy sacks up to the flaming field. Half-way there they met Jim rushing along with Mark. Bill threw them a couple of wet sacks.

Soon they were all in the flaming grass, beating frantically at the fire. Slap, slap, slap! Harriet, Jim, Frannie, Bill and Rory beat the wet sacks down on the flames, trying their hardest to put them out.

'I've got the fire out in this bit!' gasped Bill. 'Look up there, Jim – it's getting too near those sheds. You go there and beat it, and I'll work around behind you. We may save the sheds then.'

'The flames are running to that electric pole!' squealed Penny. 'Oh, quick; oh, quick!'

Rory and Harriet ran to the pole and tried to beat off the flames. 'Go and get some more wet sacks!' panted Harriet to Mark. 'Ours are getting dry with the heat. Oh my, oh my, who ever thought of firing this field today! With the grass as dry as it is, who knows where the fire will end!'

'Oh, it won't burn our farmhouse, will it!' cried Penny in fright.

'Come on, help me get some wet sacks,' said Mark, and pulled the frightened little girl along with him.

In half an hour's time nobody would have recognised any of the people who were beating out the flames. They were black with the smoke, they smelt terrible, and they were so hot and parched with thirst that they could hardly swallow.

Frannie gave up first. Her arms ached so badly with slapping at the flames that she could no longer lift them. She let her sack fall, and with tears rolling down her blackened cheeks, she staggered out of the smoke and sank down by the gate of the field. 'I can't slap any more,' she said. 'I can't do it any more!'

Harriet gave up next. She stood and looked at the burning field, shaking her head.

'It's no use,' she said. 'No use at all. The fire's like a mad thing, running this way and that!'

So it was. The wind had got up properly now, and blew in furious gusts that sent the flames careering now here and now there. There was no saving the field or the hedge at the top, which was already a blackened, twisted mass, all its green leaves gone.

Rory, Bill and Jim were trying to save the sheds from being fired. Already flames licked along one shed. Jim was beating madly at them, his trousers scorched, and his feet so hot that he could hardly walk. The two men and the boy were now so tired that they, like Harriet, could hardly lift up their arms to slap their wet sacks at the flames. But still they went on valiantly, slap, slap, slap. Rory was so horrified at the damage he had caused that he was determined not to stop fighting the fire till he dropped down with tiredness.

'We can't do any more,' said Jim at last. 'The fire's beaten us, boys.'

'No, no, let's go on!' cried poor Rory, whose face was now so black that it was like soot. 'I can't let Daddy's sheds be burnt.'

'You'll have to,' said Jim. 'And those telegraph poles too. Let's hope the fire won't jump the hedge and get into the next field.'

Everyone stood and watched the hungry fire, which crackled along the edge of the first shed, shooting out little red tongues of flames at the other two huts. There was nothing to be done. Nothing could save the sheds and the poles – and maybe the next field too would soon be in flames.

Nothing? Well, only one thing. Water would put out the flames – but where was water to come from? The nearest stream was two fields away, and it wouldn't be any good trying to cart water from it to the fire.

And then Penny gave such a squeal that everyone jumped in fright, thinking that the little girl was being burnt.

'Look, oh Look!' yelled Penny, pointing to the sky. 'RAIN! RAIN!'

Everyone looked up at the black sky. Heavy drops of rain began to fall, splashing down on the upturned, tired faces, washing patches of white in the black skins. Down and down fell the thunder-rain, while a crash suddenly sounded to the west.

'A storm!' cried Frannie. 'That will put the fire out. Oh, what a blessed mercy!'

Trembling with tiredness and relief, the exhausted little company stood there in the pouring rain, watching it put out the hungry flames. Pitter, patter, pitter, patter, down it fell, great drops as round as a ten-pence piece when they splashed on the burnt ground. Everyone was soaked. Nobody cared at all. It was marvellous, wonderful, unbelievable that the rain should have come at such a moment, when everyone had given up hope!

Penny began to cry. So did Frannie. And suddenly poor Rory burst out into great sobs too. He had been so worried, so anxious – and it had all been his fault!

'Come now,' said Harriet, putting her arm comfortingly round Rory. 'It's all right. No harm's done. None at all, except that the hedge is burnt over there, and that shed got a bit of a scorching. You come along with me and Frannie, and I'll give you all something to eat and drink. Come along now.'

So everyone went along with Harriet in the pouring rain, far too tired to run. Penny went with Rory, her hand in his, so sorry for her big brother that she could not squeeze his hand hard enough. Rory's tears had made a white channel down his blackened cheeks and he looked very strange.

Soon they were all sitting down in the kitchen, whilst Harriet, who had not stopped to clean herself, got them something to eat and drink.

Benjy and Sheila came in to see what was happening and they stared in the utmost amazement at the blacken company. Mark laughed at their astonished faces. Everyone was feeling much better already, and the adventure was beginning to seem more exciting than unpleasant, now that it had ended better than they had hoped.

'What's happened?' said Benjy at last.

'That field atop of the hill there got fired,' said Jim. 'It's a mystery how it did.'

'I fired it,' said Rory, his face red beneath its black.

'Well – you *were* a wonderful great ninny then!' said Jim. 'What'll your father say?'

'Rory doesn't need to tell him,' said Harriet, who was sorry for the boy. 'Nobody will tell on him.'

'Harriet, of course I must tell my father,' said Rory with surprise. 'You don't suppose I'd deceive him or tell him lies, do you?'

'I should jolly well think not,' said Benjy. 'Rory isn't afraid of owning up to anything. Never has been.'

'There's Daddy's car now!' said Penny. She ran to the

window and looked out, her face still black. 'Hallo, Daddy! Hallo, Mother!'

'Penny! Whatever's the matter with your face?' cried her mother. 'What *have* you been doing?'

The little girl's father and mother came to the window and looked in. They were silent with astonishment when they saw the surprising company there, all eating together, and all with black faces and scorched clothes.

Rory stood up. 'I'll tell you, Daddy,' he said, and he went out of the kitchen, and met his father at the hall door. They went together into the little study.

'I fired the top field,' said Rory. 'I–I thought it would be all right.'

'Why did you do that?' asked his father.

'Well – I thought it looked all right for firing,' said Rory. 'I know I shouldn't have done it without your permission. I–I – think I got too big for my boots, as Penny says.'

'Yes – I think you did,' said his father. 'But you seem to have gone back to your right size again, my boy. I suppose the field took fire and the sheds went up in smoke too?'

'They nearly did,' said Rory honestly. 'But the rain came just in time and saved them, Dad. There's not much damage done, except that one hedge is burnt.'

'That's lucky then,' said his father. 'We might have had a serious loss. You must never start a grass-fire unless you've got a whole lot of helpers round to beat it out when necessary, Rory. It runs like magic.'

'I know,' said Rory. 'It was dreadful. I was awfully scared. All the others came to help, and that's why we're so black and scorched. I do blame myself terribly.'

'Quite right too,' said his father. 'You were very much to blame. But I was to blame too! I've forgotten you were only a lad of fourteen, and I've made you think yourself a man. Well – you're not. You're just a lad yet – and a very good one too! But you've behaved like a man tonight, in coming to me like this, and telling me everything. Now go and wash your face.'

Rory went off, feeling his father's hand clapping him affectionately on the shoulder. 'Dad's splendid!' he thought. 'I shan't behave like that again – getting too big for my boots, and thinking I know everything!'

Everyone went to clean themselves and to put on fresh clothes, for they smelt of smoke. As Penny was just putting on a clean jersey, she gave a scream that made Sheila jump.

'Oh! Oh! What's happened to Dopey, do you think? Did he get burnt? I've not seen him for ages!'

Nobody had seen Dopey. Penny dragged on her jersey, shouting out that she must go and find him, she must, she must!

She tore out into the farmyard, and there she saw True barking frantically at a peculiar little object in the middle of the yard. It was quite black and very miserable. Penny stood and stared at it. Then she gave a yell, ran to it, and hugged it.

'*Dopey!* You're all black, just like I was! Darling Dopey, you're not burnt, are you?'

Dopey wasn't. Silly as he was, he wasn't quite so silly as that! He snuggled against Penny contentedly.

'Penny!' said Mother, appearing at the door. 'Penny! What *is* the sense of putting on perfectly clean things and then hugging a black and sooty goat? I think you must be just as mad as Dopey!'

21

Ups and Downs

The first year that the family had been at Willow Farm had been so successful that everyone had rather got into the way of thinking that farming was really quite easy. But the second year showed them that a farm had its 'downs' as well as its 'ups,' as Penny put it.

'We had all "ups" last year,' she said. 'This year we've had some "downs" – like when Daddy bought that mad bull and lost half the price he paid for it – and when Rory fired the field and we nearly lost the sheds.'

'And when Mark left the gate open and we hunted for hours for the lost horses, and Daddy had to do without them for a while,' said Sheila. 'And this year the hay isn't so good.'

'But the corn is even better,' said Rory. 'So that's an "up," isn't it? And, Sheila, your hens and ducks have done marvellously again this year, you know.'

'Except that I lost a whole brood of darling little ducklings to the rats,' said Sheila sorrowfully. That had been a great blow to her and Frannie. Twelve little yellow and black ducklings had disappeared in two nights.

Jim had said that it was rats, and he had set traps for them. But the rats were too cunning for the traps, and not one had been caught.

516

Then Bill had brought along a white ferret, a clever little creature that slipped like lightning down a rat-hole to chase the rats. The men had been waiting at other rat-holes, watching for the scared rats to come out. They had killed a good many and were well satisfied.

'Ah, rats are no good at all,' said Bill. 'Most creatures are some good – but rats are just the worst creatures ever made. They aren't even kind to their own sort. And they're too clever for anything.'

Sheila had been glad to know that the rats around the duck-pond had been killed. She loved all her baby birds and had cried bitterly when she knew so many had been eaten by the hungry rats. But in spite of the damage done to her little flock of birds, she had done extremely well with her eggs and chicks and ducklings. Mother said she was an excellent little business woman already.

'Frannie's a great help, Mother,' Sheila said, when her mother praised her. 'I think we ought to raise her wages, don't you? The rise could come out of our egg-profits.'

So Frannie's wages were raised, and the little kitchen-girl was proud and pleased. She spent her first week's rise on little presents for her many brothers and sisters. That was just like Frannie!

All the children on the farm loved the animals, both wild and tame, that lived on and around it – with the exception of the rats, of course. But the farmer used to get cross when he heard Penny or Benjy talking with delight about the rabbits on the hillside!

'Rabbits!' he would say in disgust. 'Stop raving about them, do! They've done more damage to my farm this year than anything else. I'd like to shoot the lot.'

'Oh *no*, Daddy!' Penny cried every time. 'Oh no! You can't shoot those dear little long-eared creatures with their funny little white bobtails.'

'Well, if they eat any more of my seedlings in Long Meadow, I'll shoot the whole bunch!' threatened her father.

Penny went solemnly to the hillside to warn the rabbits. Rory heard her talking to them. He was mending a gap in the hedge nearby, and Penny didn't see him.

'Rabbits,' said Penny, in her clear voice, 'you'll be shot and killed if you don't leave my Daddy's fields alone. Now, you've got plenty of grass to eat up here, and I'll bring you lettuce leaves for a treat when I can. So do leave Daddy's seedlings alone – *especially* the vetch that is growing in Long Meadow. It's going to feed the cattle, and it's very important.'

Rory laughed quietly to himself. Penny was so funny. He watched his little sister skip down the hillside as lightly as a lamb. He hoped that the rabbits would take notice of what she said, for he knew she would be very upset if they were shot.

But alas! The rabbits took no notice at all. In fact, it seemed as if they made up their minds to do as much damage as possible, as soon as they could. The very next morning the farmer came in to breakfast looking as black as thunder. Rory looked at him in surprise.

'What's up, Dad?' he asked.

'The rabbits have eaten nearly every scrap of that big field of vetch seedlings,' said his father. 'That's a serious loss. I doubt if we can plant any more seed. It's too late in the year.

I'll have to get a few guns together and do some shooting.'

Penny didn't say anything, nor did Benjy. But they both looked sad. After breakfast they went to have a look at the field. Their father was right. The vetch was almost completely spoilt, for the rabbits had eaten it right down to the ground.

'Well – you can't expect Daddy to put up with *that*,' said Benjy. 'I wonder when the rabbits will be shot.'

When the next Saturday came Daddy announced that he and three others were going to shoot the rabbits all over the farm. Penny burst into tears.

'Take Penny to see Tammylan today,' said Mother quickly to Benjy. So she and Benjy went over the hill to visit the wild man. They told him about the rabbits. Even as they told him there came the first crack of a distant gun.

'One poor little rabbit dead, never to run down the hillside any more,' said Penny with a sob.

'Penny, dear, don't take things so much to heart,' said Tammylan. 'Your father is a farmer and has to grow food for you and for his farm friends. He would be foolish to allow all his work to be wasted because he wouldn't fight his enemies: the rats, the rabbits, and many kinds of insects. What would you say if he said to you, "Penny, I'm sorry I've no food for you, because the rabbits and rats came and took it and I hadn't the heart to stop them?"'

'I'd think he was silly,' said Penny, drying her eyes, and Benjy nodded too.

'Yes, you would,' said Tammylan. 'But he isn't silly, so he is taking the quickest and kindest way of fighting his enemies. Now cheer up, and come and see my latest friend – a water-vole who will eat out of my hand!'

Penny said no more about rabbits to her father after that. She even ate rabbit-pie at dinner the next day. After all, you had to be sensible, as well as kind-hearted.

Another time the farmer complained that a whole field of potatoes had been spoilt by the pheasants that came walking among them, devouring them by the hundred. Benjy pricked up his ears at this.

'Rory, I've got an idea,' he said. 'Couldn't we train True to run round Daddy's fields and scare away the pheasants when they fly down? I'm sure we could. Do let me try to teach him.'

Rory thought it *was* a good idea – but he didn't want Benjy to do the teaching. He said he would do it himself.

'I dare say you could teach him more quickly,' he said, 'because you really are a wizard with animals – but he's my dog, and I'd rather do it, thank you, Benjy.'

So Rory began to teach True to scare off the pheasants and other birds that flew down to his father's fields. The dog, who now understood almost every word that Rory said to him, soon knew what he wanted. In a week or two, not a pheasant dared to fly down on to a field if True was anywhere about! The farmer was surprised and pleased.

'We'll buy you a new collar,' he said to True. 'You're as good as any of the children.'

'True is one of our "ups," isn't he?' said Rory proudly. True wagged his tail. He didn't know what an 'up' was, but he felt sure it was something good.

'And Dopey is one of our "downs,"' said Sheila. Penny protested at once.

'He isn't, he isn't. Why do you say that?'

'Only because he went and butted one of my coops over, let out the hen and her chicks, and then chased the poor old hen into the pond,' said Sheila.

'And yesterday he got hold of one of the piglets by its curly tail and wouldn't let go,' said Benjy. 'The pig squealed the place down. I do think it's time Dopey had a smacking again, Penny. Scamper never does anything like that. He's always perfectly good.'

'Well – I don't like creatures that are always perfectly good,' said Penny. 'I prefer Dopey. Anyway, he'll soon be a proper goat, and then Jim says he'll have to go and live in the field with the cows. I *shall* miss him.'

'He'll be a jolly good miss, that's all I can say,' said Rory. 'How I shall look forward to missing him!'

22

Happy Days

Mark came to spend part of his summer holidays at Willow Farm. Since the adventure of the lost horses he had been much more careful, and was now almost as responsible as the farm children. He always adored staying at the farm, and loved all the animals as much as they did.

'You know, even when there's nothing at all happening, it's lovely to be on a farm,' he told Rory. 'It's exciting, of course, when you buy a new bull, or make the hay, or harvest the corn – but even an ordinary peaceful day is lovely, I think.'

It was. The bees hummed loudly as they went to and from the hive. The children liked to think of the golden honey being stored there. Benjy had become extremely good at handling the bees, and his father had made him responsible for them. They did not sting him at all. Rory had been stung once, and Mark twice, but nobody else.

The humming of the bees, the baaing of the sheep, the cluck of the hens, and the quack of the ducks sounded all day long at the farm. Everyone was used to the noise, and hardly noticed it except when they left the farm to go to the town – and then they missed all the familiar sounds very much.

Then there were the shouts of the men at work, coming suddenly on the air – an unexpected whinny from a waiting horse, and a stamp of hoofs – a mooing from a cow, and a squeal from a pig. Sometimes there was the clatter of a pail, or the sound of children's running feet, coming home from school. It was a happy farm, with everyone doing his work well, and everyone helping the other.

Mother used to laugh at the way the animals and birds came to the house. This always astonished visitors too. The hens came regularly to the kitchen door, and were as regularly shooed away by Harriet. Mr By-Himself sometimes did a bit of shooing when he felt like it, but the hens did not really fear him. If there was no one in the kitchen they would walk right in and peck about.

Sometimes they would go into the house by the open French windows of the sitting-room, clucking importantly. If Mother had visitors, the visitors would say 'How sweet!' But Mother didn't think so, and out would go the hens at top speed.

Once one of the ducks brought all her little yellow ducklings into the house, much to Penny's delight.

'Mother, the duck-pond is almost dried up, and I expect the duck wants to find the bath for her ducks to swim on,' said Penny. 'Oh, Mother, do let me run the bath full for them, *please*!'

But to Penny's great disappointment she was not allowed to, and the duck had to take her string of youngsters to the stream, where they all bobbed and swam to their hearts' content.

The big carthorses often came into the farmyard and stood there whilst Jim or Bill went to have a word with Harriet. If they thought Penny was anywhere about they would wander to the house, and put their heads in at the door or the window. It always gave the children a real thrill to look up and see the big brown head looking in, the large eyes asking silently for a lump of sugar.

'Oh! Darling! Wait a minute, wait a minute! I'll just get you some sugar!' Penny would say, dropping her knitting or her book at once. And the patient horse would stand there, blinking long-lashed eyes, his head almost filling the window. Once Captain even went into the hall, and knocked over the umbrella stand with such a crash that he backed out hastily, stepping on the foot-scraper and smashing it to bits.

'Don't be cross with him, Mother!' begged Benjy when he heard about it. Benjy had been in bed with a cold at the time. 'Mother, I'm sure Captain came to look for me. He must have wondered why I didn't groom him. I'll pay for a new foot-scraper.'

'Oh, I think I can manage that!' said Mother, with a laugh. 'So long as you hurry up and get better, Benjy. I don't want cows and horses and sheep tramping up the stairs all day long to ask how you are!'

The sheep never came over to the house, except Hoppitty and Jumpity, who had been brought up by hand. They ran in and out continually, though Mother always chased them away. She did her best to make the children keep the doors shut, but except for Mark, who always shut gates and doors behind him, wherever he was, the farm children left the house-doors open. Penny secretly loved the animals coming into the house, and one of her happiest memories was going into the sitting-room one day and finding Hoppitty, Jumpity and Dopey lying asleep on the old rug in front of the fire! The little girl had lain down beside them and gone to sleep too.

'Well, what a heap of tired creatures!' Harriet had said, when she came in to lay the tea. 'I'm surprised you don't give them a place in your bed, that I am, Penny!'

Penny had thought that was a splendid idea, but Mother had said 'no' so decidedly that Penny hadn't even bothered to ask twice.

'Willow Farm is such a friendly place,' Mark said, dozens of times. 'Whenever I come I feel as if the hens cluck "Good morning!" to me, and the ducks say "Hallo!" The horses say "What, you again!" and the pigs squeal out, "Here's Mark! Here's Mark!" And the . . .'

'The children say, "Oh, what a bore – here's that tiresome boy again!"' said Rory with a grin.

Even Paul Pry, the new bullock, took to being friendly enough to pay a call at the house. He usually went to the kitchen, because, for some reason or other, he had taken a great fancy to Harriet. He would arrive there, and stand at the door, his big head lowered, looking anxiously into the kitchen, waiting for Harriet to appear. He only once attempted to go right into the kitchen, much to the astonishment and fright of Mr By-Himself, who was fast asleep on a chair. He awoke to find Paul Pry standing over him, breathing hard.

Mr By-Himself leapt straight into the air, and spat so loudly that the bullock was scared. He backed hastily and knocked over the kitchen table. It was full of saucepans and pans that Frannie was to clean. They went over with a crash that brought Frannie and Harriet and Mother out of the dairy at a run.

'Paul Pry!' exclaimed Harriet in wrath. 'Who told *you* to

come into the kitchen then? Knocking over my table like that! Out you go, and don't you dare to come and see me again!'

And out went the poor bullock as meekly as a lamb, sad that Harriet was cross with him. But he was back again two days later, staring in at the door for his beloved Harriet.

'Well, there's one thing,' said the farmer, with a laugh, 'if ever Paul Pry goes mad like Stamper, we shall know who can deal with him. Harriet would put him right with a thwack from her broom. To see her chase the bullock away is the funniest sight in the world. And yet I think she is very fond of him.'

That was the nice part of Willow Farm. Men, women, children and animals were all fond of one another. The creatures trusted their masters and mistresses, and never expected or got anything but kindness and understanding. Nobody slacked, nobody shirked his work, everyone did his bit.

And so Willow Farm, in spite of more 'downs' than 'ups' that second year, prospered and did well. New cow-sheds were built – beautiful places, airy and clean. New machinery was bought and admired, put to use and then cleaned and stored until next time. New animals were born, named and loved. New fields were cleaned, ploughed and sown.

'It's a family farm,' said Rory happily. 'We've all got our jobs and we try to do them well. Daddy, aren't you glad you gave up your London work and came here, to Willow Farm?'

'Very glad,' said his father. 'I've seen you all grow healthy and strong. I've seen you doing work that matters. I've watched you learning good lessons as you handle the animals and help to till the soil. You've had to use your muscles and you've had to use your brains. You've grown up complete and whole, with no nonsense in you. I'm proud of you all.'

'I hope we'll never have to leave,' said Benjy. 'I couldn't bear to have to live in town now, Daddy. I hope Willow Farm never fails.'

'There's no reason why it should,' said the farmer. 'After all, ours is a mixed farm, and there is no waste anywhere.'

'That's true,' said Rory. 'We grow corn and it feeds the hens we want to keep. We grow fodder and it feeds the cows whose milk we need. They give us cream and butter and cheese, and the skim milk goes to the pigs and the calves. The hens in turn give us eggs.'

'It's a pity we can't grow our own clothes,' said Penny. 'Then we could almost live on the farm without buying a single thing.'

'Well, the second year is over,' said the farmer. 'We've made mistakes, and sometimes had misfortune and bad luck – but here we all are, happy and healthy, with the farm growing bigger than ever. Good luck to Willow Farm!'

And that is what we all say too – good luck to Willow Farm. We will peep in at the window before we say good-bye and see them all sitting round the fire there, one wintry Sunday afternoon.

There is Rory, big and strong, with Sheila beside him, adding up her egg-book. And there is Benjy, nursing Scamper as usual. And there, on the rug, is little Penny, who has been allowed to have Dopey in for a treat. He is trying to bite True's ears, but the dog will not let him.

527

Outside there is the tread of feet coming to the door. The sound makes Penny jump up and go to the window. 'It's Mark – and Tammylan! They've come to tea. Hallo, Mark! Hallo, Tammylan! Wait a minute till I open the door!'

She flies to open it, and it would be nice if we could slip in too. But the door is closed and we are left outside alone.

Not quite alone! A hen pecks at our legs, and a horse whinnies softly from the stables. Davey's sheep baa in their folds and Rascal barks in the distance. The first star shines out in the sky and we must go.

Goodbye, Willow Farm! May you always be the same friendly place that we know and love so well.